ROB GUILLORY'S

FARMHAND

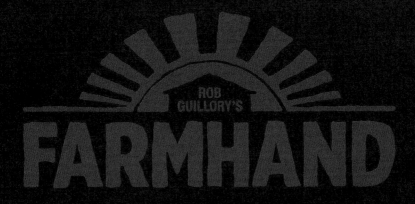

VOLUME 3
ROOTS OF ALL EVIL

Created, Written and Drawn by
ROB GUILLORY

Colors by
TAYLOR WELLS
(Chapters 1 & 2)

JEREMY TREECE
(Chapter 3)

RICO RENZI
(Chapters 4 & 5)

Letters by
KODY CHAMBERLAIN

Graphic Design by
BURTON DURAND

IMAGE COMICS, INC. • Robert Kirkman, Chief Operating Officer • Erik Larsen, Chief Financial Officer • Todd McFarlane, President • Marc Silvestri, Chief Executive Officer • Jim Valentino, Vice President • Eric Stephenson, Publisher / Chief Creative Officer • Jeff Boison, Director of Publishing Planning & Book Trade Sales • Chris Ross, Director of Digital Sales • Jeff Stang, Director of Direct Market Sales • Kat Salazar, Director of PR & Marketing • Drew Gill, Art Director • Heather Doornink, Production Director • Nicole Lapalme, Controller • IMAGECOMICS.COM

DreamWorks Trolls TrollsTopia FARMHAND

DEDICATION

For Mom and Dad.

John Jennings for lending an ear.
Jeremy Treece and
Rico Renzi for all the help.

And to my April for sharing the journey.

CHAPTER 11

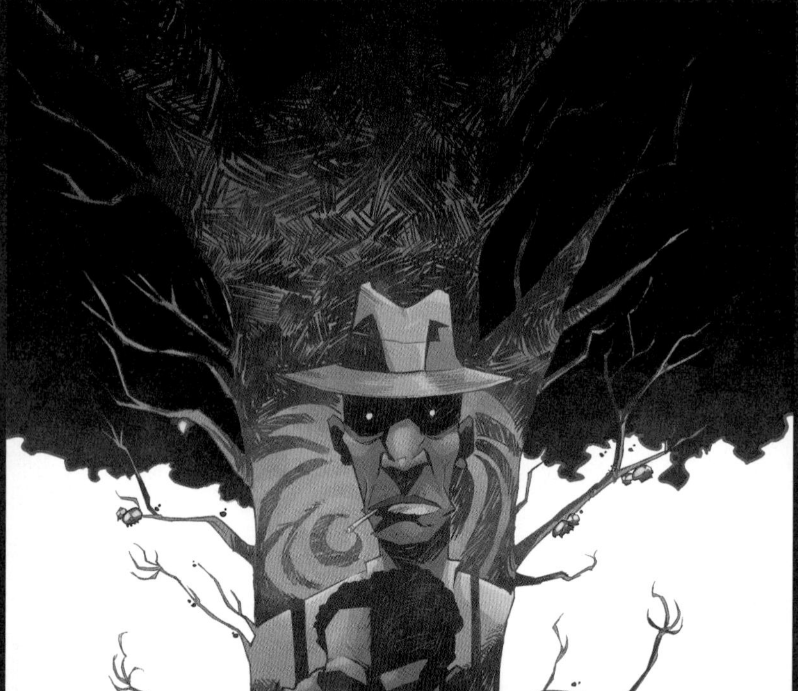
ROB!
2014
TAYLOR
WELLS

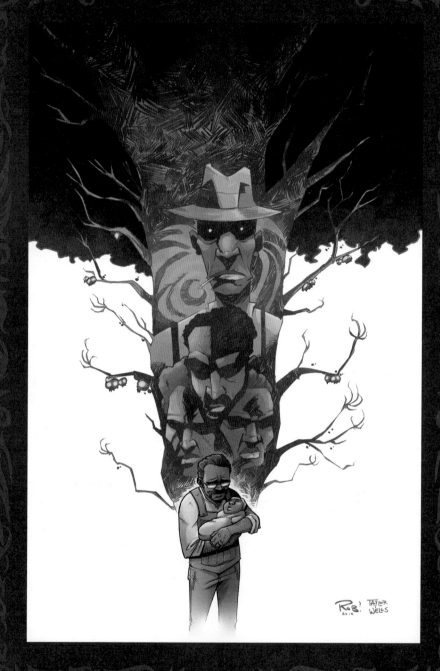

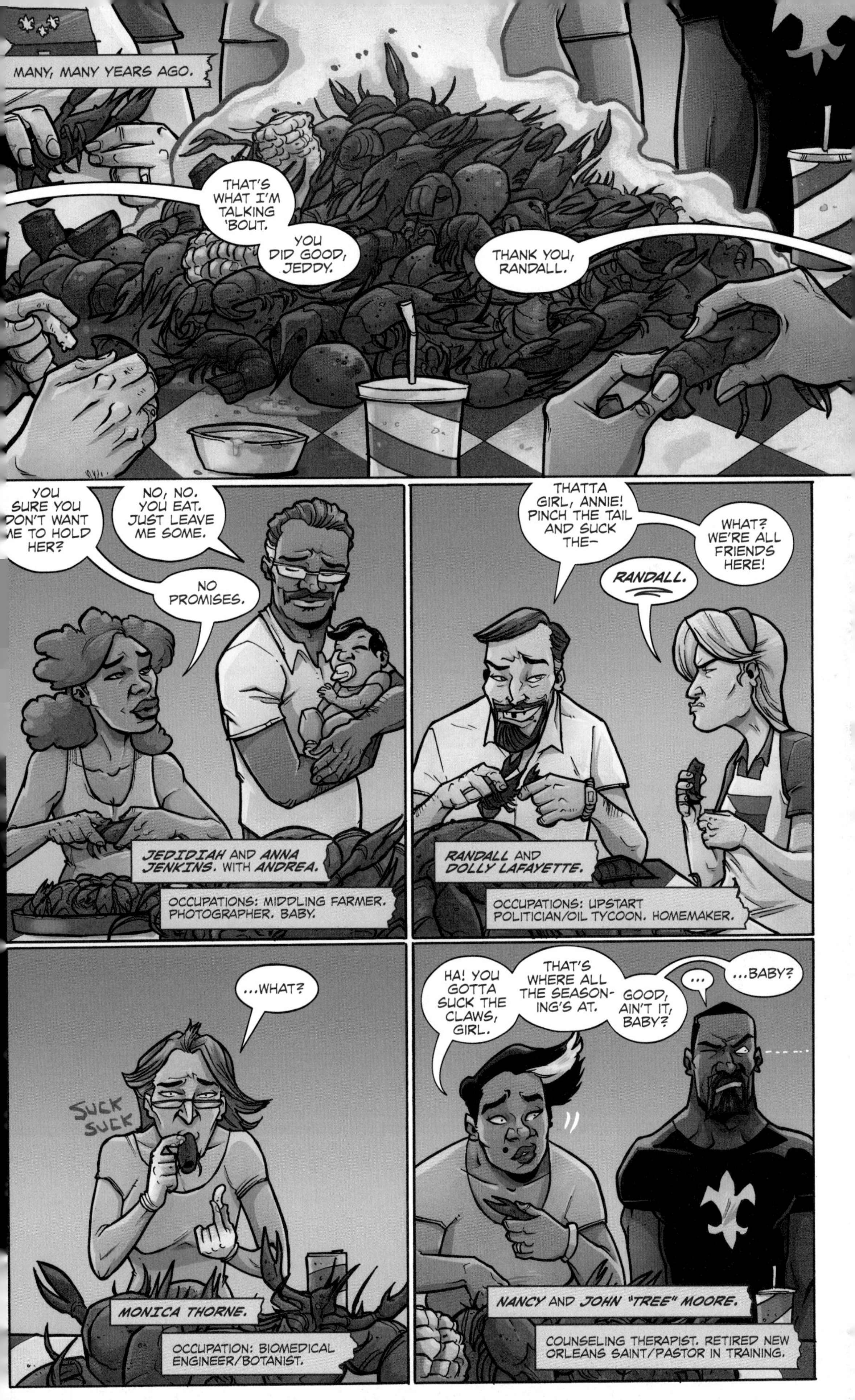
MANY, MANY YEARS AGO.
THAT'S WHAT I'M TALKING 'BOUT.
YOU DID GOOD, JEDDY.
THANK YOU, RANDALL.
YOU SURE YOU DON'T WANT ME TO HOLD HER?
NO, NO. YOU EAT. JUST LEAVE ME SOME.
NO PROMISES.
JEDIDIAH AND ANNA JENKINS. WITH ANDREA.
OCCUPATIONS: MIDDLING FARMER. PHOTOGRAPHER. BABY.
THATTA GIRL, ANNIE! PINCH THE TAIL AND SUCK THE–
RANDALL.
WHAT? WE'RE ALL FRIENDS HERE!
RANDALL AND DOLLY LAFAYETTE.
OCCUPATIONS: UPSTART POLITICIAN/OIL TYCOON. HOMEMAKER.
...WHAT?
SUCK SUCK
MONICA THORNE.
OCCUPATION: BIOMEDICAL ENGINEER/BOTANIST.
HA! YOU GOTTA SUCK THE CLAWS, GIRL.
THAT'S WHERE ALL THE SEASON-ING'S AT.
GOOD, AIN'T IT, BABY?
...
...BABY?
NANCY AND JOHN "TREE" MOORE.
COUNSELING THERAPIST. RETIRED NEW ORLEANS SAINT/PASTOR IN TRAINING.

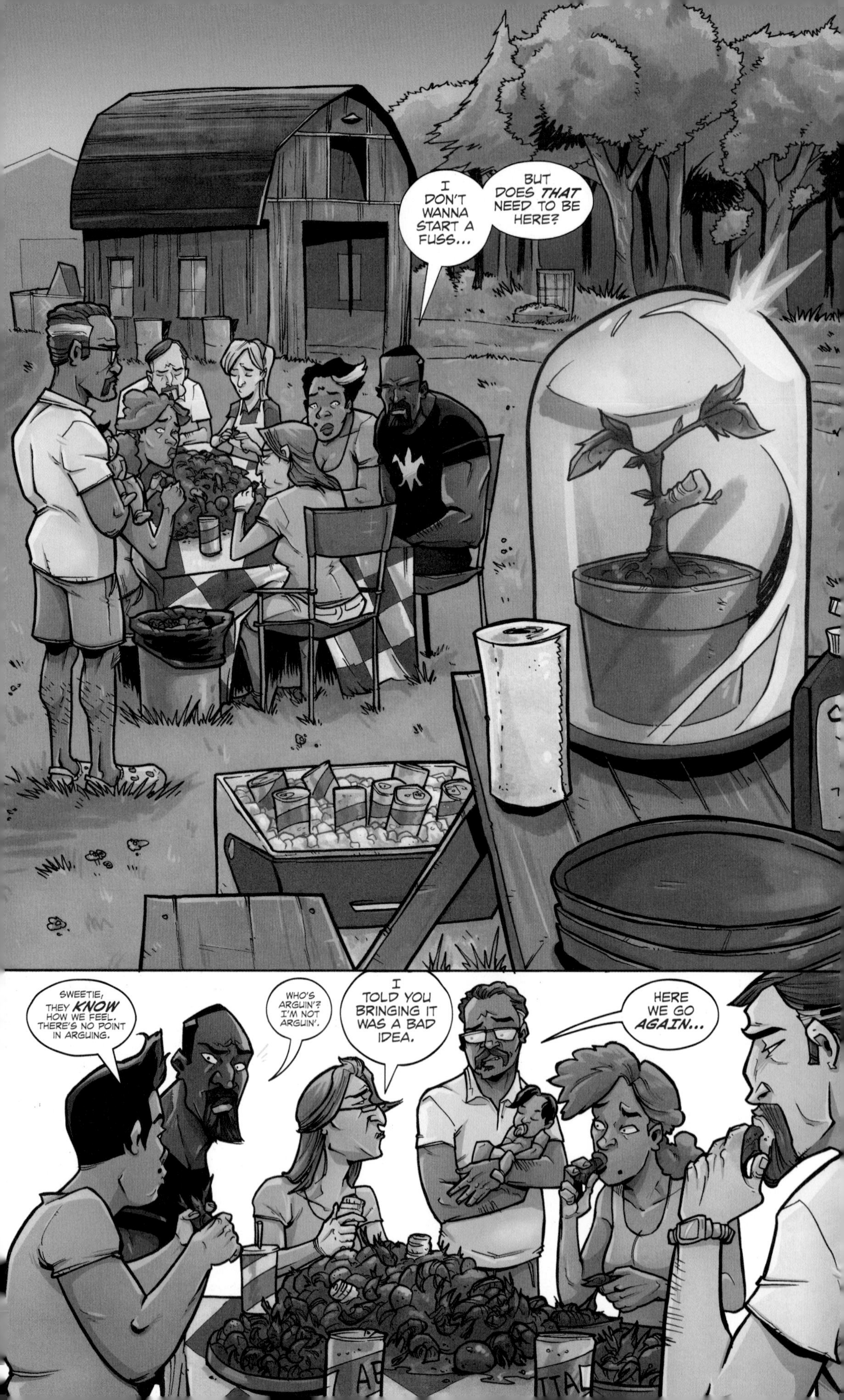
I DON'T WANNA START A FUSS...
BUT DOES *THAT* NEED TO BE HERE?
SWEETIE, THEY *KNOW* HOW WE FEEL. THERE'S NO POINT IN ARGUING.
WHO'S ARGUIN'? I'M NOT ARGUIN'.
I TOLD YOU BRINGING IT WAS A BAD IDEA.
HERE WE GO *AGAIN...*

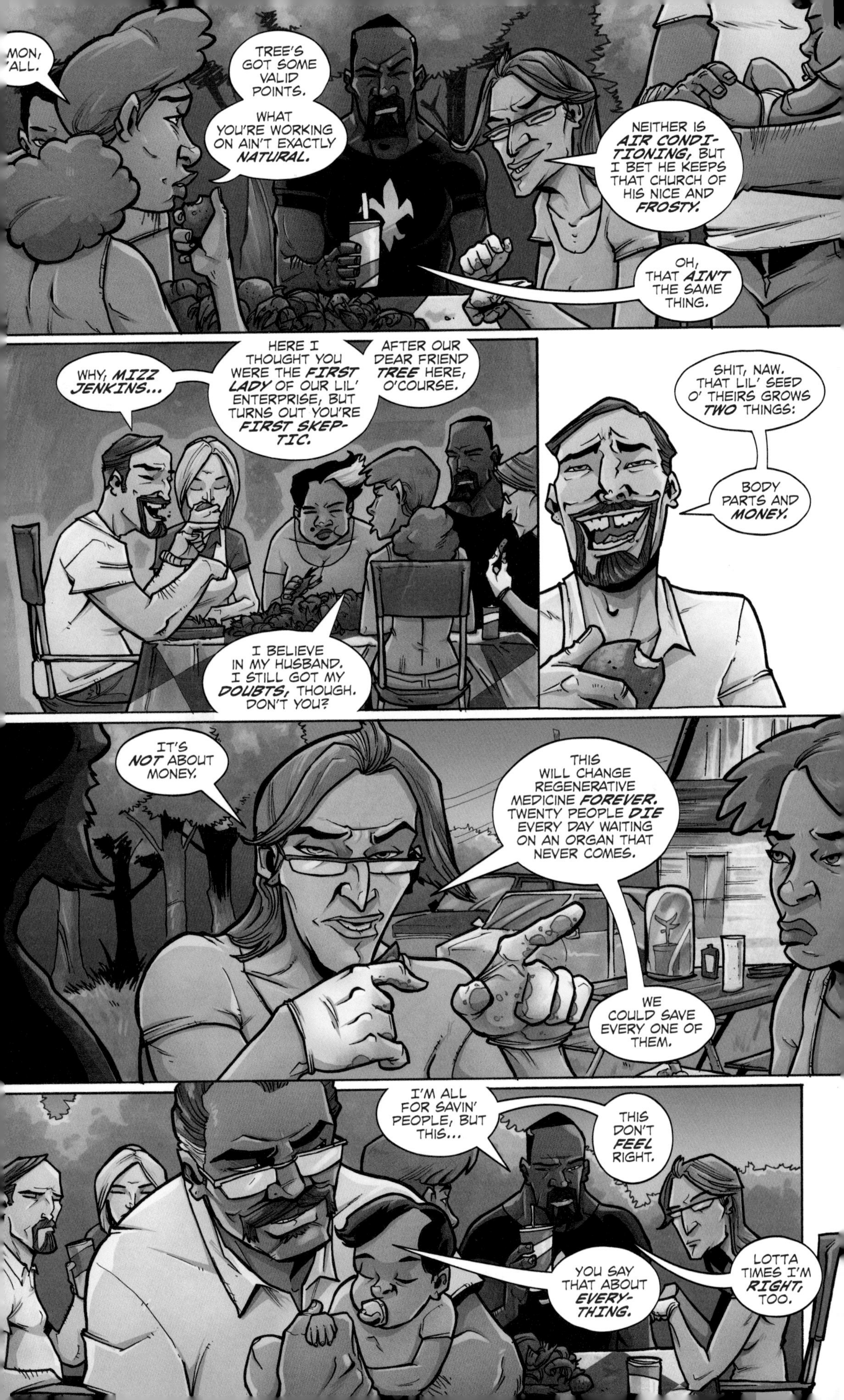

MON, ’ALL.
TREE’S GOT SOME VALID POINTS.
WHAT YOU’RE WORKING ON AIN’T EXACTLY NATURAL.
NEITHER IS AIR CONDI-TIONING, BUT I BET HE KEEPS THAT CHURCH OF HIS NICE AND FROSTY.
OH, THAT AIN’T THE SAME THING.
WHY, MIZZ JENKINS...
HERE I THOUGHT YOU WERE THE FIRST LADY OF OUR LIL’ ENTERPRISE, BUT TURNS OUT YOU’RE FIRST SKEP-TIC.
AFTER OUR DEAR FRIEND TREE HERE, O’COURSE.
I BELIEVE IN MY HUSBAND. I STILL GOT MY DOUBTS, THOUGH. DON’T YOU?
SHIT, NAW. THAT LIL’ SEED O’ THEIRS GROWS TWO THINGS:
BODY PARTS AND MONEY.
IT’S NOT ABOUT MONEY.
THIS WILL CHANGE REGENERATIVE MEDICINE FOREVER. TWENTY PEOPLE DIE EVERY DAY WAITING ON AN ORGAN THAT NEVER COMES.
WE COULD SAVE EVERY ONE OF THEM.
I’M ALL FOR SAVIN’ PEOPLE, BUT THIS...
THIS DON’T FEEL RIGHT.
YOU SAY THAT ABOUT EVERY-THING.
LOTTA TIMES I’M RIGHT, TOO.

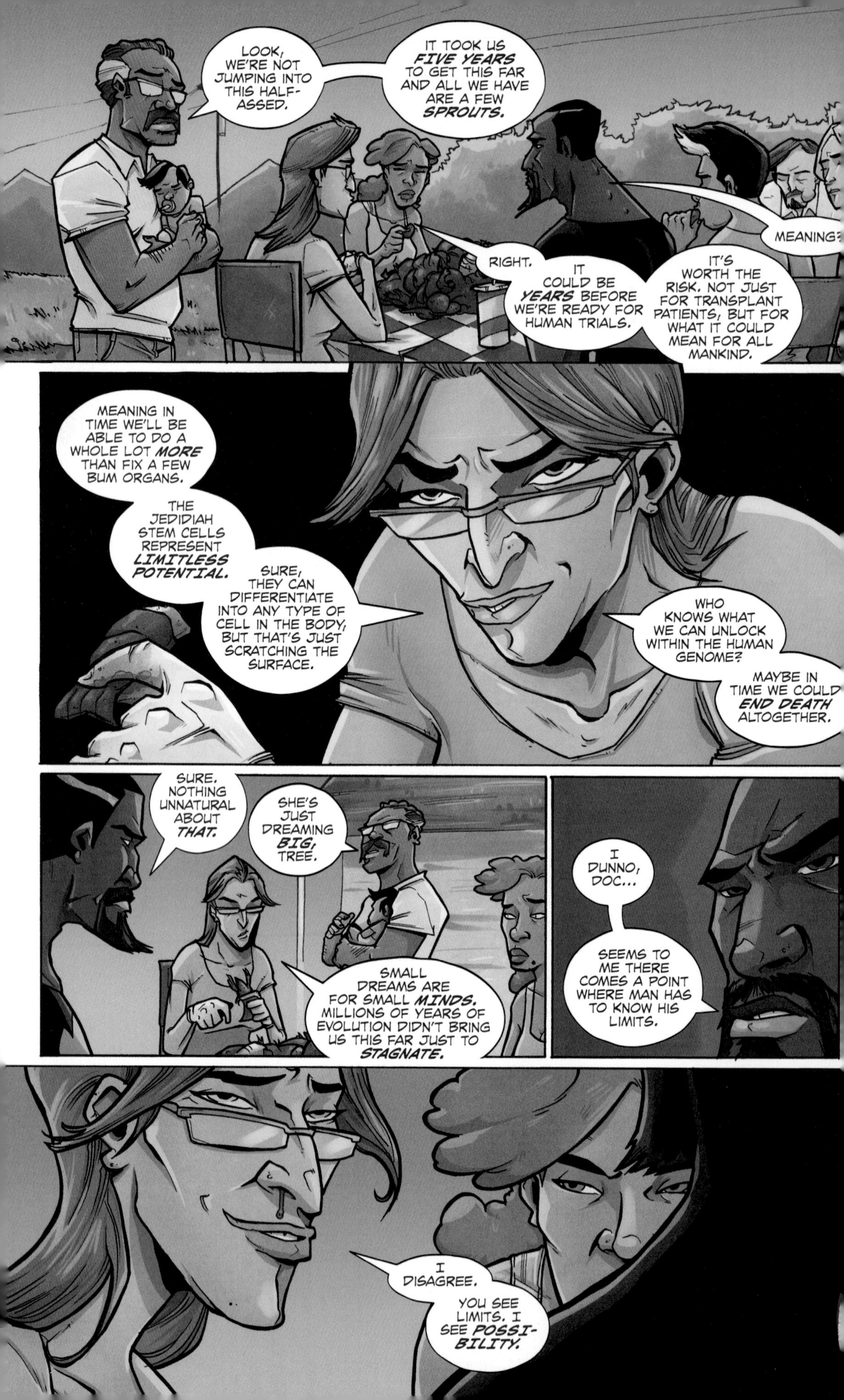
LOOK, WE'RE NOT JUMPING INTO THIS HALF-ASSED.
IT TOOK US FIVE YEARS TO GET THIS FAR AND ALL WE HAVE ARE A FEW SPROUTS.
MEANING?
RIGHT.
IT COULD BE YEARS BEFORE WE'RE READY FOR HUMAN TRIALS.
IT'S WORTH THE RISK. NOT JUST FOR TRANSPLANT PATIENTS, BUT FOR WHAT IT COULD MEAN FOR ALL MANKIND.
MEANING IN TIME WE'LL BE ABLE TO DO A WHOLE LOT MORE THAN FIX A FEW BUM ORGANS.
THE JEDIDIAH STEM CELLS REPRESENT LIMITLESS POTENTIAL.
SURE, THEY CAN DIFFERENTIATE INTO ANY TYPE OF CELL IN THE BODY, BUT THAT'S JUST SCRATCHING THE SURFACE.
WHO KNOWS WHAT WE CAN UNLOCK WITHIN THE HUMAN GENOME?
MAYBE IN TIME WE COULD END DEATH ALTOGETHER.
SURE. NOTHING UNNATURAL ABOUT THAT.
SHE'S JUST DREAMING BIG, TREE.
SMALL DREAMS ARE FOR SMALL MINDS. MILLIONS OF YEARS OF EVOLUTION DIDN'T BRING US THIS FAR JUST TO STAGNATE.
I DUNNO, DOC...
SEEMS TO ME THERE COMES A POINT WHERE MAN HAS TO KNOW HIS LIMITS.
I DISAGREE.
YOU SEE LIMITS. I SEE POSSI-BILITY.

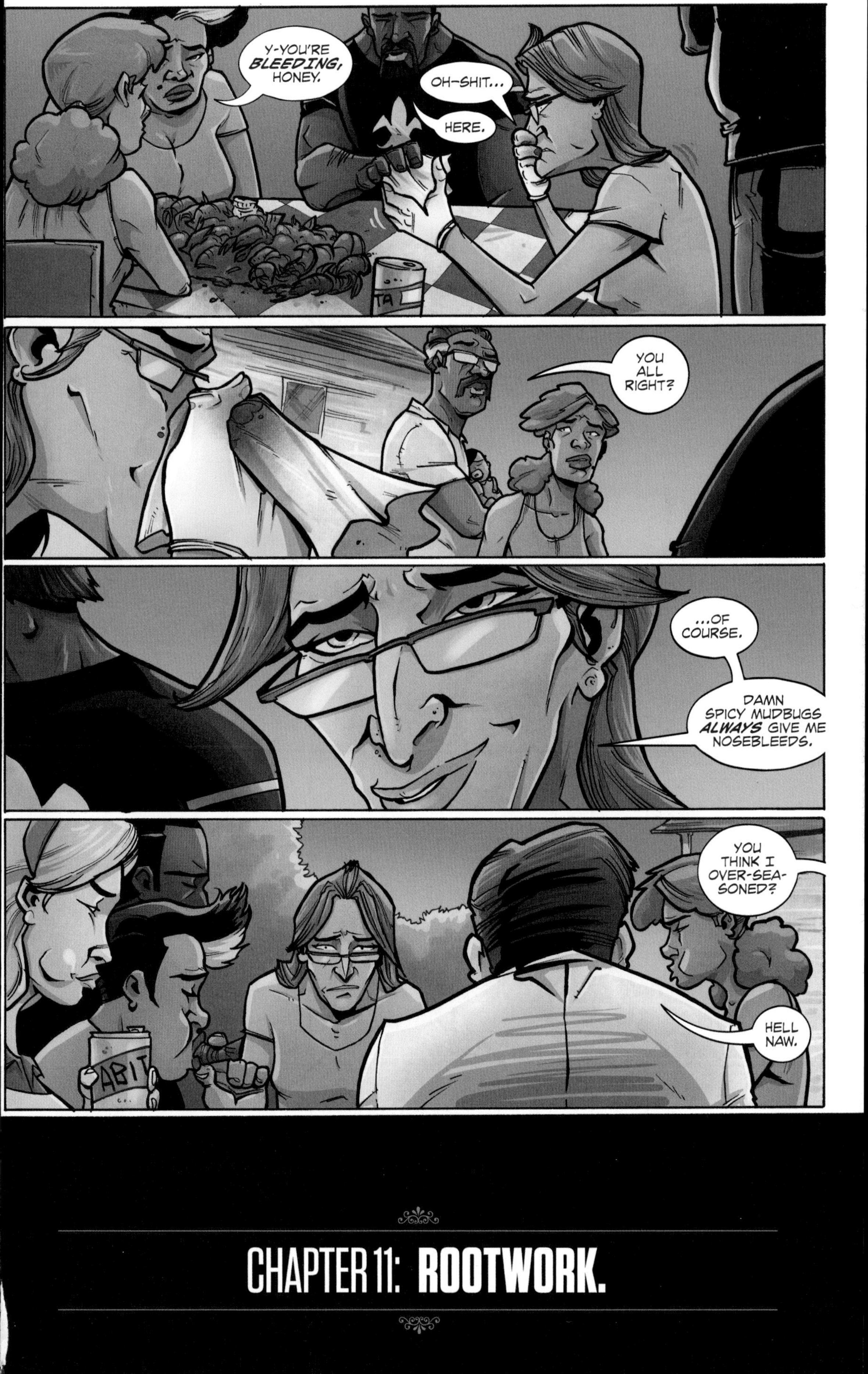
Y-YOU'RE *BLEEDING,* HONEY.
OH–SHIT...
HERE.
YOU ALL RIGHT?
...OF COURSE.
DAMN SPICY MUDBUGS *ALWAYS* GIVE ME NOSEBLEEDS.
YOU THINK I OVER-SEA-SONED?
HELL NAW.

CHAPTER 11: **ROOTWORK.**

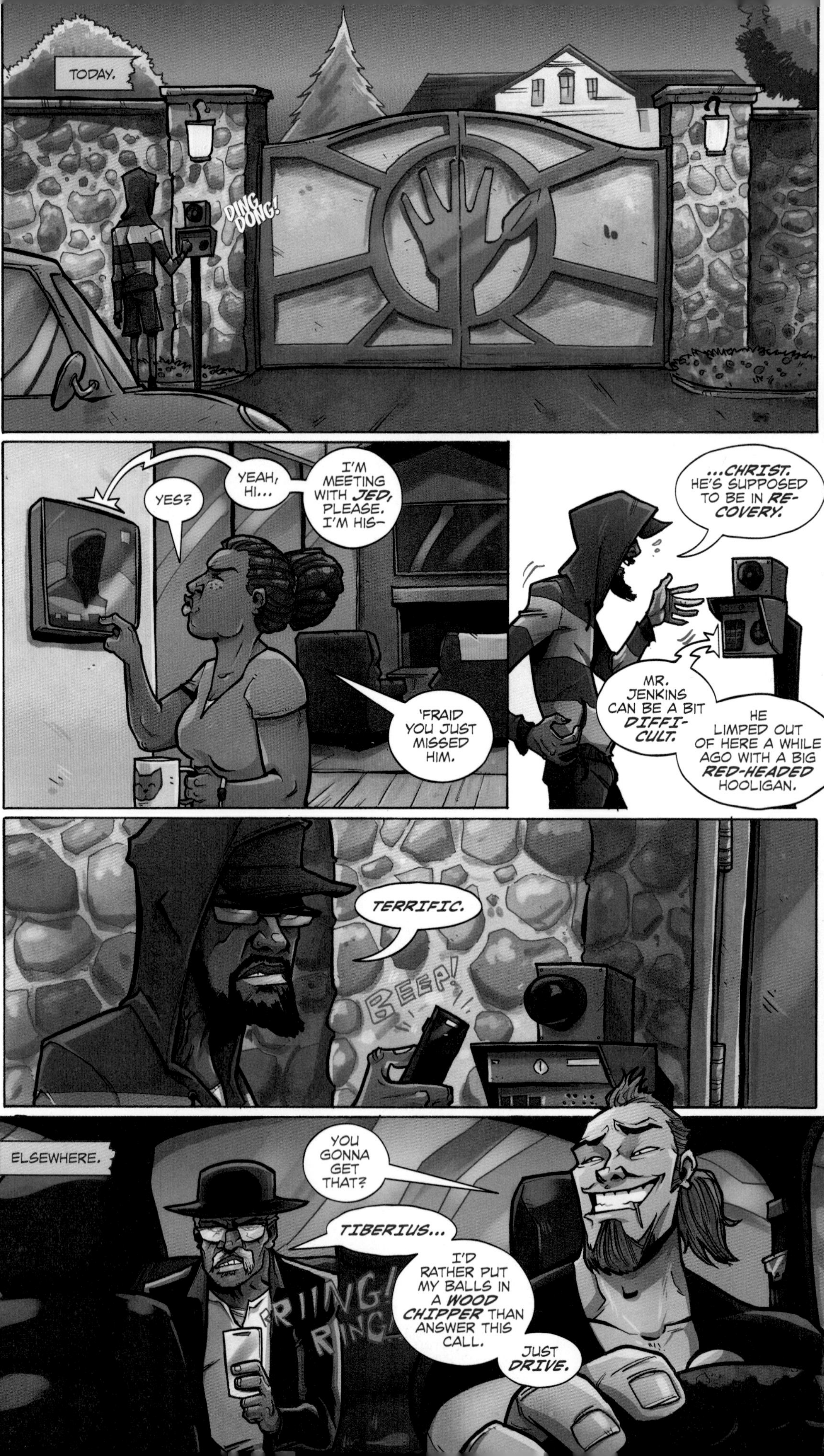
TODAY.
DING DONG!
YES?
YEAH, HI...
I'M MEETING WITH JED, PLEASE. I'M HIS-
'FRAID YOU JUST MISSED HIM.
...CHRIST. HE'S SUPPOSED TO BE IN RE-COVERY.
MR. JENKINS CAN BE A BIT DIFFI-CULT.
HE LIMPED OUT OF HERE A WHILE AGO WITH A BIG RED-HEADED HOOLIGAN.
TERRIFIC.
BEEP!
ELSEWHERE.
YOU GONNA GET THAT?
TIBERIUS...
I'D RATHER PUT MY BALLS IN A WOOD CHIPPER THAN ANSWER THIS CALL.
JUST DRIVE.
RIIING! RING!

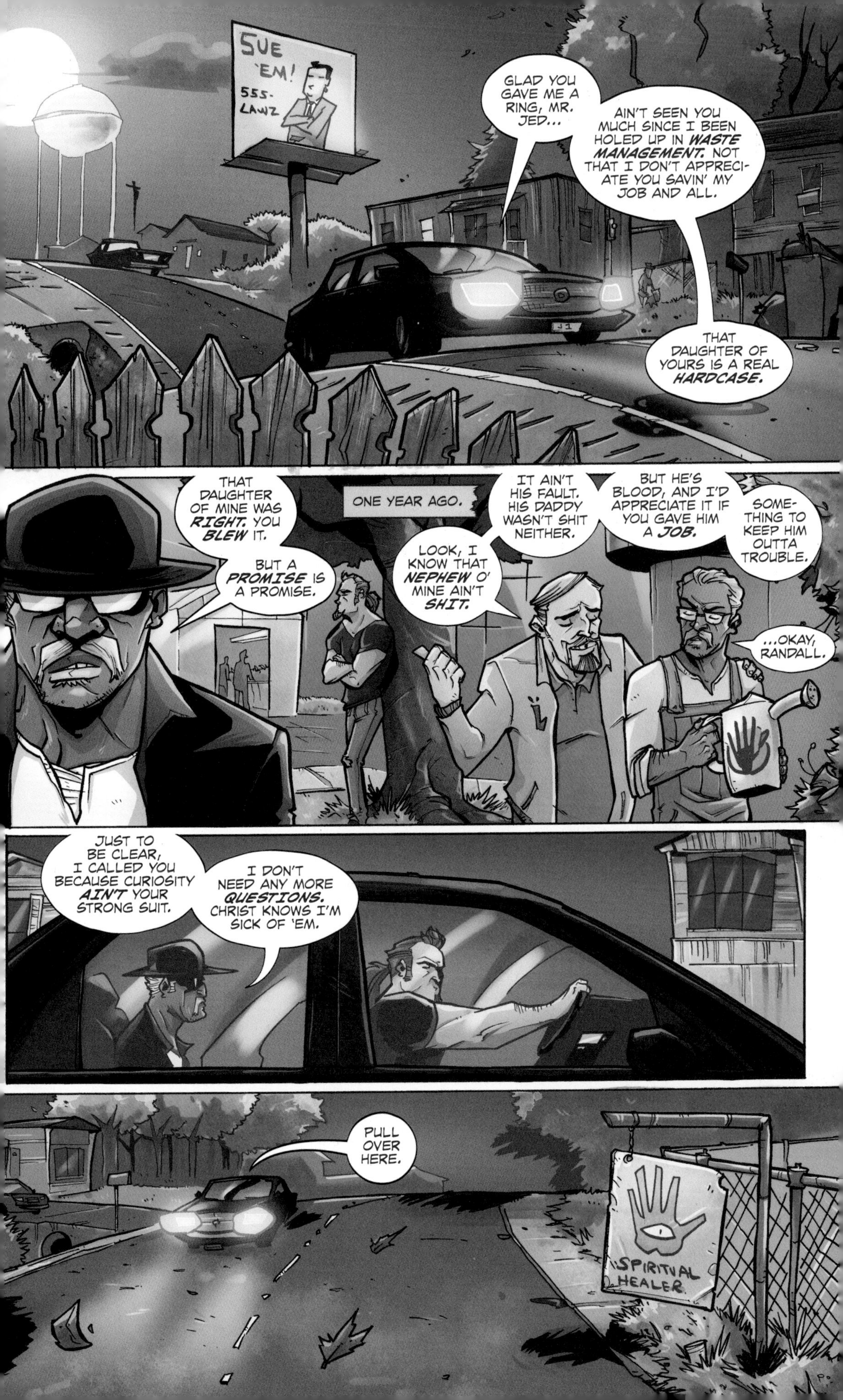
SUE 'EM! 555-LAWZ
GLAD YOU GAVE ME A RING, MR. JED...
AIN'T SEEN YOU MUCH SINCE I BEEN HOLED UP IN WASTE MANAGEMENT. NOT THAT I DON'T APPRECIATE YOU SAVIN' MY JOB AND ALL.
THAT DAUGHTER OF YOURS IS A REAL HARDCASE.
THAT DAUGHTER OF MINE WAS RIGHT. YOU BLEW IT.
BUT A PROMISE IS A PROMISE.
ONE YEAR AGO.
LOOK, I KNOW THAT NEPHEW O' MINE AIN'T SHIT.
IT AIN'T HIS FAULT. HIS DADDY WASN'T SHIT NEITHER.
BUT HE'S BLOOD, AND I'D APPRECIATE IT IF YOU GAVE HIM A JOB.
SOMETHING TO KEEP HIM OUTTA TROUBLE.
...OKAY, RANDALL.
JUST TO BE CLEAR, I CALLED YOU BECAUSE CURIOSITY AIN'T YOUR STRONG SUIT.
I DON'T NEED ANY MORE QUESTIONS. CHRIST KNOWS I'M SICK OF 'EM.
PULL OVER HERE.
SPIRITUAL HEALER

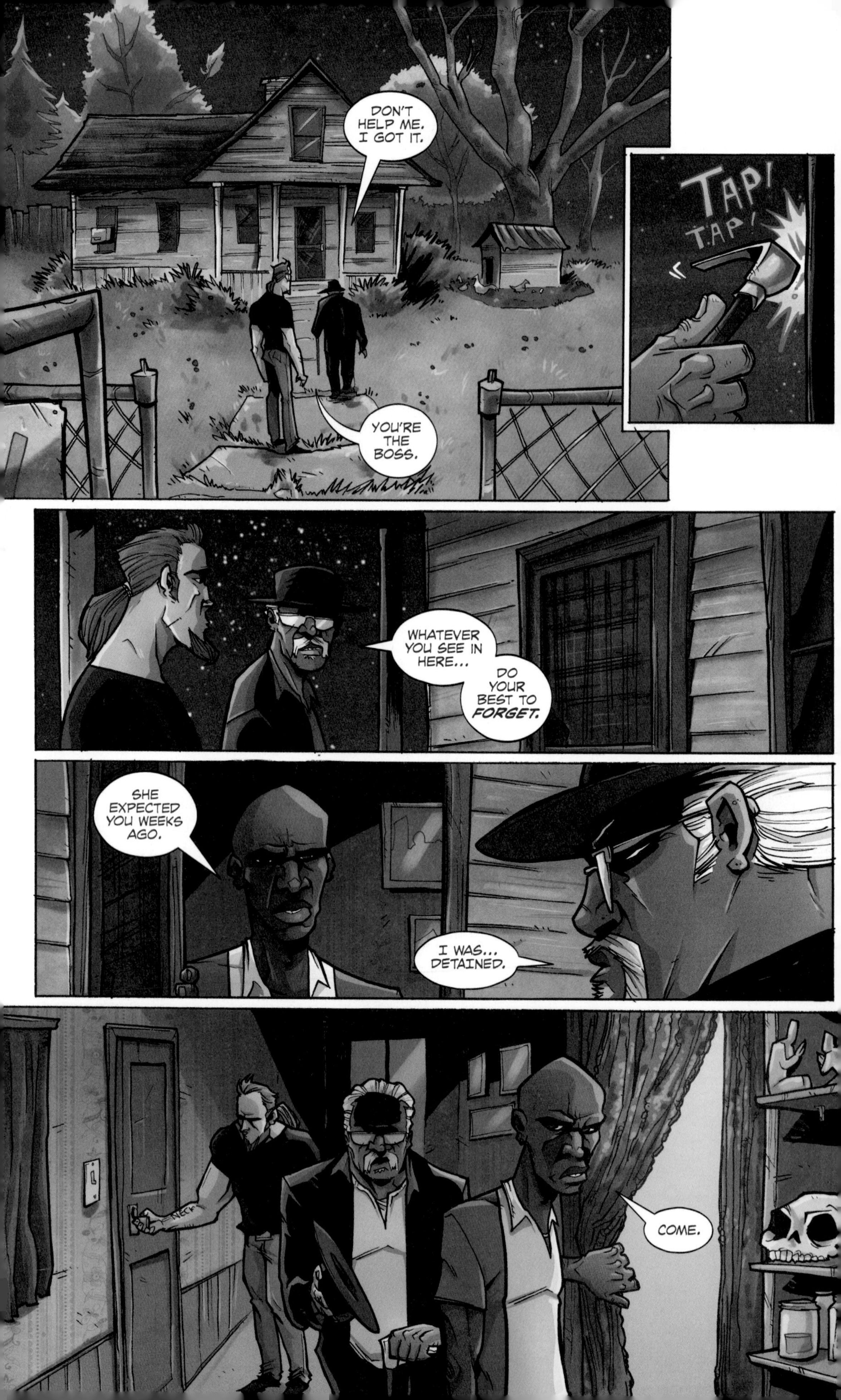
DON'T HELP ME. I GOT IT.
YOU'RE THE BOSS.
TAP! TAP!
WHATEVER YOU SEE IN HERE...
DO YOUR BEST TO FORGET.
SHE EXPECTED YOU WEEKS AGO.
I WAS... DETAINED.
COME.

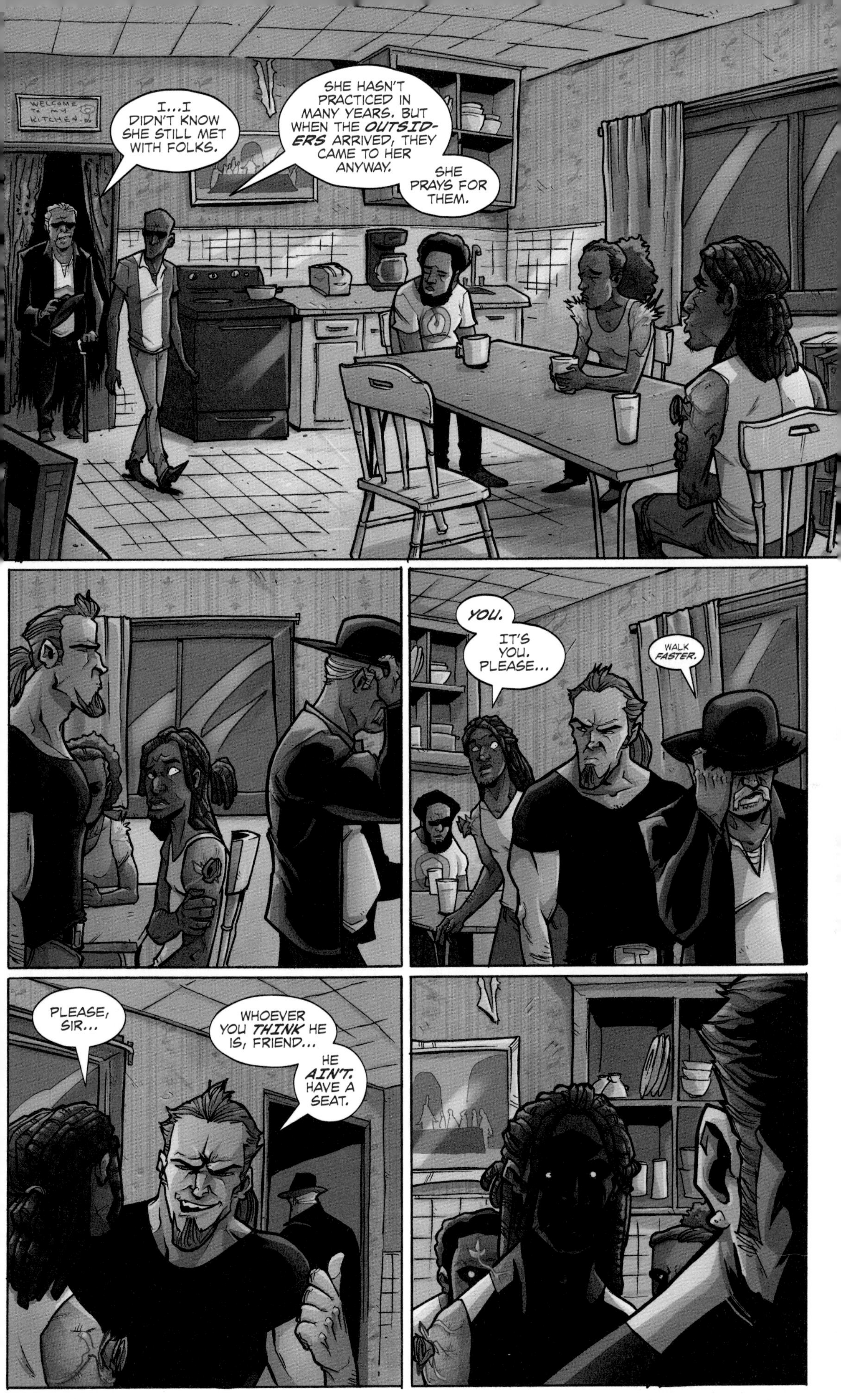
WELCOME TO MY KITCHEN
I...I DIDN'T KNOW SHE STILL MET WITH FOLKS.
SHE HASN'T PRACTICED IN MANY YEARS. BUT WHEN THE *OUTSIDERS* ARRIVED, THEY CAME TO HER ANYWAY.
SHE PRAYS FOR THEM.
YOU.
IT'S YOU. PLEASE...
WALK *FASTER.*
PLEASE, SIR...
WHOEVER YOU *THINK* HE IS, FRIEND...
HE *AIN'T.* HAVE A SEAT.

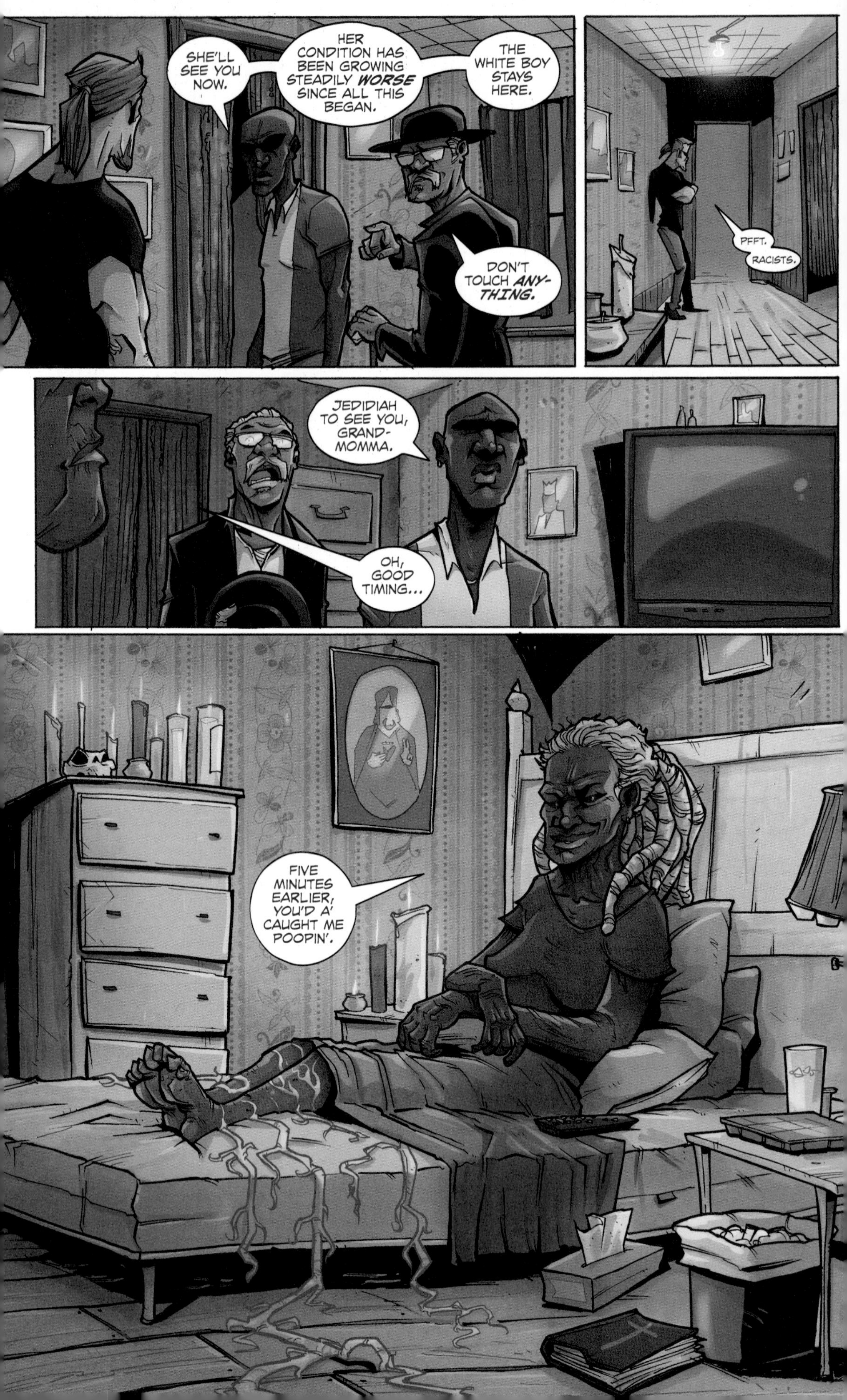
SHE'LL SEE YOU NOW.
HER CONDITION HAS BEEN GROWING STEADILY WORSE SINCE ALL THIS BEGAN.
THE WHITE BOY STAYS HERE.
DON'T TOUCH ANYTHING.
PFFT.
RACISTS.
JEDIDIAH TO SEE YOU, GRAND-MOMMA.
OH, GOOD TIMING...
FIVE MINUTES EARLIER, YOU'D A' CAUGHT ME POOPIN'.

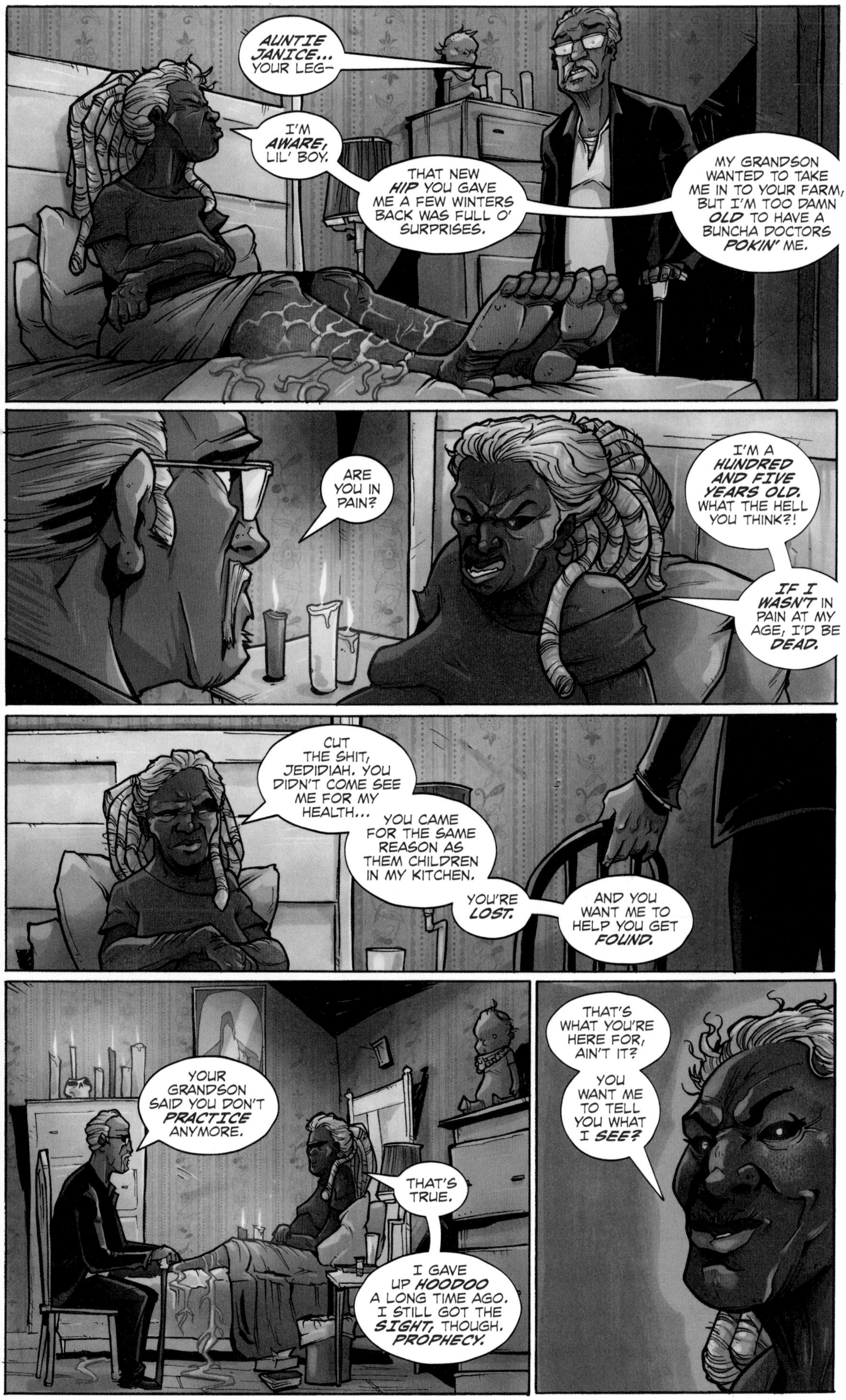
AUNTIE JANICE... YOUR LEG—
I'M AWARE, LIL' BOY.
THAT NEW HIP YOU GAVE ME A FEW WINTERS BACK WAS FULL O' SURPRISES.
MY GRANDSON WANTED TO TAKE ME IN TO YOUR FARM, BUT I'M TOO DAMN OLD TO HAVE A BUNCHA DOCTORS POKIN' ME.
ARE YOU IN PAIN?
I'M A HUNDRED AND FIVE YEARS OLD. WHAT THE HELL YOU THINK?!
IF I WASN'T IN PAIN AT MY AGE, I'D BE DEAD.
CUT THE SHIT, JEDIDIAH. YOU DIDN'T COME SEE ME FOR MY HEALTH...
YOU CAME FOR THE SAME REASON AS THEM CHILDREN IN MY KITCHEN.
YOU'RE LOST.
AND YOU WANT ME TO HELP YOU GET FOUND.
YOUR GRANDSON SAID YOU DON'T PRACTICE ANYMORE.
THAT'S TRUE.
I GAVE UP HOODOO A LONG TIME AGO. I STILL GOT THE SIGHT, THOUGH. PROPHECY.
THAT'S WHAT YOU'RE HERE FOR, AIN'T IT?
YOU WANT ME TO TELL YOU WHAT I SEE?

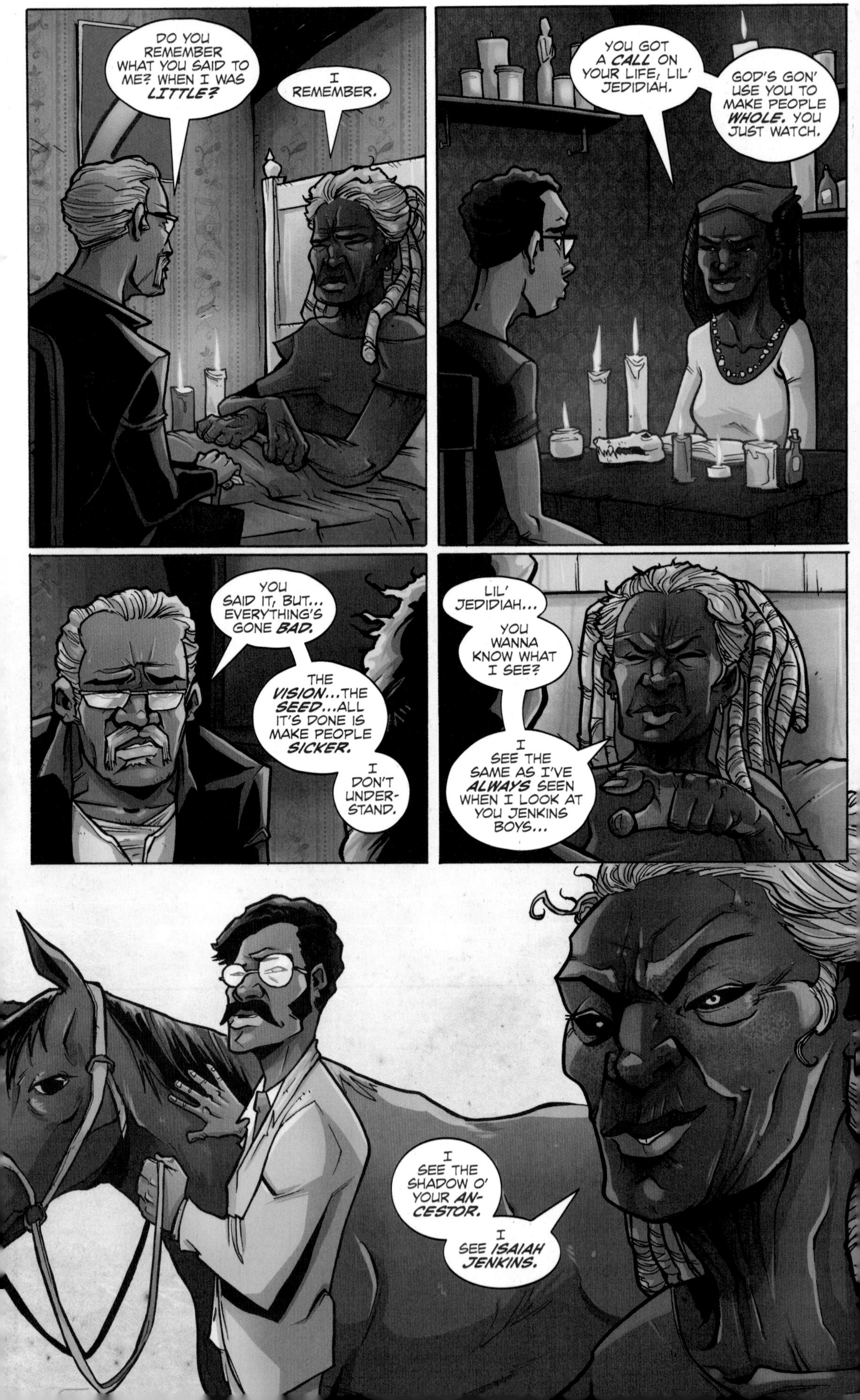

DO YOU REMEMBER WHAT YOU SAID TO ME? WHEN I WAS *LITTLE?*
I REMEMBER.
YOU GOT A *CALL* ON YOUR LIFE, LIL' JEDIDIAH.
GOD'S GON' USE YOU TO MAKE PEOPLE *WHOLE.* YOU JUST WATCH.
YOU SAID IT, BUT... EVERYTHING'S GONE *BAD.*
THE *VISION*...THE *SEED*...ALL IT'S DONE IS MAKE PEOPLE *SICKER.*
I DON'T UNDER-STAND.
LIL' JEDIDIAH...
YOU WANNA KNOW WHAT I SEE?
I SEE THE SAME AS I'VE *ALWAYS* SEEN WHEN I LOOK AT YOU JENKINS BOYS...
I SEE THE SHADOW O' YOUR *AN-CESTOR.*
I SEE *ISAIAH JENKINS.*

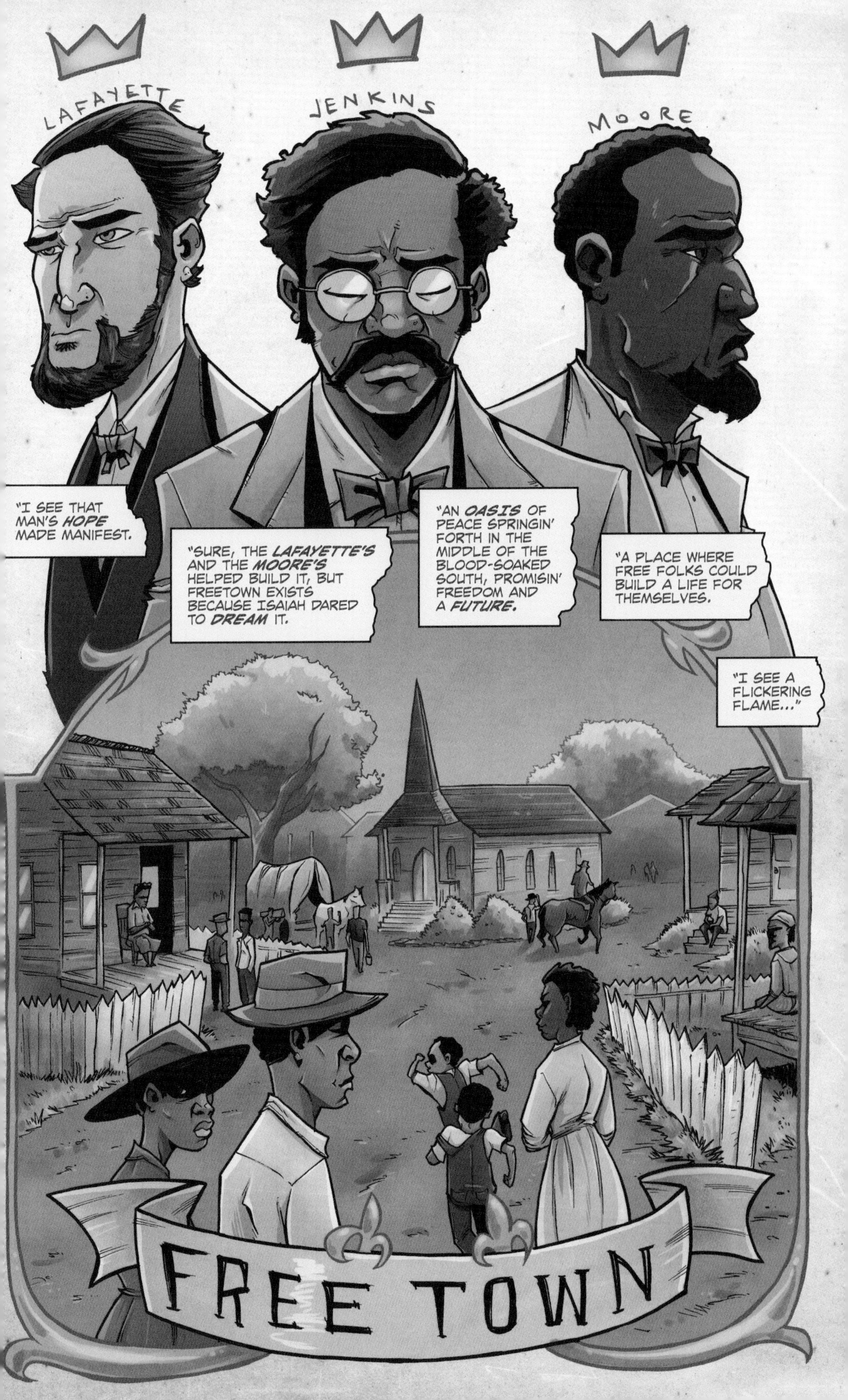
LAFAYETTE
JENKINS
MOORE
"I SEE THAT MAN'S *HOPE* MADE MANIFEST.
"SURE, THE *LAFAYETTE'S* AND THE *MOORE'S* HELPED BUILD IT, BUT FREETOWN EXISTS BECAUSE ISAIAH DARED TO *DREAM* IT.
"AN *OASIS* OF PEACE SPRINGIN' FORTH IN THE MIDDLE OF THE BLOOD-SOAKED SOUTH, PROMISIN' FREEDOM AND A *FUTURE.*
"A PLACE WHERE FREE FOLKS COULD BUILD A LIFE FOR THEMSELVES.
"I SEE A FLICKERING FLAME..."
FREE TOWN

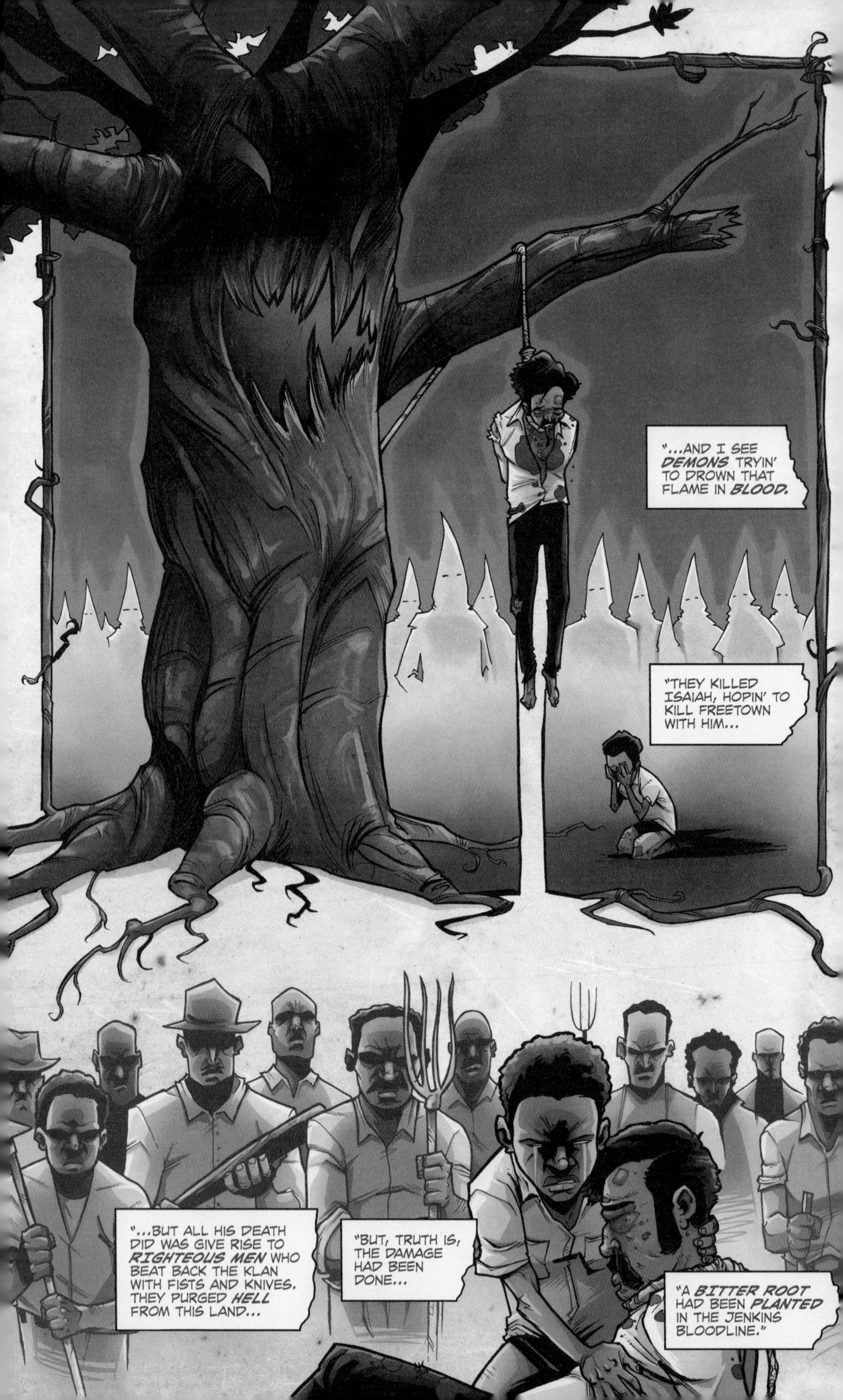
"...AND I SEE DEMONS TRYIN' TO DROWN THAT FLAME IN BLOOD.
"THEY KILLED ISAIAH, HOPIN' TO KILL FREETOWN WITH HIM...
"...BUT ALL HIS DEATH DID WAS GIVE RISE TO RIGHTEOUS MEN WHO BEAT BACK THE KLAN WITH FISTS AND KNIVES. THEY PURGED HELL FROM THIS LAND...
"BUT, TRUTH IS, THE DAMAGE HAD BEEN DONE...
"A BITTER ROOT HAD BEEN PLANTED IN THE JENKINS BLOODLINE."

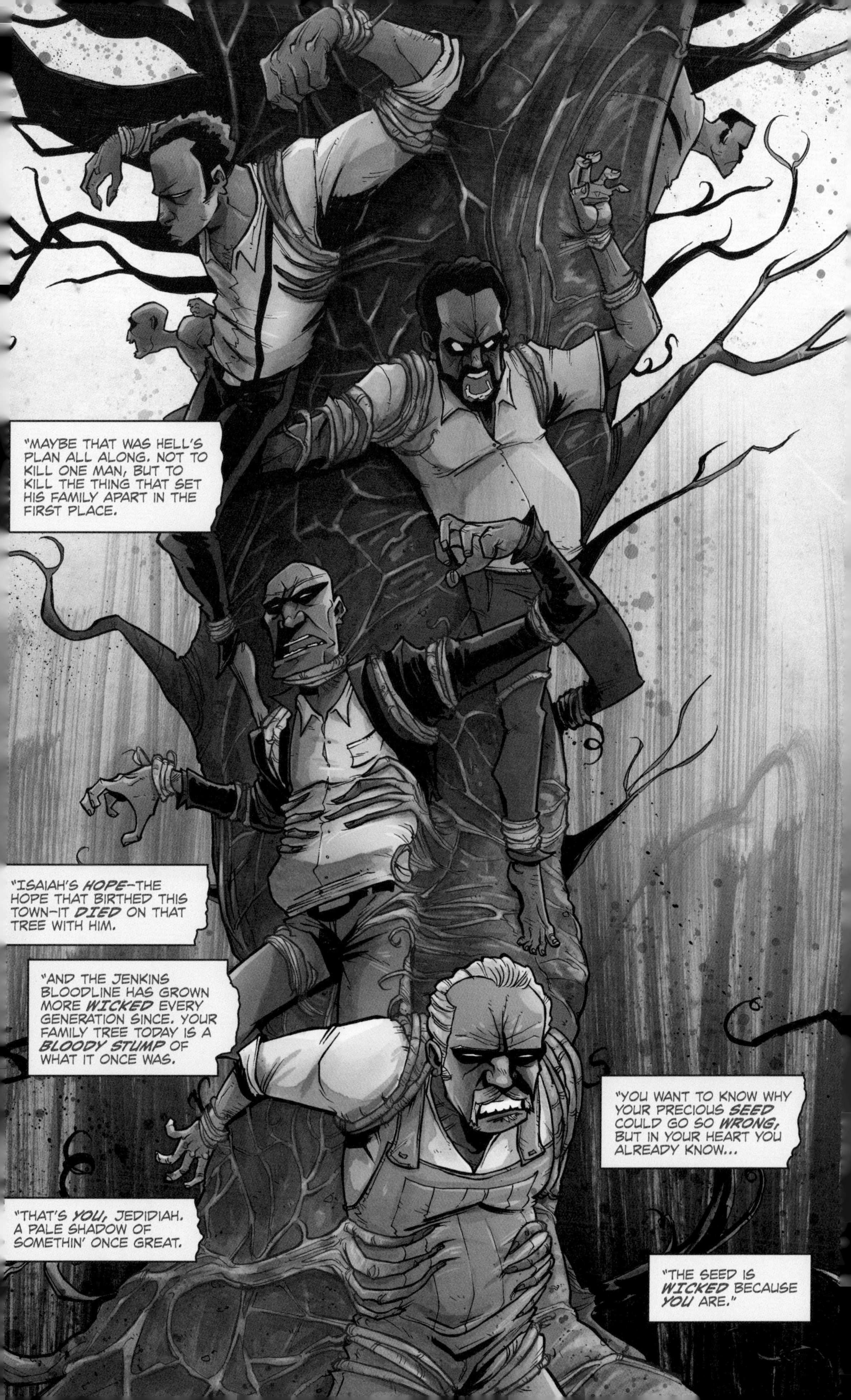
"MAYBE THAT WAS HELL'S PLAN ALL ALONG. NOT TO KILL ONE MAN, BUT TO KILL THE THING THAT SET HIS FAMILY APART IN THE FIRST PLACE.
"ISAIAH'S *HOPE*--THE HOPE THAT BIRTHED THIS TOWN--IT *DIED* ON THAT TREE WITH HIM.
"AND THE JENKINS BLOODLINE HAS GROWN MORE *WICKED* EVERY GENERATION SINCE. YOUR FAMILY TREE TODAY IS A *BLOODY STUMP* OF WHAT IT ONCE WAS.
"YOU WANT TO KNOW WHY YOUR PRECIOUS *SEED* COULD GO SO *WRONG*, BUT IN YOUR HEART YOU ALREADY KNOW...
"THAT'S *YOU,* JEDIDIAH. A PALE SHADOW OF SOMETHIN' ONCE GREAT.
"THE SEED IS *WICKED* BECAUSE *YOU* ARE."

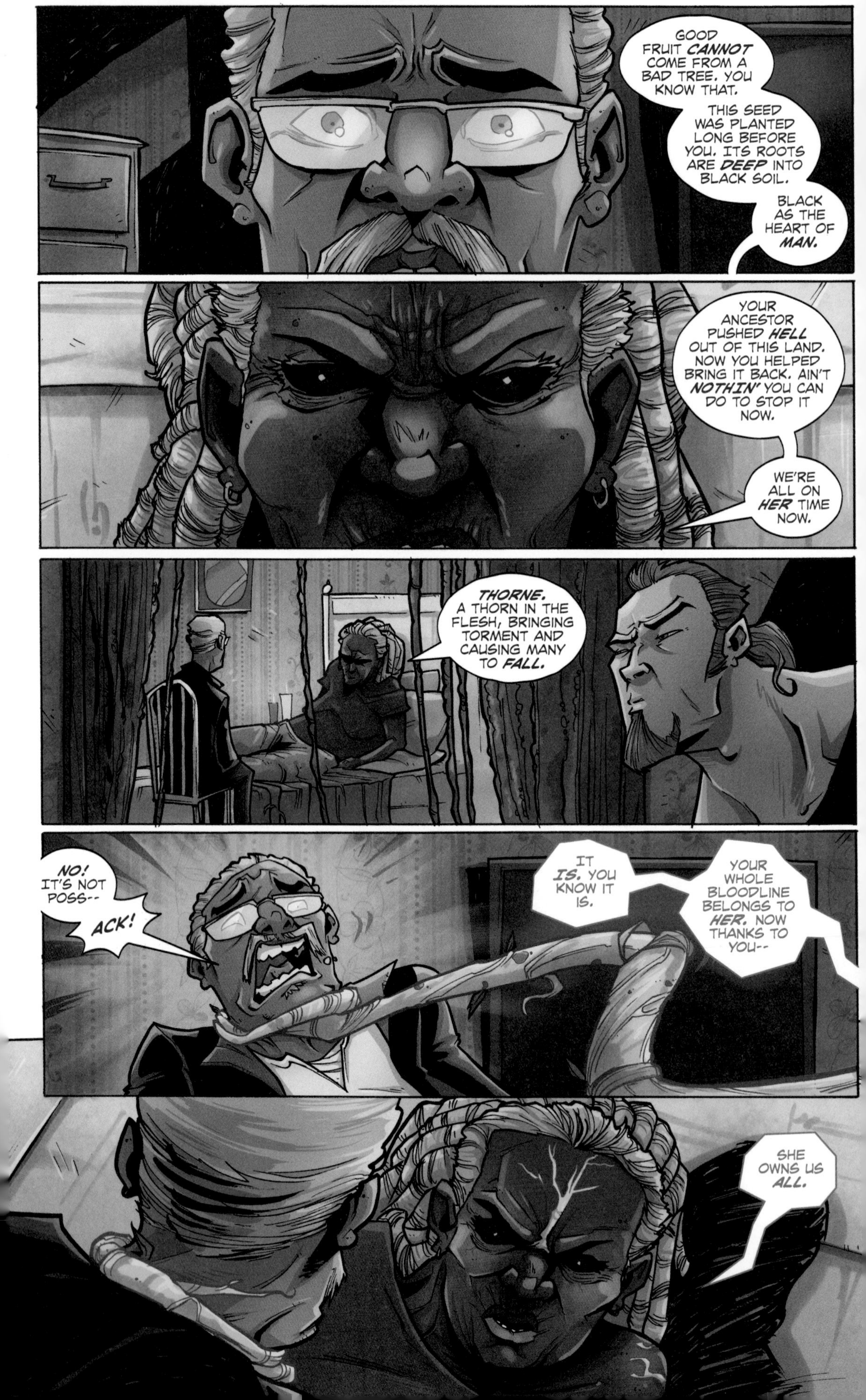
GOOD FRUIT CANNOT COME FROM A BAD TREE. YOU KNOW THAT.
THIS SEED WAS PLANTED LONG BEFORE YOU. ITS ROOTS ARE DEEP INTO BLACK SOIL.
BLACK AS THE HEART OF MAN.
YOUR ANCESTOR PUSHED HELL OUT OF THIS LAND. NOW YOU HELPED BRING IT BACK. AIN'T NOTHIN' YOU CAN DO TO STOP IT NOW.
WE'RE ALL ON HER TIME NOW.
THORNE. A THORN IN THE FLESH, BRINGING TORMENT AND CAUSING MANY TO FALL.
NO! IT'S NOT POSS--
ACK!
IT IS. YOU KNOW IT IS.
YOUR WHOLE BLOODLINE BELONGS TO HER. NOW THANKS TO YOU--
SHE OWNS US ALL.

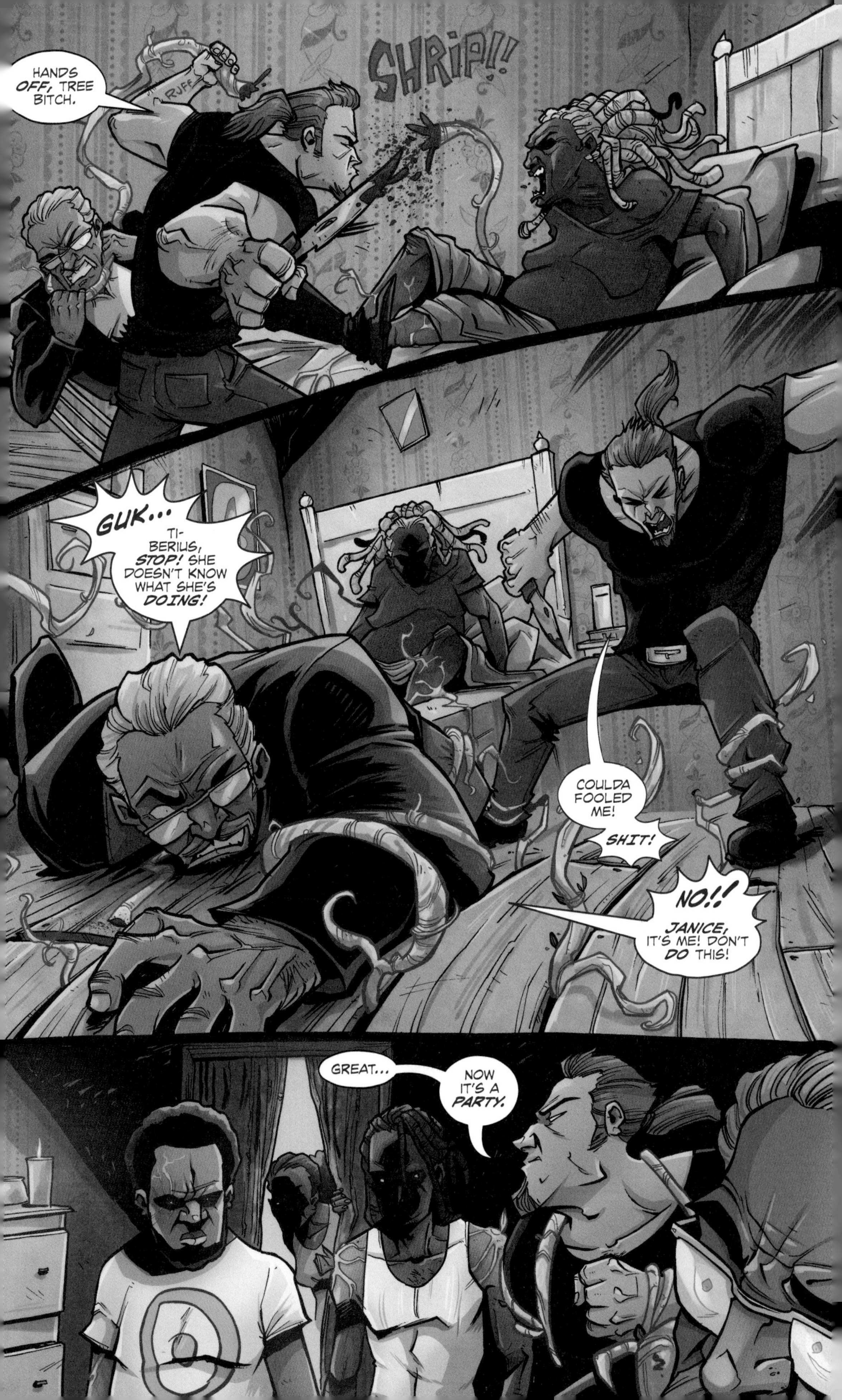
HANDS OFF, TREE BITCH.
SHRIP!!
GUK...
TI-BERIUS, STOP! SHE DOESN'T KNOW WHAT SHE'S DOING!
COULDA FOOLED ME!
SHIT!
NO!!
JANICE, IT'S ME! DON'T DO THIS!
GREAT...
NOW IT'S A PARTY.

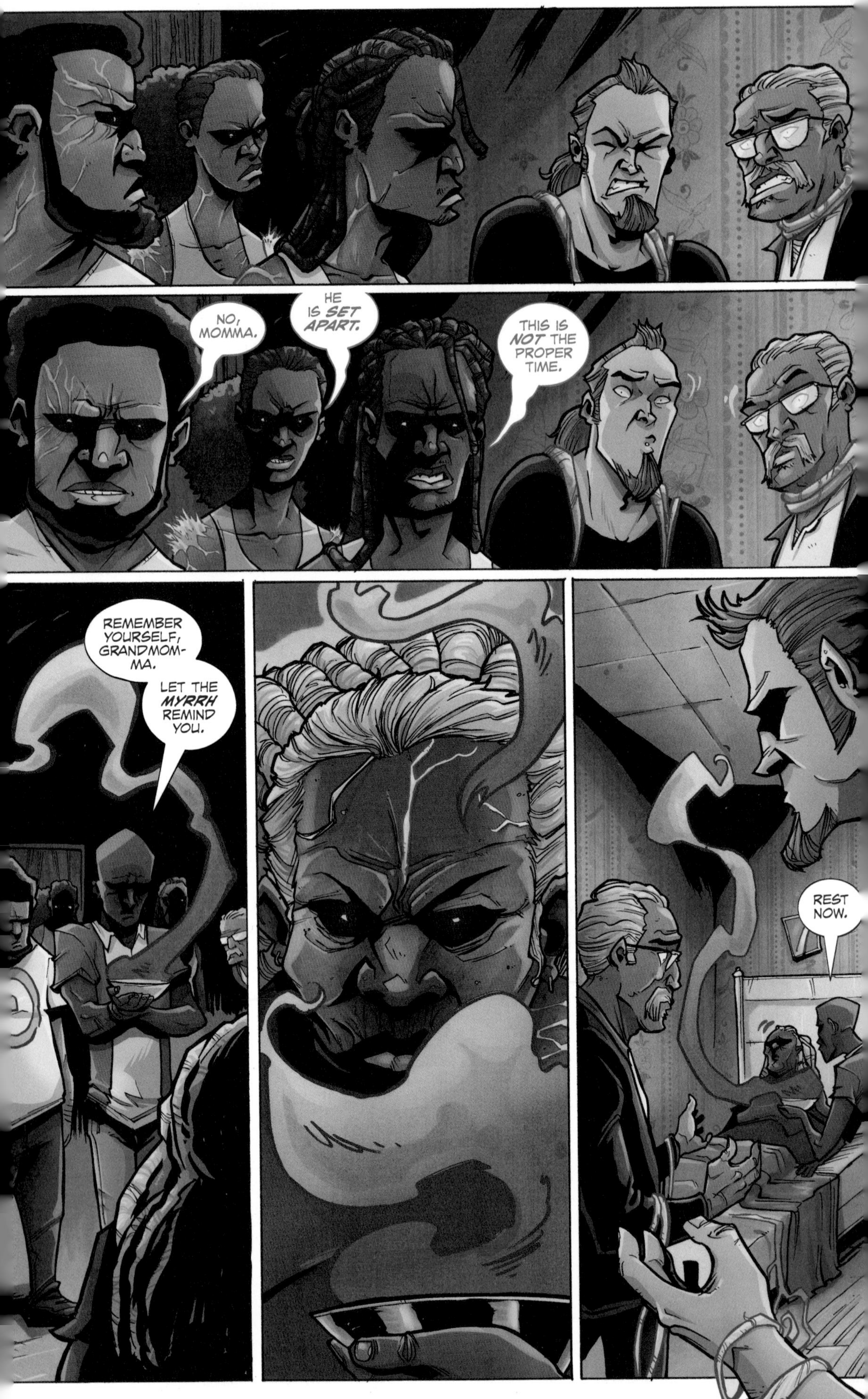
NO, MOMMA.
HE IS SET APART.
THIS IS NOT THE PROPER TIME.
REMEMBER YOURSELF, GRANDMOM-MA.
LET THE MYRRH REMIND YOU.
REST NOW.

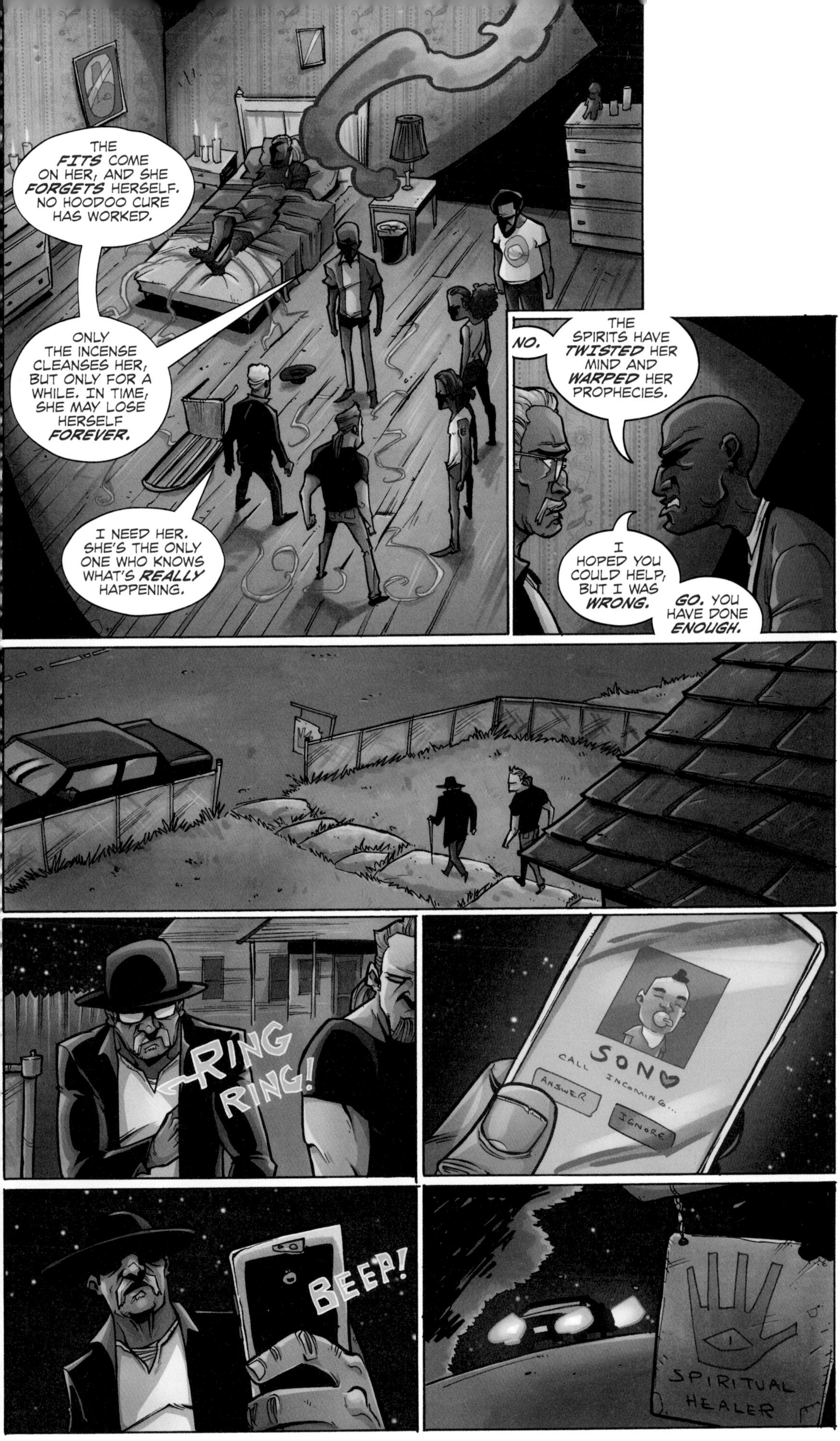
THE FITS COME ON HER, AND SHE FORGETS HERSELF. NO HOODOO CURE HAS WORKED.
ONLY THE INCENSE CLEANSES HER, BUT ONLY FOR A WHILE. IN TIME, SHE MAY LOSE HERSELF FOREVER.
I NEED HER. SHE'S THE ONLY ONE WHO KNOWS WHAT'S REALLY HAPPENING.
NO.
THE SPIRITS HAVE TWISTED HER MIND AND WARPED HER PROPHECIES.
I HOPED YOU COULD HELP, BUT I WAS WRONG.
GO. YOU HAVE DONE ENOUGH.
RING RING!
SON
CALL INCOMING...
ANSWER
IGNORE
BEEP!
SPIRITUAL HEALER

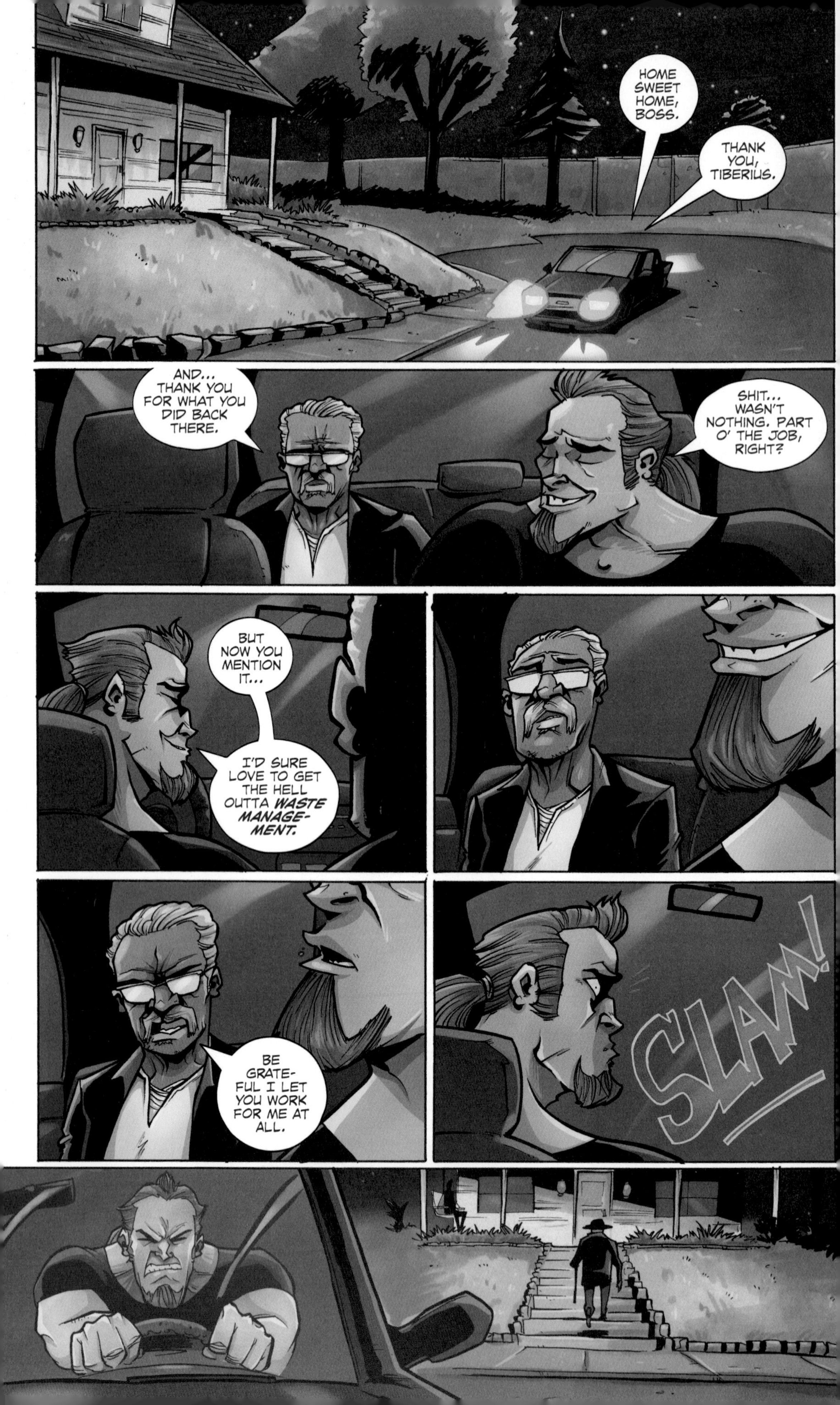
HOME SWEET HOME, BOSS.
THANK YOU, TIBERIUS.
AND... THANK YOU FOR WHAT YOU DID BACK THERE.
SHIT... WASN'T NOTHING. PART O' THE JOB, RIGHT?
BUT NOW YOU MENTION IT...
I'D SURE LOVE TO GET THE HELL OUTTA WASTE MANAGE-MENT.
BE GRATE-FUL I LET YOU WORK FOR ME AT ALL.
SLAM!

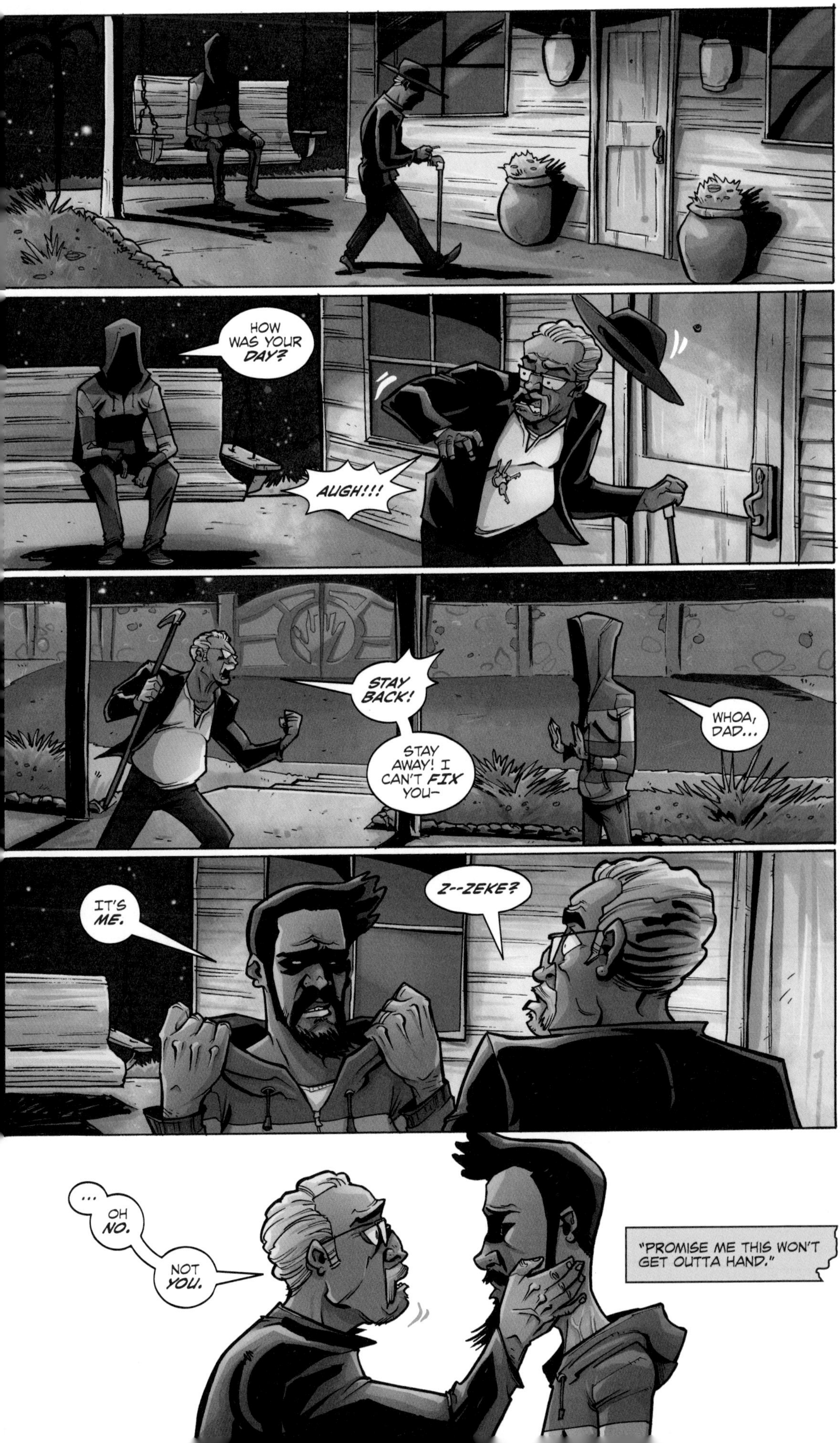
HOW WAS YOUR DAY?
AUGH!!!
STAY BACK!
STAY AWAY! I CAN'T FIX YOU–
WHOA, DAD...
IT'S ME.
Z--ZEKE?
... OH NO.
NOT YOU.
"PROMISE ME THIS WON'T GET OUTTA HAND."

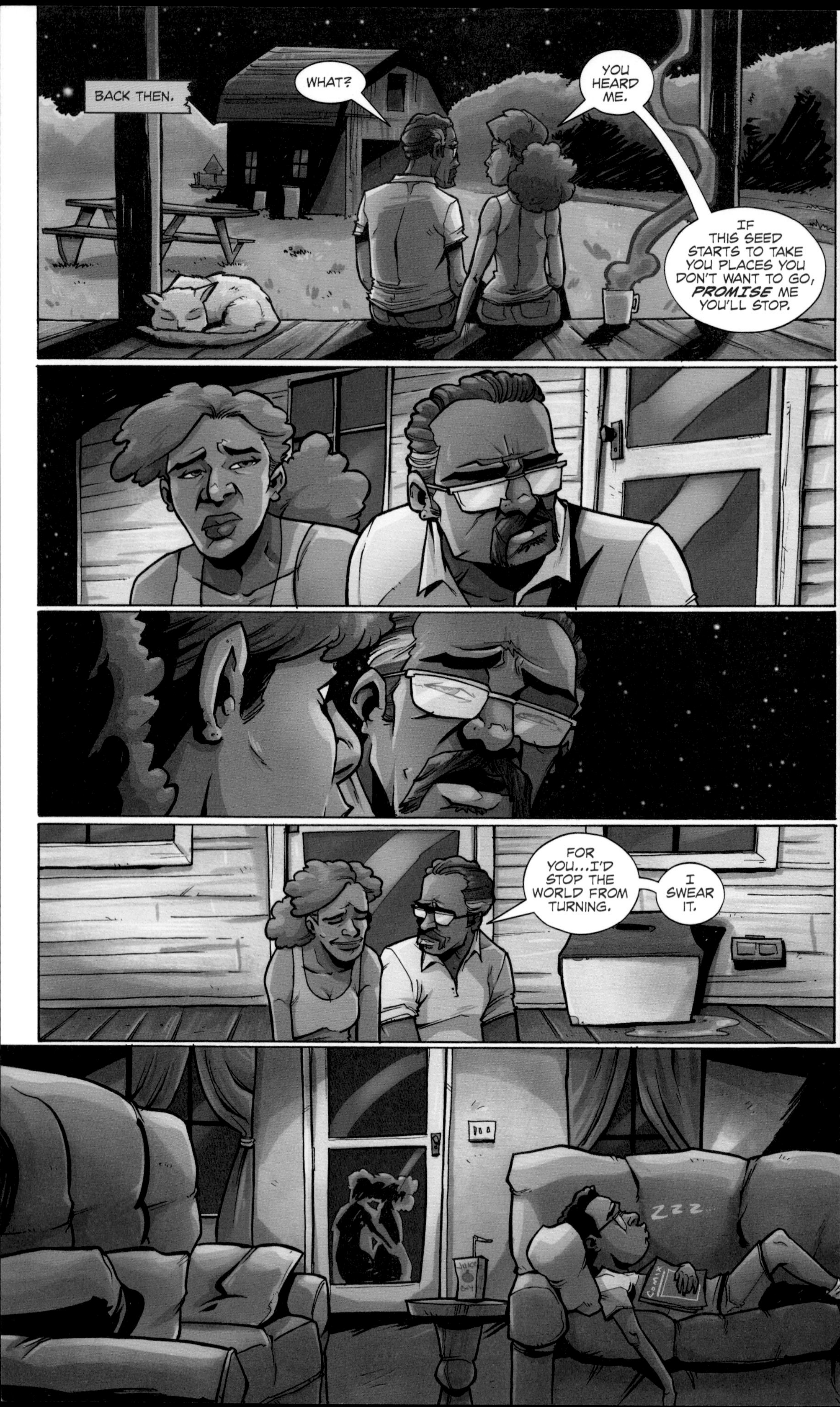
BACK THEN.
WHAT?
YOU HEARD ME.
IF THIS SEED STARTS TO TAKE YOU PLACES YOU DON'T WANT TO GO, **PROMISE** ME YOU'LL STOP.
FOR YOU...I'D STOP THE WORLD FROM TURNING.
I SWEAR IT.
ZZZ...

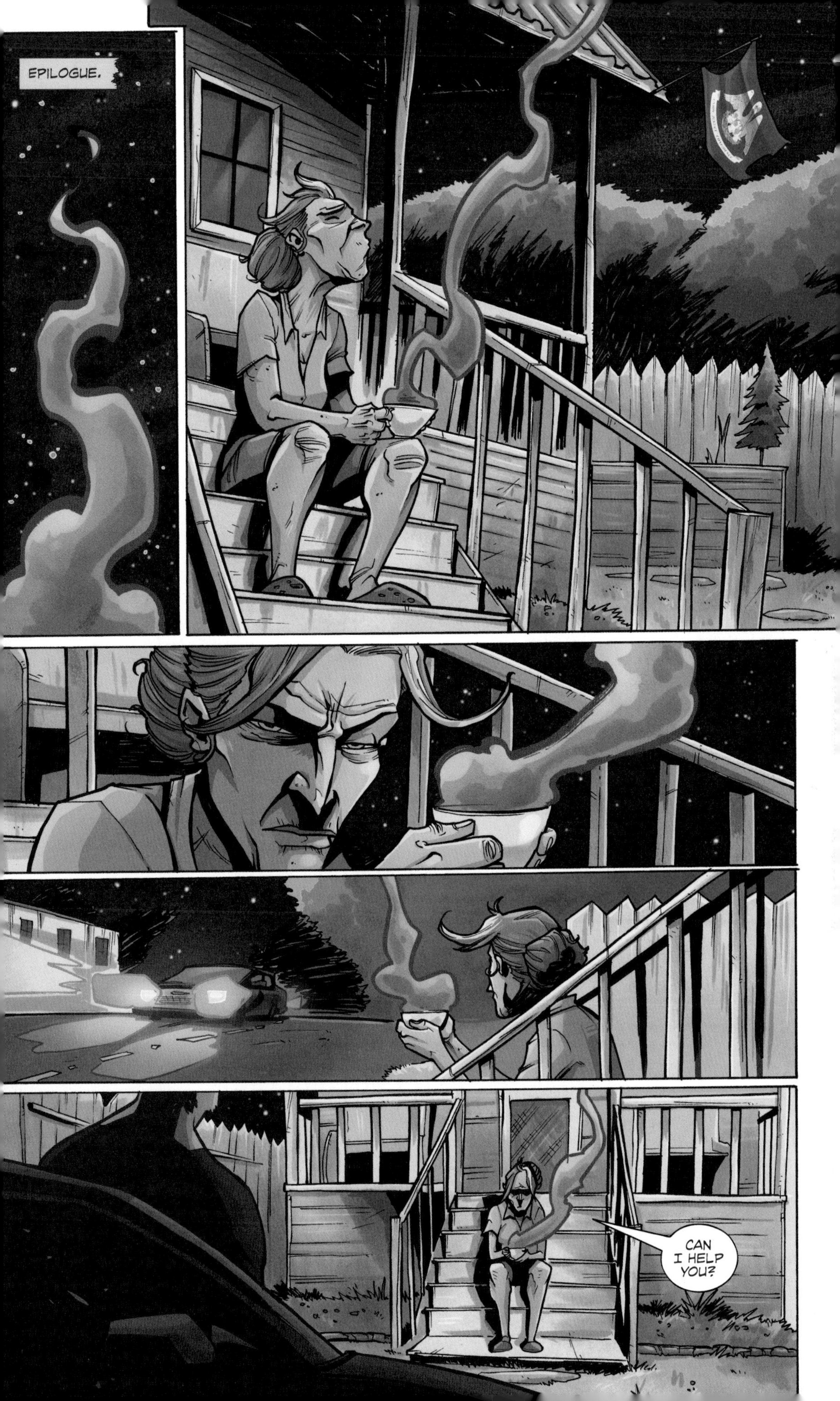
EPILOGUE.
CAN I HELP YOU?

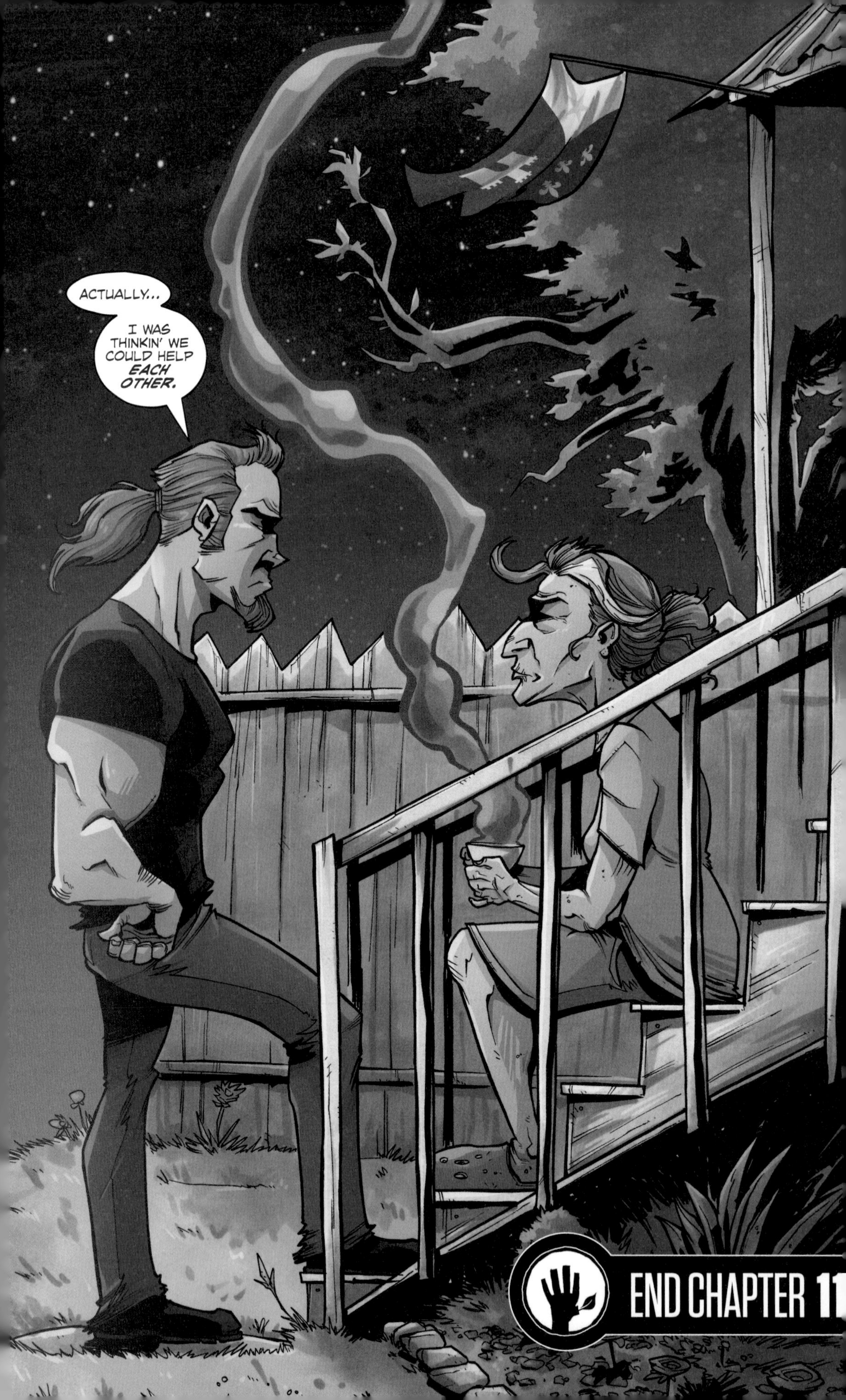
ACTUALLY... I WAS THINKIN' WE COULD HELP *EACH OTHER.*
END CHAPTER 11

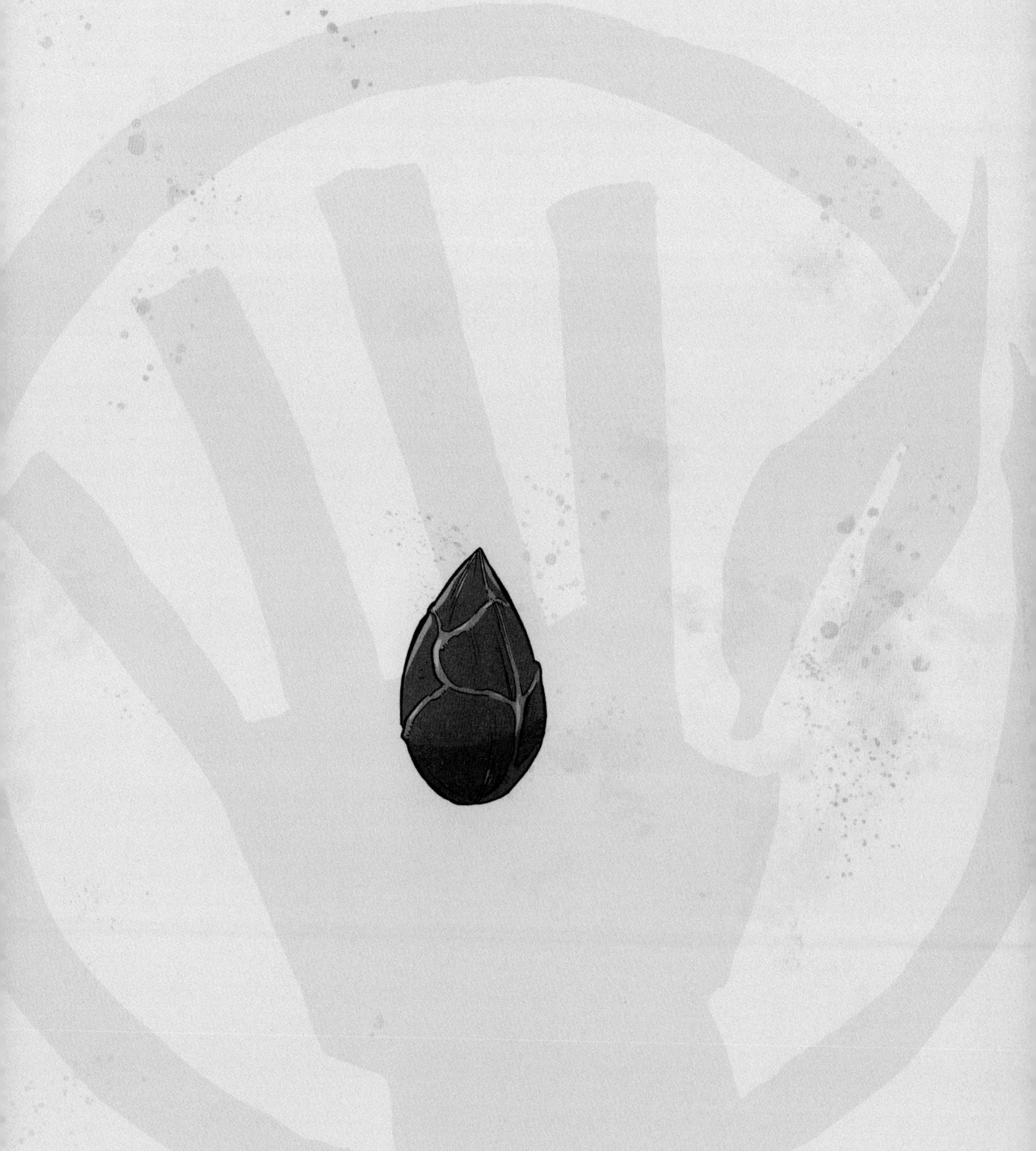

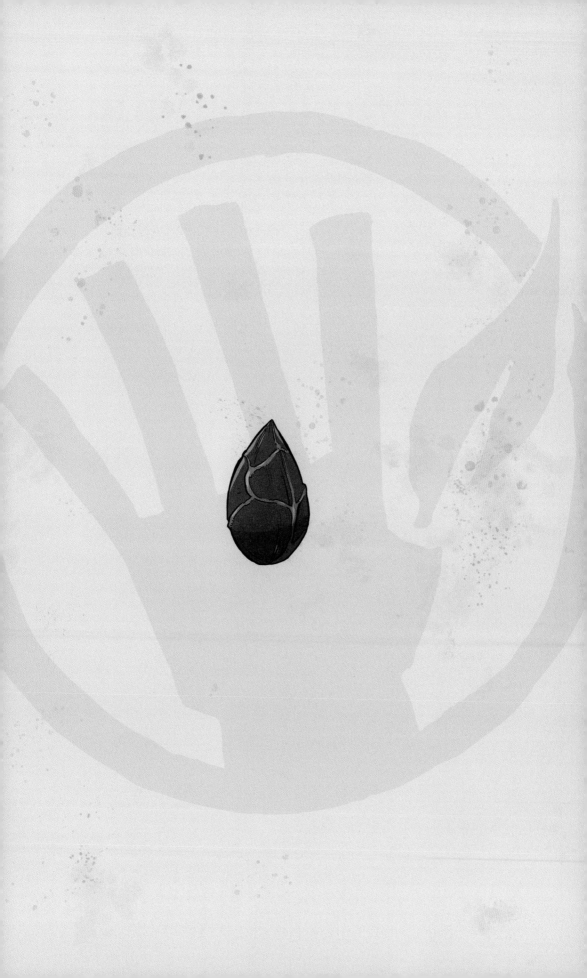

CHAPTER 12

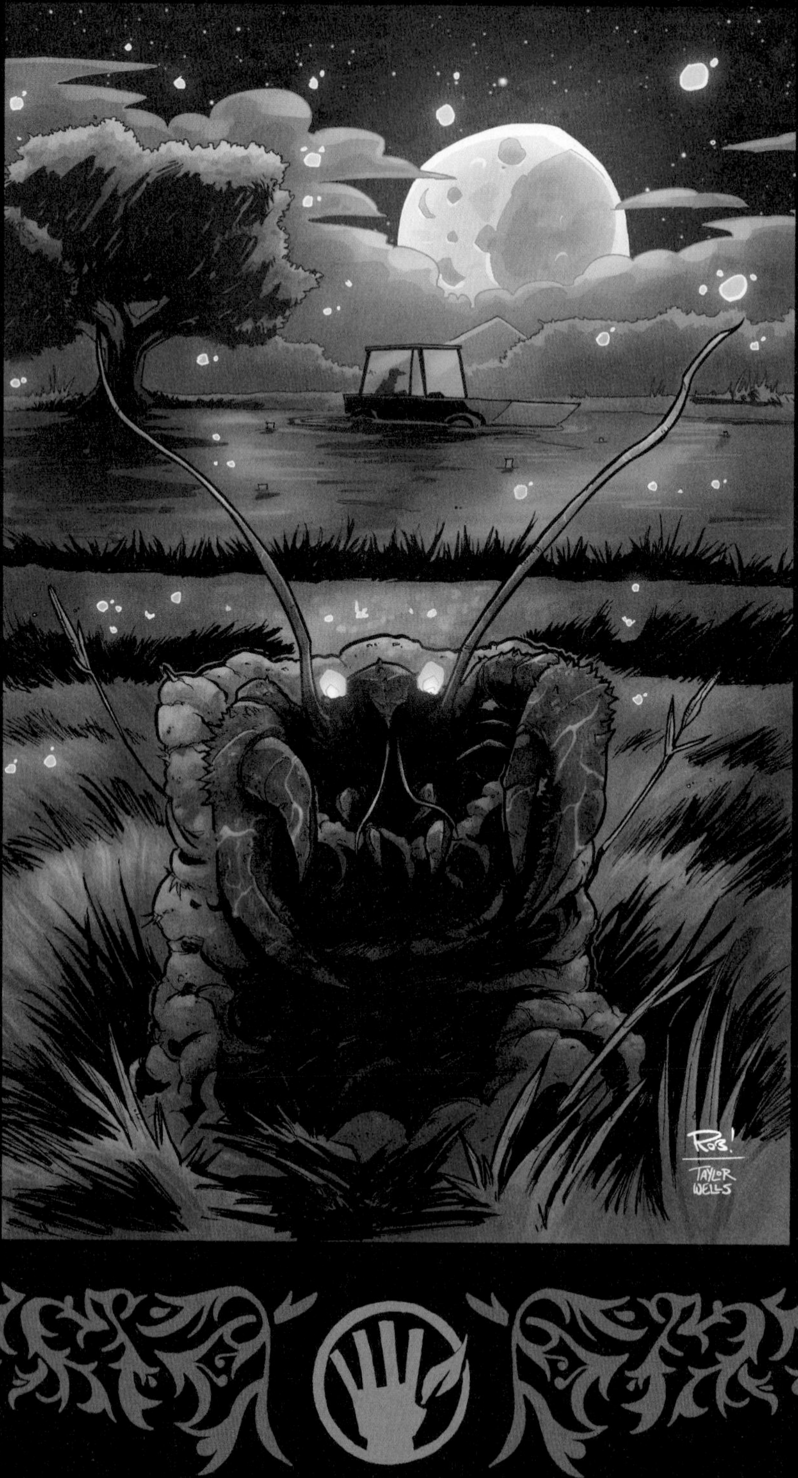
ROB!
TAYLOR
WELLS

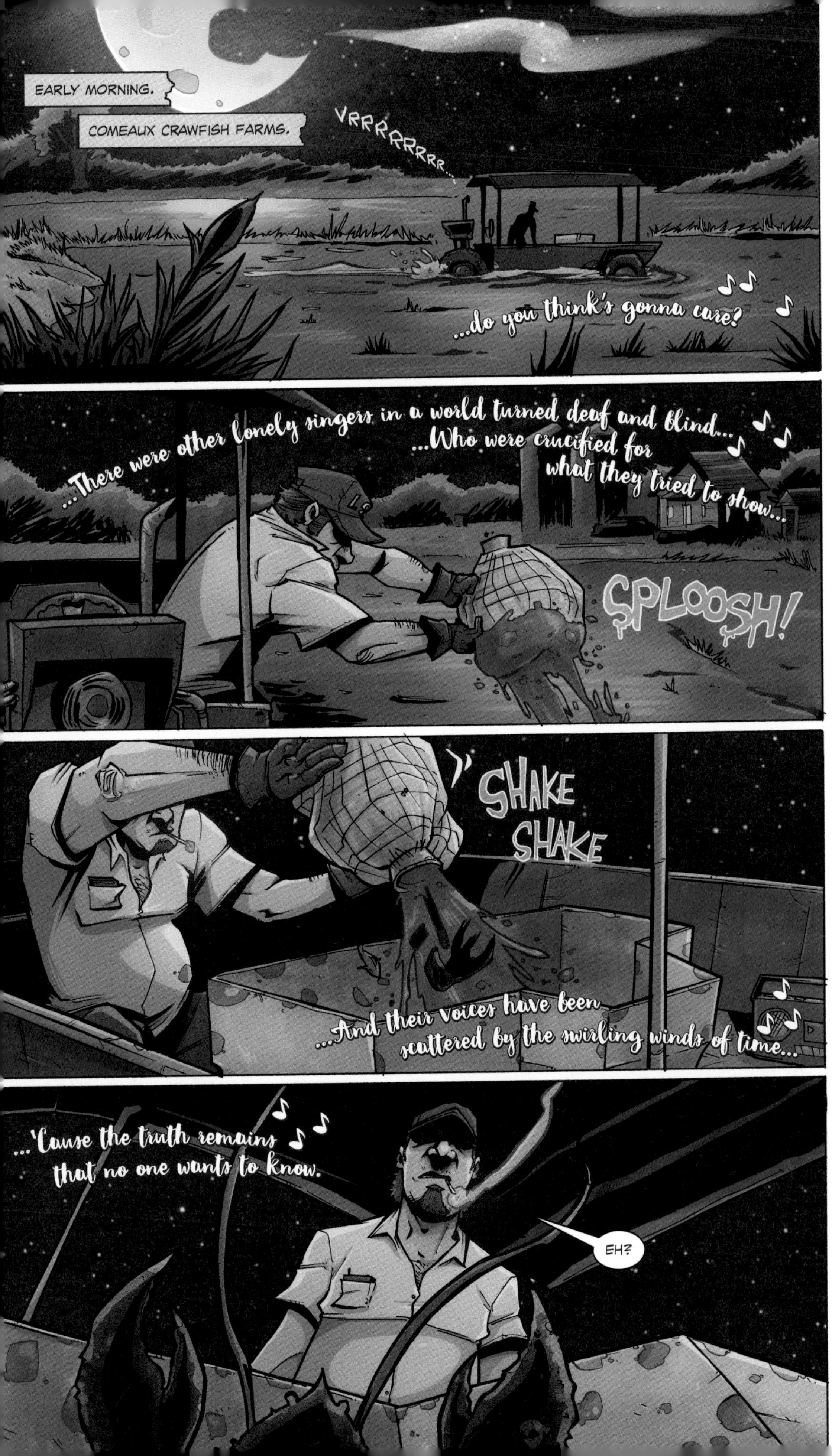

EARLY MORNING.
COMEAUX CRAWFISH FARMS.
VRRRRRRRRR...
...do you think's gonna care?
...There were other lonely singers in a world turned deaf and blind...
...Who were crucified for what they tried to show...
SPLOOSH!
SHAKE SHAKE
...And their voices have been scattered by the swirling winds of time...
...'Cause the truth remains that no one wants to know.
EH?

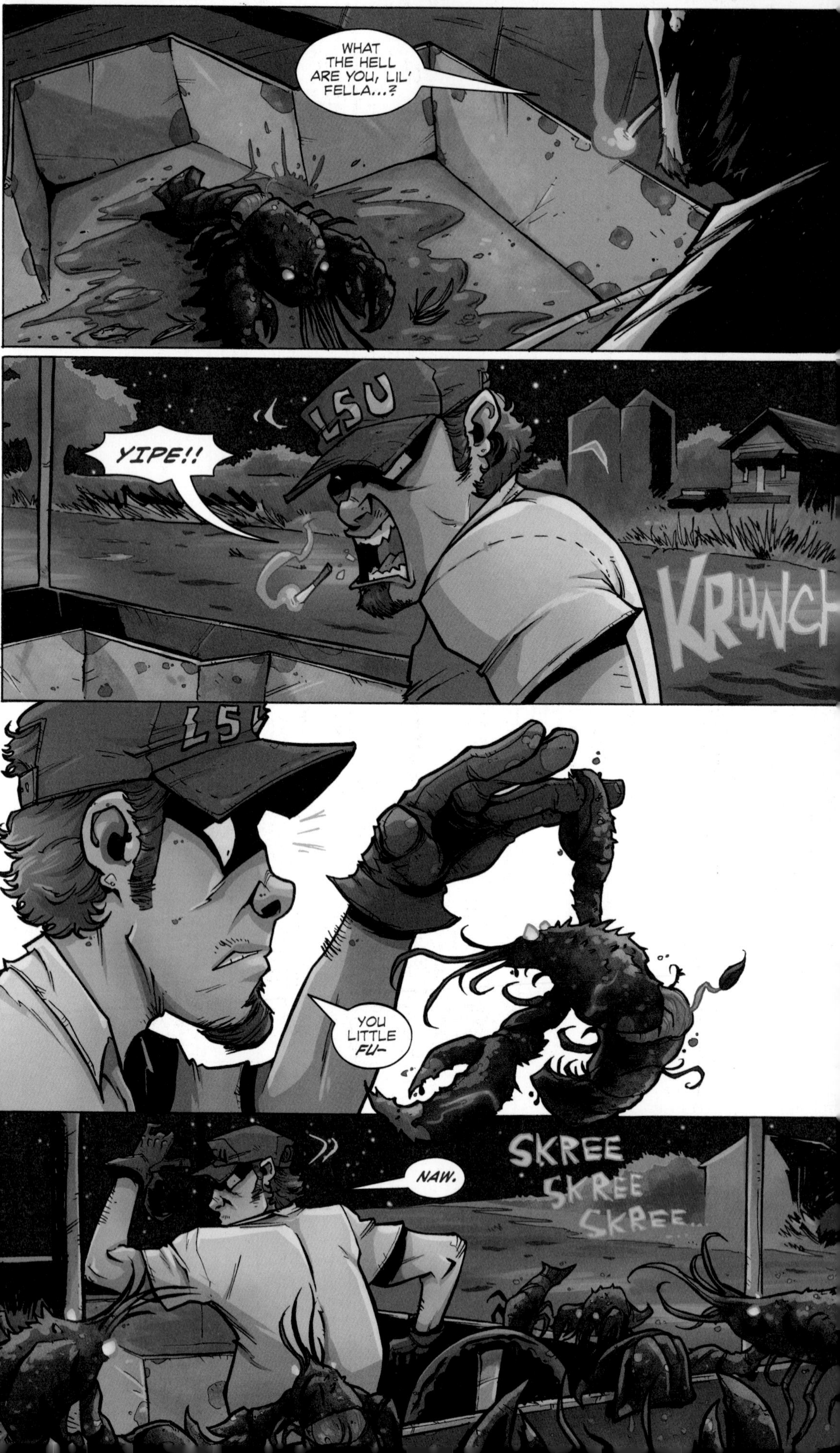
WHAT THE HELL ARE YOU, LIL' FELLA...?
YIPE!!
KRUNCH
YOU LITTLE FU-
NAW.
SKREE
SKREE
SKREE...

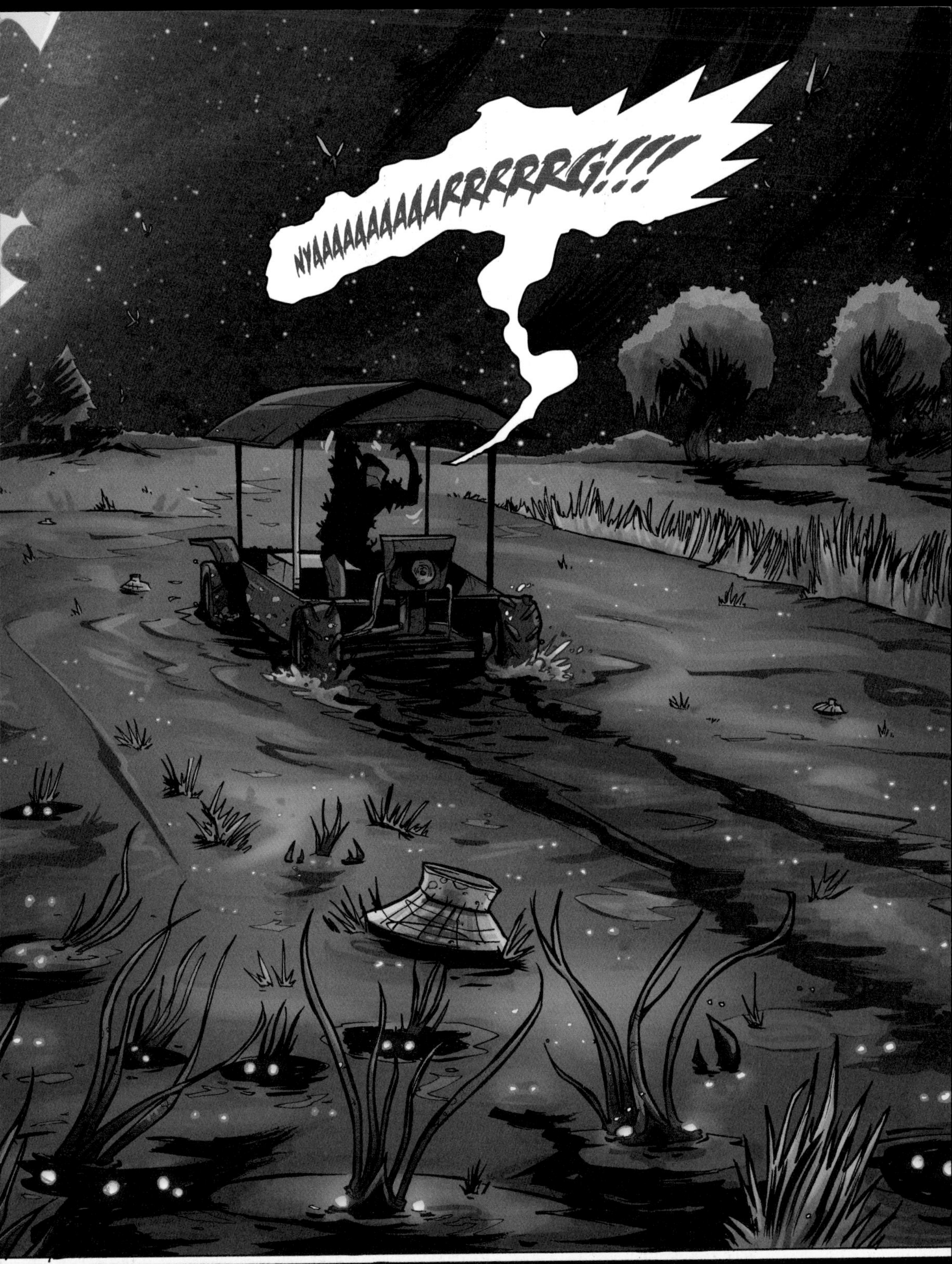
NYAAAAAAAAARRRRRG!!!

CHAPTER 12: THE EARTH DIVER.

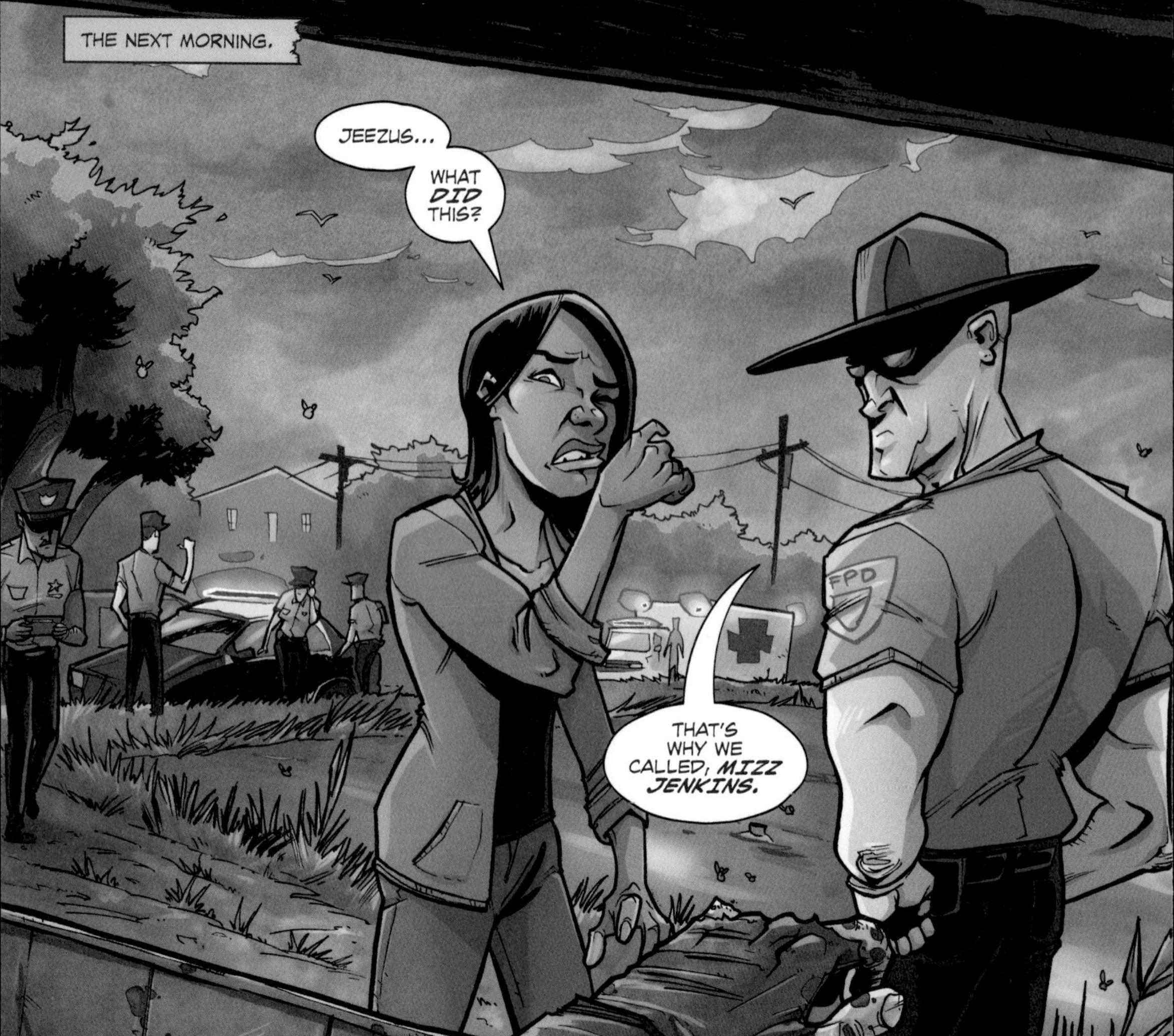
THE NEXT MORNING.
JEEZUS...
WHAT *DID* THIS?
THAT'S WHY WE CALLED, *MIZZ JENKINS.*

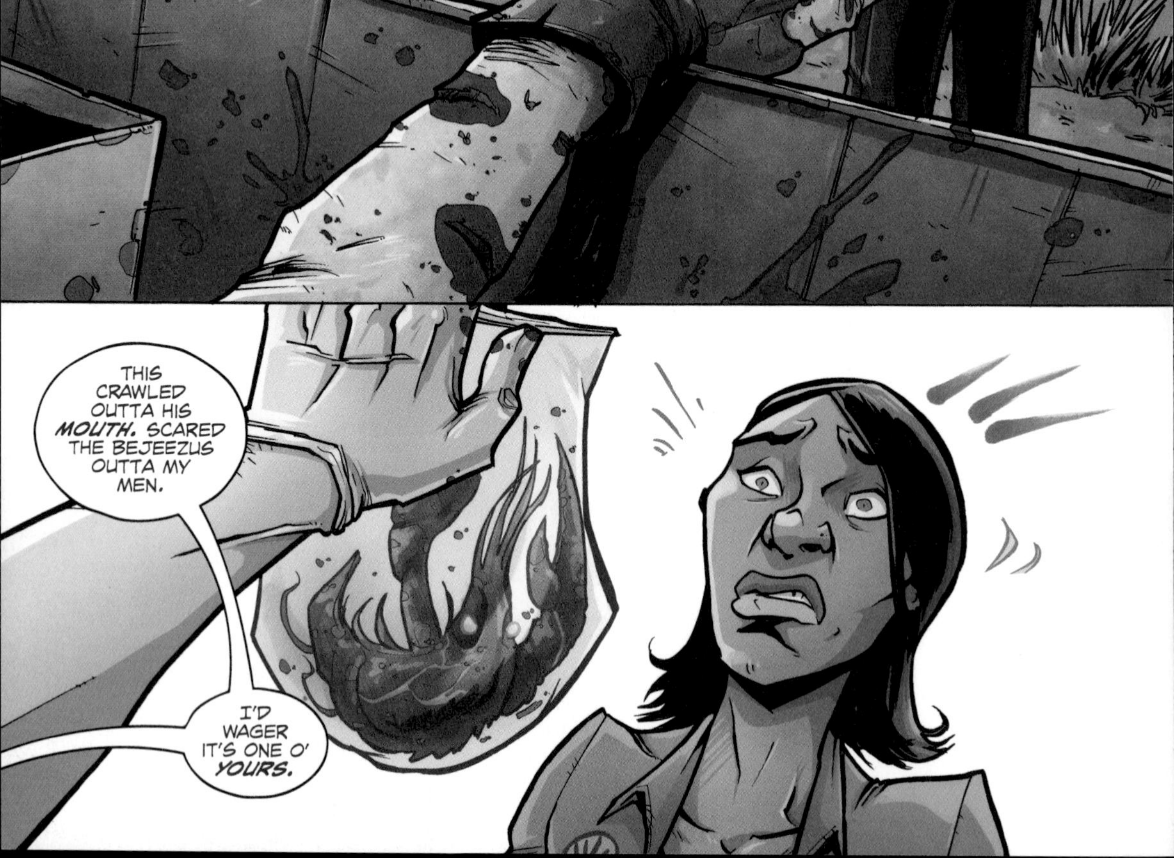
THIS CRAWLED OUTTA HIS *MOUTH.* SCARED THE BEJEEZUS OUTTA MY MEN.
I'D WAGER IT'S ONE O' *YOURS.*

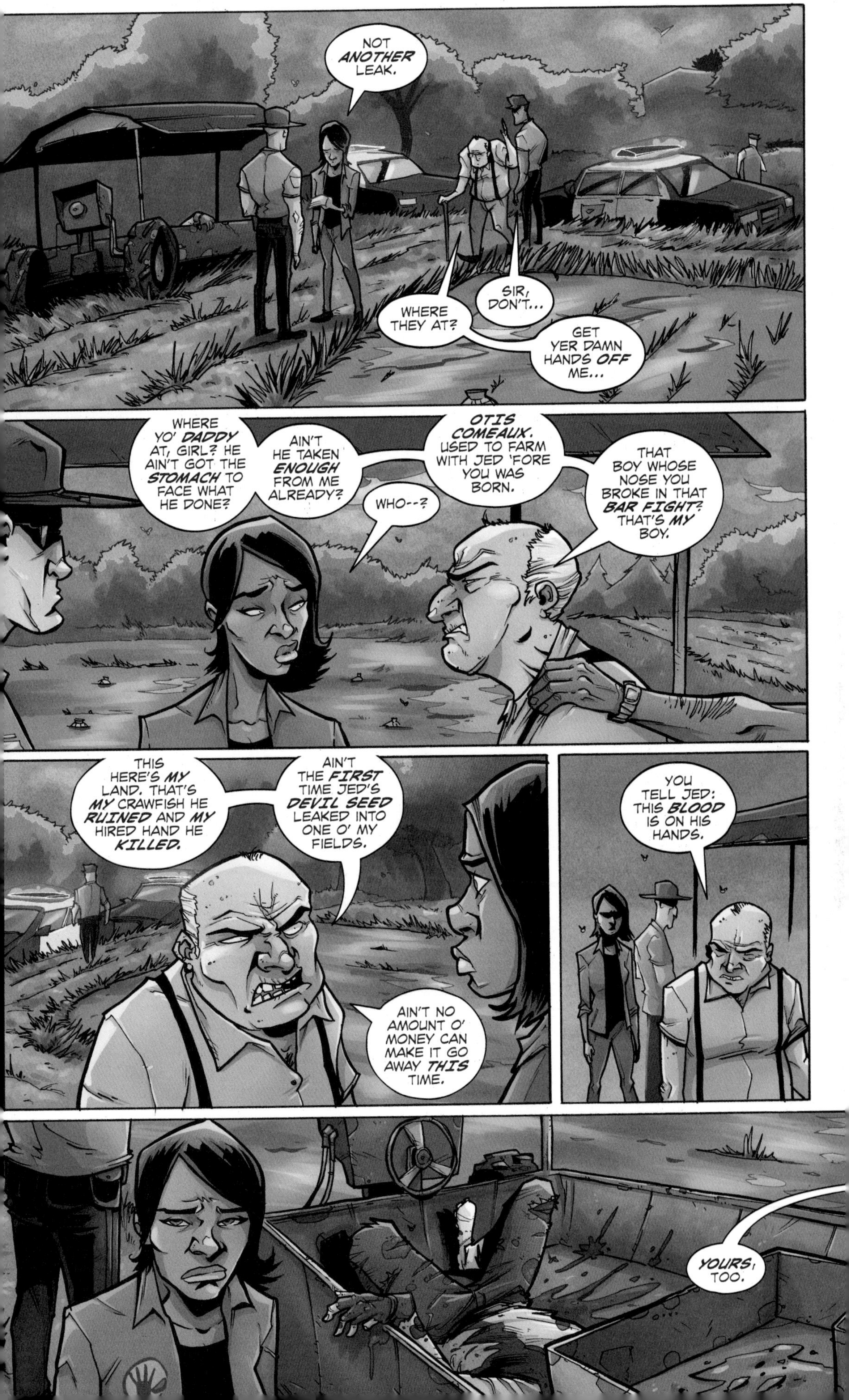
NOT ANOTHER LEAK.
WHERE THEY AT?
SIR, DON'T...
GET YER DAMN HANDS OFF ME...
WHERE YO' DADDY AT, GIRL? HE AIN'T GOT THE STOMACH TO FACE WHAT HE DONE?
AIN'T HE TAKEN ENOUGH FROM ME ALREADY?
WHO--?
OTIS COMEAUX. USED TO FARM WITH JED 'FORE YOU WAS BORN.
THAT BOY WHOSE NOSE YOU BROKE IN THAT BAR FIGHT? THAT'S MY BOY.
THIS HERE'S MY LAND. THAT'S MY CRAWFISH HE RUINED AND MY HIRED HAND HE KILLED.
AIN'T THE FIRST TIME JED'S DEVIL SEED LEAKED INTO ONE O' MY FIELDS.
AIN'T NO AMOUNT O' MONEY CAN MAKE IT GO AWAY THIS TIME.
YOU TELL JED: THIS BLOOD IS ON HIS HANDS.
YOURS, TOO.

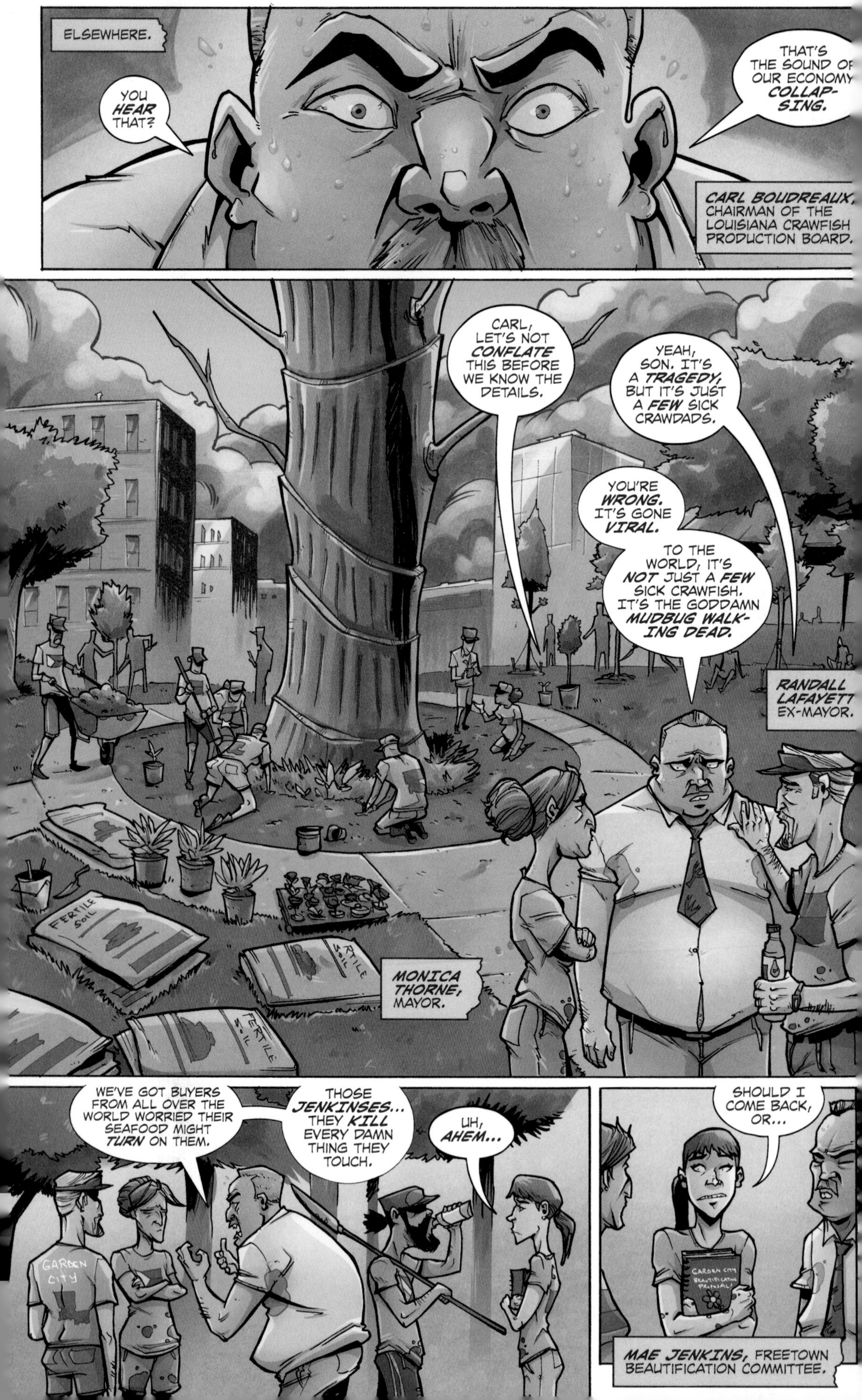

ELSEWHERE.
YOU HEAR THAT?
THAT'S THE SOUND OF OUR ECONOMY COLLAPSING.
CARL BOUDREAUX, CHAIRMAN OF THE LOUISIANA CRAWFISH PRODUCTION BOARD.
CARL, LET'S NOT CONFLATE THIS BEFORE WE KNOW THE DETAILS.
YEAH, SON. IT'S A TRAGEDY, BUT IT'S JUST A FEW SICK CRAWDADS.
YOU'RE WRONG. IT'S GONE VIRAL.
TO THE WORLD, IT'S NOT JUST A FEW SICK CRAWFISH. IT'S THE GODDAMN MUDBUG WALKING DEAD.
RANDALL LAFAYETT, EX-MAYOR.
FERTILE SOIL
MONICA THORNE, MAYOR.
WE'VE GOT BUYERS FROM ALL OVER THE WORLD WORRIED THEIR SEAFOOD MIGHT TURN ON THEM.
THOSE JENKINSES... THEY KILL EVERY DAMN THING THEY TOUCH.
UH, AHEM...
GARDEN CITY
SHOULD I COME BACK, OR...
MAE JENKINS, FREETOWN BEAUTIFICATION COMMITTEE.

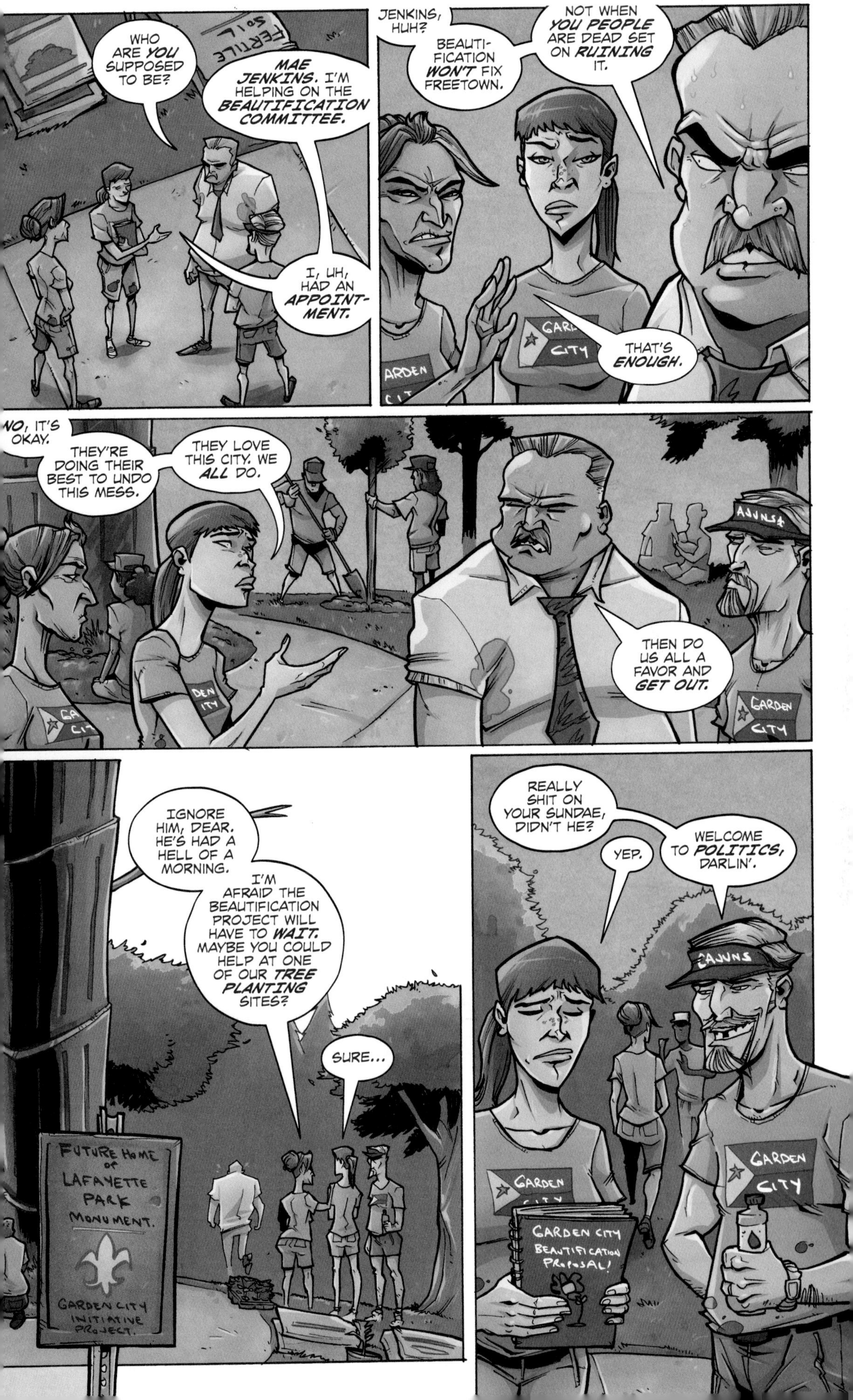
FERTILE SOIL
WHO ARE YOU SUPPOSED TO BE?
MAE JENKINS. I'M HELPING ON THE BEAUTIFICATION COMMITTEE.
I, UH, HAD AN APPOINTMENT.
JENKINS, HUH?
BEAUTIFICATION WON'T FIX FREETOWN.
NOT WHEN YOU PEOPLE ARE DEAD SET ON RUINING IT.
GARDEN CITY
THAT'S ENOUGH.
NO, IT'S OKAY.
THEY'RE DOING THEIR BEST TO UNDO THIS MESS.
THEY LOVE THIS CITY. WE ALL DO.
CAJUNS
THEN DO US ALL A FAVOR AND GET OUT.
GARDEN CITY
IGNORE HIM, DEAR. HE'S HAD A HELL OF A MORNING.
I'M AFRAID THE BEAUTIFICATION PROJECT WILL HAVE TO WAIT. MAYBE YOU COULD HELP AT ONE OF OUR TREE PLANTING SITES?
SURE...
FUTURE HOME OF LAFAYETTE PARK MONUMENT.
GARDEN CITY INITIATIVE PROJECT.
REALLY SHIT ON YOUR SUNDAE, DIDN'T HE?
YEP.
WELCOME TO POLITICS, DARLIN'.
CAJUNS
GARDEN CITY
GARDEN CITY BEAUTIFICATION PROPOSAL!

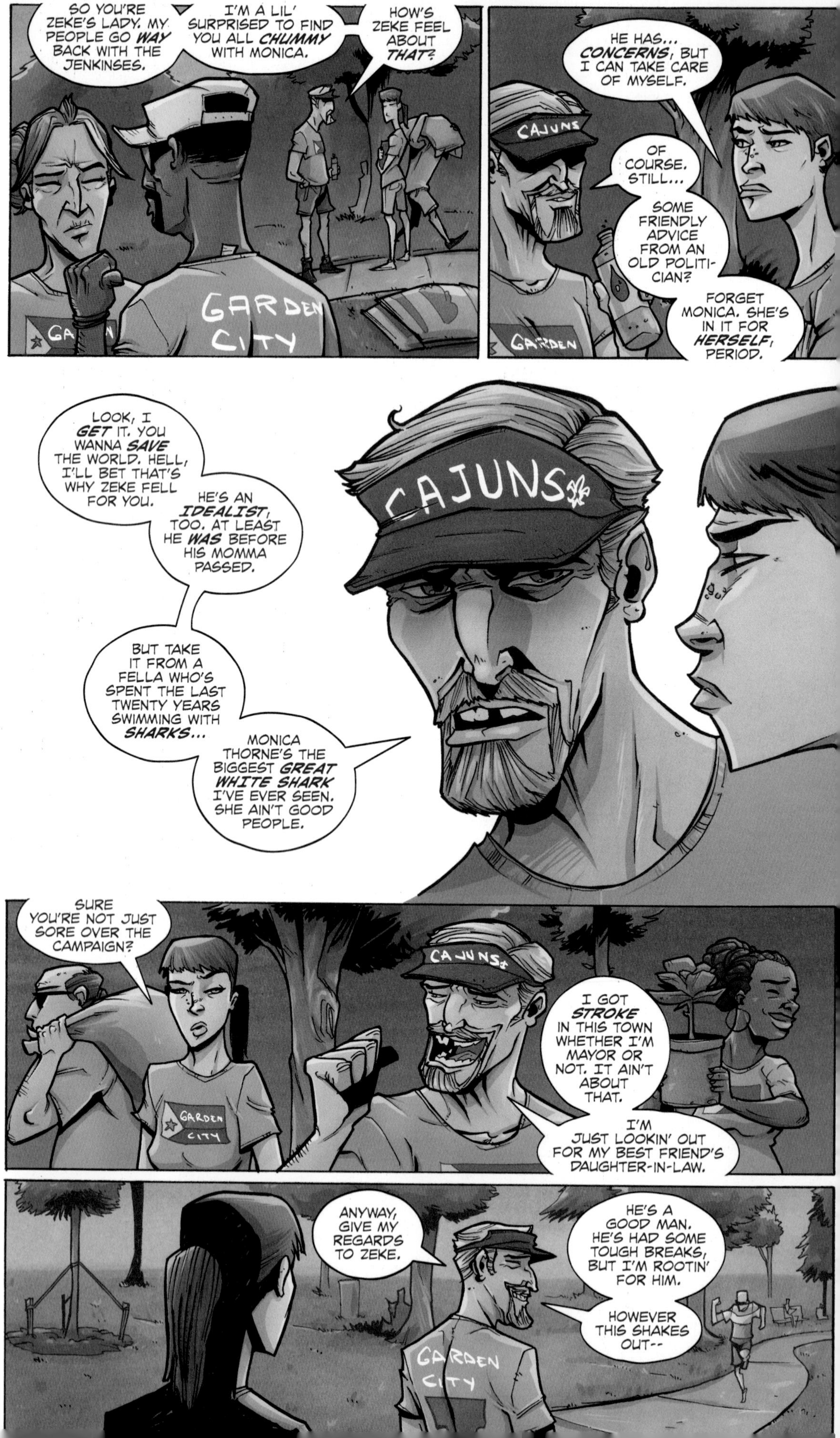

SO YOU'RE ZEKE'S LADY. MY PEOPLE GO WAY BACK WITH THE JENKINSES.
I'M A LIL' SURPRISED TO FIND YOU ALL CHUMMY WITH MONICA.
HOW'S ZEKE FEEL ABOUT THAT?
GARDEN CITY
HE HAS... CONCERNS, BUT I CAN TAKE CARE OF MYSELF.
CAJUNS
OF COURSE. STILL...
SOME FRIENDLY ADVICE FROM AN OLD POLITICIAN?
FORGET MONICA. SHE'S IN IT FOR HERSELF, PERIOD.
GARDEN
LOOK, I GET IT. YOU WANNA SAVE THE WORLD. HELL, I'LL BET THAT'S WHY ZEKE FELL FOR YOU.
HE'S AN IDEALIST, TOO. AT LEAST HE WAS BEFORE HIS MOMMA PASSED.
BUT TAKE IT FROM A FELLA WHO'S SPENT THE LAST TWENTY YEARS SWIMMING WITH SHARKS...
MONICA THORNE'S THE BIGGEST GREAT WHITE SHARK I'VE EVER SEEN. SHE AIN'T GOOD PEOPLE.
CAJUNS
SURE YOU'RE NOT JUST SORE OVER THE CAMPAIGN?
CAJUNS
GARDEN CITY
I GOT STROKE IN THIS TOWN WHETHER I'M MAYOR OR NOT. IT AIN'T ABOUT THAT.
I'M JUST LOOKIN' OUT FOR MY BEST FRIEND'S DAUGHTER-IN-LAW.
ANYWAY, GIVE MY REGARDS TO ZEKE.
HE'S A GOOD MAN. HE'S HAD SOME TOUGH BREAKS, BUT I'M ROOTIN' FOR HIM.
HOWEVER THIS SHAKES OUT--
GARDEN CITY

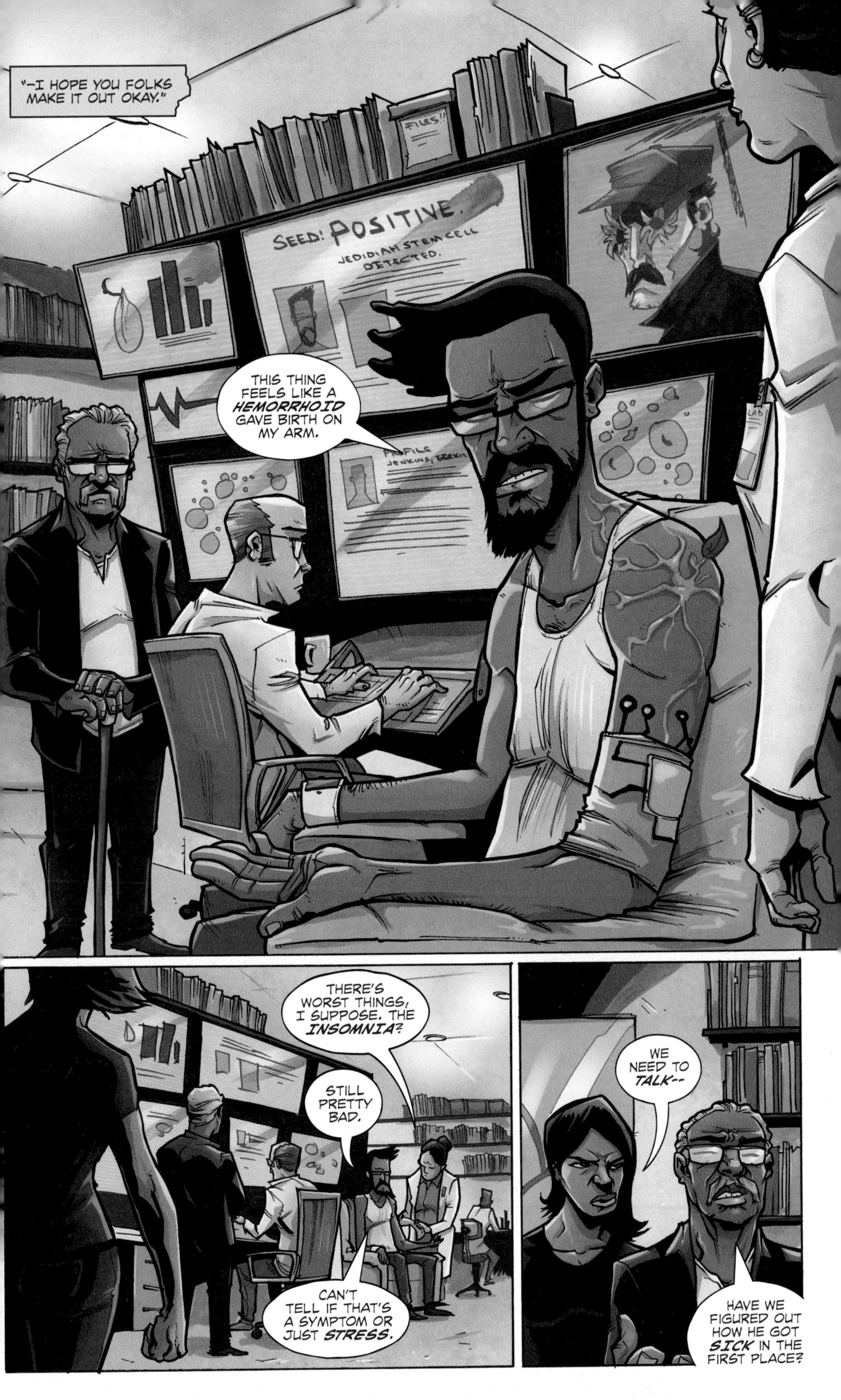
"–I HOPE YOU FOLKS MAKE IT OUT OKAY."
SEED: POSITIVE. JEDIDIAH STEM CELL DETECTED.
THIS THING FEELS LIKE A HEMORRHOID GAVE BIRTH ON MY ARM.
THERE'S WORST THINGS, I SUPPOSE. THE INSOMNIA?
STILL PRETTY BAD.
CAN'T TELL IF THAT'S A SYMPTOM OR JUST STRESS.
WE NEED TO TALK--
HAVE WE FIGURED OUT HOW HE GOT SICK IN THE FIRST PLACE?

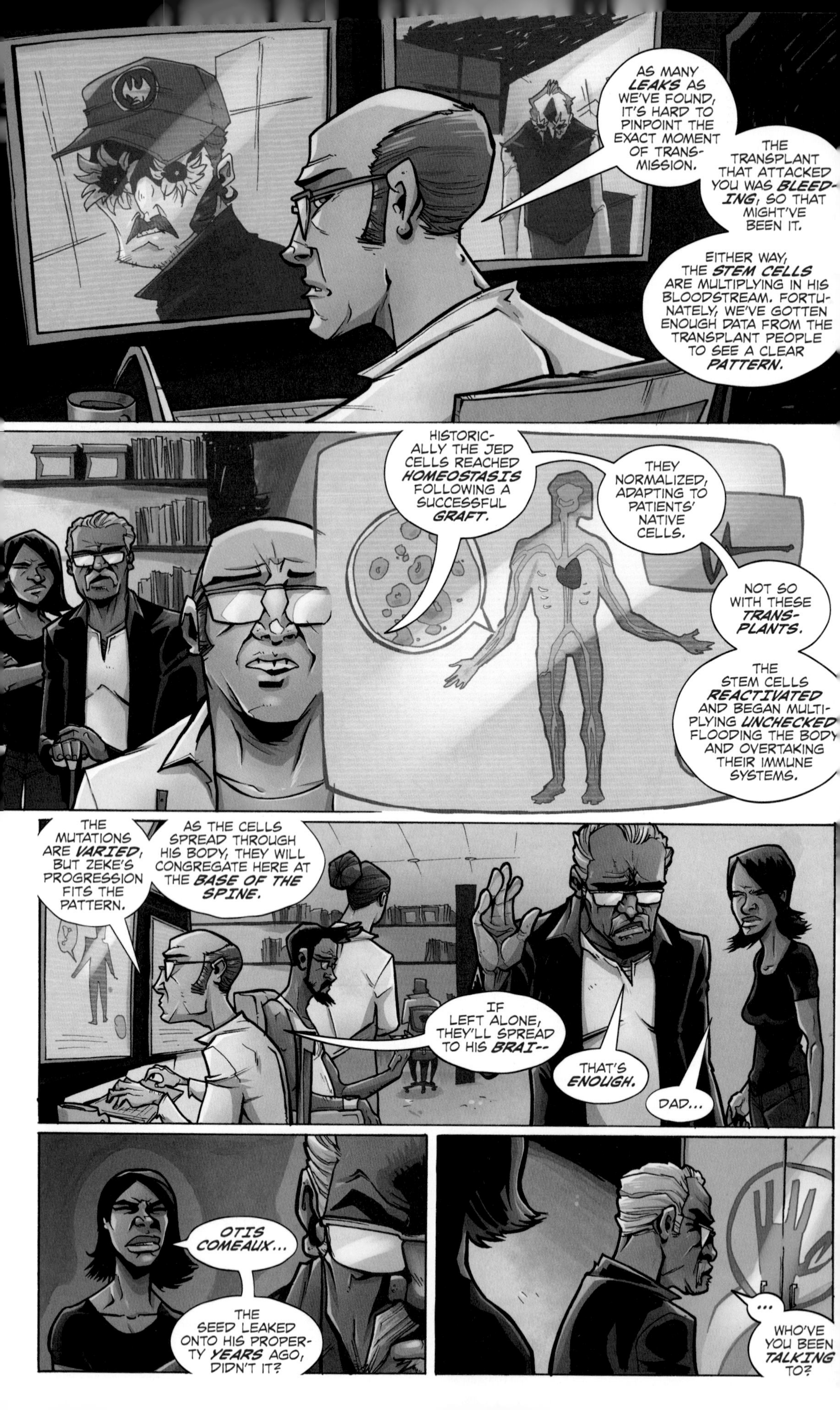
AS MANY LEAKS AS WE'VE FOUND, IT'S HARD TO PINPOINT THE EXACT MOMENT OF TRANS-MISSION.
THE TRANSPLANT THAT ATTACKED YOU WAS BLEED-ING, SO THAT MIGHT'VE BEEN IT.
EITHER WAY, THE STEM CELLS ARE MULTIPLYING IN HIS BLOODSTREAM. FORTU-NATELY, WE'VE GOTTEN ENOUGH DATA FROM THE TRANSPLANT PEOPLE TO SEE A CLEAR PATTERN.
HISTORIC-ALLY THE JED CELLS REACHED HOMEOSTASIS FOLLOWING A SUCCESSFUL GRAFT.
THEY NORMALIZED, ADAPTING TO PATIENTS' NATIVE CELLS.
NOT SO WITH THESE TRANS-PLANTS.
THE STEM CELLS REACTIVATED AND BEGAN MULTI-PLYING UNCHECKED FLOODING THE BODY AND OVERTAKING THEIR IMMUNE SYSTEMS.
THE MUTATIONS ARE VARIED, BUT ZEKE'S PROGRESSION FITS THE PATTERN.
AS THE CELLS SPREAD THROUGH HIS BODY, THEY WILL CONGREGATE HERE AT THE BASE OF THE SPINE.
IF LEFT ALONE, THEY'LL SPREAD TO HIS BRAI--
THAT'S ENOUGH.
DAD...
OTIS COMEAUX...
THE SEED LEAKED ONTO HIS PROPER-TY YEARS AGO, DIDN'T IT?
...
WHO'VE YOU BEEN TALKING TO?

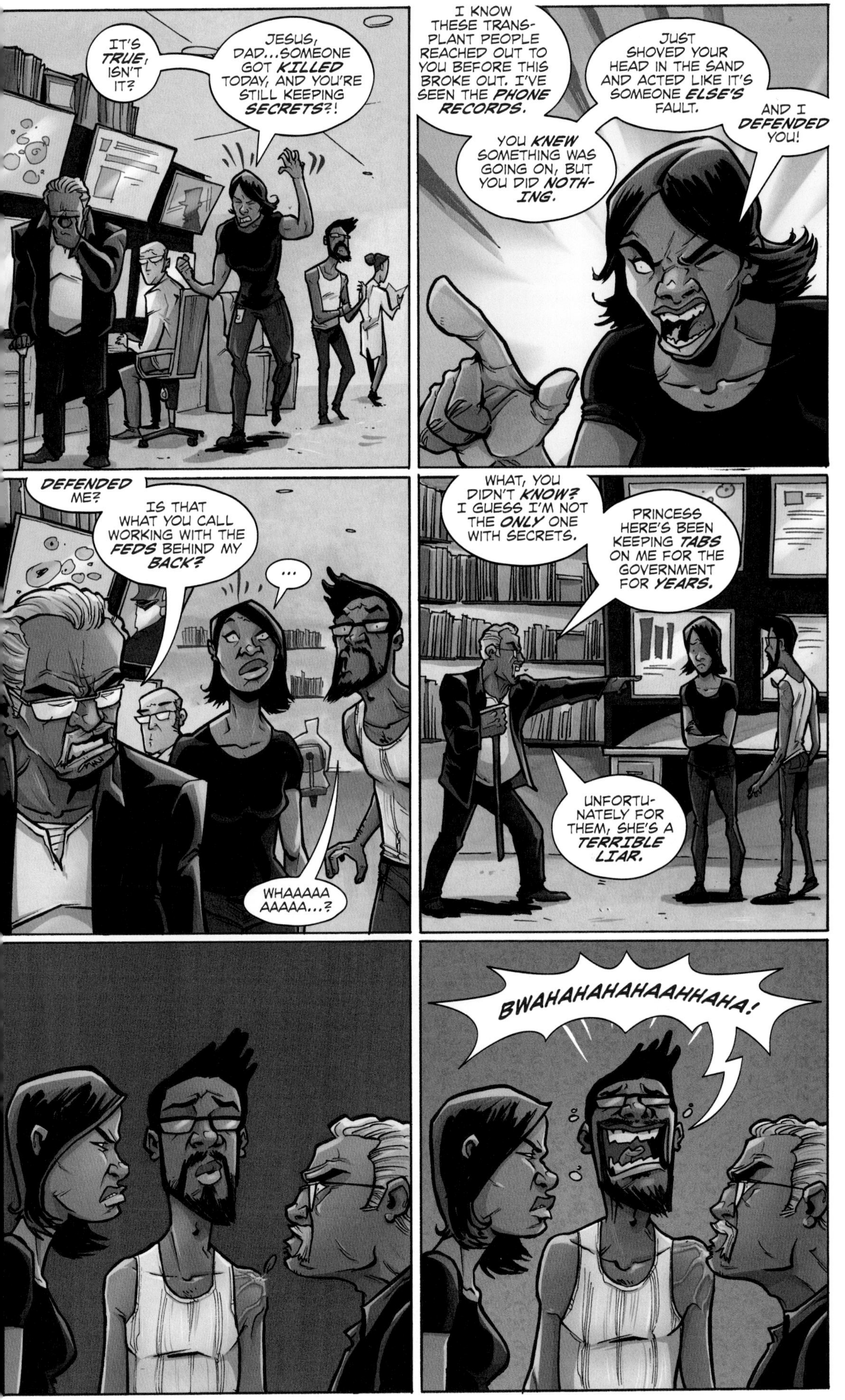

IT'S TRUE, ISN'T IT?
JESUS, DAD...SOMEONE GOT KILLED TODAY, AND YOU'RE STILL KEEPING SECRETS?!
I KNOW THESE TRANS-PLANT PEOPLE REACHED OUT TO YOU BEFORE THIS BROKE OUT. I'VE SEEN THE PHONE RECORDS.
YOU KNEW SOMETHING WAS GOING ON, BUT YOU DID NOTH-ING.
JUST SHOVED YOUR HEAD IN THE SAND AND ACTED LIKE IT'S SOMEONE ELSE'S FAULT.
AND I DEFENDED YOU!
DEFENDED ME?
IS THAT WHAT YOU CALL WORKING WITH THE FEDS BEHIND MY BACK?
...
WHAAAAA AAAAA...?
WHAT, YOU DIDN'T KNOW? I GUESS I'M NOT THE ONLY ONE WITH SECRETS.
PRINCESS HERE'S BEEN KEEPING TABS ON ME FOR THE GOVERNMENT FOR YEARS.
UNFORTU-NATELY FOR THEM, SHE'S A TERRIBLE LIAR.
BWAHAHAHAHAAHHAHA!

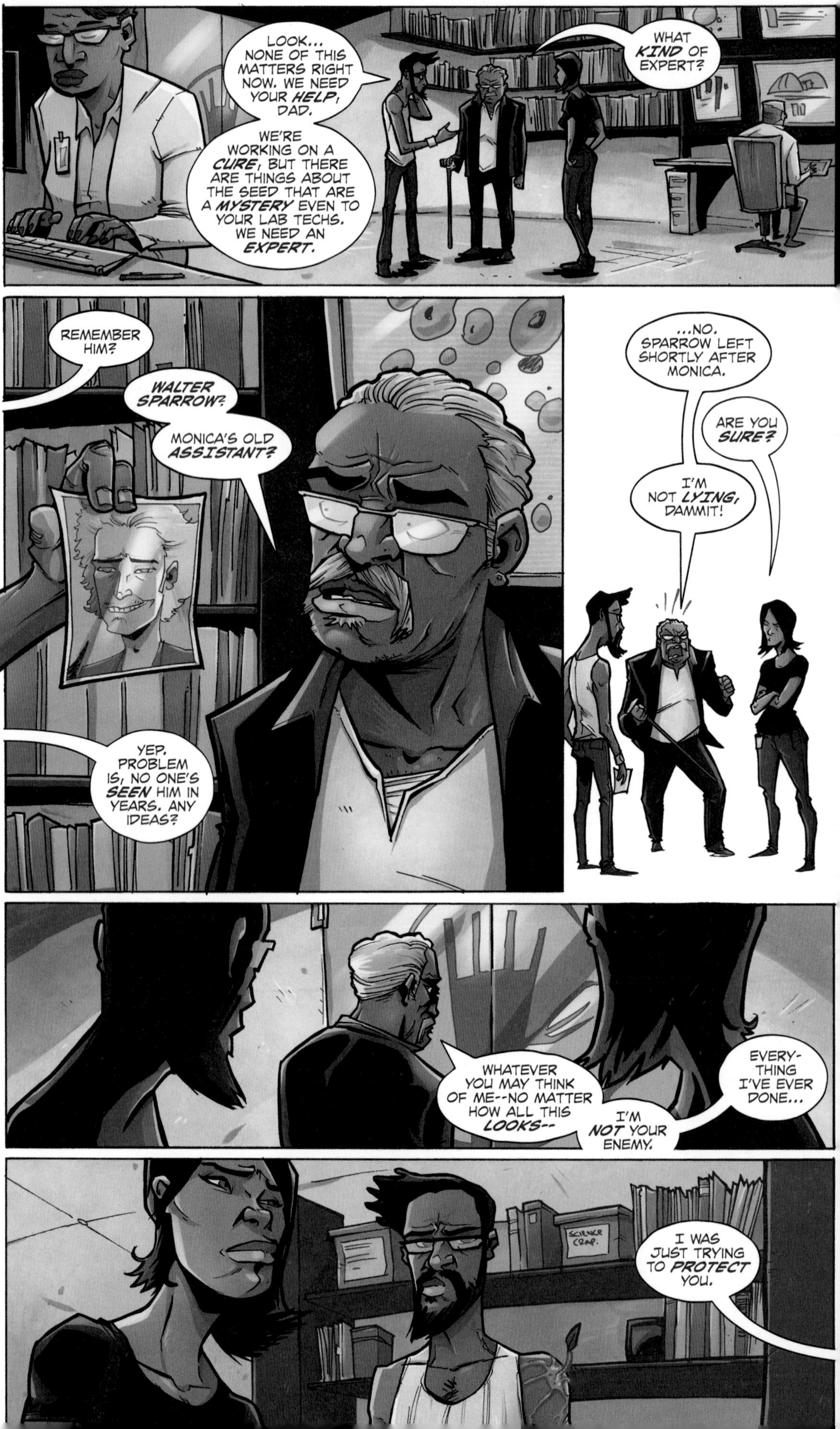

LOOK... NONE OF THIS MATTERS RIGHT NOW. WE NEED YOUR HELP, DAD.
WE'RE WORKING ON A CURE, BUT THERE ARE THINGS ABOUT THE SEED THAT ARE A MYSTERY EVEN TO YOUR LAB TECHS. WE NEED AN EXPERT.
WHAT KIND OF EXPERT?
REMEMBER HIM?
WALTER SPARROW?
MONICA'S OLD ASSISTANT?
YEP. PROBLEM IS, NO ONE'S SEEN HIM IN YEARS. ANY IDEAS?
...NO. SPARROW LEFT SHORTLY AFTER MONICA.
ARE YOU SURE?
I'M NOT LYING, DAMMIT!
WHATEVER YOU MAY THINK OF ME--NO MATTER HOW ALL THIS LOOKS--
I'M NOT YOUR ENEMY.
EVERY-THING I'VE EVER DONE...
SCIENCE CRAP.
I WAS JUST TRYING TO PROTECT YOU.

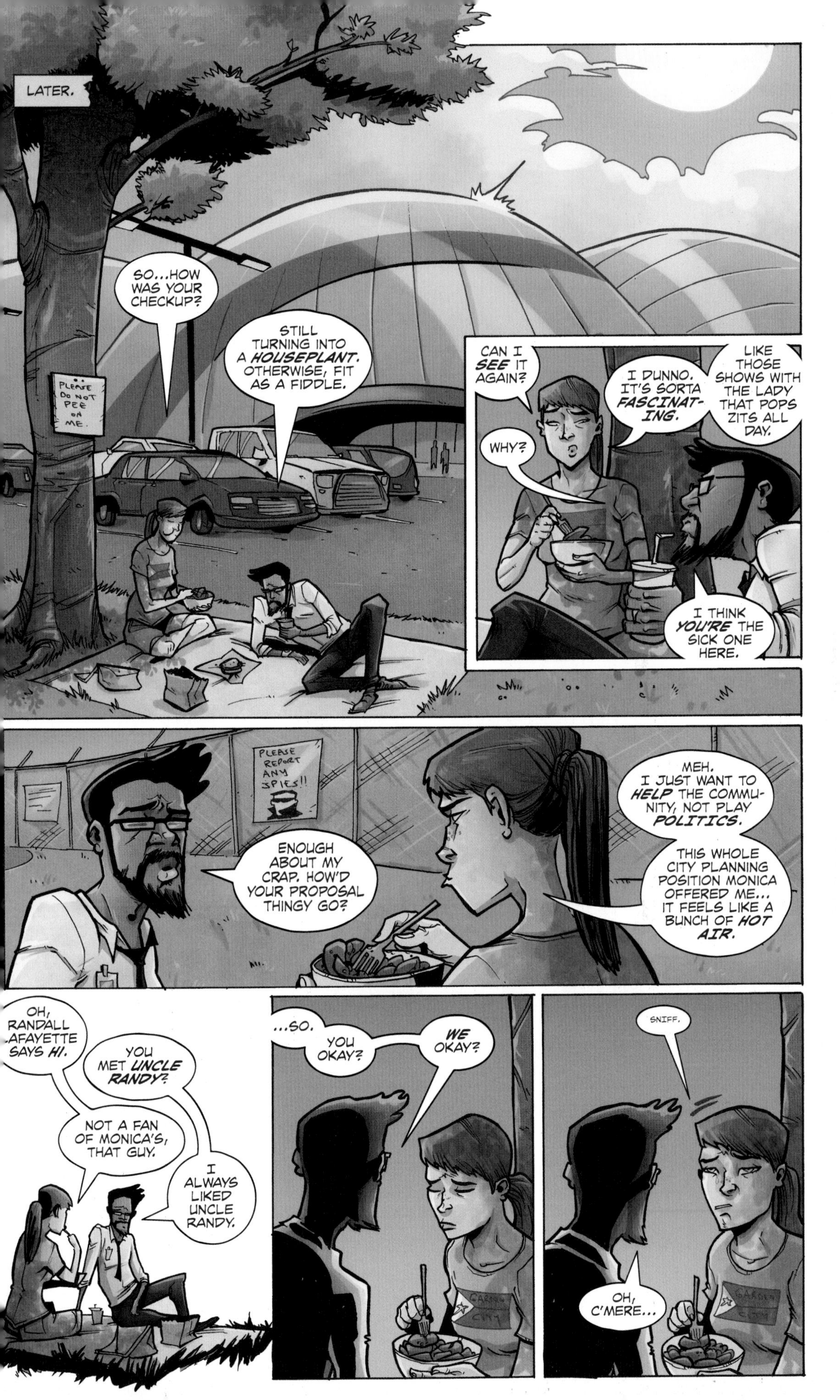
LATER.
SO...HOW WAS YOUR CHECKUP?
STILL TURNING INTO A HOUSEPLANT. OTHERWISE, FIT AS A FIDDLE.
PLEASE DO NOT PEE ON ME.
CAN I SEE IT AGAIN?
WHY?
I DUNNO. IT'S SORTA FASCINATING.
LIKE THOSE SHOWS WITH THE LADY THAT POPS ZITS ALL DAY.
I THINK YOU'RE THE SICK ONE HERE.
PLEASE REPORT ANY SPIES!!
ENOUGH ABOUT MY CRAP. HOW'D YOUR PROPOSAL THINGY GO?
MEH. I JUST WANT TO HELP THE COMMUNITY, NOT PLAY POLITICS.
THIS WHOLE CITY PLANNING POSITION MONICA OFFERED ME... IT FEELS LIKE A BUNCH OF HOT AIR.
OH, RANDALL LAFAYETTE SAYS HI.
YOU MET UNCLE RANDY?
NOT A FAN OF MONICA'S, THAT GUY.
I ALWAYS LIKED UNCLE RANDY.
...SO.
YOU OKAY?
WE OKAY?
SNIFF.
OH, C'MERE...

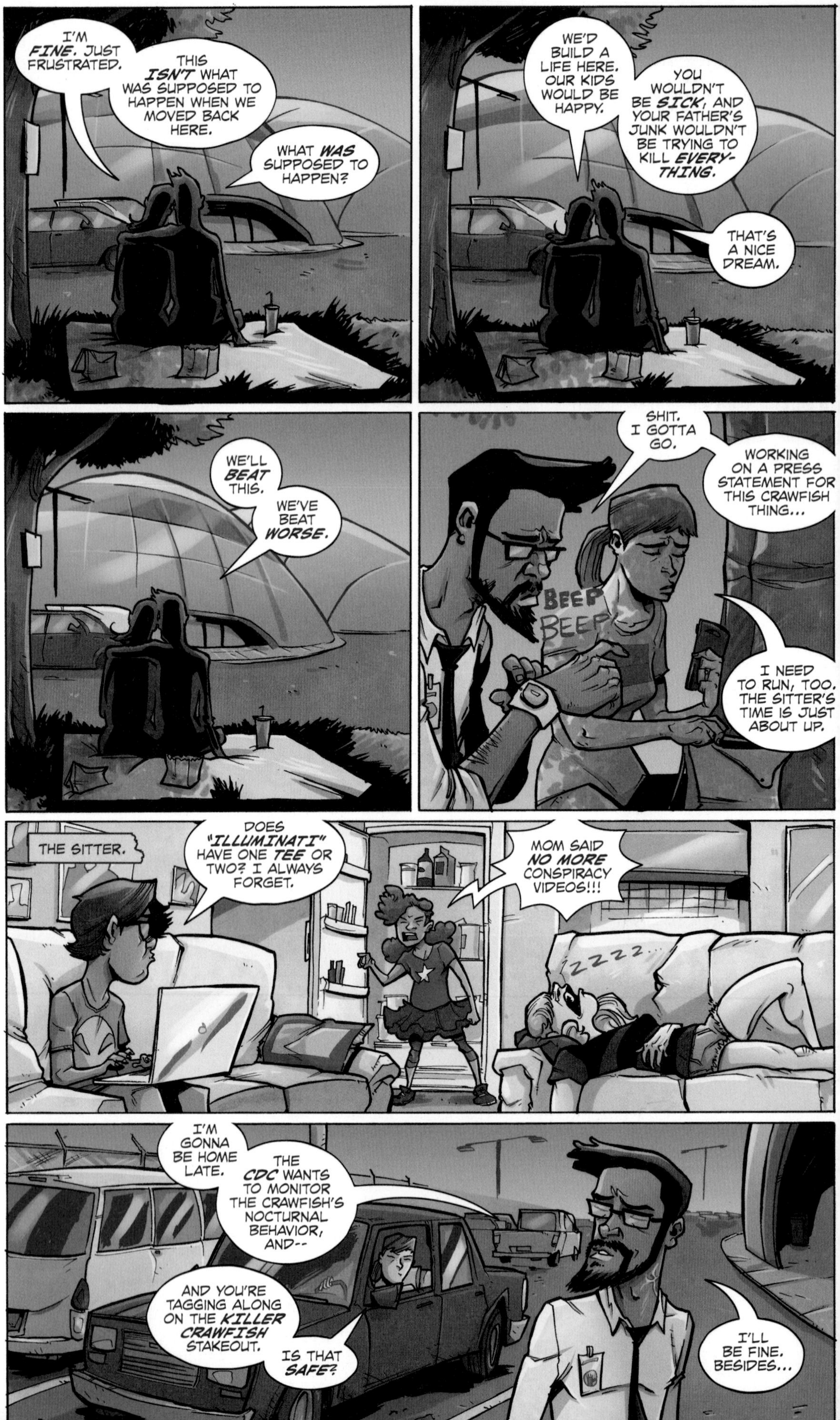
I'M FINE. JUST FRUSTRATED.
THIS ISN'T WHAT WAS SUPPOSED TO HAPPEN WHEN WE MOVED BACK HERE.
WHAT WAS SUPPOSED TO HAPPEN?
WE'D BUILD A LIFE HERE. OUR KIDS WOULD BE HAPPY.
YOU WOULDN'T BE SICK, AND YOUR FATHER'S JUNK WOULDN'T BE TRYING TO KILL EVERYTHING.
THAT'S A NICE DREAM.
WE'LL BEAT THIS.
WE'VE BEAT WORSE.
SHIT. I GOTTA GO.
WORKING ON A PRESS STATEMENT FOR THIS CRAWFISH THING...
BEEP BEEP
I NEED TO RUN, TOO. THE SITTER'S TIME IS JUST ABOUT UP.
THE SITTER.
DOES "ILLUMINATI" HAVE ONE TEE OR TWO? I ALWAYS FORGET.
MOM SAID NO MORE CONSPIRACY VIDEOS!!!
ZZZZ...
I'M GONNA BE HOME LATE.
THE CDC WANTS TO MONITOR THE CRAWFISH'S NOCTURNAL BEHAVIOR, AND--
AND YOU'RE TAGGING ALONG ON THE KILLER CRAWFISH STAKEOUT.
IS THAT SAFE?
I'LL BE FINE. BESIDES...

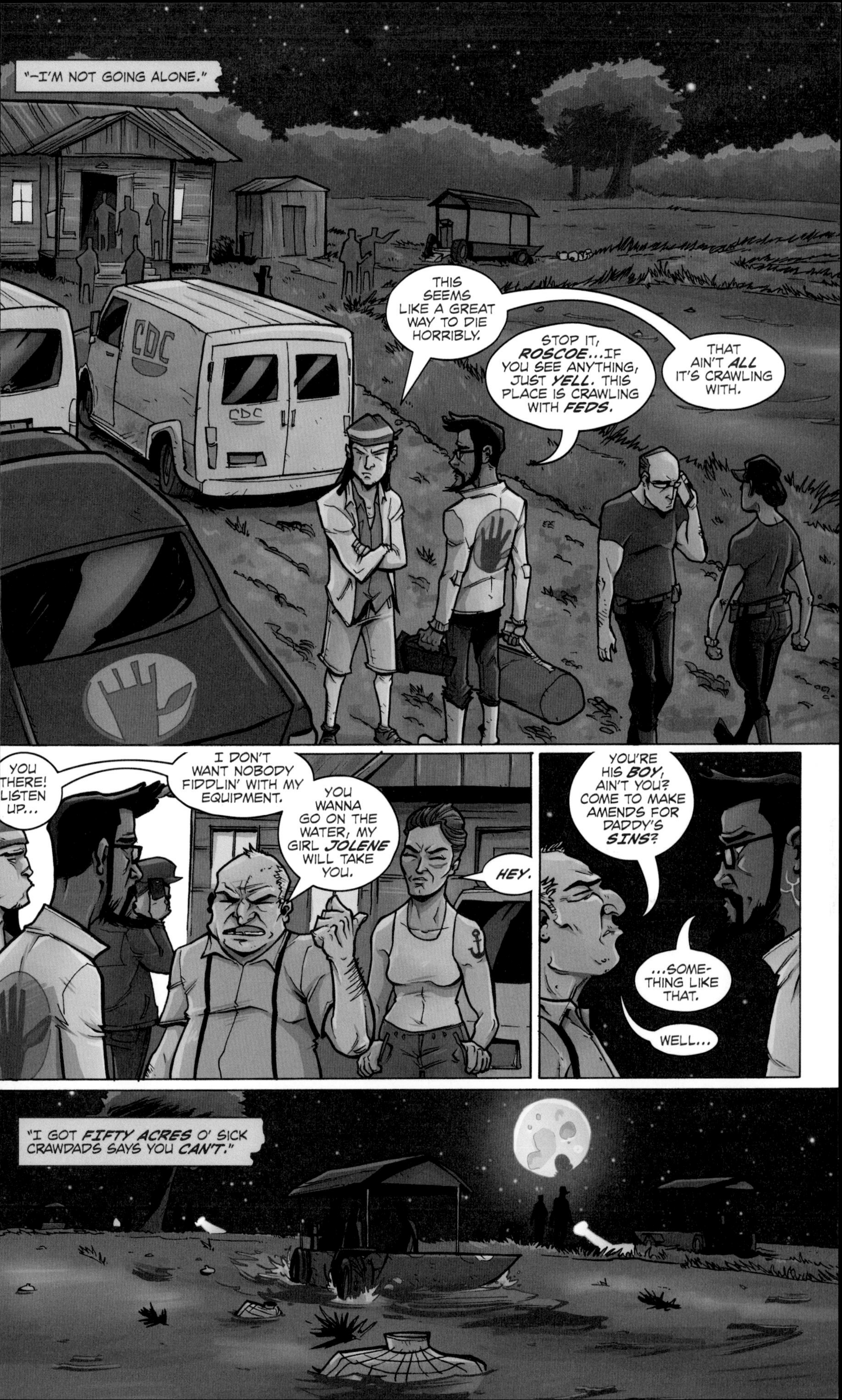
"–I'M NOT GOING ALONE."
THIS SEEMS LIKE A GREAT WAY TO DIE HORRIBLY.
STOP IT, ROSCOE...IF YOU SEE ANYTHING, JUST YELL. THIS PLACE IS CRAWLING WITH FEDS.
THAT AIN'T ALL IT'S CRAWLING WITH.
CDC
CDC
YOU THERE! LISTEN UP...
I DON'T WANT NOBODY FIDDLIN' WITH MY EQUIPMENT.
YOU WANNA GO ON THE WATER, MY GIRL JOLENE WILL TAKE YOU.
HEY.
YOU'RE HIS BOY, AIN'T YOU? COME TO MAKE AMENDS FOR DADDY'S SINS?
...SOMETHING LIKE THAT.
WELL...
"I GOT FIFTY ACRES O' SICK CRAWDADS SAYS YOU CAN'T."

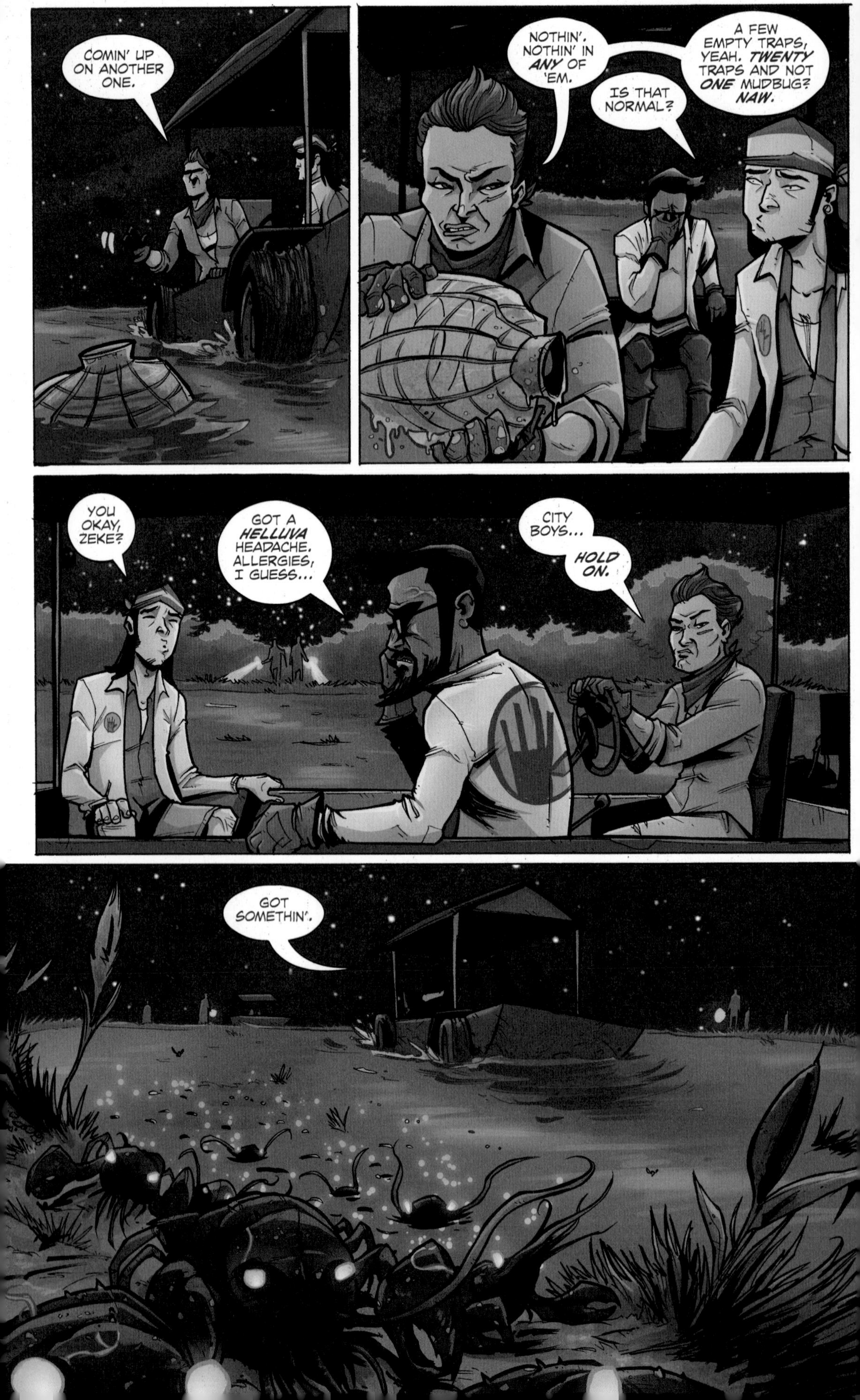
COMIN' UP ON ANOTHER ONE.
NOTHIN'. NOTHIN' IN ANY OF 'EM.
IS THAT NORMAL?
A FEW EMPTY TRAPS, YEAH. TWENTY TRAPS AND NOT ONE MUDBUG? NAW.
YOU OKAY, ZEKE?
GOT A HELLUVA HEADACHE. ALLERGIES, I GUESS...
CITY BOYS...
HOLD ON.
GOT SOMETHIN'.

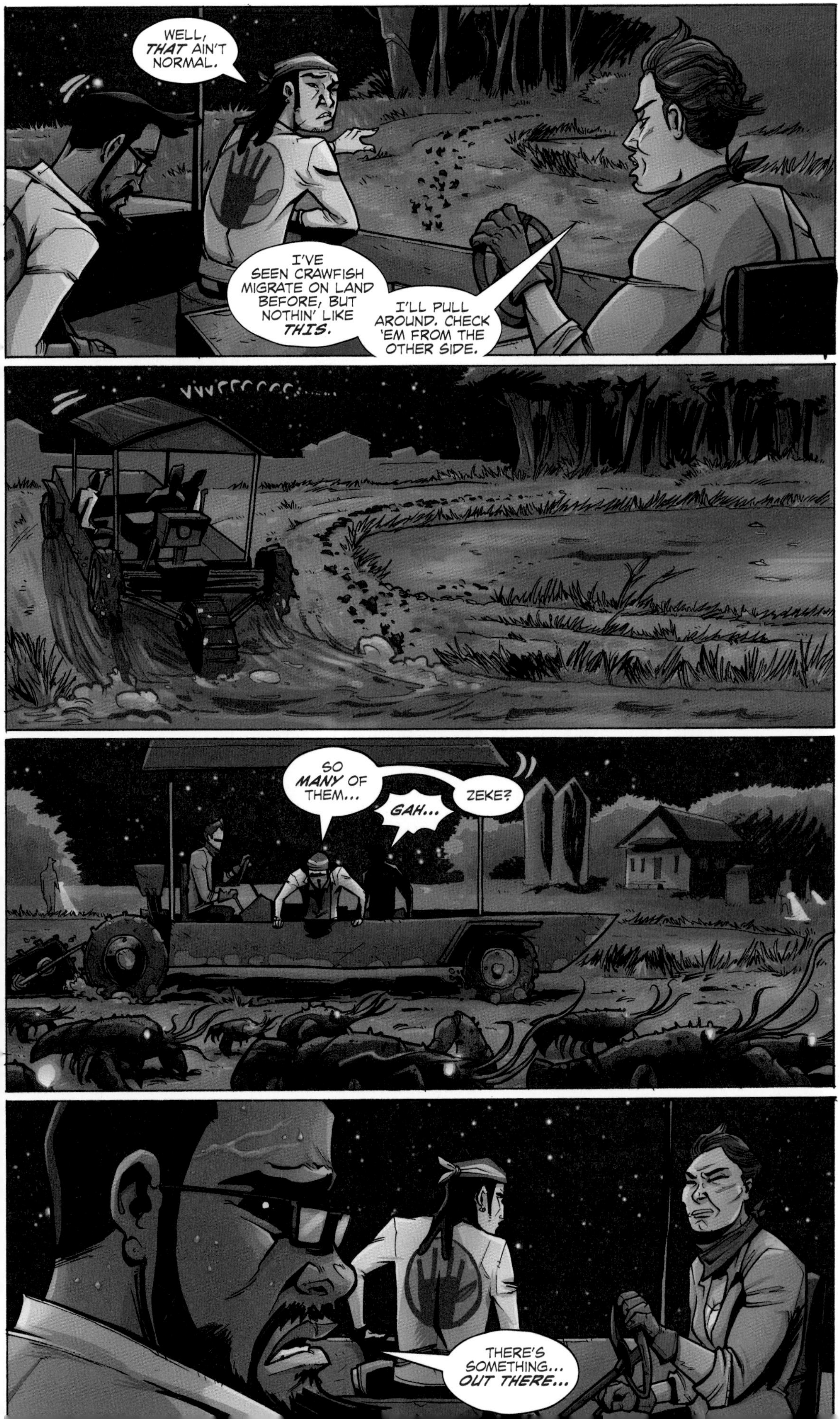
WELL, THAT AIN'T NORMAL.
I'VE SEEN CRAWFISH MIGRATE ON LAND BEFORE, BUT NOTHIN' LIKE THIS.
I'LL PULL AROUND. CHECK 'EM FROM THE OTHER SIDE.
VVVRRRRRR......
SO MANY OF THEM...
GAH...
ZEKE?
THERE'S SOMETHING... OUT THERE...

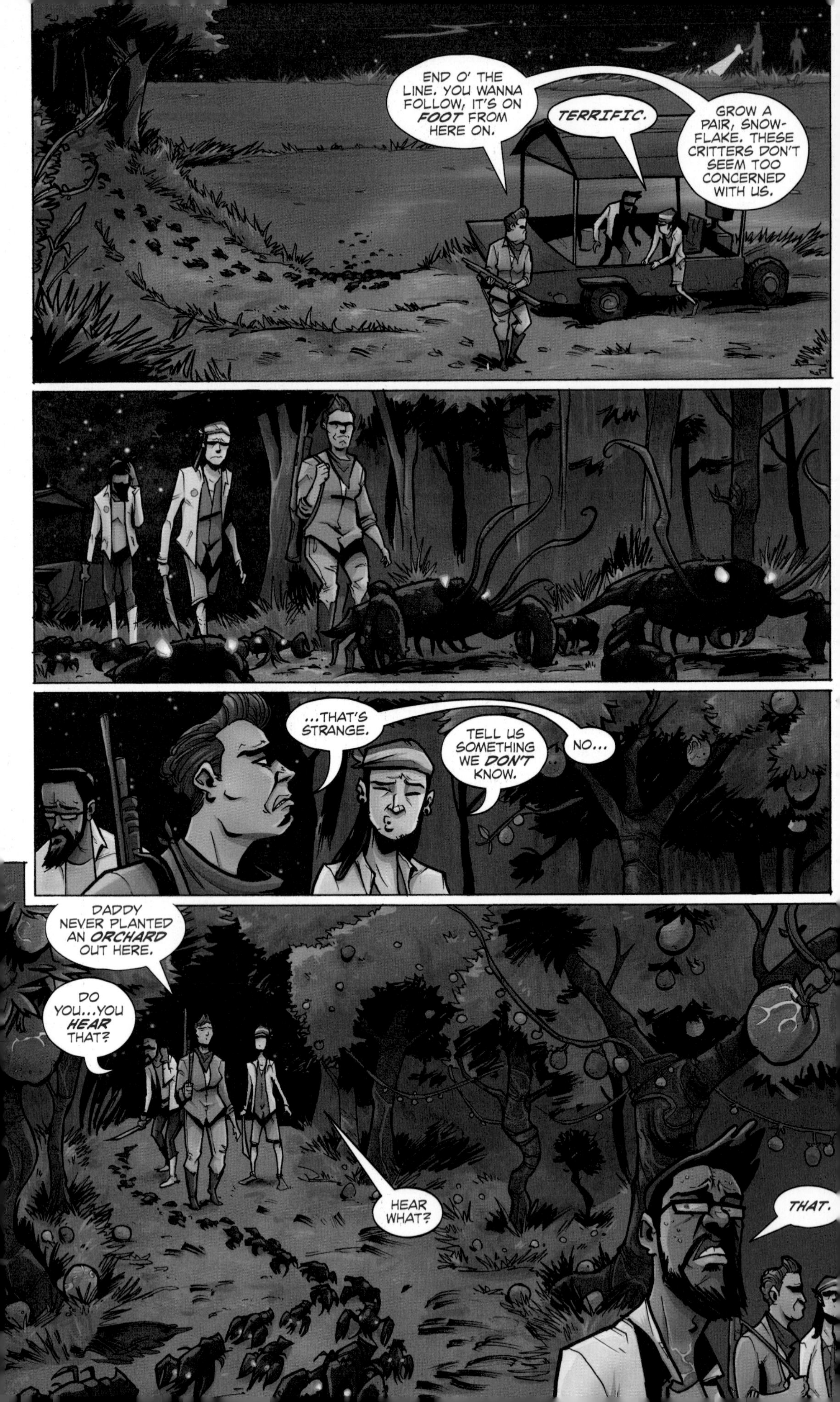
END O' THE LINE. YOU WANNA FOLLOW, IT'S ON *FOOT* FROM HERE ON.
TERRIFIC.
GROW A PAIR, SNOW-FLAKE. THESE CRITTERS DON'T SEEM TOO CONCERNED WITH US.
...THAT'S STRANGE.
TELL US SOMETHING WE *DON'T* KNOW.
NO...
DADDY NEVER PLANTED AN *ORCHARD* OUT HERE.
DO YOU...YOU *HEAR* THAT?
HEAR WHAT?
THAT.

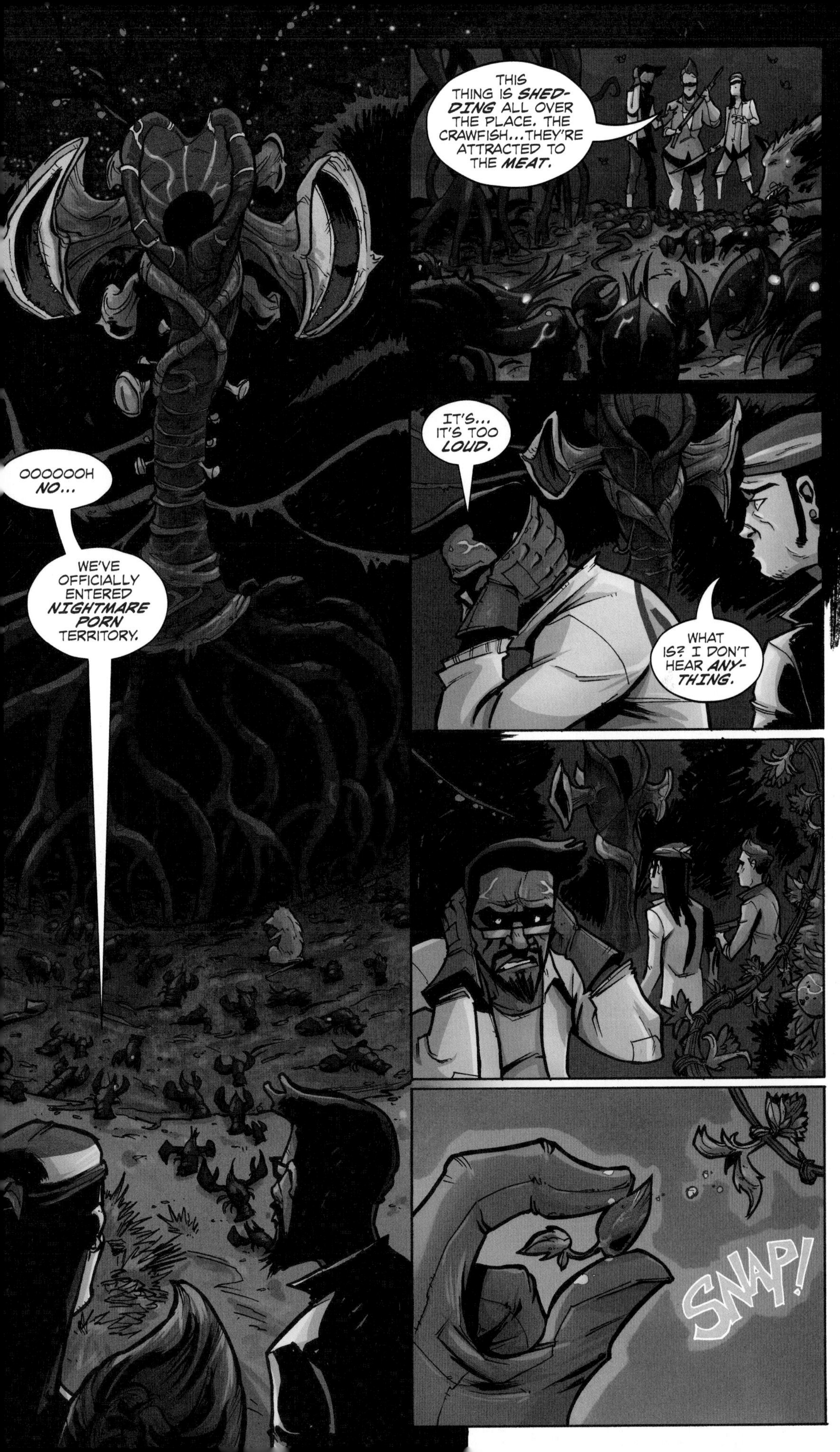
OOOOOOH NO...
WE'VE OFFICIALLY ENTERED NIGHTMARE PORN TERRITORY.
THIS THING IS SHEDDING ALL OVER THE PLACE. THE CRAWFISH...THEY'RE ATTRACTED TO THE MEAT.
IT'S... IT'S TOO LOUD.
WHAT IS? I DON'T HEAR ANYTHING.
SNAP!

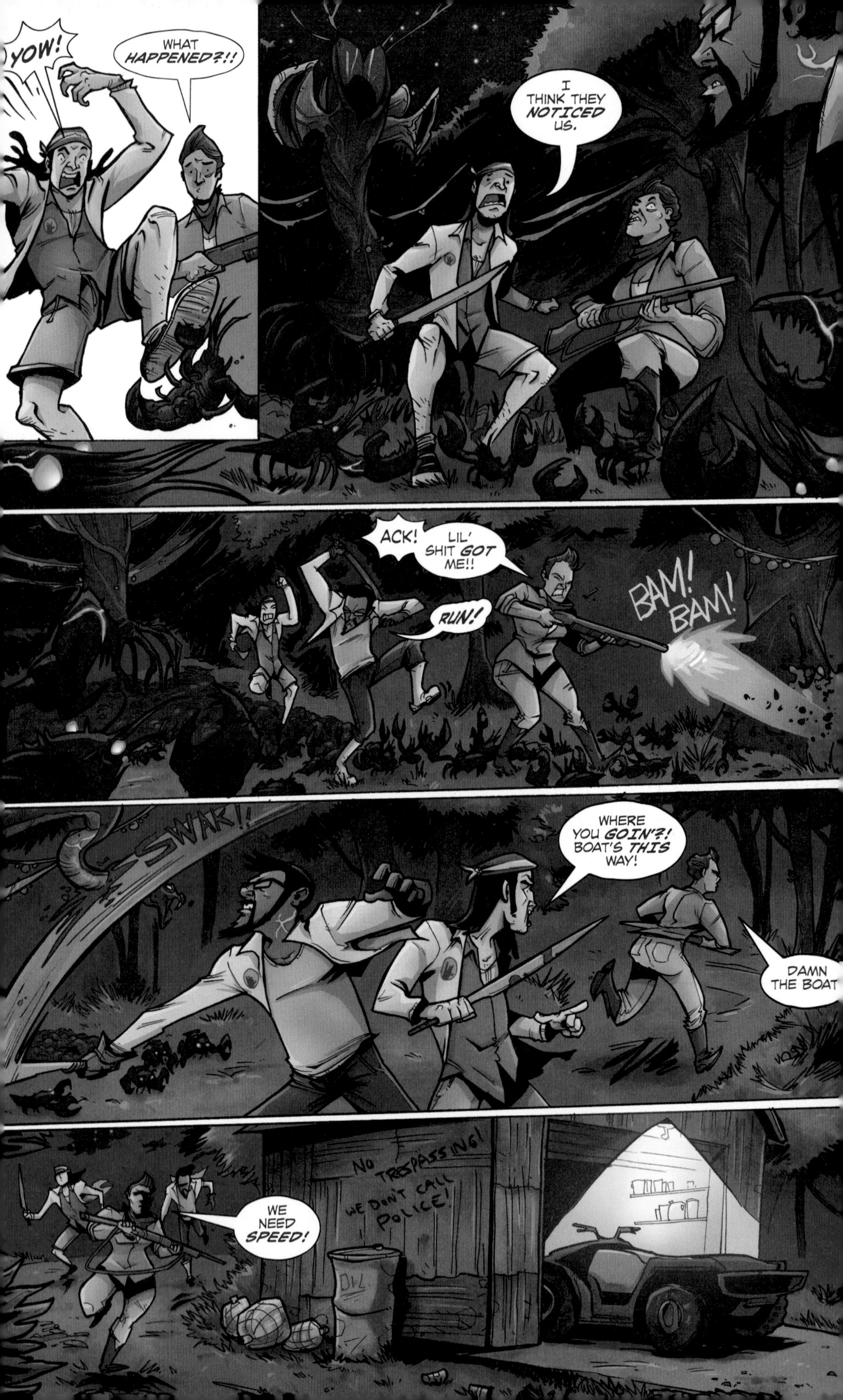
YOW!
WHAT HAPPENED?!!
I THINK THEY NOTICED US.
ACK!
LIL' SHIT GOT ME!!
RUN!
BAM! BAM!
SWAK!!
WHERE YOU GOIN'?! BOAT'S THIS WAY!
DAMN THE BOAT
NO TRESPASSING!
WE DON'T CALL POLICE!
WE NEED SPEED!
OIL

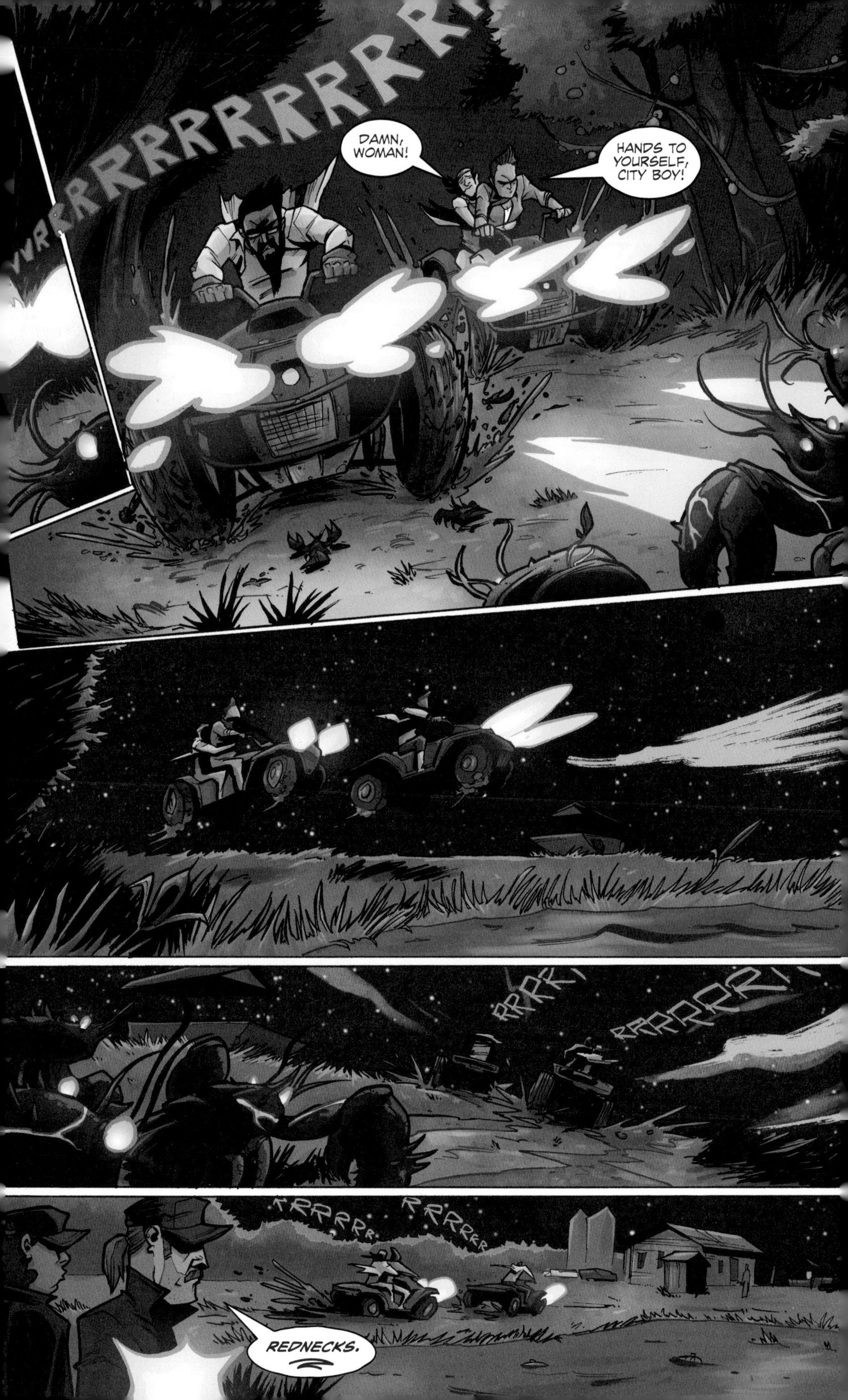
VVRRRRRRRRRRRR
DAMN, WOMAN!
HANDS TO YOURSELF, CITY BOY!
RRRRR
RRRRRRRR
RRRRRRR
RRRRRRR
REDNECKS.

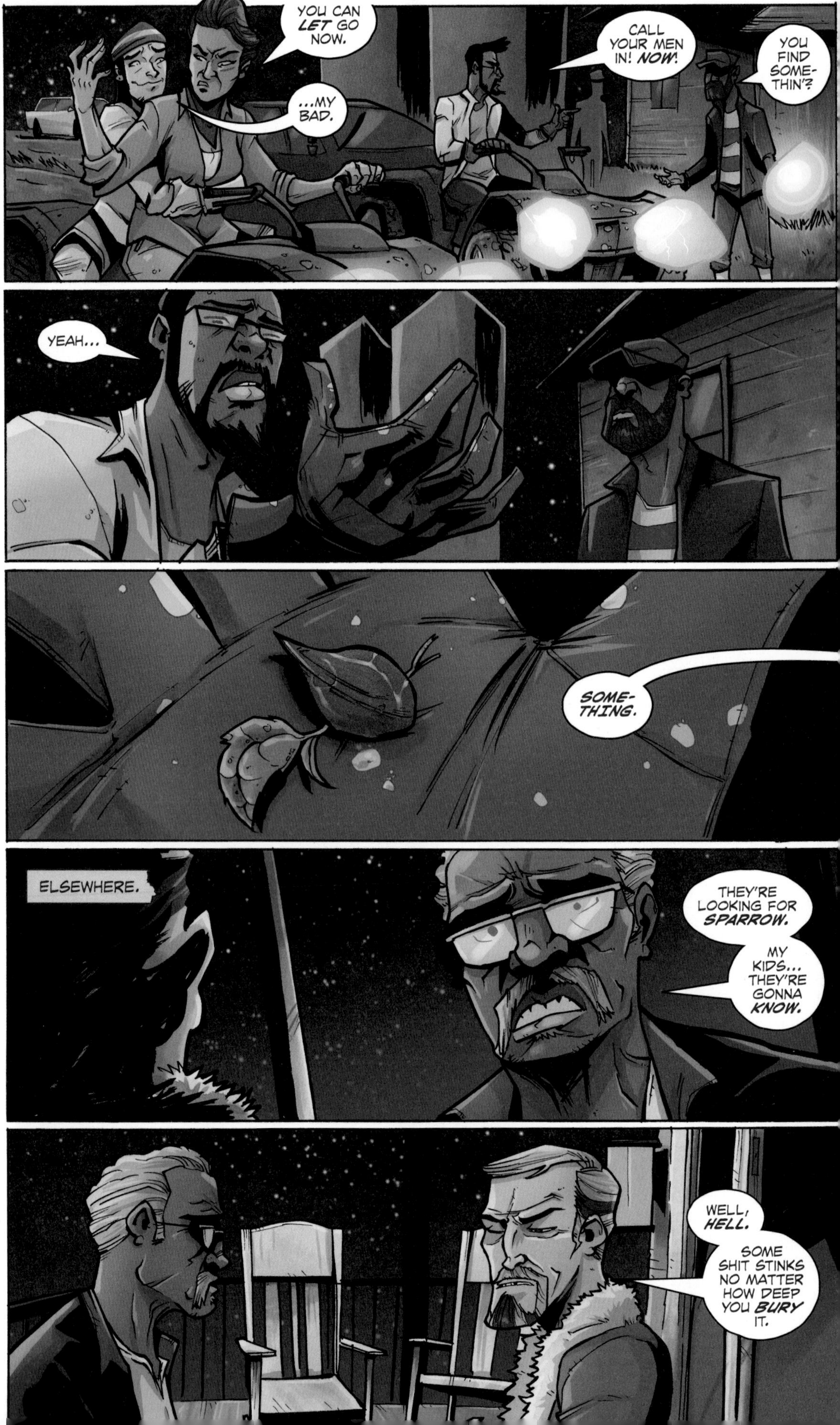
YOU CAN LET GO NOW.
...MY BAD.
CALL YOUR MEN IN! NOW!
YOU FIND SOME-THIN'?
YEAH...
SOME-THING.
ELSEWHERE.
THEY'RE LOOKING FOR SPARROW.
MY KIDS... THEY'RE GONNA KNOW.
WELL, HELL.
SOME SHIT STINKS NO MATTER HOW DEEP YOU BURY IT.

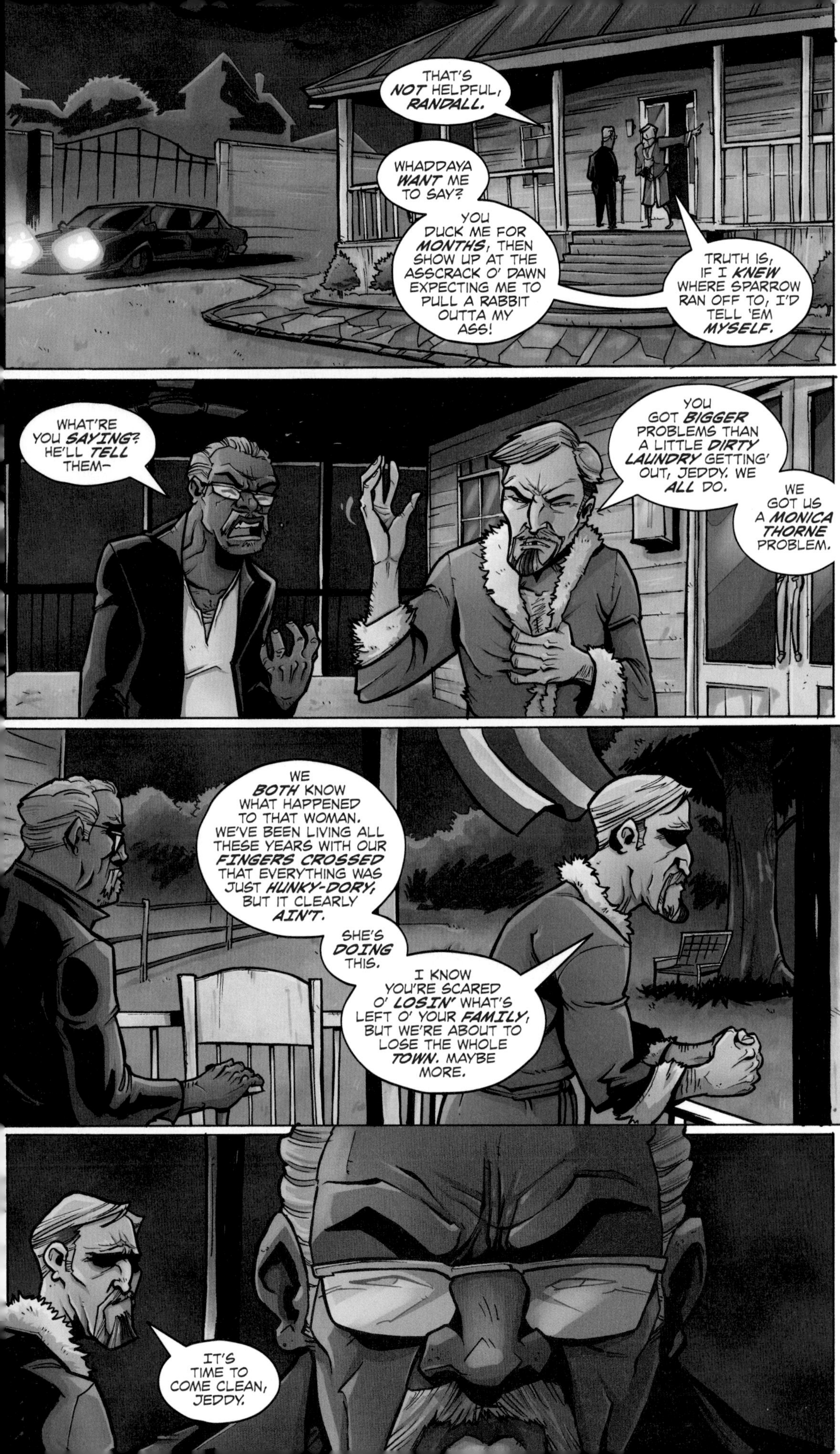
THAT'S NOT HELPFUL, RANDALL.
WHADDAYA WANT ME TO SAY?
YOU DUCK ME FOR MONTHS, THEN SHOW UP AT THE ASSCRACK O' DAWN EXPECTING ME TO PULL A RABBIT OUTTA MY ASS!
TRUTH IS, IF I KNEW WHERE SPARROW RAN OFF TO, I'D TELL 'EM MYSELF.
WHAT'RE YOU SAYING? HE'LL TELL THEM–
YOU GOT BIGGER PROBLEMS THAN A LITTLE DIRTY LAUNDRY GETTING' OUT, JEDDY. WE ALL DO.
WE GOT US A MONICA THORNE PROBLEM.
WE BOTH KNOW WHAT HAPPENED TO THAT WOMAN. WE'VE BEEN LIVING ALL THESE YEARS WITH OUR FINGERS CROSSED THAT EVERYTHING WAS JUST HUNKY-DORY, BUT IT CLEARLY AIN'T.
SHE'S DOING THIS.
I KNOW YOU'RE SCARED O' LOSIN' WHAT'S LEFT O' YOUR FAMILY, BUT WE'RE ABOUT TO LOSE THE WHOLE TOWN. MAYBE MORE.
IT'S TIME TO COME CLEAN, JEDDY.

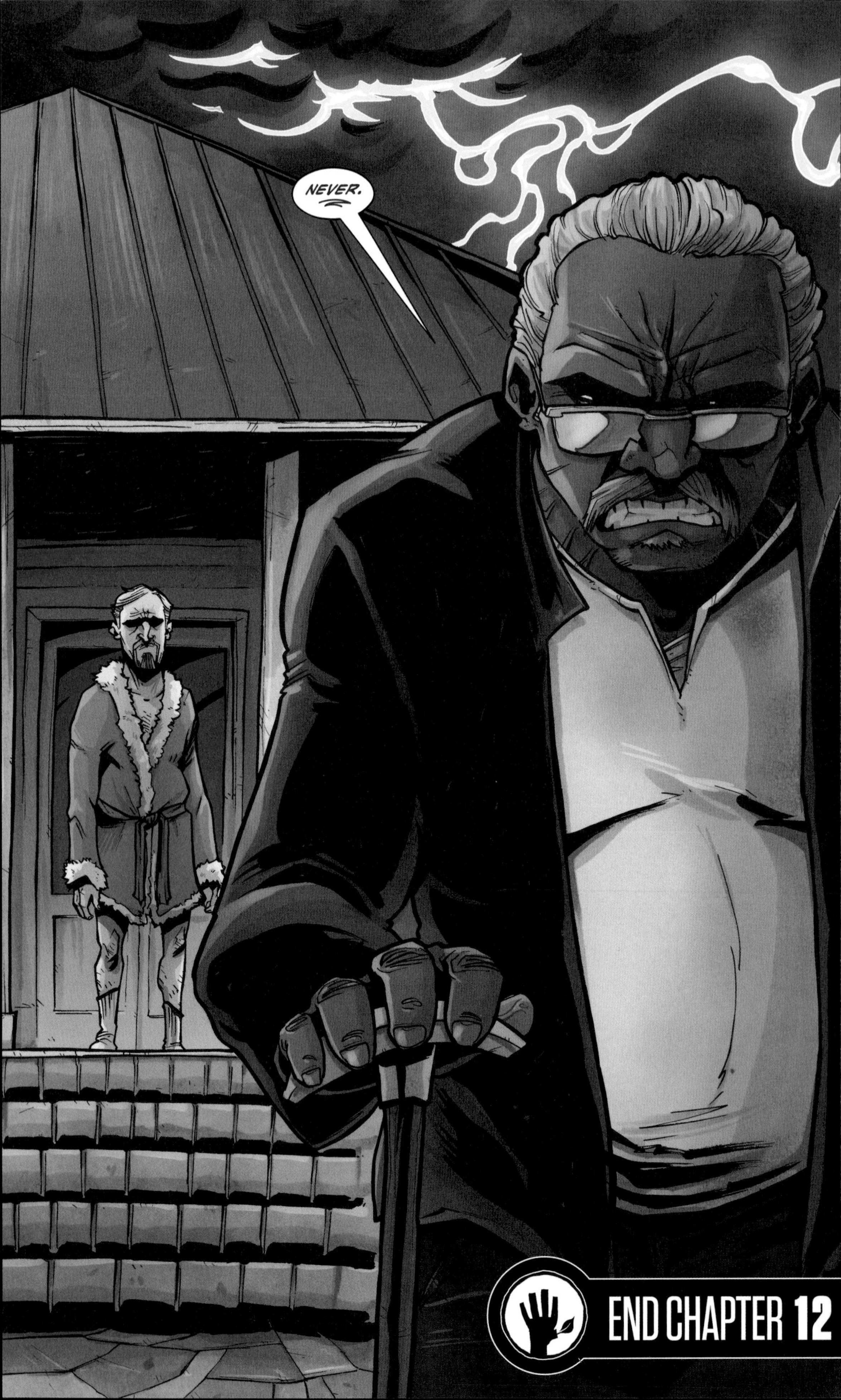
NEVER.
END CHAPTER 12

CHAPTER 13

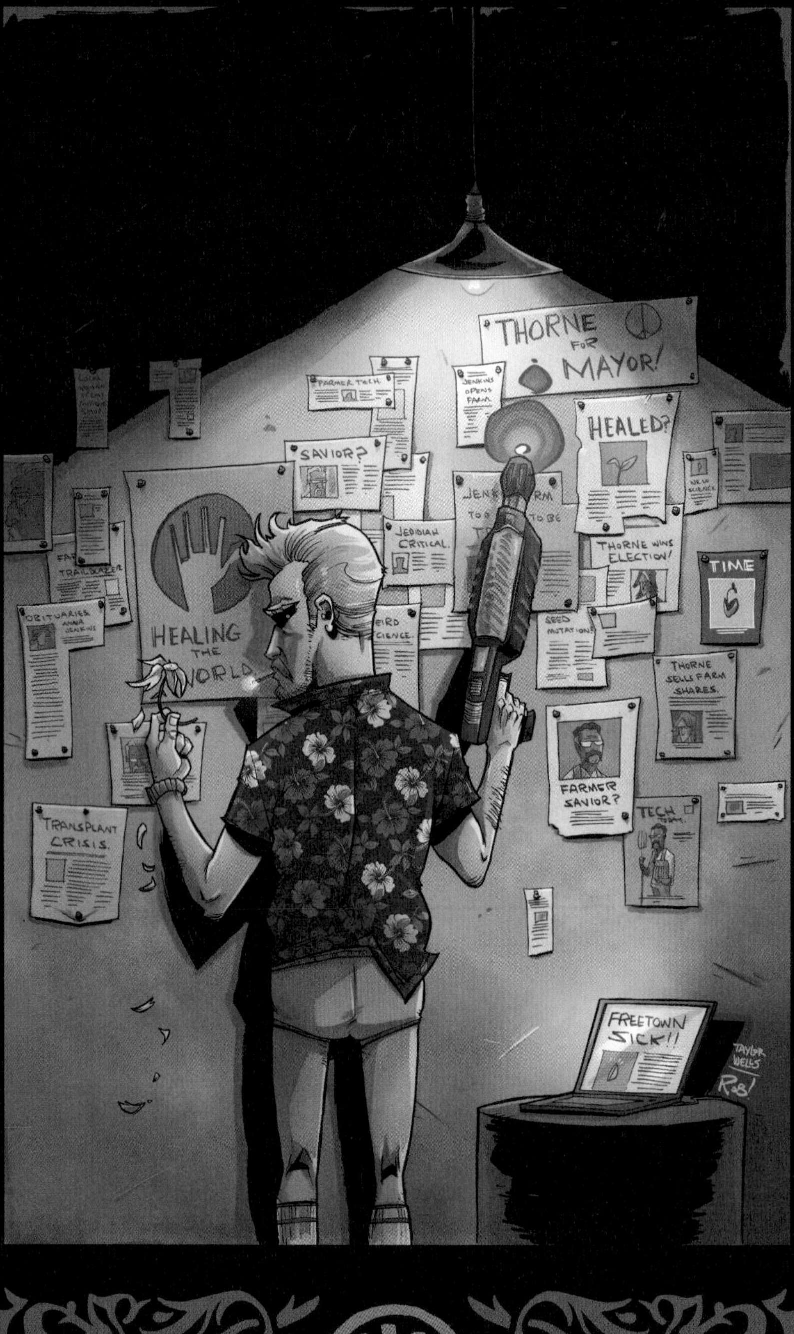
THORNE FOR MAYOR!
JENKINS OPENS FARM.
FARMER TECH
HEALED?
SAVIOR?
HEALING THE WORLD
JEDIDIAN CRITICAL.
THORNE WINS ELECTION!
TIME
SEED MUTATION!
THORNE SELLS FARM SHARES.
OBITUARIES ANNA JENKINS
FARMER SAVIOR?
TECH TODAY
TRANSPLANT CRISIS.
FREETOWN SICK!!

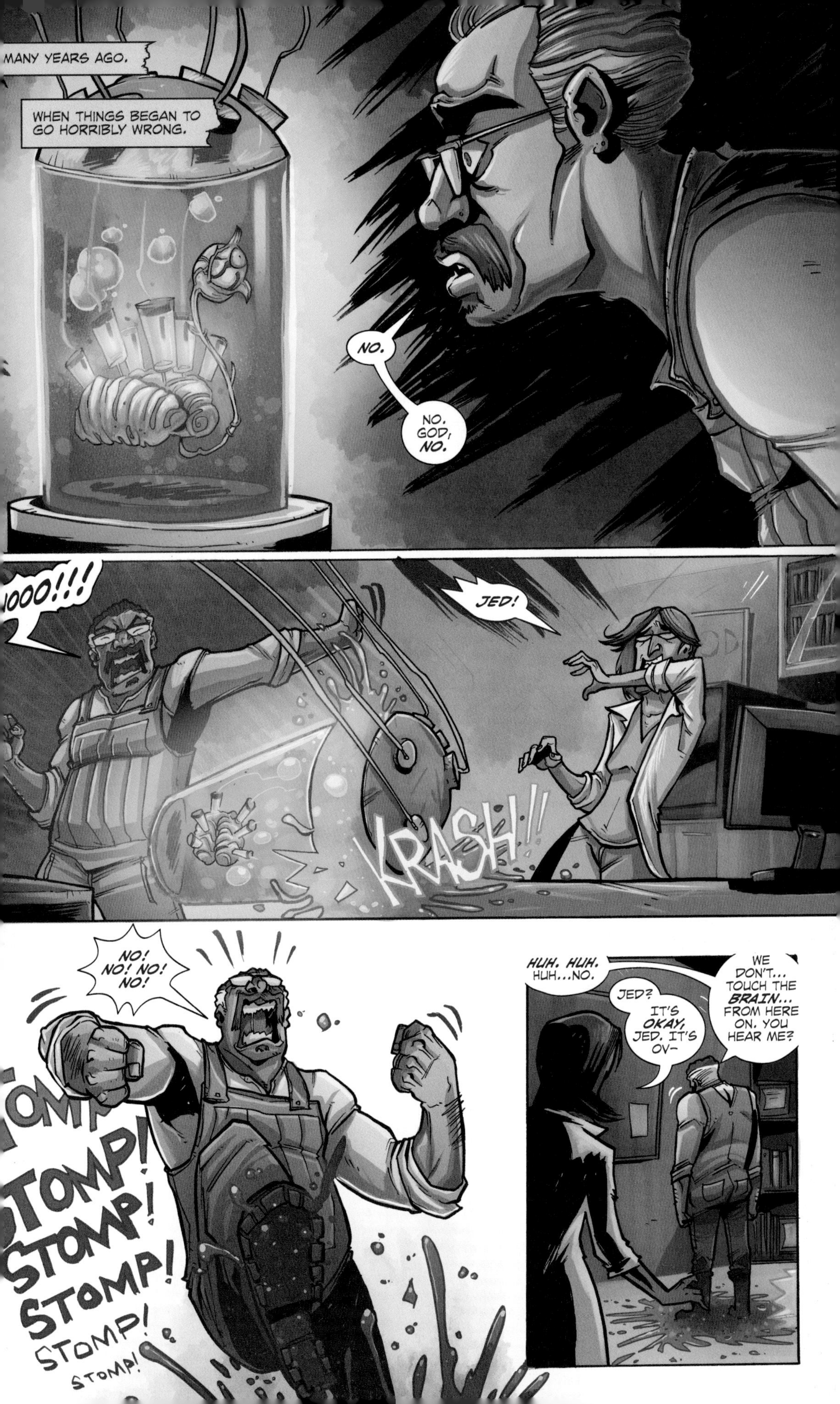
MANY YEARS AGO.
WHEN THINGS BEGAN TO GO HORRIBLY WRONG.
NO.
NO. GOD, NO.
NOOO!!!
JED!
KRASH!!
NO! NO! NO! NO!
STOMP! STOMP! STOMP! STOMP! STOMP! STOMP!
HUH. HUH. HUH...NO.
JED?
IT'S OKAY, JED. IT'S OV-
WE DON'T... TOUCH THE BRAIN... FROM HERE ON. YOU HEAR ME?

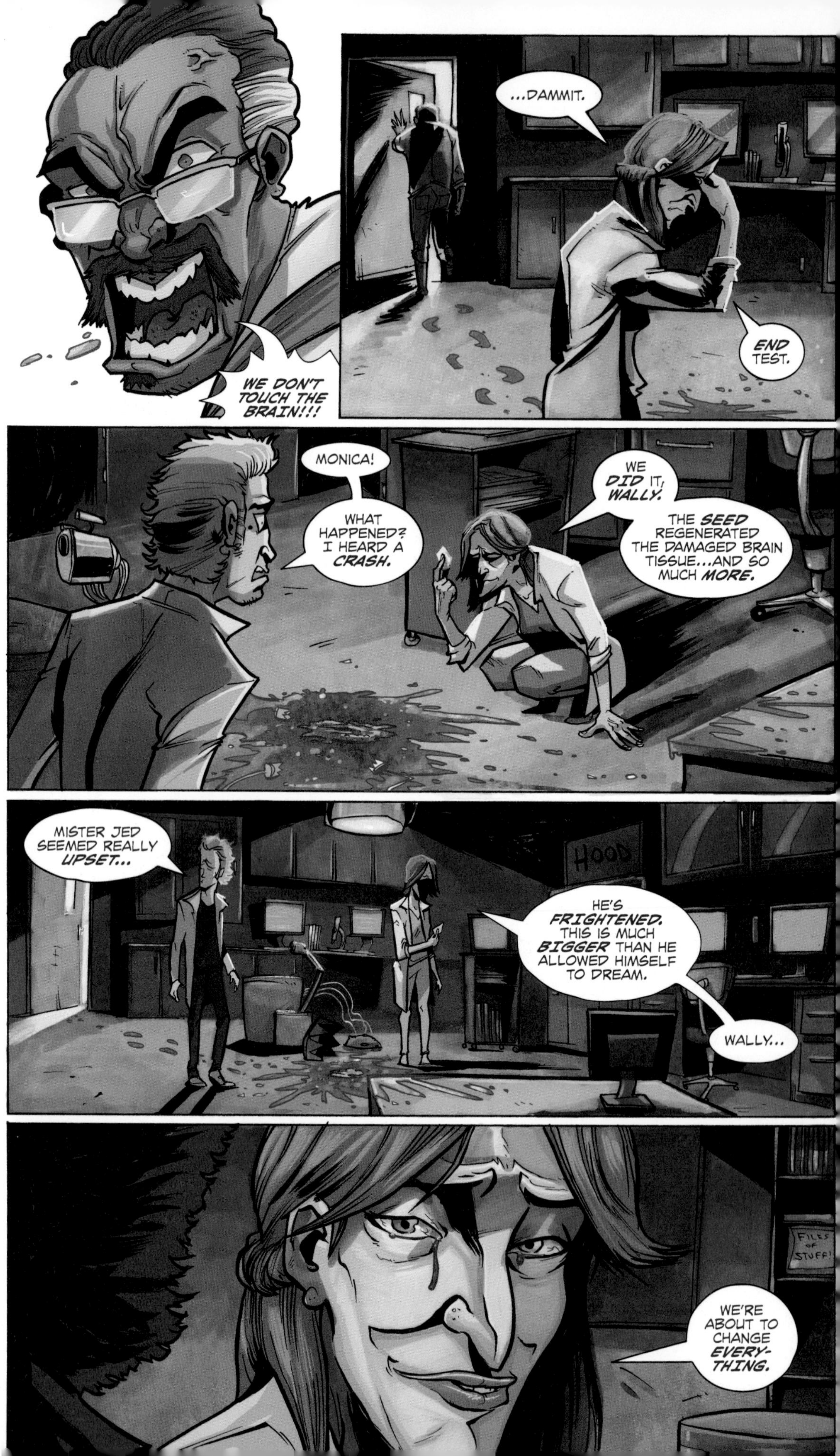
WE DON'T TOUCH THE BRAIN!!!
...DAMMIT.
END TEST.
MONICA!
WHAT HAPPENED? I HEARD A CRASH.
WE DID IT, WALLY.
THE SEED REGENERATED THE DAMAGED BRAIN TISSUE...AND SO MUCH MORE.
MISTER JED SEEMED REALLY UPSET...
HOOD
HE'S FRIGHTENED. THIS IS MUCH BIGGER THAN HE ALLOWED HIMSELF TO DREAM.
WALLY...
FILES OF STUFF!
WE'RE ABOUT TO CHANGE EVERY-THING.

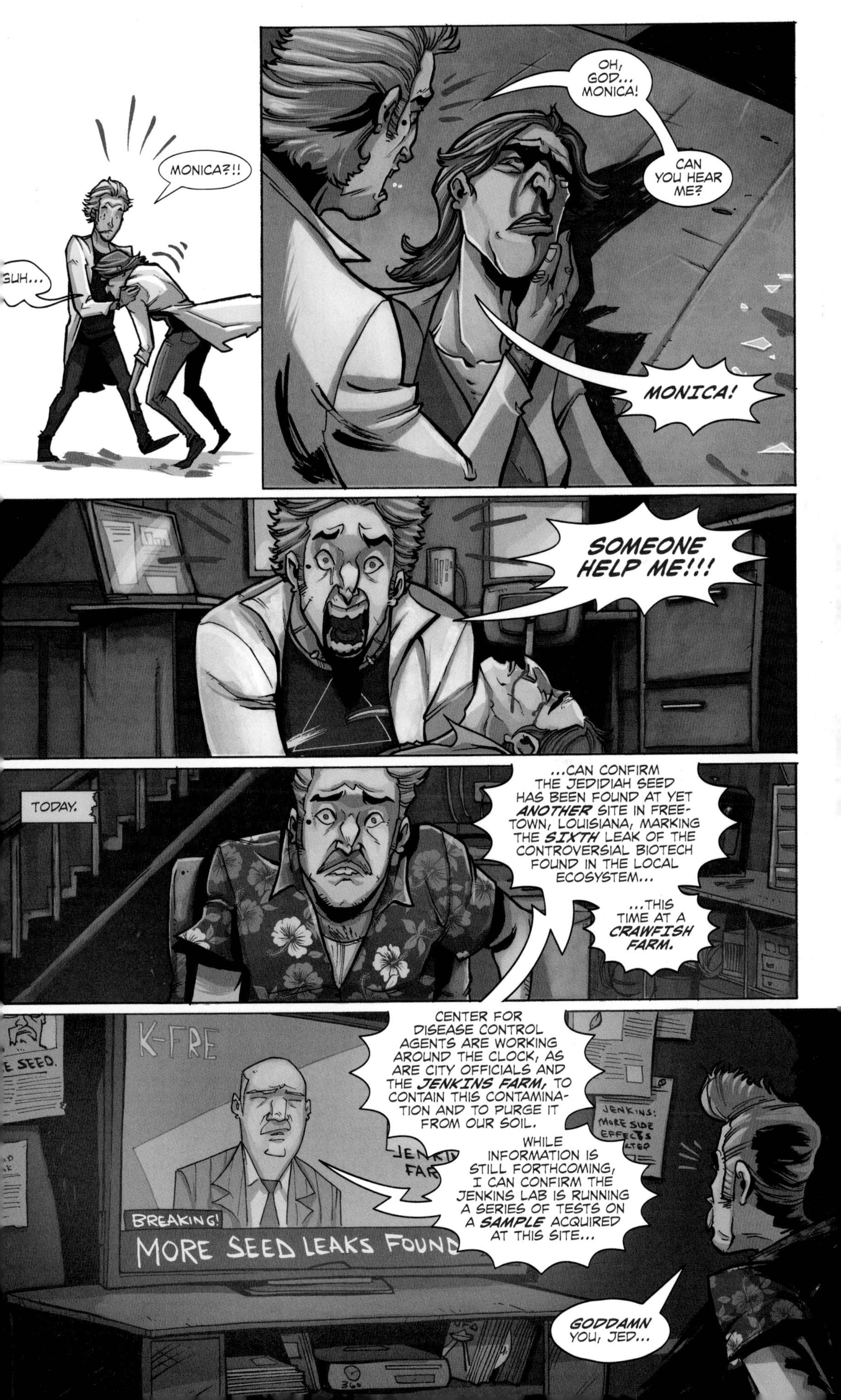
MONICA?!!
GUH...
OH, GOD... MONICA!
CAN YOU HEAR ME?
MONICA!
SOMEONE HELP ME!!!
TODAY.
...CAN CONFIRM THE JEDIDIAH SEED HAS BEEN FOUND AT YET ANOTHER SITE IN FREE-TOWN, LOUISIANA, MARKING THE SIXTH LEAK OF THE CONTROVERSIAL BIOTECH FOUND IN THE LOCAL ECOSYSTEM...
...THIS TIME AT A CRAWFISH FARM.
K-FRE
BREAKING!
MORE SEED LEAKS FOUND
CENTER FOR DISEASE CONTROL AGENTS ARE WORKING AROUND THE CLOCK, AS ARE CITY OFFICIALS AND THE JENKINS FARM, TO CONTAIN THIS CONTAMINATION AND TO PURGE IT FROM OUR SOIL.
WHILE INFORMATION IS STILL FORTHCOMING, I CAN CONFIRM THE JENKINS LAB IS RUNNING A SERIES OF TESTS ON A SAMPLE ACQUIRED AT THIS SITE...
GODDAMN YOU, JED...

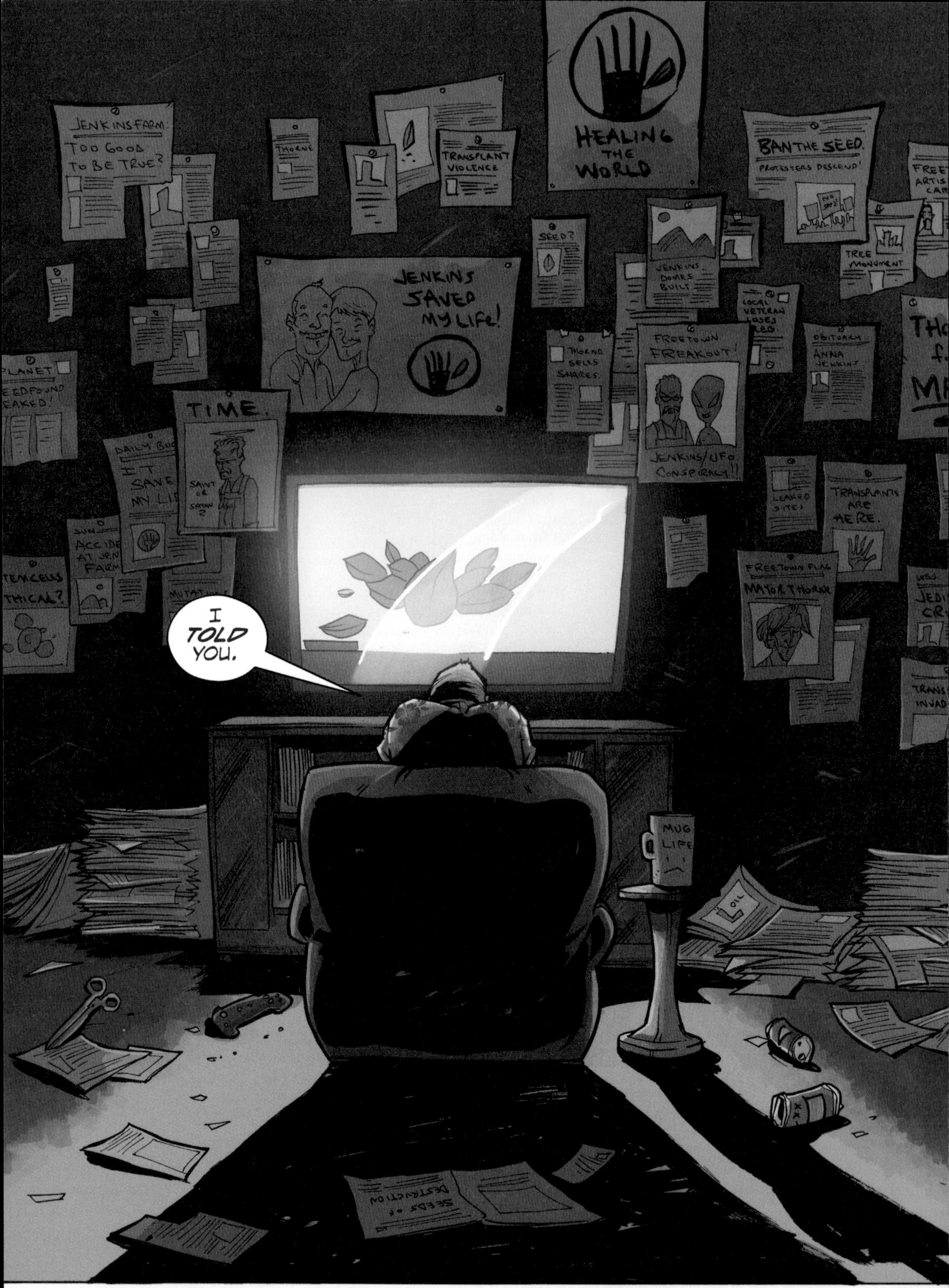

I TOLD YOU.
JENKINS FARM: TOO GOOD TO BE TRUE?
THORNE
TRANSPLANT VIOLENCE
HEALING THE WORLD
BAN THE SEED.
PROTESTERS DESCEND!
SEED?
JENKINS SAVED MY LIFE!
JENKINS DOMES BUILT
TREE MONUMENT
THORNE SELLS SHARES.
FREETOWN FREAKOUT!
JENKINS/UFO CONSPIRACY!!
OBITUARY ANNA JENKINS
TIME.
SAINT OR SATAN?
LEAKED SITES
TRANSPLANTS ARE HERE.
FREETOWN FLAG
MAYOR THORNE
MUG LIFE
SEEDS of DESTRUCTION

CHAPTER 13: **THE WIZ.**

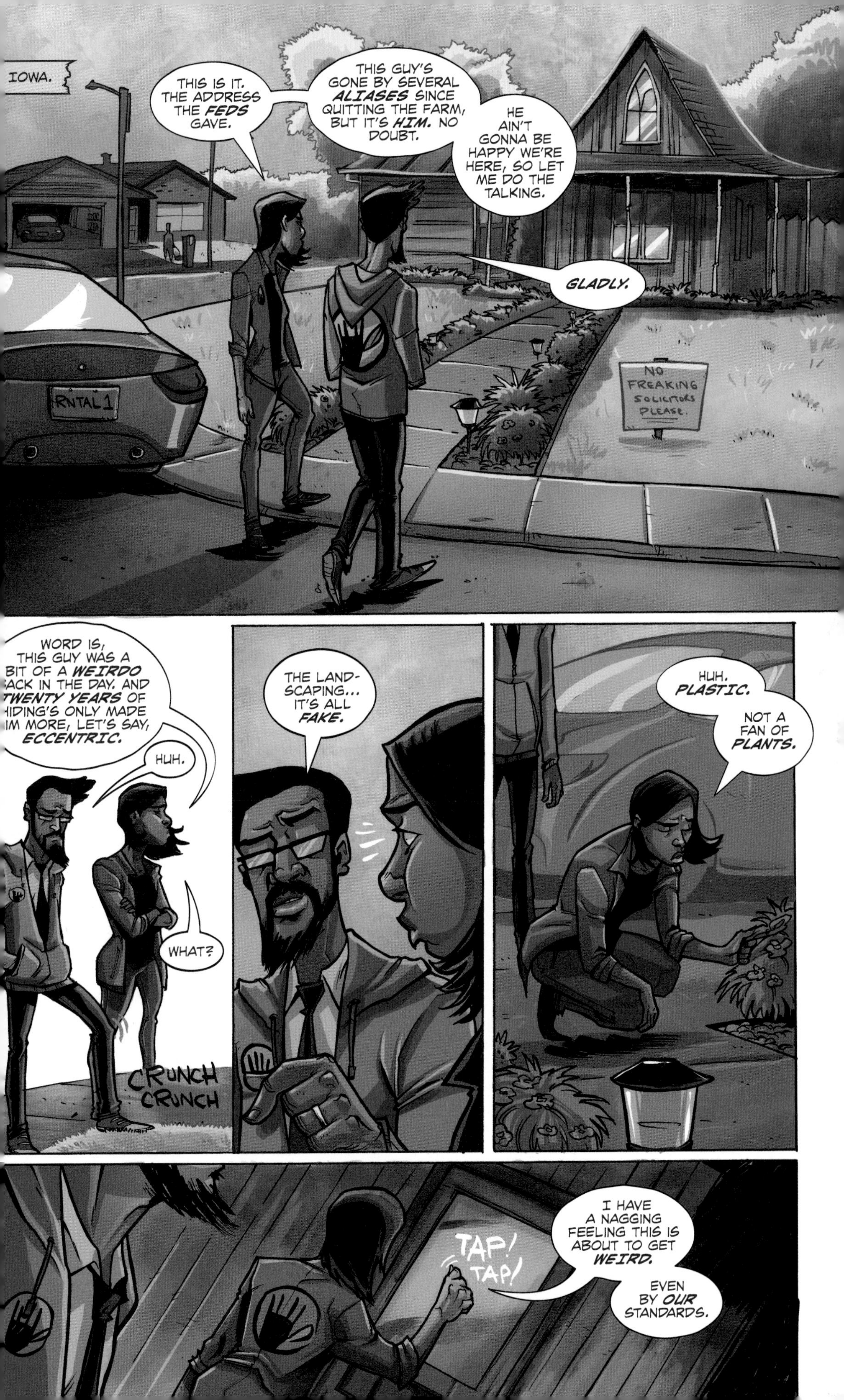
IOWA.
THIS IS IT. THE ADDRESS THE FEDS GAVE.
THIS GUY'S GONE BY SEVERAL ALIASES SINCE QUITTING THE FARM, BUT IT'S HIM. NO DOUBT.
HE AIN'T GONNA BE HAPPY WE'RE HERE, SO LET ME DO THE TALKING.
GLADLY.
RNTAL1
NO FREAKING SOLICITORS PLEASE.
WORD IS, THIS GUY WAS A BIT OF A WEIRDO ACK IN THE DAY. AND WENTY YEARS OF IDING'S ONLY MADE IM MORE, LET'S SAY, ECCENTRIC.
HUH.
WHAT?
CRUNCH CRUNCH
THE LAND-SCAPING... IT'S ALL FAKE.
HUH. PLASTIC.
NOT A FAN OF PLANTS.
TAP! TAP!
I HAVE A NAGGING FEELING THIS IS ABOUT TO GET WEIRD.
EVEN BY OUR STANDARDS.

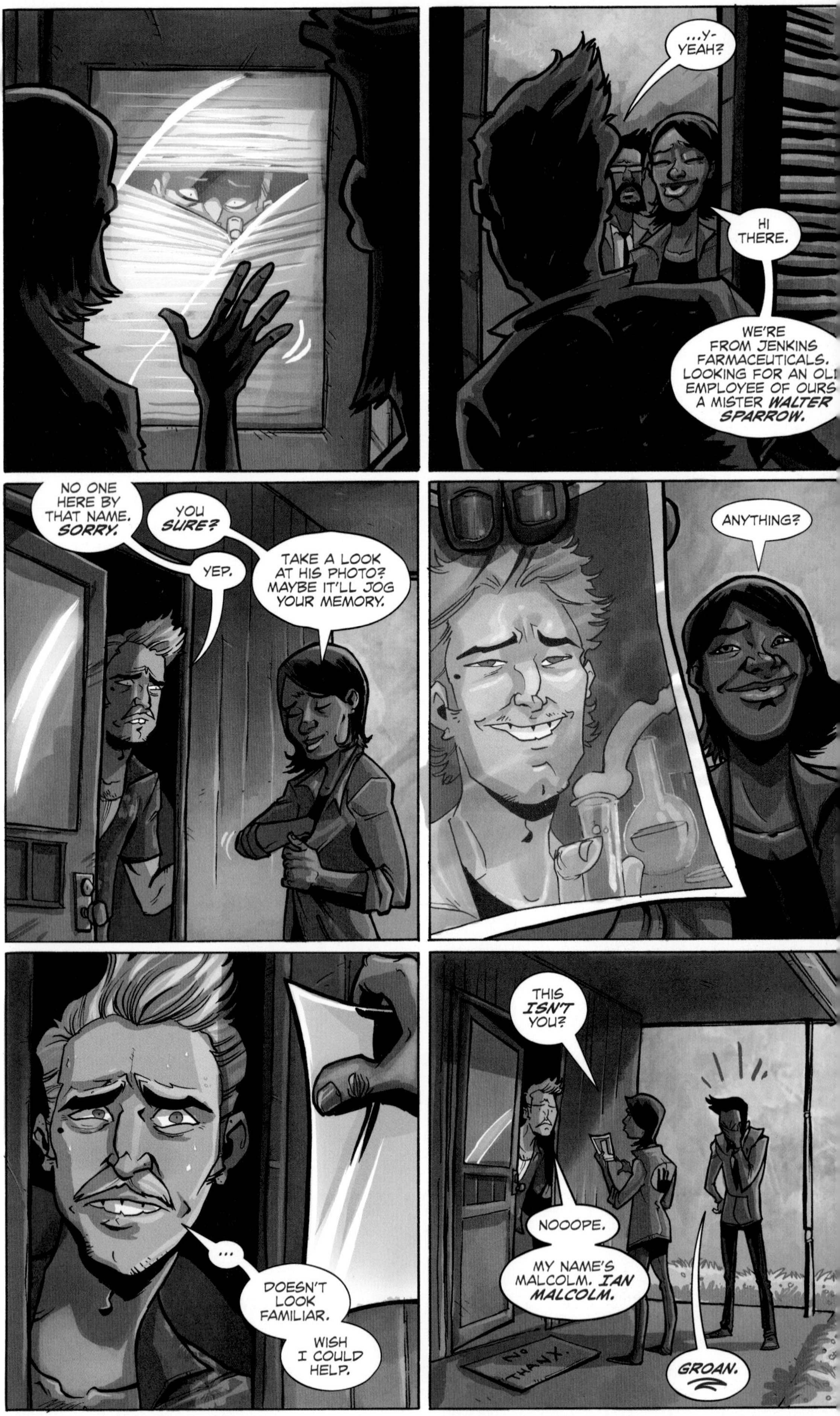
...Y-
YEAH?
HI THERE.
WE'RE FROM JENKINS FARMACEUTICALS. LOOKING FOR AN OLD EMPLOYEE OF OURS A MISTER WALTER SPARROW.
NO ONE HERE BY THAT NAME. SORRY.
YOU SURE?
YEP.
TAKE A LOOK AT HIS PHOTO? MAYBE IT'LL JOG YOUR MEMORY.
ANYTHING?
...
DOESN'T LOOK FAMILIAR.
WISH I COULD HELP.
THIS ISN'T YOU?
NOOOPE.
MY NAME'S MALCOLM. IAN MALCOLM.
GROAN.
NO THANX

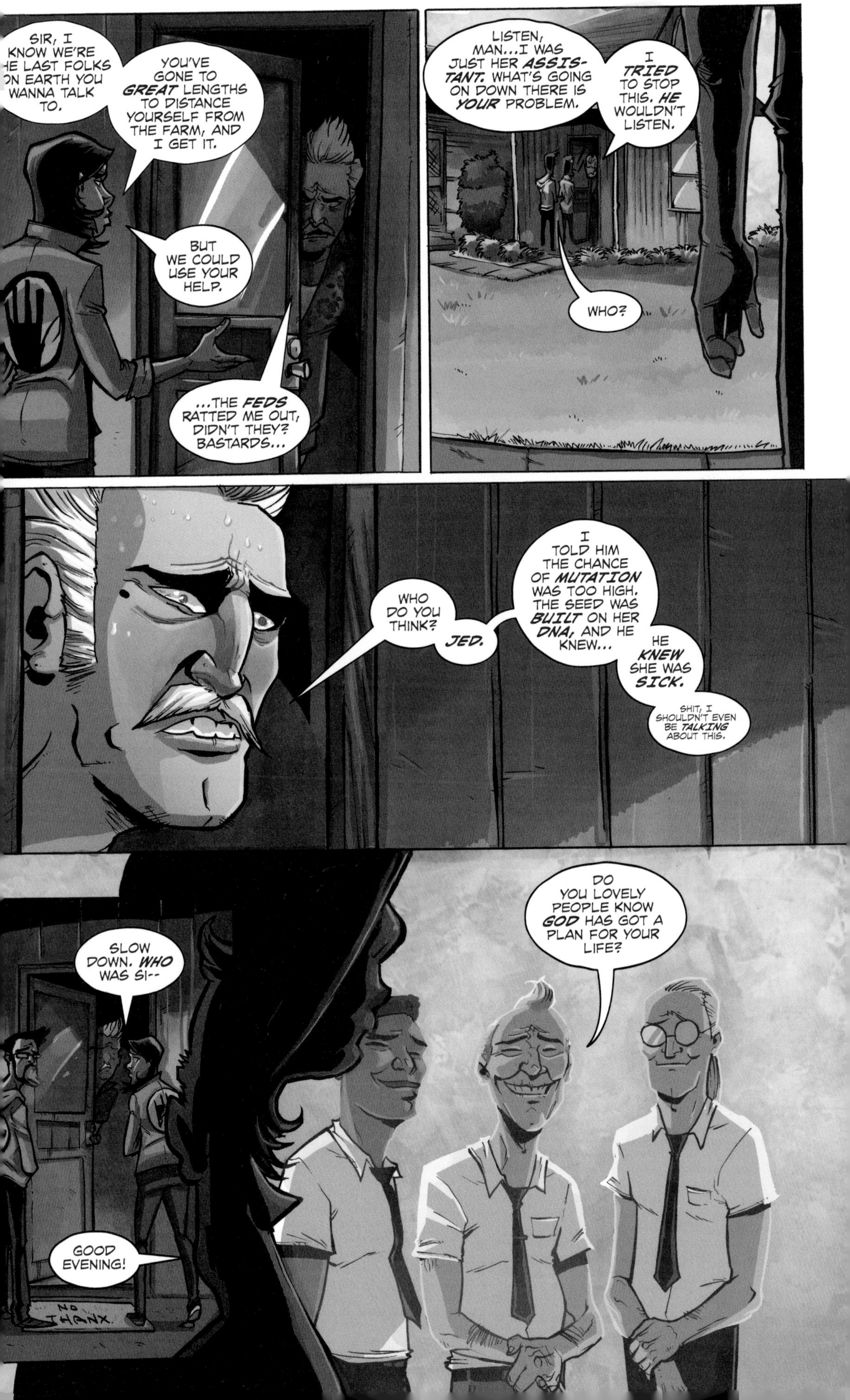
SIR, I KNOW WE'RE THE LAST FOLKS ON EARTH YOU WANNA TALK TO.
YOU'VE GONE TO GREAT LENGTHS TO DISTANCE YOURSELF FROM THE FARM, AND I GET IT.
BUT WE COULD USE YOUR HELP.
...THE FEDS RATTED ME OUT, DIDN'T THEY? BASTARDS...
LISTEN, MAN...I WAS JUST HER ASSISTANT. WHAT'S GOING ON DOWN THERE IS YOUR PROBLEM.
I TRIED TO STOP THIS. HE WOULDN'T LISTEN.
WHO?
WHO DO YOU THINK? JED.
I TOLD HIM THE CHANCE OF MUTATION WAS TOO HIGH. THE SEED WAS BUILT ON HER DNA, AND HE KNEW...
HE KNEW SHE WAS SICK.
SHIT, I SHOULDN'T EVEN BE TALKING ABOUT THIS.
SLOW DOWN. WHO WAS SI--
GOOD EVENING!
DO YOU LOVELY PEOPLE KNOW GOD HAS GOT A PLAN FOR YOUR LIFE?
NO THANX

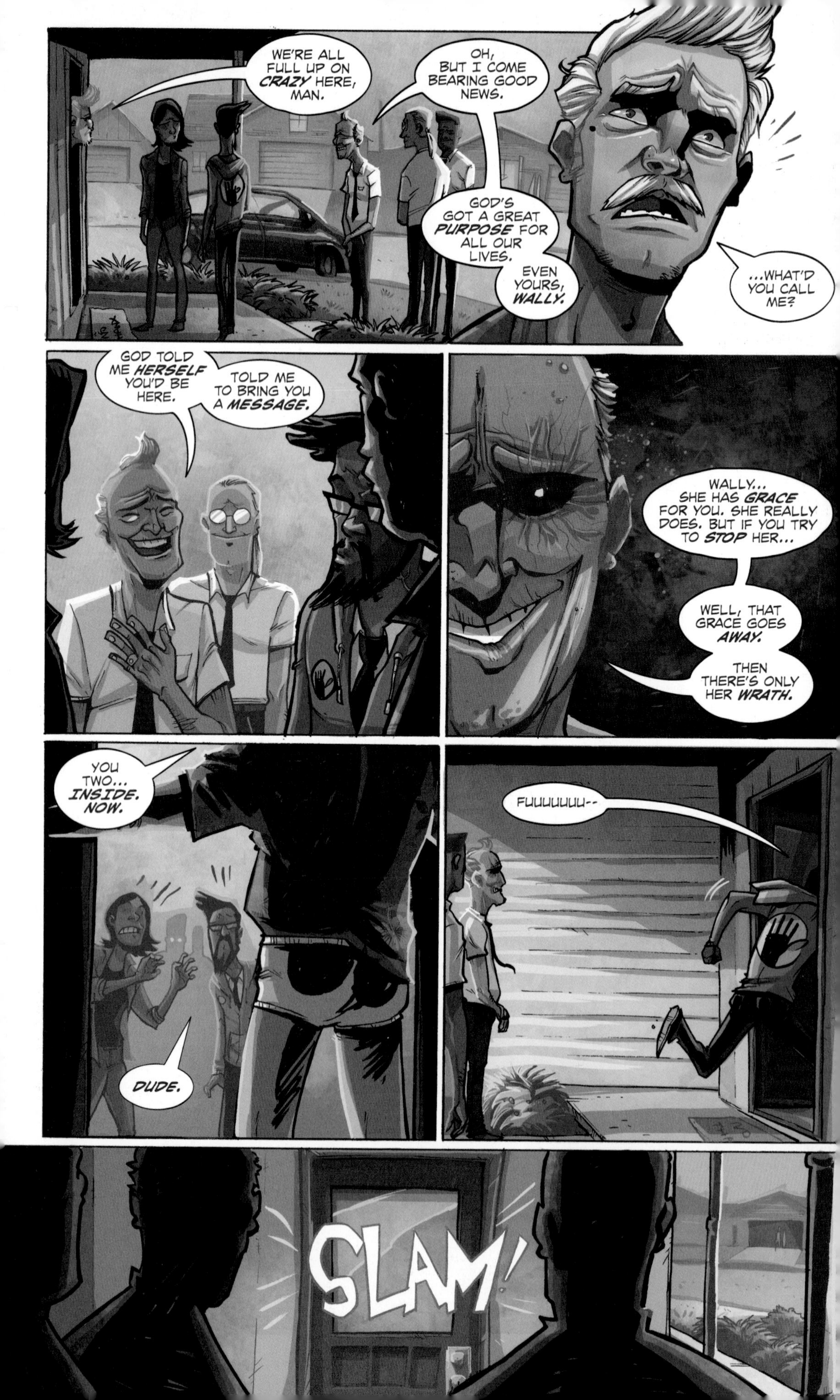
WE'RE ALL FULL UP ON CRAZY HERE, MAN.
OH, BUT I COME BEARING GOOD NEWS.
GOD'S GOT A GREAT PURPOSE FOR ALL OUR LIVES.
EVEN YOURS, WALLY.
...WHAT'D YOU CALL ME?
GOD TOLD ME HERSELF YOU'D BE HERE.
TOLD ME TO BRING YOU A MESSAGE.
WALLY... SHE HAS GRACE FOR YOU. SHE REALLY DOES. BUT IF YOU TRY TO STOP HER...
WELL, THAT GRACE GOES AWAY.
THEN THERE'S ONLY HER WRATH.
YOU TWO... INSIDE. NOW.
DUDE.
FUUUUUUU--
SLAM!

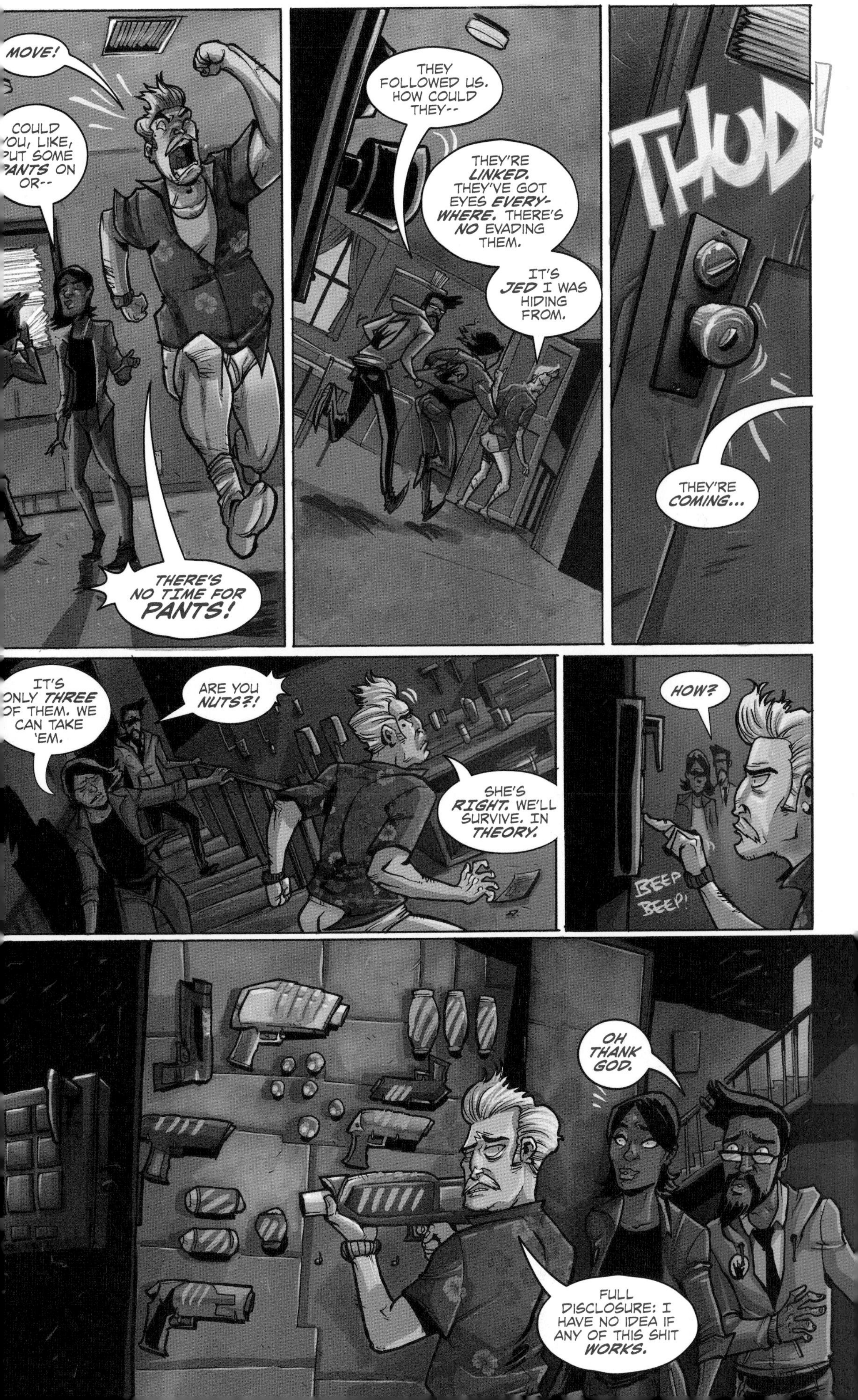
MOVE!
COULD YOU, LIKE, PUT SOME PANTS ON OR--
THERE'S NO TIME FOR PANTS!
THEY FOLLOWED US. HOW COULD THEY--
THEY'RE LINKED. THEY'VE GOT EYES EVERY-WHERE. THERE'S NO EVADING THEM.
IT'S JED I WAS HIDING FROM.
THUD!
THEY'RE COMING...
IT'S ONLY THREE OF THEM. WE CAN TAKE 'EM.
ARE YOU NUTS?!
SHE'S RIGHT. WE'LL SURVIVE. IN THEORY.
HOW?
BEEP BEEP!
OH THANK GOD.
FULL DISCLOSURE: I HAVE NO IDEA IF ANY OF THIS SHIT WORKS.

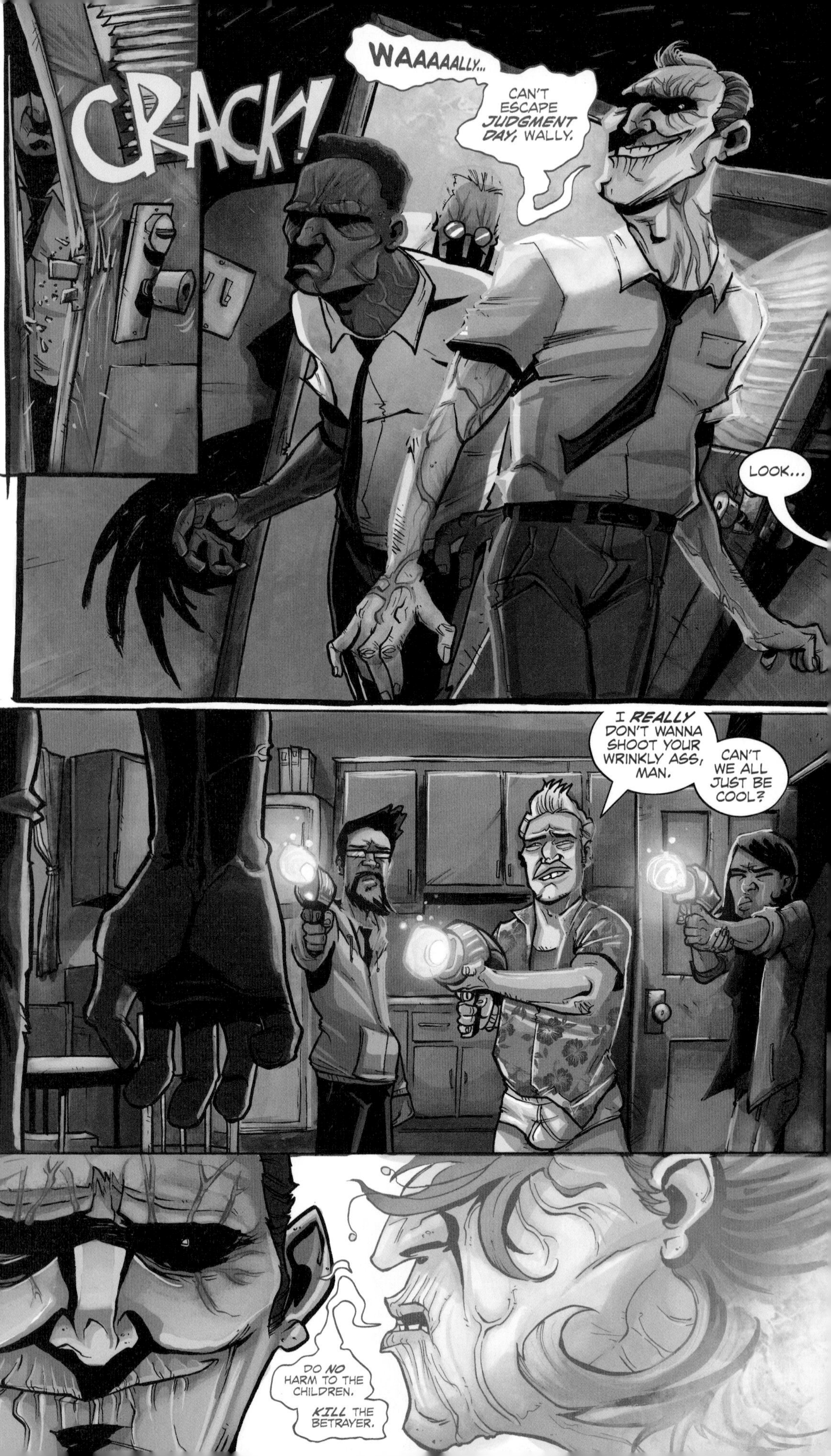
CRACK!
WAAAAALLY...
CAN'T ESCAPE JUDGMENT DAY, WALLY.
LOOK...
I REALLY DON'T WANNA SHOOT YOUR WRINKLY ASS, MAN.
CAN'T WE ALL JUST BE COOL?
DO NO HARM TO THE CHILDREN.
KILL THE BETRAYER.

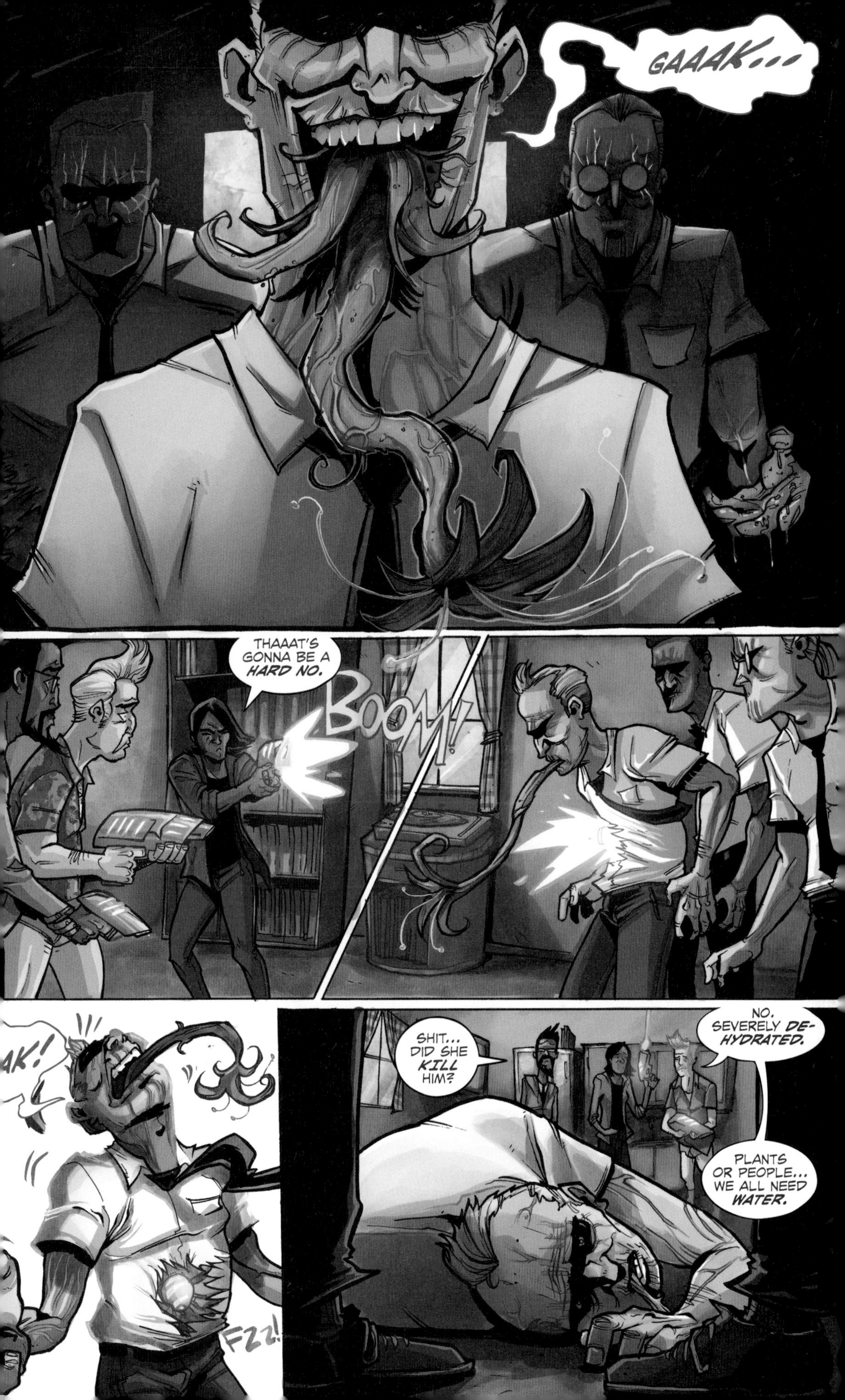
GAAAK...
THAAAT'S GONNA BE A HARD NO.
BOOM!
AK!
FZZ!
SHIT... DID SHE KILL HIM?
NO. SEVERELY DE-HYDRATED.
PLANTS OR PEOPLE... WE ALL NEED WATER.

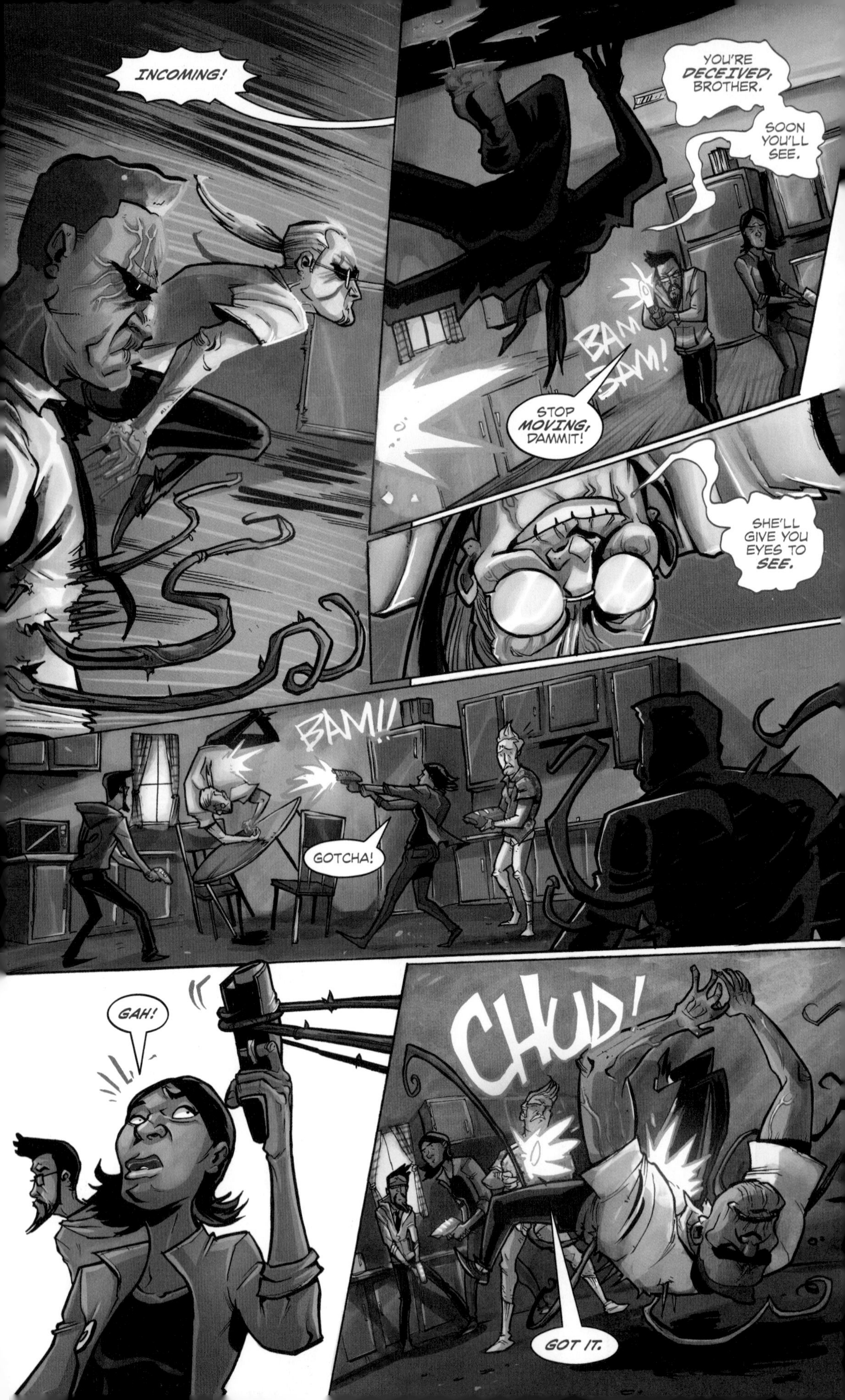
INCOMING!
YOU'RE DECEIVED, BROTHER.
SOON YOU'LL SEE.
BAM BAM!
STOP MOVING, DAMMIT!
SHE'LL GIVE YOU EYES TO SEE.
BAM!!
GOTCHA!
GAH!
CHUD!
GOT IT.

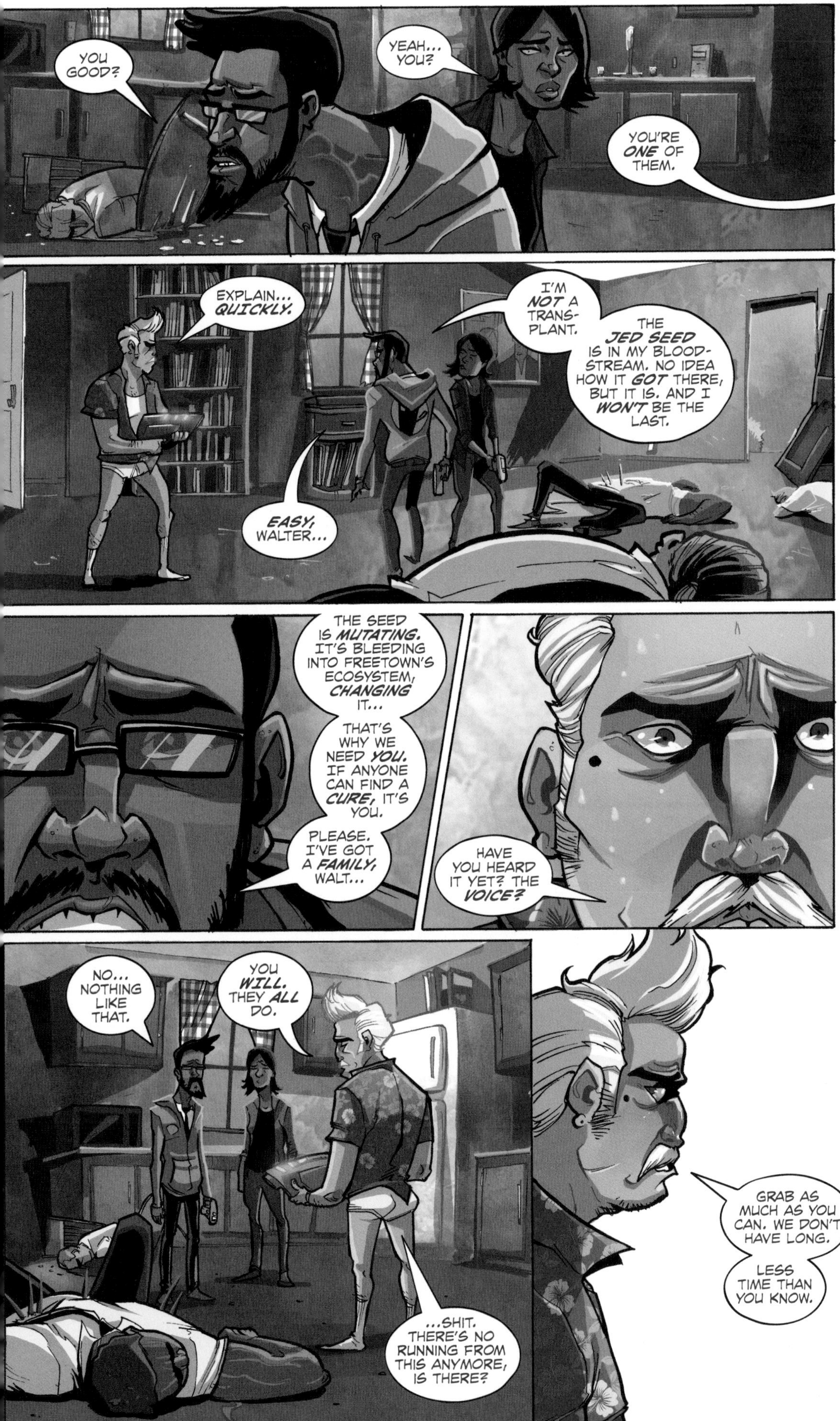
YOU GOOD?
YEAH... YOU?
YOU'RE ONE OF THEM.
EXPLAIN... QUICKLY.
EASY, WALTER...
I'M NOT A TRANSPLANT.
THE JED SEED IS IN MY BLOODSTREAM. NO IDEA HOW IT GOT THERE, BUT IT IS. AND I WON'T BE THE LAST.
THE SEED IS MUTATING. IT'S BLEEDING INTO FREETOWN'S ECOSYSTEM, CHANGING IT...
THAT'S WHY WE NEED YOU. IF ANYONE CAN FIND A CURE, IT'S YOU.
PLEASE. I'VE GOT A FAMILY, WALT...
HAVE YOU HEARD IT YET? THE VOICE?
NO... NOTHING LIKE THAT.
YOU WILL. THEY ALL DO.
...SHIT. THERE'S NO RUNNING FROM THIS ANYMORE, IS THERE?
GRAB AS MUCH AS YOU CAN. WE DON'T HAVE LONG.
LESS TIME THAN YOU KNOW.

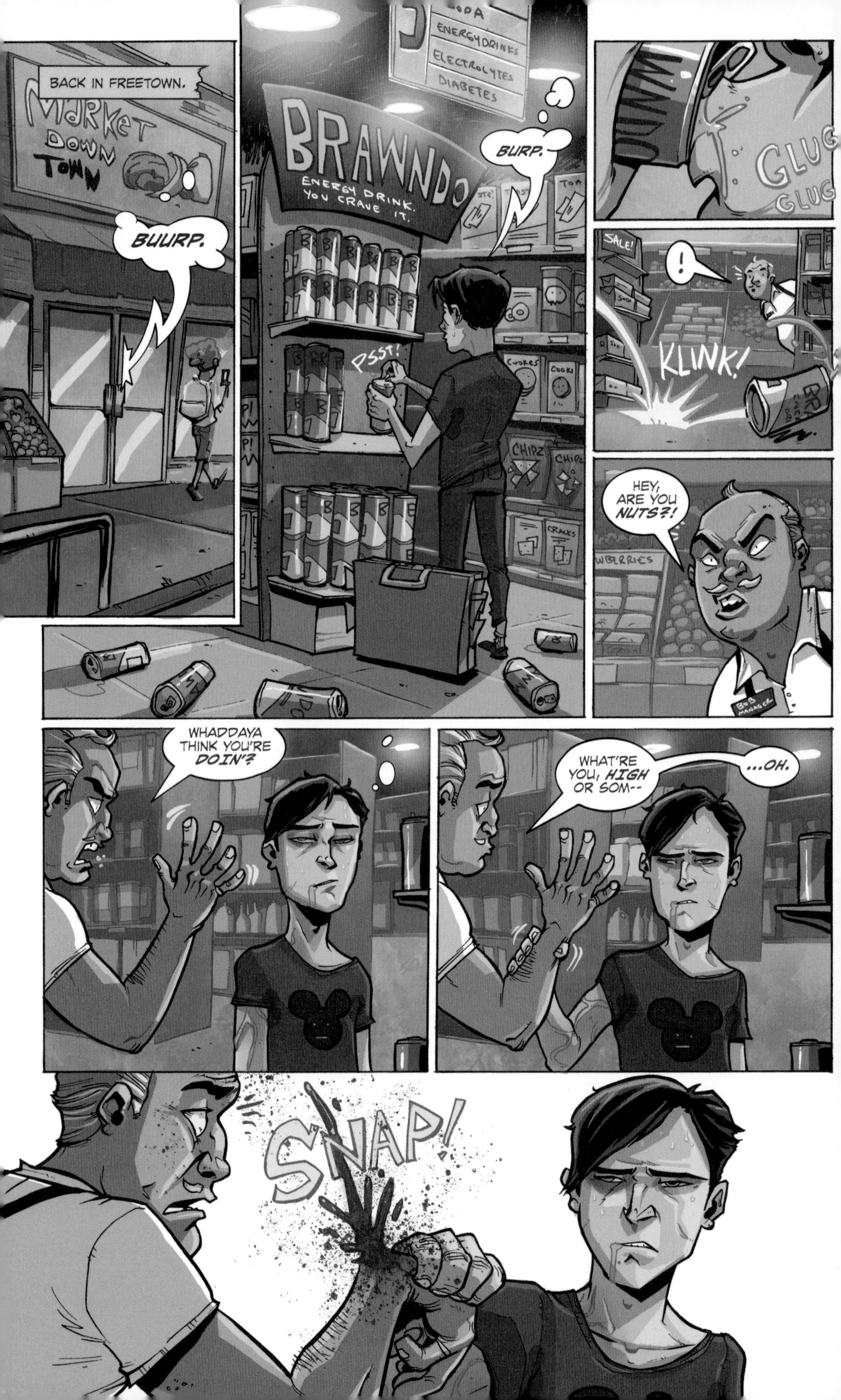
BACK IN FREETOWN.
MARKET DOWN TOWN
BUURP.
SODA
ENERGY DRINKS
ELECTROLYTES
DIABETES
BRAWNDO
ENERGY DRINK. YOU CRAVE IT.
BURP.
PSST!
CHIPZ
GLUG
GLUG
SALE!
!
KLINK!
HEY, ARE YOU NUTS?!
BOB MANAGER
WHADDAYA THINK YOU'RE DOIN'?
WHAT'RE YOU, HIGH OR SOM--
...OH.
SNAP!

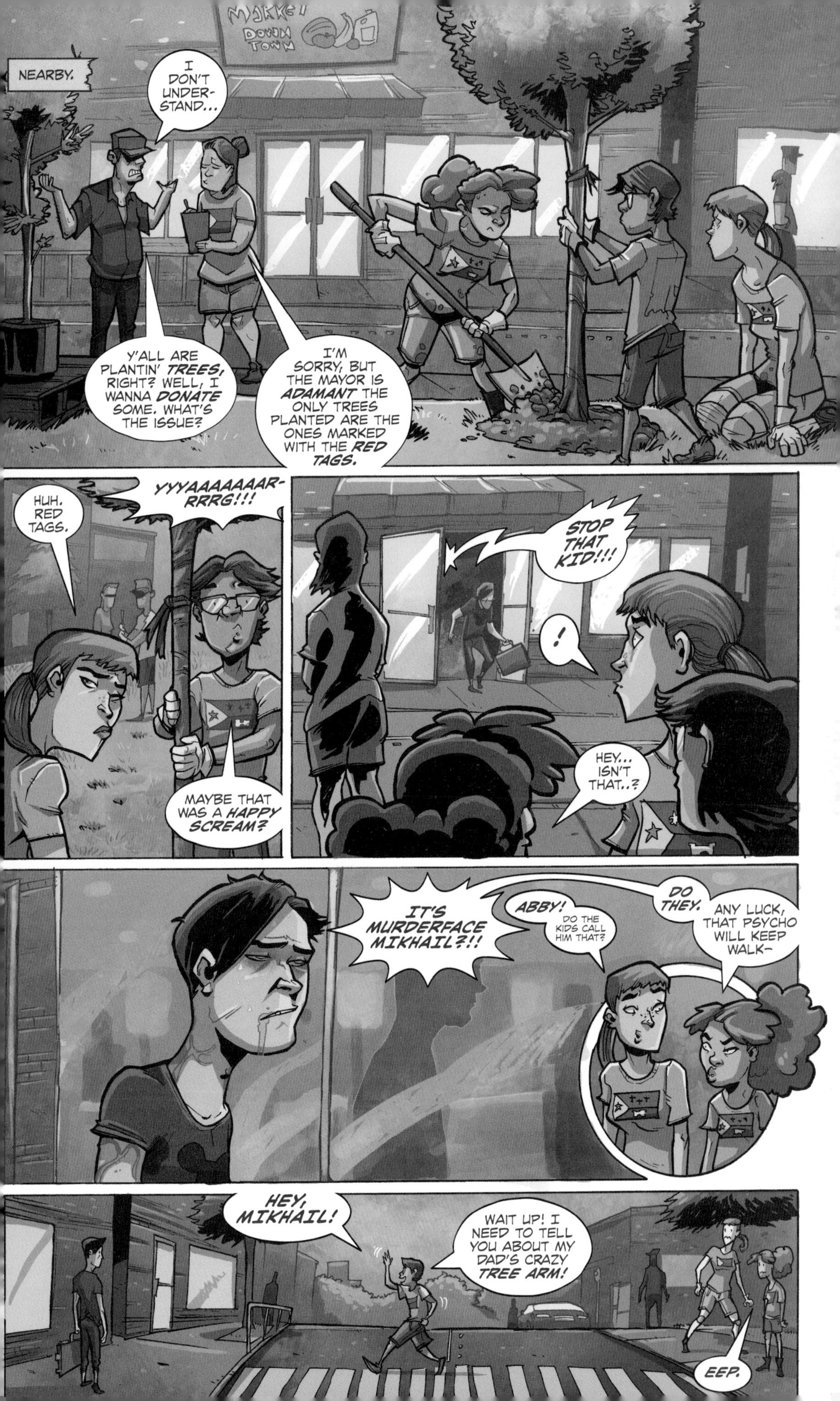
MARKET DOWN TOWN
NEARBY.
I DON'T UNDER-STAND...
Y'ALL ARE PLANTIN' TREES, RIGHT? WELL, I WANNA DONATE SOME. WHAT'S THE ISSUE?
I'M SORRY, BUT THE MAYOR IS ADAMANT THE ONLY TREES PLANTED ARE THE ONES MARKED WITH THE RED TAGS.
HUH. RED TAGS.
YYYAAAAAAAR-RRRG!!!
MAYBE THAT WAS A HAPPY SCREAM?
STOP THAT KID!!!
!
HEY... ISN'T THAT..?
IT'S MURDERFACE MIKHAIL?!!
ABBY!
DO THE KIDS CALL HIM THAT?
DO THEY.
ANY LUCK, THAT PSYCHO WILL KEEP WALK-
HEY, MIKHAIL!
WAIT UP! I NEED TO TELL YOU ABOUT MY DAD'S CRAZY TREE ARM!
EEP.

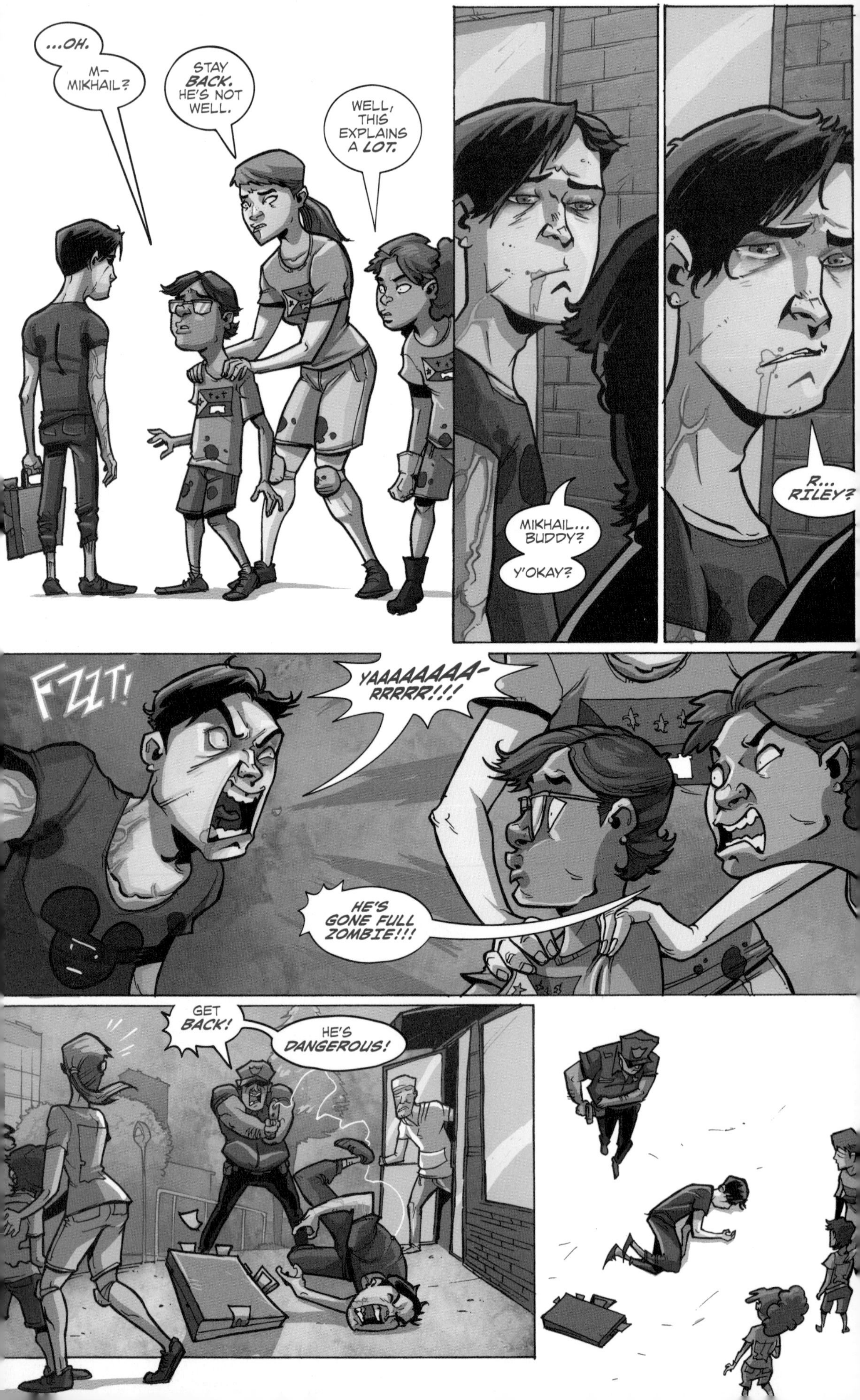
...OH.
M– MIKHAIL?
STAY BACK. HE'S NOT WELL.
WELL, THIS EXPLAINS A LOT.
MIKHAIL... BUDDY?
Y'OKAY?
R... RILEY?
FZZT!
YAAAAAAAA-RRRRR!!!
HE'S GONE FULL ZOMBIE!!!
GET BACK!
HE'S DANGEROUS!

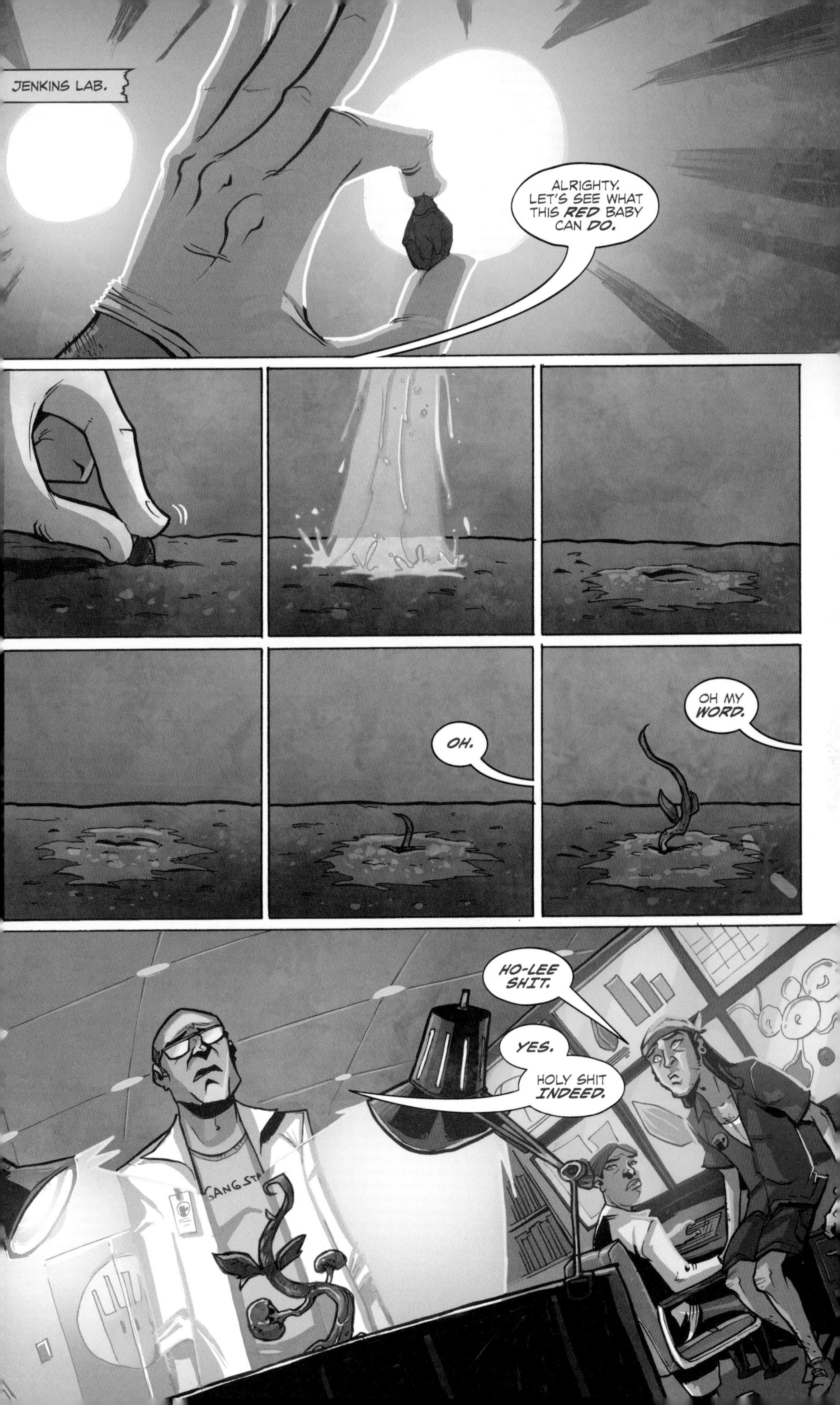

JENKINS LAB.
ALRIGHTY. LET'S SEE WHAT THIS RED BABY CAN DO.
OH.
OH MY WORD.
HO-LEE SHIT.
YES.
HOLY SHIT INDEED.

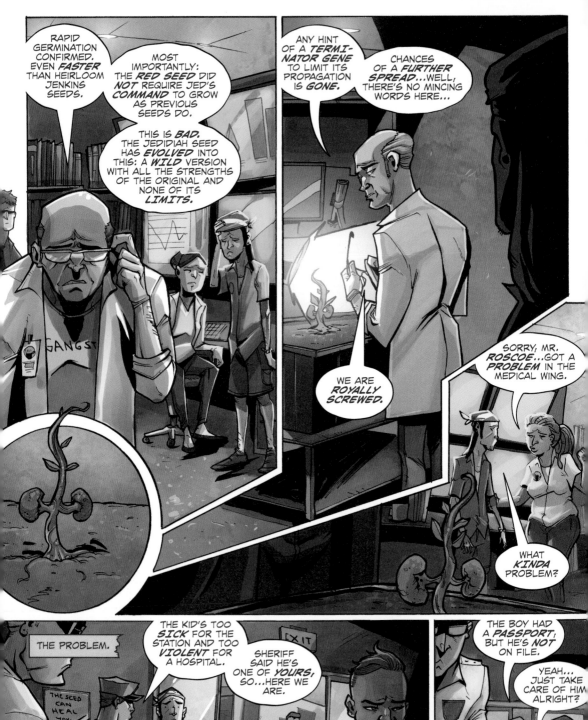

RAPID GERMINATION CONFIRMED. EVEN *FASTER* THAN HEIRLOOM JENKINS SEEDS.

MOST IMPORTANTLY: THE *RED SEED* DID *NOT* REQUIRE JED'S *COMMAND* TO GROW AS PREVIOUS SEEDS DO.

THIS IS *BAD.* THE JEDIDIAH SEED HAS *EVOLVED* INTO THIS: A *WILD* VERSION WITH ALL THE STRENGTHS OF THE ORIGINAL AND NONE OF ITS *LIMITS.*

ANY HINT OF A *TERMI-NATOR GENE* TO LIMIT ITS PROPAGATION IS *GONE.*

CHANCES OF A *FURTHER SPREAD*...WELL, THERE'S NO MINCING WORDS HERE...

WE ARE *ROYALLY SCREWED.*

SORRY, MR. *ROSCOE*...GOT A *PROBLEM* IN THE MEDICAL WING.

WHAT *KINDA* PROBLEM?

GANGST

THE PROBLEM.

THE KID'S TOO *SICK* FOR THE STATION AND TOO *VIOLENT* FOR A HOSPITAL.

SHERIFF SAID HE'S ONE OF *YOURS,* SO...HERE WE ARE.

THE SEED CAN HEAL YOU.

EXIT

WELL, *SHIT.*

THE BOY HAD A *PASSPORT,* BUT HE'S *NOT* ON FILE.

YEAH... JUST TAKE CARE OF HIM ALRIGHT?

PARAM

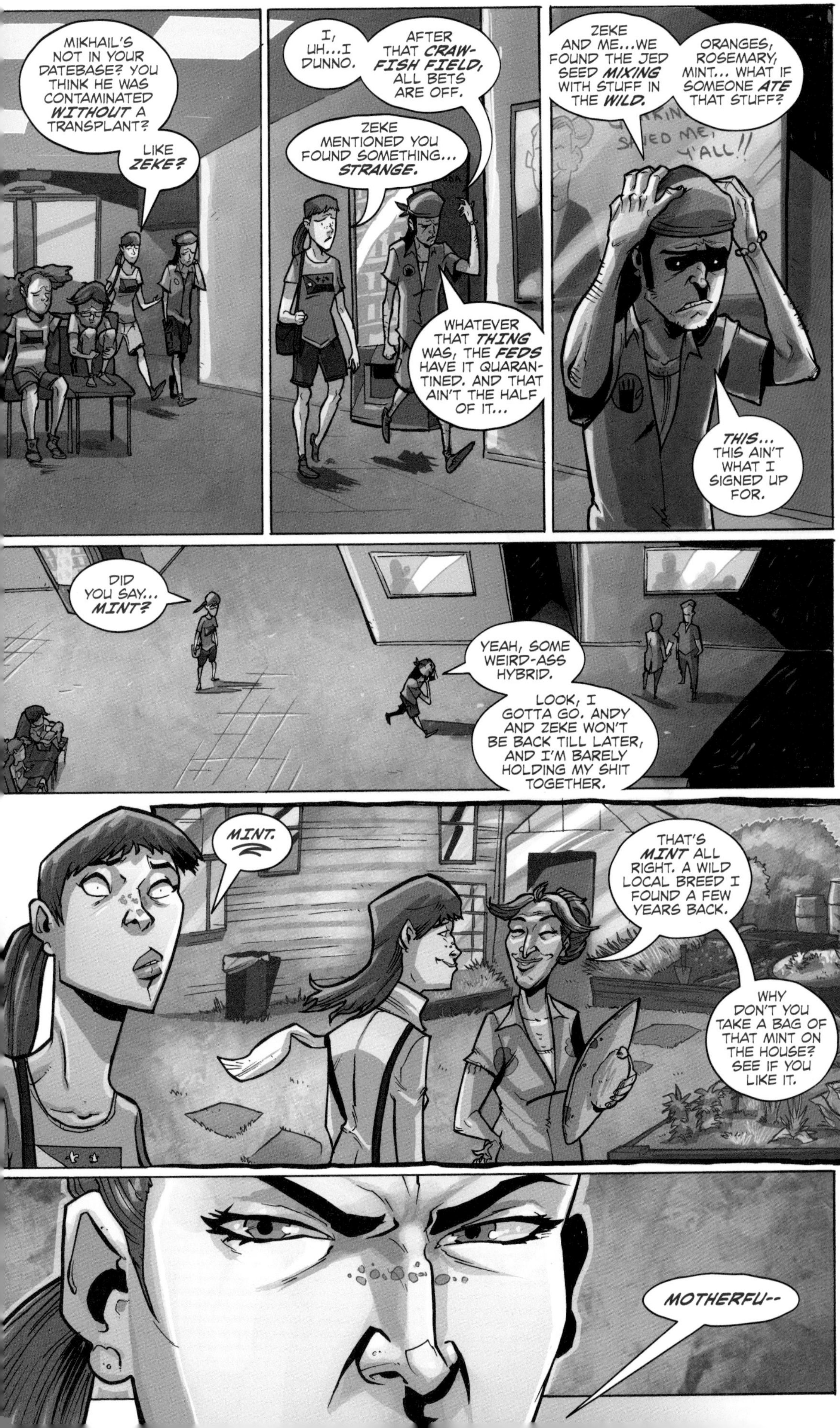

MIKHAIL'S NOT IN YOUR DATEBASE? YOU THINK HE WAS CONTAMINATED *WITHOUT* A TRANSPLANT?
LIKE *ZEKE?*
I, UH...I DUNNO.
AFTER THAT *CRAWFISH FIELD,* ALL BETS ARE OFF.
ZEKE MENTIONED YOU FOUND SOMETHING... *STRANGE.*
WHATEVER THAT *THING* WAS, THE *FEDS* HAVE IT QUARANTINED. AND THAT AIN'T THE HALF OF IT...
ZEKE AND ME...WE FOUND THE JED SEED *MIXING* WITH STUFF IN THE *WILD.*
ORANGES, ROSEMARY, MINT... WHAT IF SOMEONE *ATE* THAT STUFF?
THIS... THIS AIN'T WHAT I SIGNED UP FOR.
DID YOU SAY... *MINT?*
YEAH, SOME WEIRD-ASS HYBRID.
LOOK, I GOTTA GO. ANDY AND ZEKE WON'T BE BACK TILL LATER, AND I'M BARELY HOLDING MY SHIT TOGETHER.
MINT.
THAT'S *MINT* ALL RIGHT. A WILD LOCAL BREED I FOUND A FEW YEARS BACK.
WHY DON'T YOU TAKE A BAG OF THAT MINT ON THE HOUSE? SEE IF YOU LIKE IT.
MOTHERFU--

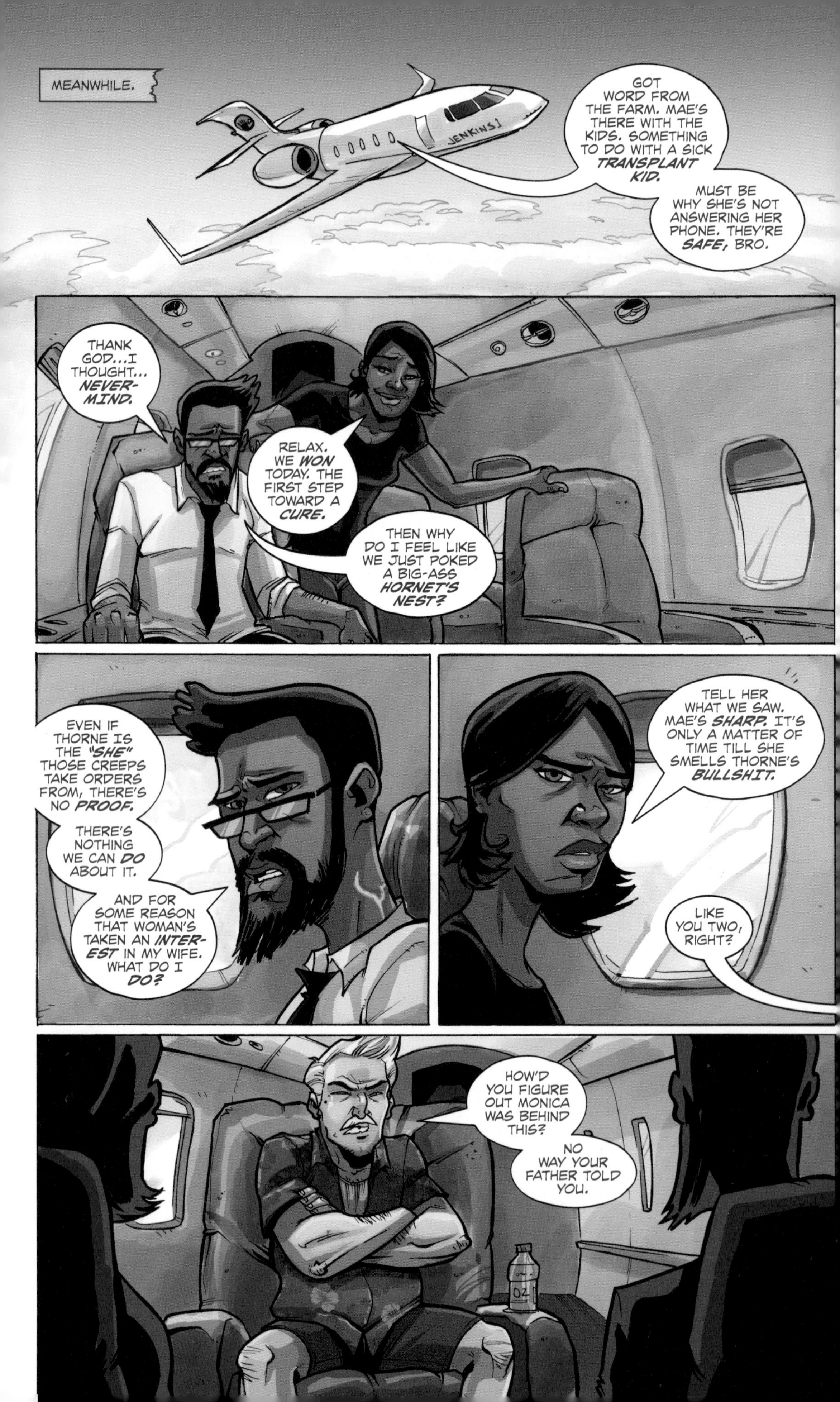
MEANWHILE.
JENKINS 1
GOT WORD FROM THE FARM. MAE'S THERE WITH THE KIDS. SOMETHING TO DO WITH A SICK ***TRANSPLANT KID.***
MUST BE WHY SHE'S NOT ANSWERING HER PHONE. THEY'RE ***SAFE,*** BRO.
THANK GOD...I THOUGHT... ***NEVER-MIND.***
RELAX. WE ***WON*** TODAY. THE FIRST STEP TOWARD A ***CURE.***
THEN WHY DO I FEEL LIKE WE JUST POKED A BIG-ASS ***HORNET'S NEST?***
EVEN IF THORNE IS THE ***"SHE"*** THOSE CREEPS TAKE ORDERS FROM, THERE'S NO ***PROOF.***
THERE'S NOTHING WE CAN ***DO*** ABOUT IT.
AND FOR SOME REASON THAT WOMAN'S TAKEN AN ***INTER-EST*** IN MY WIFE. WHAT DO I ***DO?***
TELL HER WHAT WE SAW. MAE'S ***SHARP.*** IT'S ONLY A MATTER OF TIME TILL SHE SMELLS THORNE'S ***BULLSHIT.***
LIKE YOU TWO, RIGHT?
HOW'D YOU FIGURE OUT MONICA WAS BEHIND THIS?
NO WAY YOUR FATHER TOLD YOU.

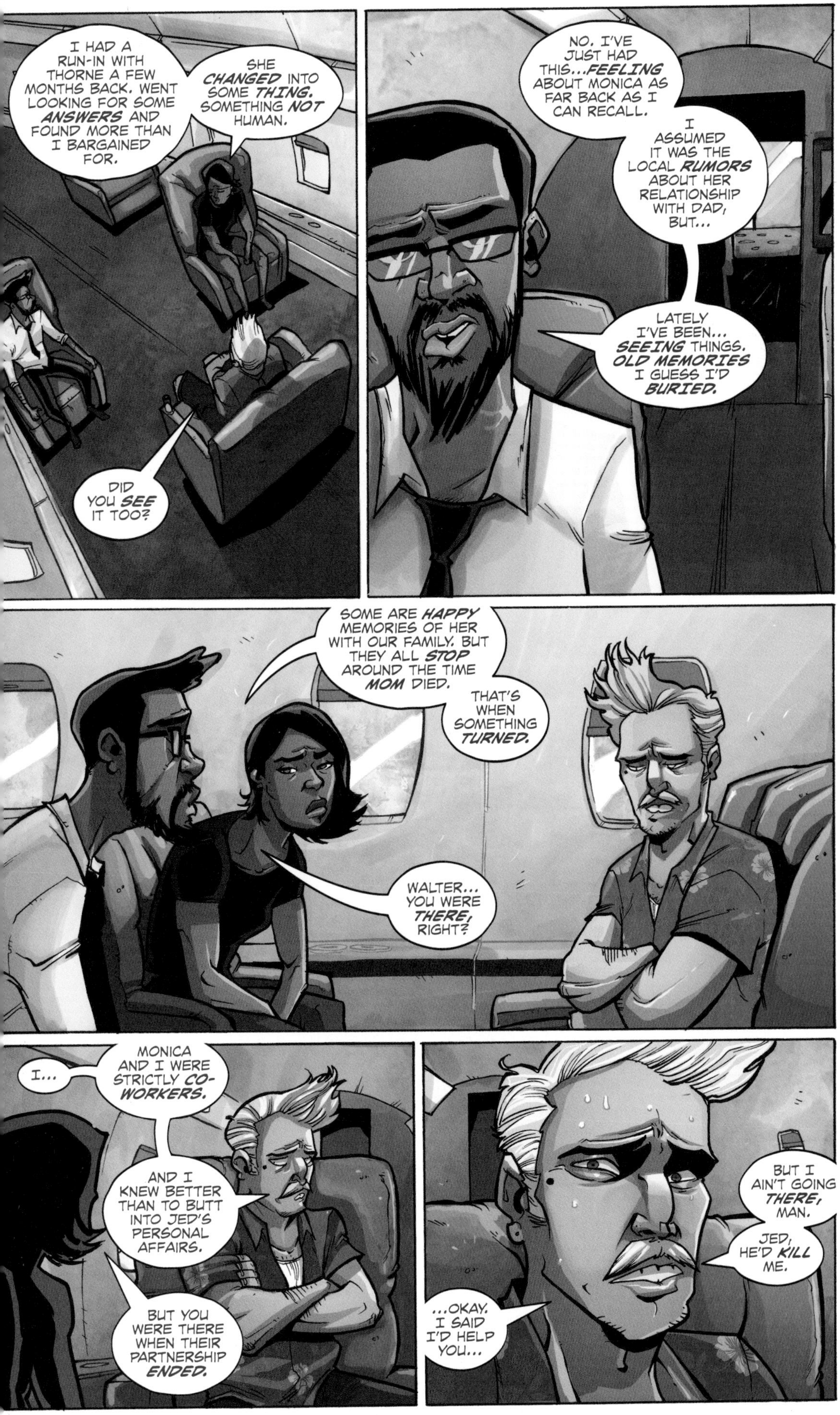
I HAD A RUN-IN WITH THORNE A FEW MONTHS BACK. WENT LOOKING FOR SOME ANSWERS AND FOUND MORE THAN I BARGAINED FOR.
SHE CHANGED INTO SOME THING. SOMETHING NOT HUMAN.
DID YOU SEE IT TOO?
NO. I'VE JUST HAD THIS...FEELING ABOUT MONICA AS FAR BACK AS I CAN RECALL.
I ASSUMED IT WAS THE LOCAL RUMORS ABOUT HER RELATIONSHIP WITH DAD, BUT...
LATELY I'VE BEEN... SEEING THINGS. OLD MEMORIES I GUESS I'D BURIED.
SOME ARE HAPPY MEMORIES OF HER WITH OUR FAMILY. BUT THEY ALL STOP AROUND THE TIME MOM DIED.
THAT'S WHEN SOMETHING TURNED.
WALTER... YOU WERE THERE, RIGHT?
I...
MONICA AND I WERE STRICTLY CO-WORKERS.
AND I KNEW BETTER THAN TO BUTT INTO JED'S PERSONAL AFFAIRS.
BUT YOU WERE THERE WHEN THEIR PARTNERSHIP ENDED.
...OKAY. I SAID I'D HELP YOU...
BUT I AIN'T GOING THERE, MAN.
JED, HE'D KILL ME.

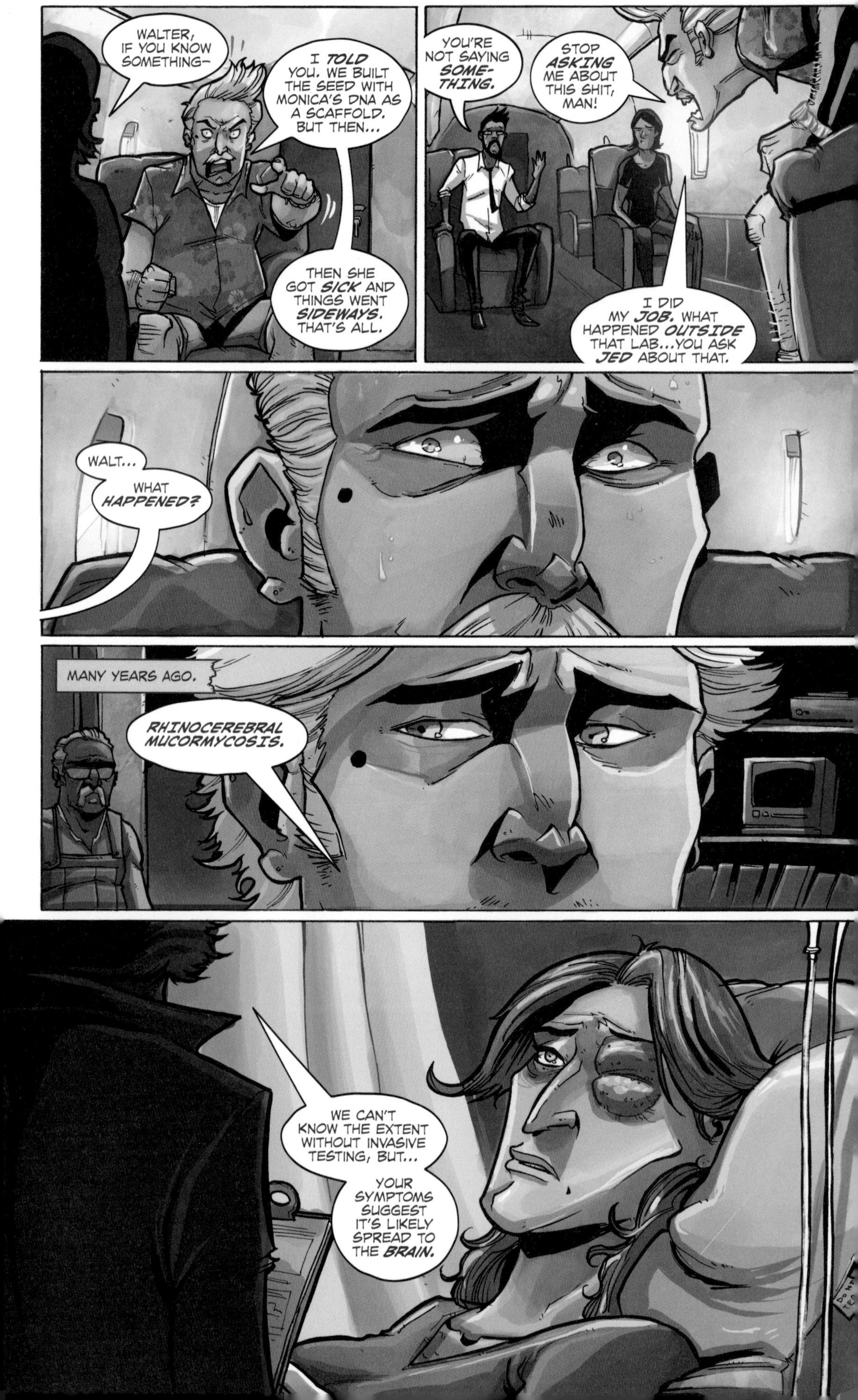
WALTER, IF YOU KNOW SOMETHING–
I TOLD YOU. WE BUILT THE SEED WITH MONICA'S DNA AS A SCAFFOLD. BUT THEN...
THEN SHE GOT SICK AND THINGS WENT SIDEWAYS. THAT'S ALL.
YOU'RE NOT SAYING SOMETHING.
STOP ASKING ME ABOUT THIS SHIT, MAN!
I DID MY JOB. WHAT HAPPENED OUTSIDE THAT LAB...YOU ASK JED ABOUT THAT.
WALT...
WHAT HAPPENED?
MANY YEARS AGO.
RHINOCEREBRAL MUCORMYCOSIS.
WE CAN'T KNOW THE EXTENT WITHOUT INVASIVE TESTING, BUT...
YOUR SYMPTOMS SUGGEST IT'S LIKELY SPREAD TO THE BRAIN.

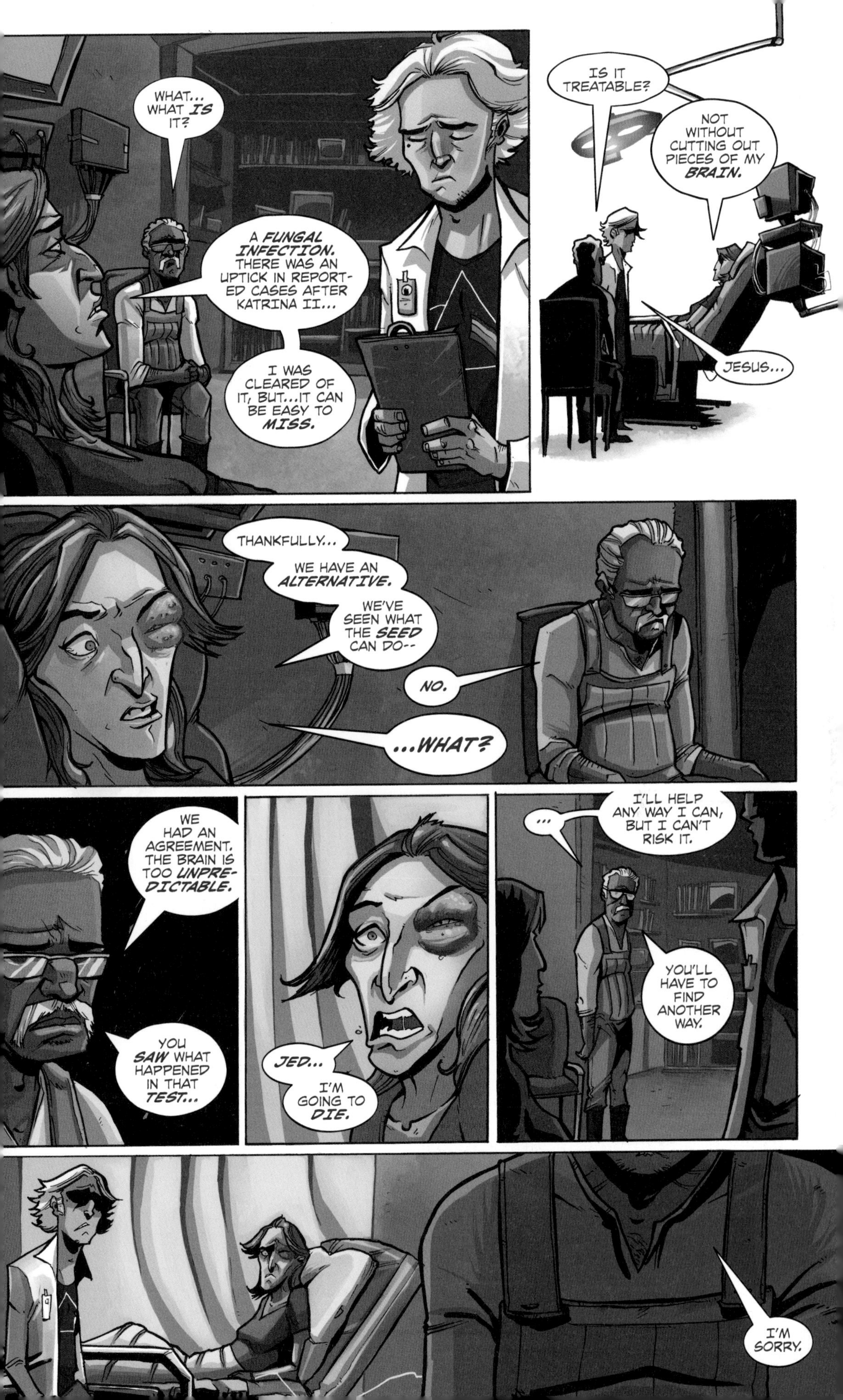
WHAT... WHAT IS IT?
A FUNGAL INFECTION. THERE WAS AN UPTICK IN REPORTED CASES AFTER KATRINA II...
I WAS CLEARED OF IT, BUT...IT CAN BE EASY TO MISS.
IS IT TREATABLE?
NOT WITHOUT CUTTING OUT PIECES OF MY BRAIN.
JESUS...
THANKFULLY...
WE HAVE AN ALTERNATIVE.
WE'VE SEEN WHAT THE SEED CAN DO--
NO.
...WHAT?
WE HAD AN AGREEMENT. THE BRAIN IS TOO UNPREDICTABLE.
YOU SAW WHAT HAPPENED IN THAT TEST...
JED...
I'M GOING TO DIE.
...
I'LL HELP ANY WAY I CAN, BUT I CAN'T RISK IT.
YOU'LL HAVE TO FIND ANOTHER WAY.
I'M SORRY.

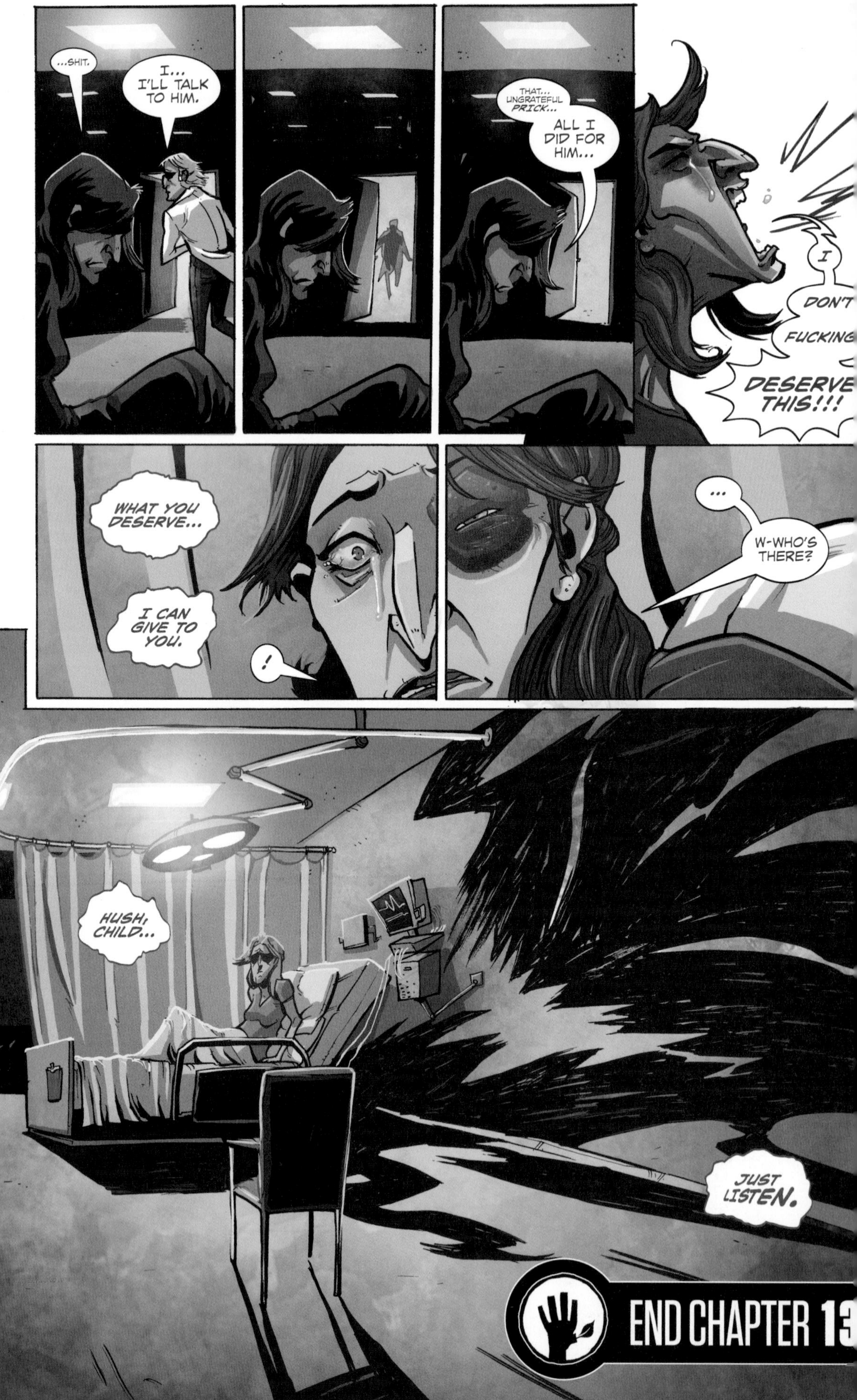
...SHIT.
I... I'LL TALK TO HIM.
THAT... UNGRATEFUL PRICK...
ALL I DID FOR HIM...
I DON'T FUCKING DESERVE THIS!!!
WHAT YOU DESERVE...
I CAN GIVE TO YOU.
!
...
W-WHO'S THERE?
HUSH, CHILD...
JUST LISTEN.
END CHAPTER 13

CHAPTER 14

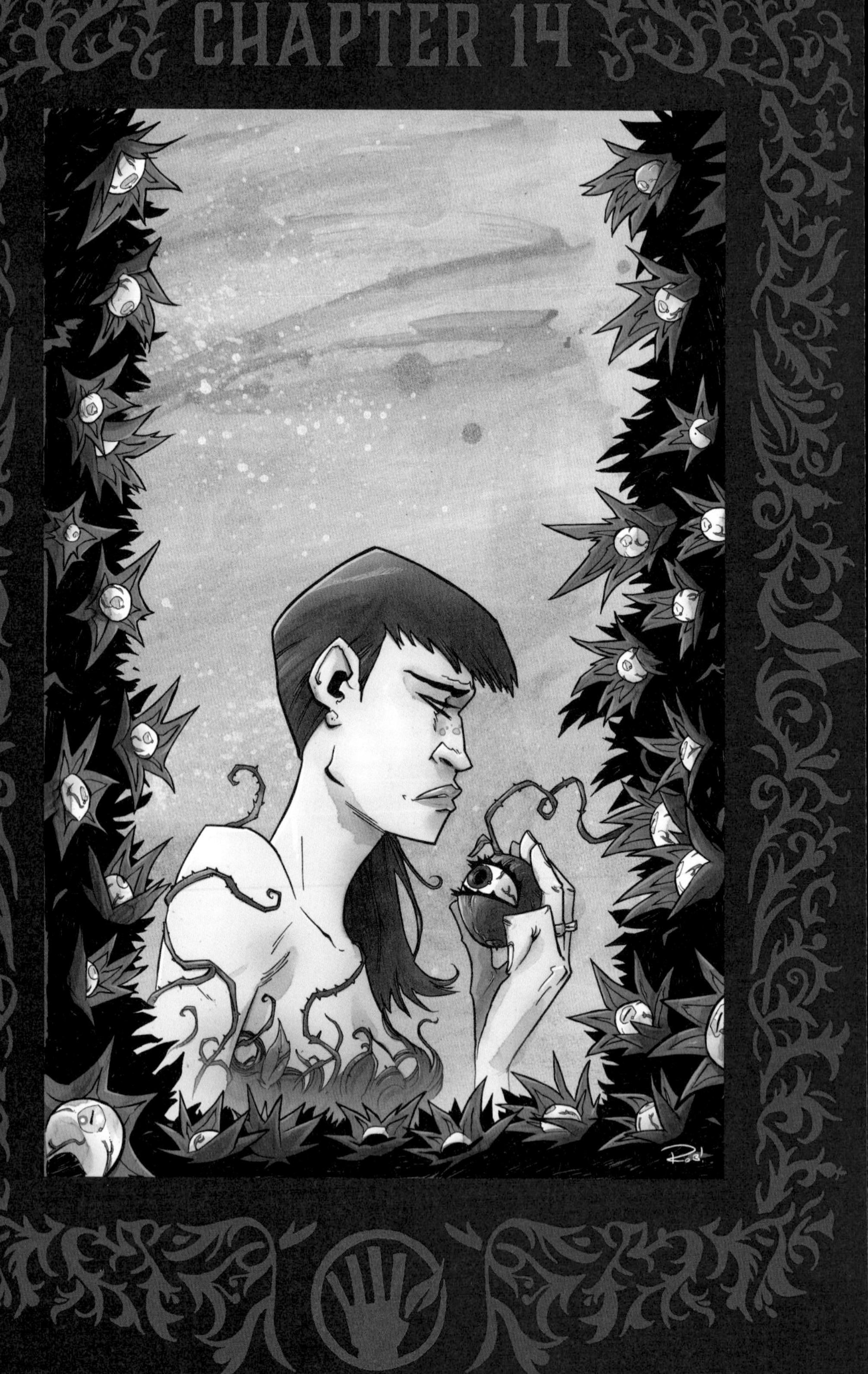

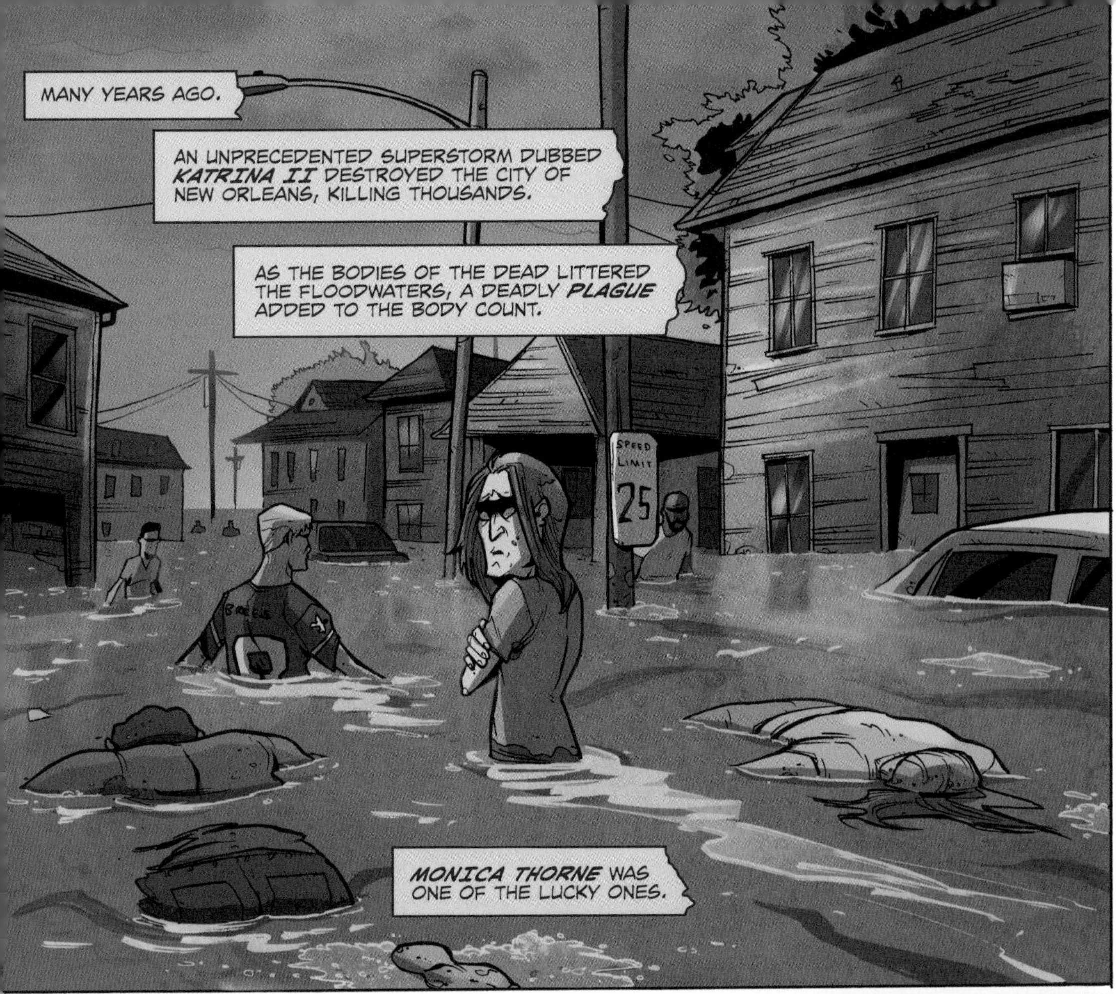
MANY YEARS AGO.
AN UNPRECEDENTED SUPERSTORM DUBBED *KATRINA II* DESTROYED THE CITY OF NEW ORLEANS, KILLING THOUSANDS.
AS THE BODIES OF THE DEAD LITTERED THE FLOODWATERS, A DEADLY *PLAGUE* ADDED TO THE BODY COUNT.
SPEED LIMIT 25
MONICA THORNE WAS ONE OF THE LUCKY ONES.

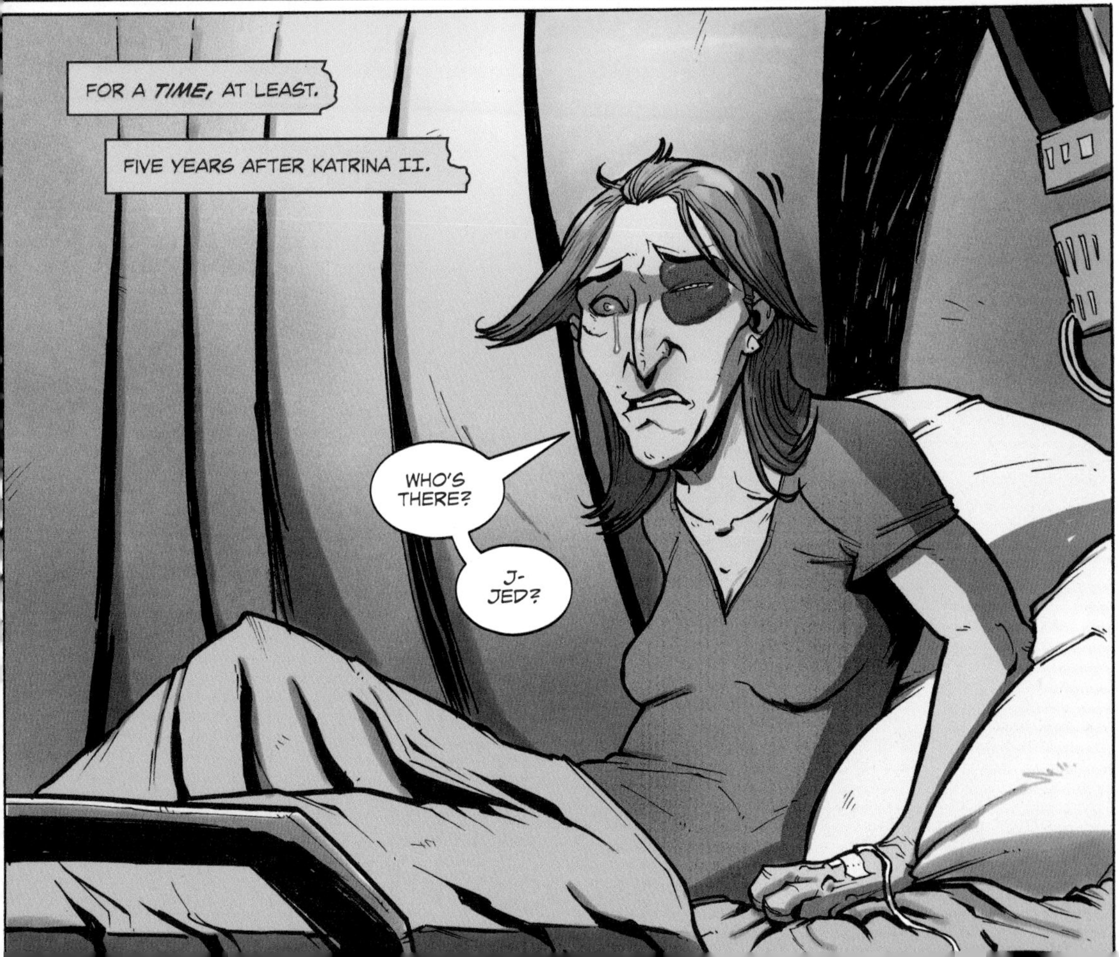
FOR A *TIME,* AT LEAST.
FIVE YEARS AFTER KATRINA II.
WHO'S THERE?
J-JED?

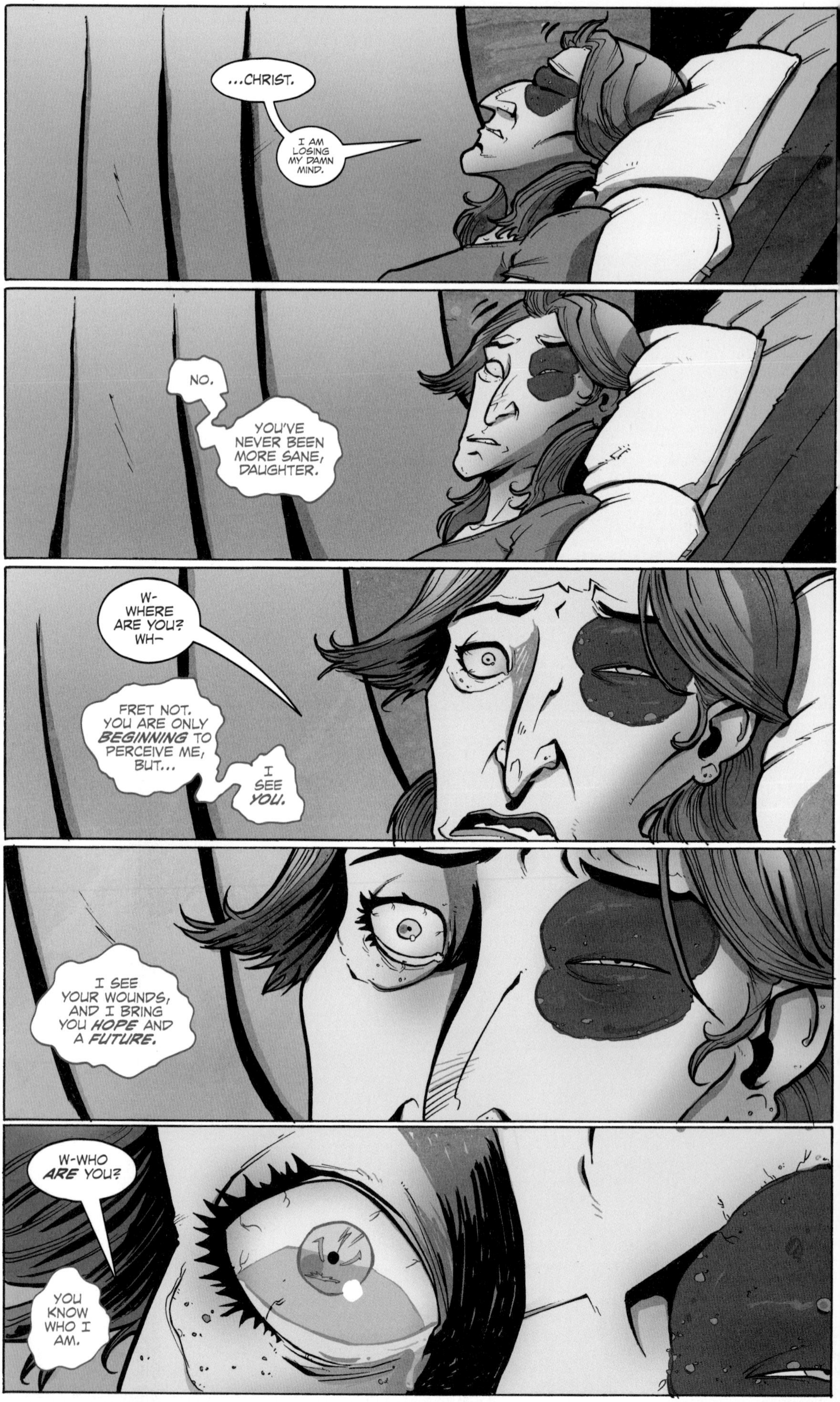
...CHRIST.
I AM LOSING MY DAMN MIND.
NO.
YOU'VE NEVER BEEN MORE SANE, DAUGHTER.
W-WHERE ARE YOU? WH–
FRET NOT. YOU ARE ONLY *BEGINNING* TO PERCEIVE ME, BUT...
I SEE *YOU.*
I SEE YOUR WOUNDS, AND I BRING YOU *HOPE* AND A *FUTURE.*
W-WHO *ARE* YOU?
YOU KNOW WHO I AM.

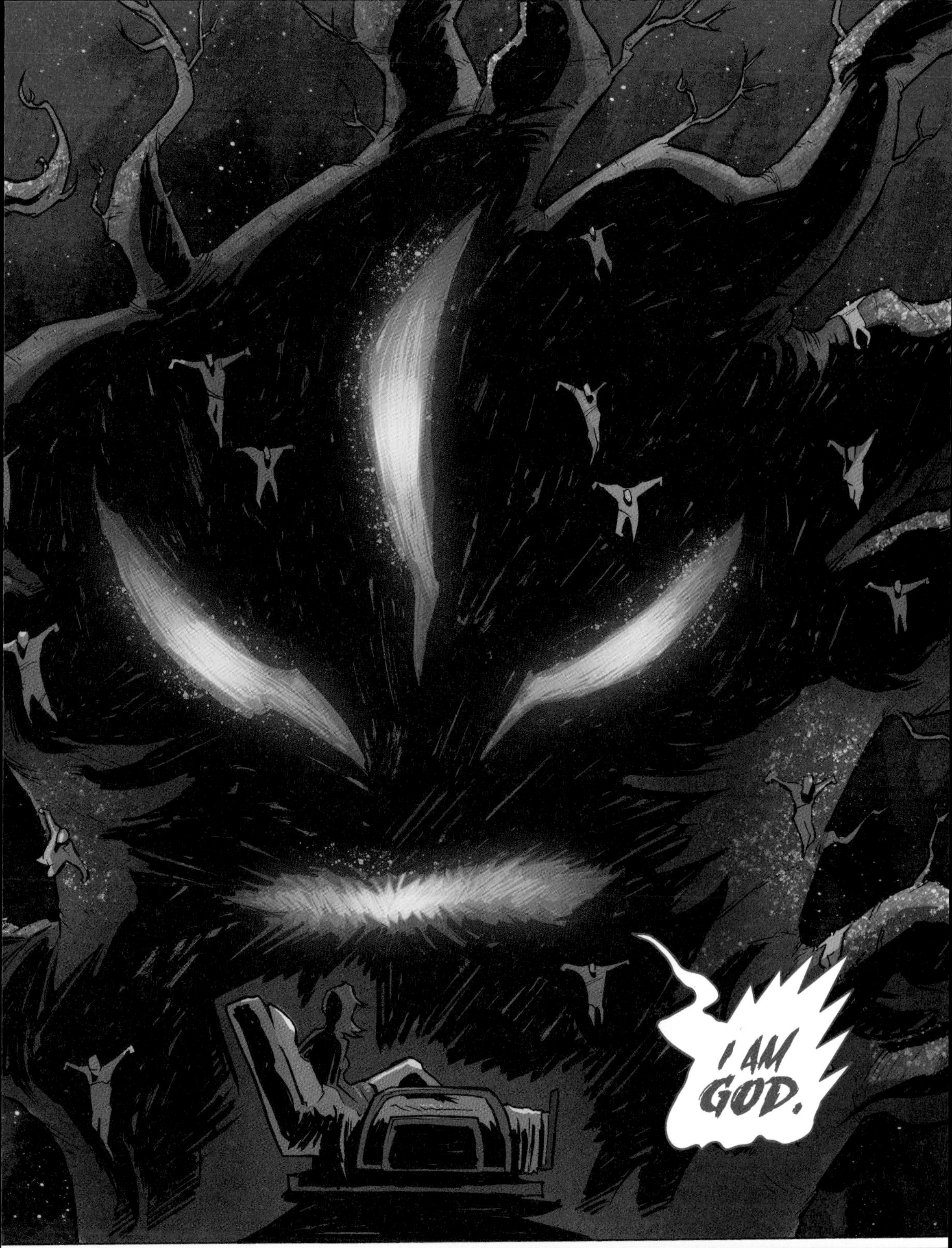
I AM GOD.

CHAPTER 14: **THE VOICE.**

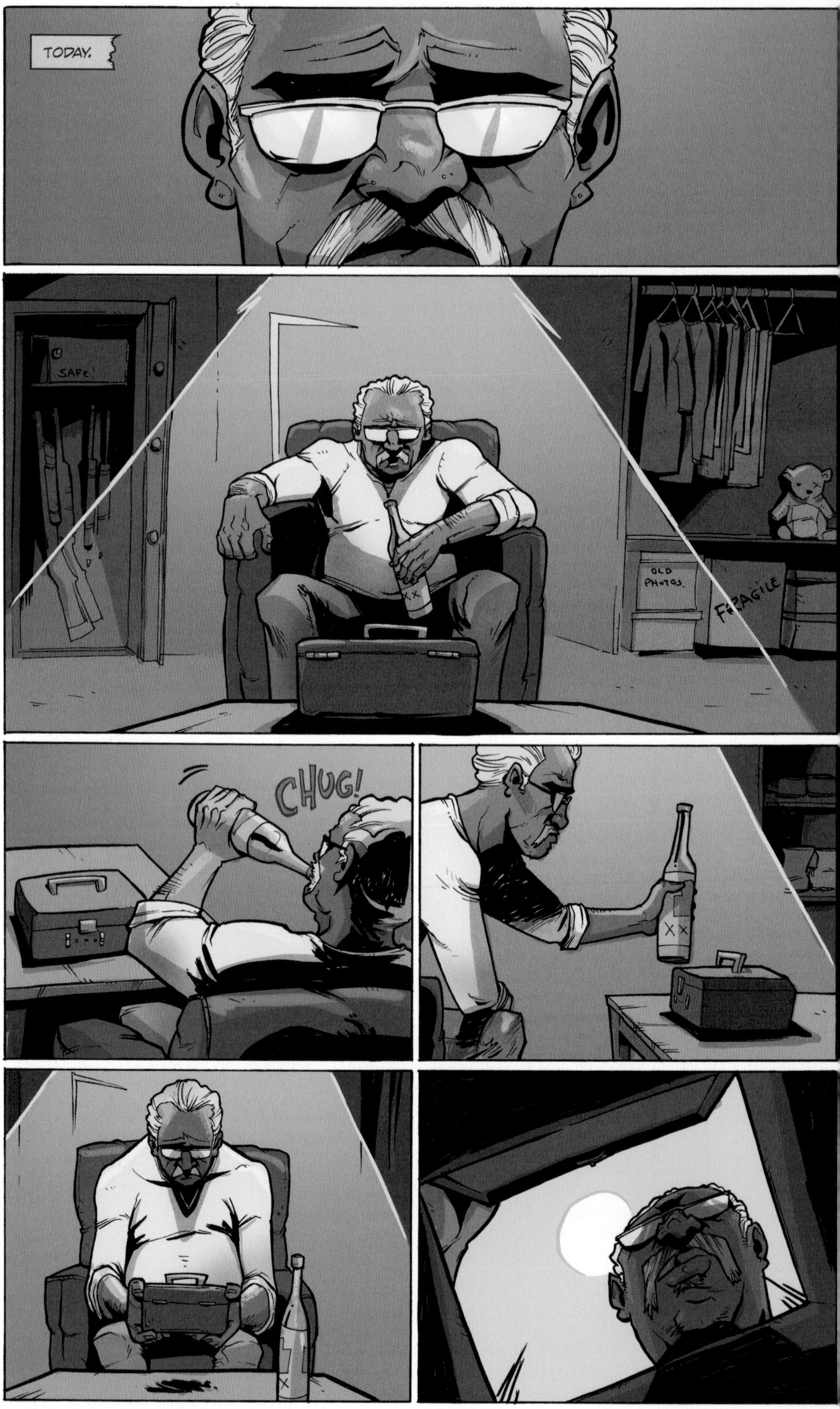
TODAY.
SAFE!
OLD PHOTOS.
FRAGILE
CHUG!

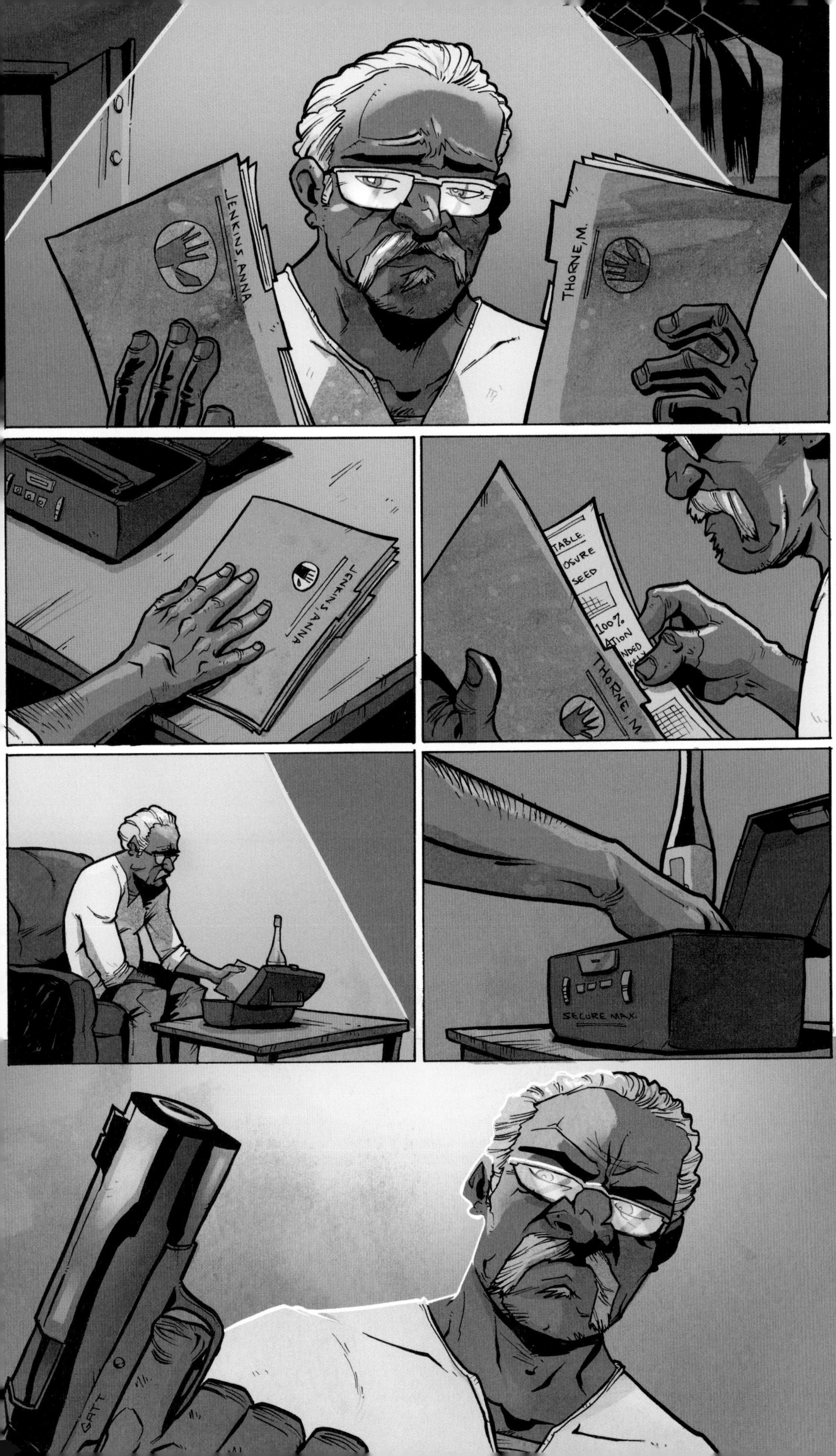
JENKINS, ANNA
THORNE, M.
JENKINS, ANNA
TABLE.
OSURE
SEED
100%
ATION
NDED
THORNE, M.
SECURE MAX.
GATT

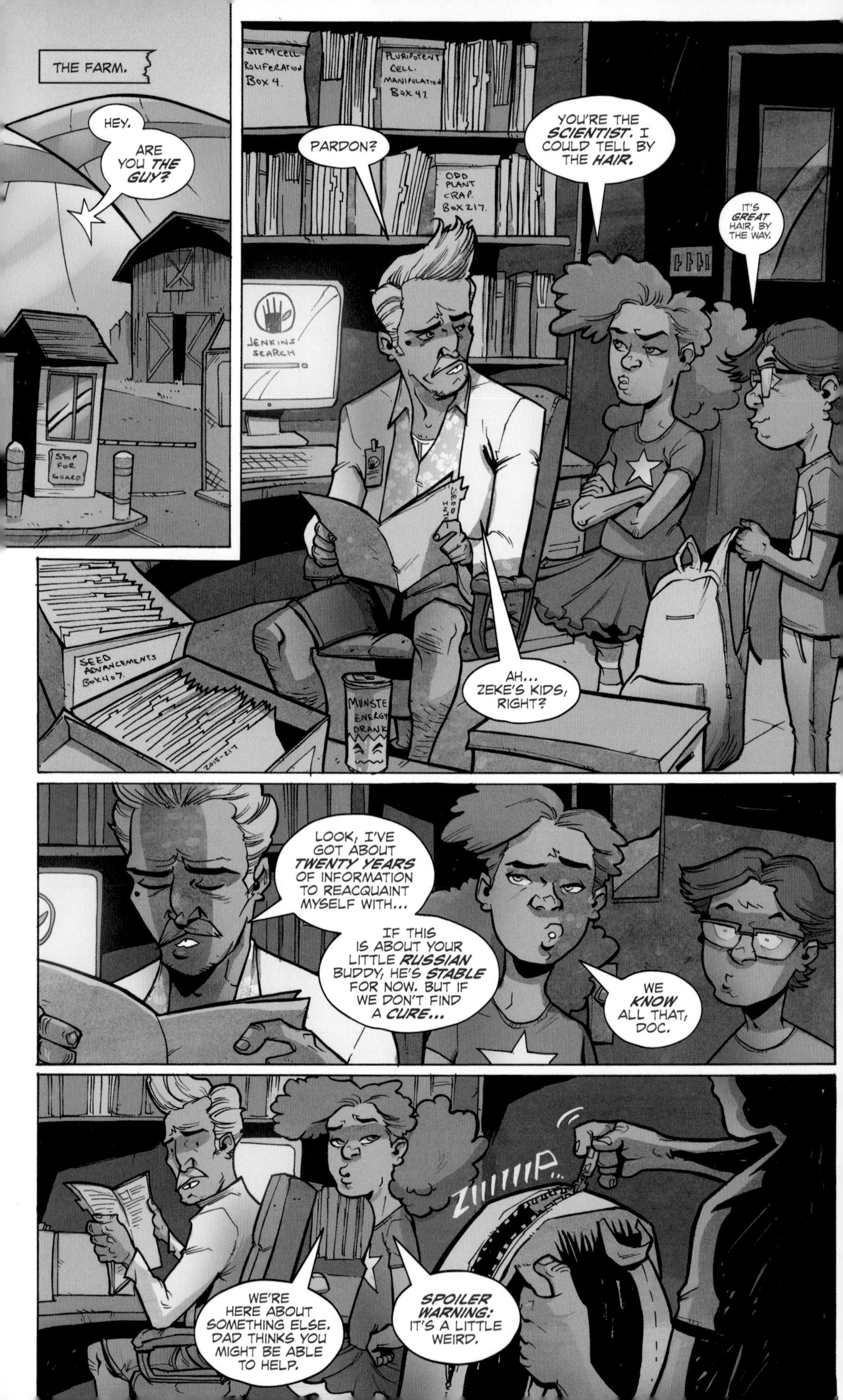

THE FARM.
HEY.
ARE YOU THE GUY?
STOP FOR GUARD!
STEM CELL PROLIFERATION BOX 4.
PLURIPOTENT CELL MANIPULATION BOX 41.
PARDON?
ODD PLANT CRAP. BOX 217.
YOU'RE THE SCIENTIST. I COULD TELL BY THE HAIR.
IT'S GREAT HAIR, BY THE WAY.
JENKINS SEARCH
SEED INFO
SEED ADVANCEMENTS BOX 407.
2015-217
MUNSTER ENERGY DRANK
AH... ZEKE'S KIDS, RIGHT?
LOOK, I'VE GOT ABOUT TWENTY YEARS OF INFORMATION TO REACQUAINT MYSELF WITH...
IF THIS IS ABOUT YOUR LITTLE RUSSIAN BUDDY, HE'S STABLE FOR NOW. BUT IF WE DON'T FIND A CURE...
WE KNOW ALL THAT, DOC.
ZIIIIIP...
WE'RE HERE ABOUT SOMETHING ELSE. DAD THINKS YOU MIGHT BE ABLE TO HELP.
SPOILER WARNING: IT'S A LITTLE WEIRD.

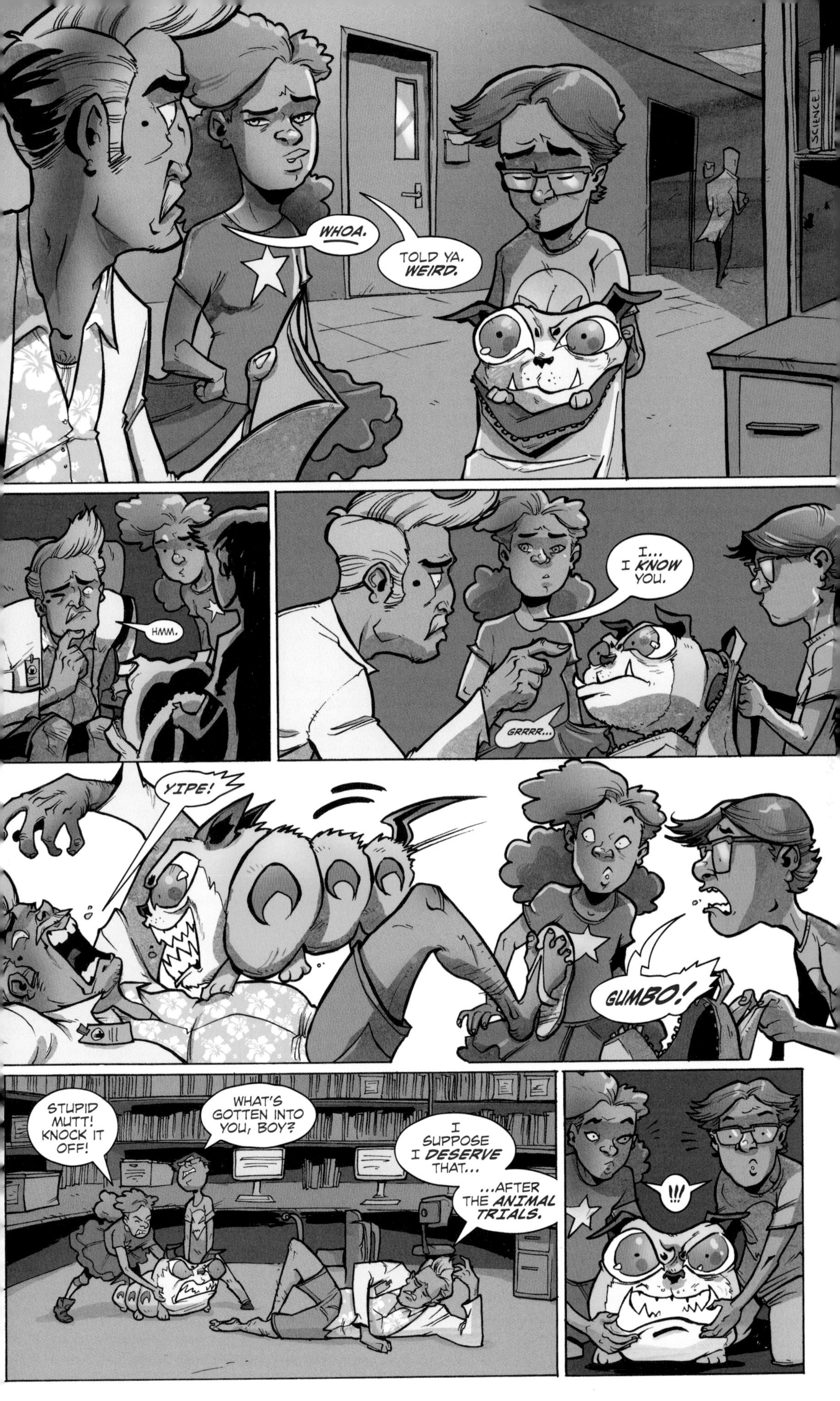

SCIENCE!
WHOA.
TOLD YA. WEIRD.
HMM.
I... I KNOW YOU.
GRRRR...
YIPE!
GUMBO!
STUPID MUTT! KNOCK IT OFF!
WHAT'S GOTTEN INTO YOU, BOY?
I SUPPOSE I DESERVE THAT...
...AFTER THE ANIMAL TRIALS.
!!!

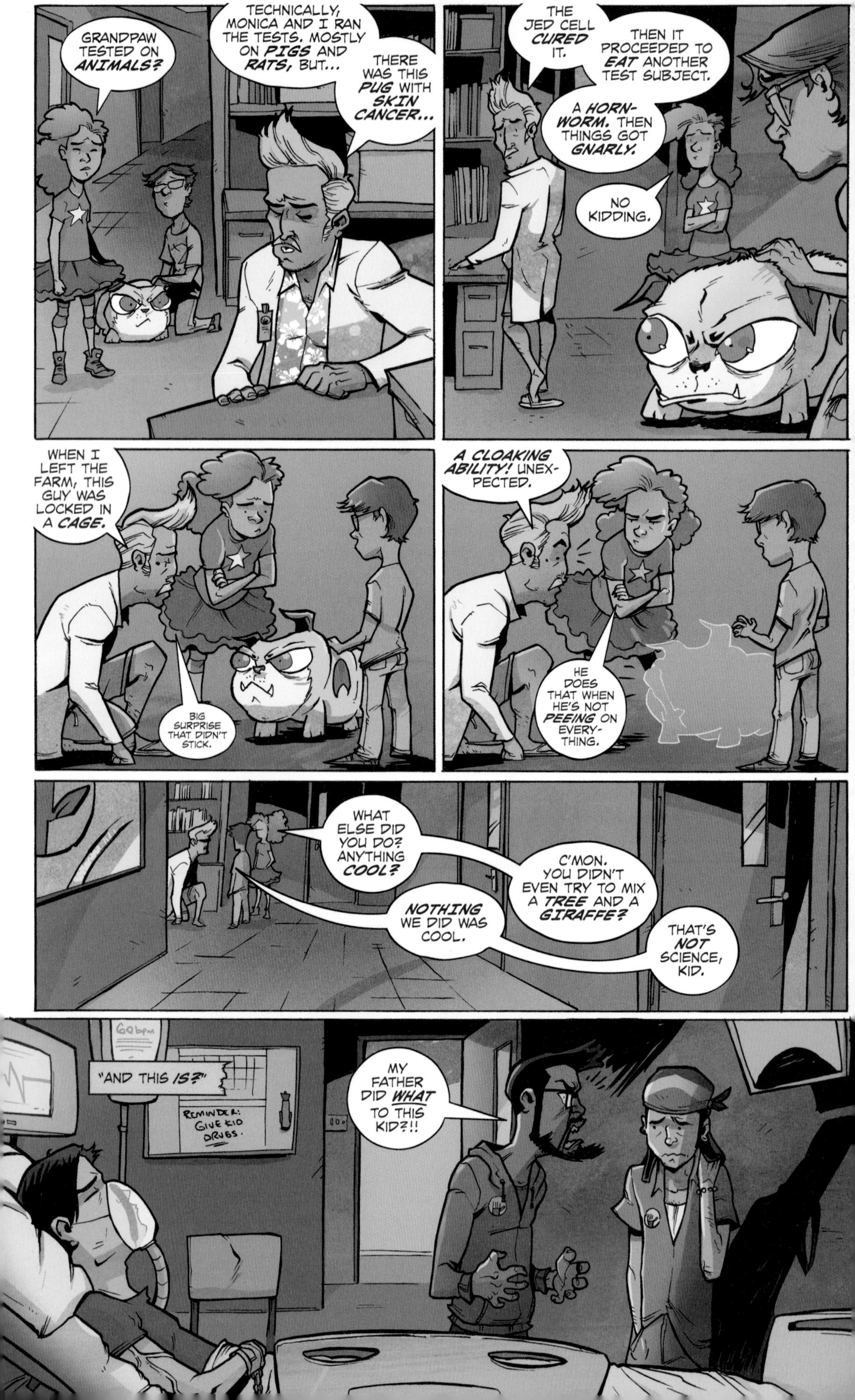
GRANDPAW TESTED ON ANIMALS?
TECHNICALLY, MONICA AND I RAN THE TESTS. MOSTLY ON PIGS AND RATS, BUT...
THERE WAS THIS PUG WITH SKIN CANCER...
THE JED CELL CURED IT.
THEN IT PROCEEDED TO EAT ANOTHER TEST SUBJECT.
A HORN-WORM. THEN THINGS GOT GNARLY.
NO KIDDING.
WHEN I LEFT THE FARM, THIS GUY WAS LOCKED IN A CAGE.
BIG SURPRISE THAT DIDN'T STICK.
A CLOAKING ABILITY! UNEX-PECTED.
HE DOES THAT WHEN HE'S NOT PEEING ON EVERY-THING.
WHAT ELSE DID YOU DO? ANYTHING COOL?
NOTHING WE DID WAS COOL.
C'MON. YOU DIDN'T EVEN TRY TO MIX A TREE AND A GIRAFFE?
THAT'S NOT SCIENCE, KID.
60bpm
"AND THIS IS?"
REMINDER: GIVE KID DRUGS.
MY FATHER DID WHAT TO THIS KID?!!

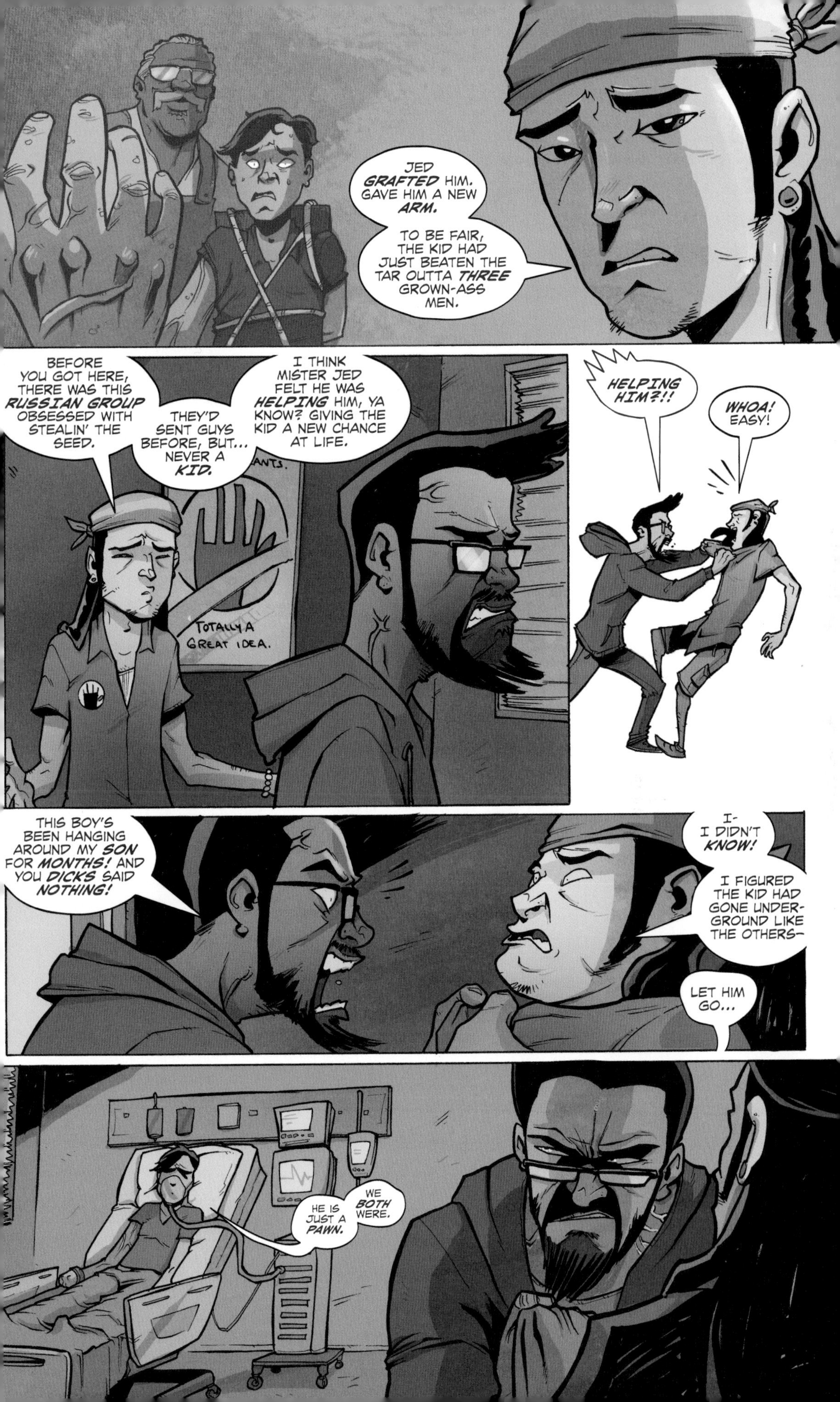

JED *GRAFTED* HIM. GAVE HIM A NEW *ARM.*
TO BE FAIR, THE KID HAD JUST BEATEN THE TAR OUTTA *THREE* GROWN-ASS MEN.
BEFORE YOU GOT HERE, THERE WAS THIS *RUSSIAN GROUP* OBSESSED WITH STEALIN' THE SEED.
THEY'D SENT GUYS BEFORE, BUT... NEVER A *KID.*
I THINK MISTER JED FELT HE WAS *HELPING* HIM, YA KNOW? GIVING THE KID A NEW CHANCE AT LIFE.
TOTALLY A GREAT IDEA.
HELPING HIM?!!
WHOA! EASY!
THIS BOY'S BEEN HANGING AROUND MY *SON* FOR *MONTHS!* AND YOU *DICKS* SAID *NOTHING!*
I- I DIDN'T *KNOW!*
I FIGURED THE KID HAD GONE UNDER-GROUND LIKE THE OTHERS—
LET HIM GO...
HE IS JUST A *PAWN.*
WE *BOTH* WERE.

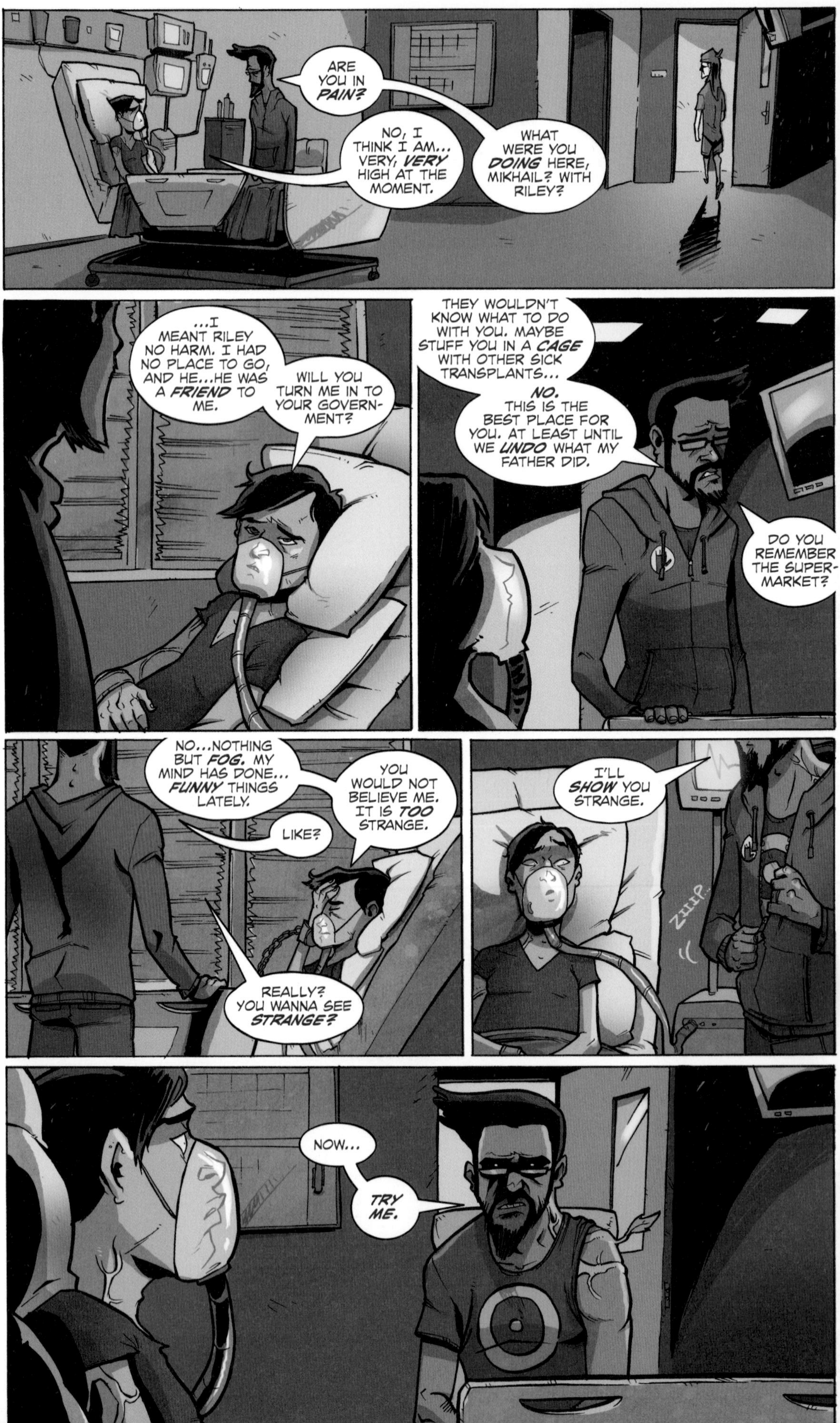
ARE YOU IN PAIN?
NO, I THINK I AM... VERY, VERY HIGH AT THE MOMENT.
WHAT WERE YOU DOING HERE, MIKHAIL? WITH RILEY?
...I MEANT RILEY NO HARM. I HAD NO PLACE TO GO, AND HE...HE WAS A FRIEND TO ME.
WILL YOU TURN ME IN TO YOUR GOVERNMENT?
THEY WOULDN'T KNOW WHAT TO DO WITH YOU. MAYBE STUFF YOU IN A CAGE WITH OTHER SICK TRANSPLANTS...
NO. THIS IS THE BEST PLACE FOR YOU. AT LEAST UNTIL WE UNDO WHAT MY FATHER DID.
DO YOU REMEMBER THE SUPER-MARKET?
NO...NOTHING BUT FOG. MY MIND HAS DONE... FUNNY THINGS LATELY.
LIKE?
YOU WOULD NOT BELIEVE ME. IT IS TOO STRANGE.
REALLY? YOU WANNA SEE STRANGE?
I'LL SHOW YOU STRANGE.
ZIIIP.
NOW...
TRY ME.

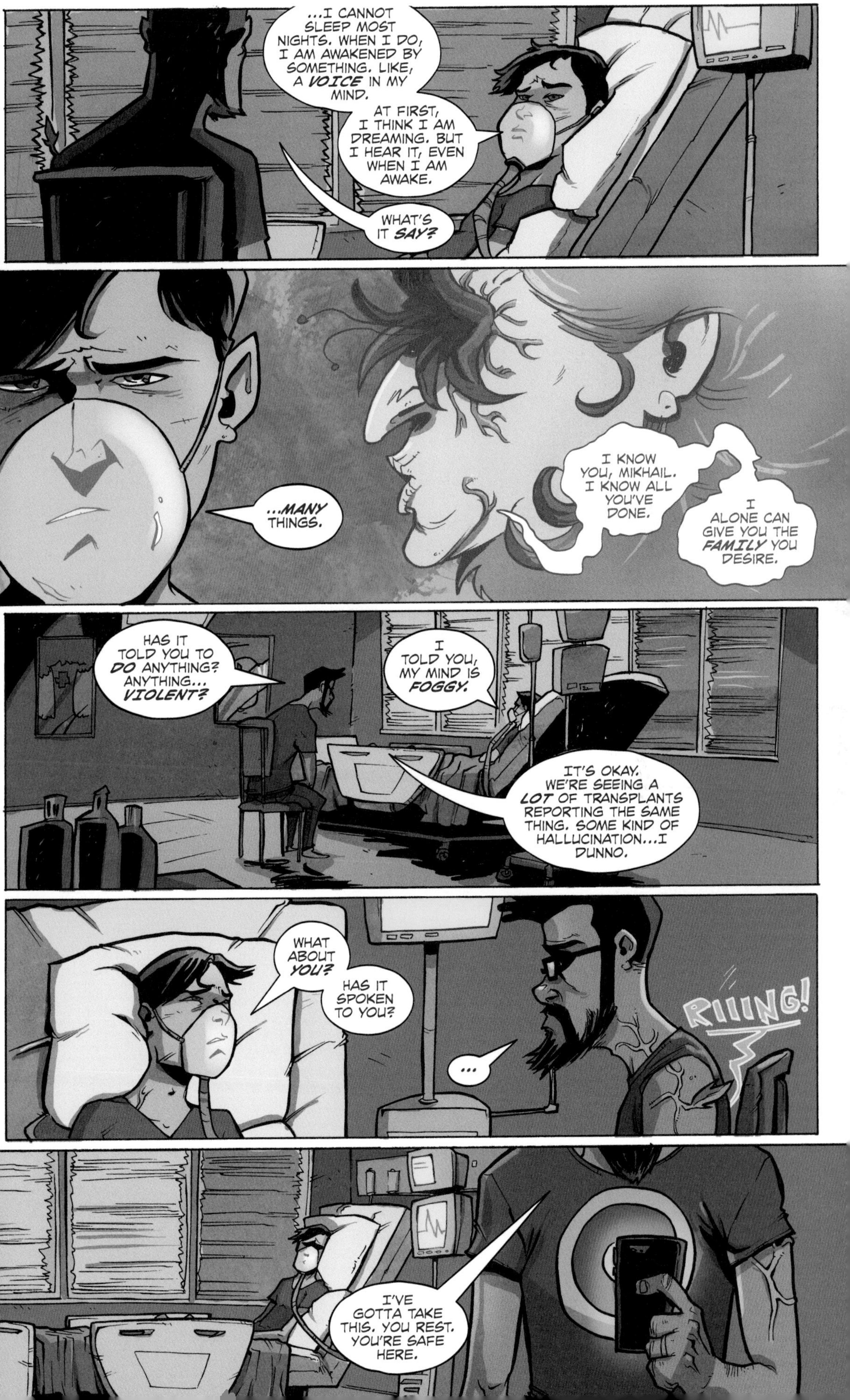

...I CANNOT SLEEP MOST NIGHTS. WHEN I DO, I AM AWAKENED BY SOMETHING. LIKE, A VOICE IN MY MIND.
AT FIRST, I THINK I AM DREAMING. BUT I HEAR IT, EVEN WHEN I AM AWAKE.
WHAT'S IT SAY?
...MANY THINGS.
I KNOW YOU, MIKHAIL. I KNOW ALL YOU'VE DONE.
I ALONE CAN GIVE YOU THE FAMILY YOU DESIRE.
HAS IT TOLD YOU TO DO ANYTHING? ANYTHING... VIOLENT?
I TOLD YOU, MY MIND IS FOGGY.
IT'S OKAY. WE'RE SEEING A LOT OF TRANSPLANTS REPORTING THE SAME THING. SOME KIND OF HALLUCINATION...I DUNNO.
WHAT ABOUT YOU?
HAS IT SPOKEN TO YOU?
...
RIIING!
I'VE GOTTA TAKE THIS. YOU REST. YOU'RE SAFE HERE.

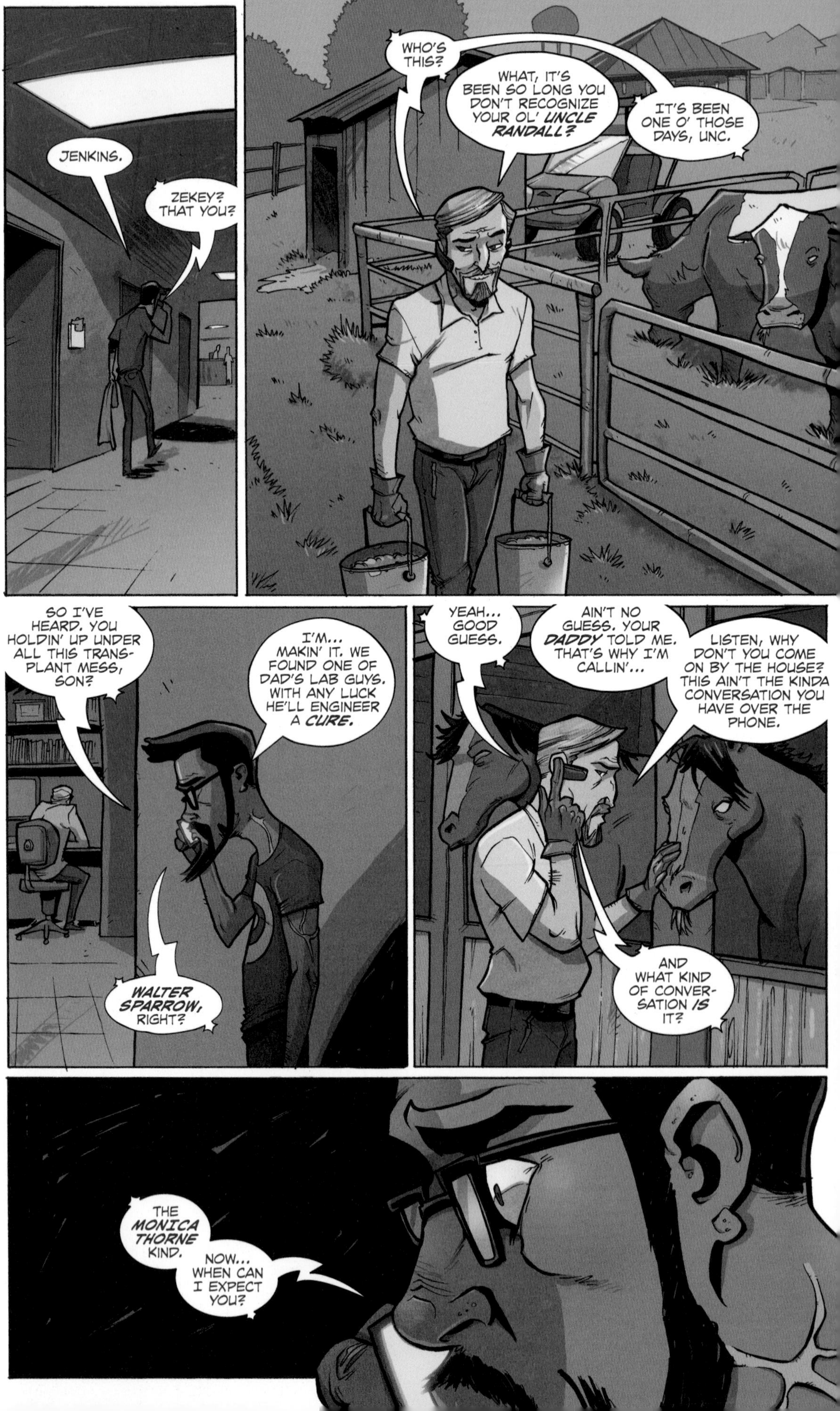
JENKINS.
ZEKEY? THAT YOU?
WHO'S THIS?
WHAT, IT'S BEEN SO LONG YOU DON'T RECOGNIZE YOUR OL' UNCLE RANDALL?
IT'S BEEN ONE O' THOSE DAYS, UNC.
SO I'VE HEARD. YOU HOLDIN' UP UNDER ALL THIS TRANS-PLANT MESS, SON?
I'M... MAKIN' IT. WE FOUND ONE OF DAD'S LAB GUYS. WITH ANY LUCK HE'LL ENGINEER A CURE.
WALTER SPARROW, RIGHT?
YEAH... GOOD GUESS.
AIN'T NO GUESS. YOUR DADDY TOLD ME. THAT'S WHY I'M CALLIN'...
LISTEN, WHY DON'T YOU COME ON BY THE HOUSE? THIS AIN'T THE KINDA CONVERSATION YOU HAVE OVER THE PHONE.
AND WHAT KIND OF CONVER-SATION IS IT?
THE MONICA THORNE KIND.
NOW... WHEN CAN I EXPECT YOU?

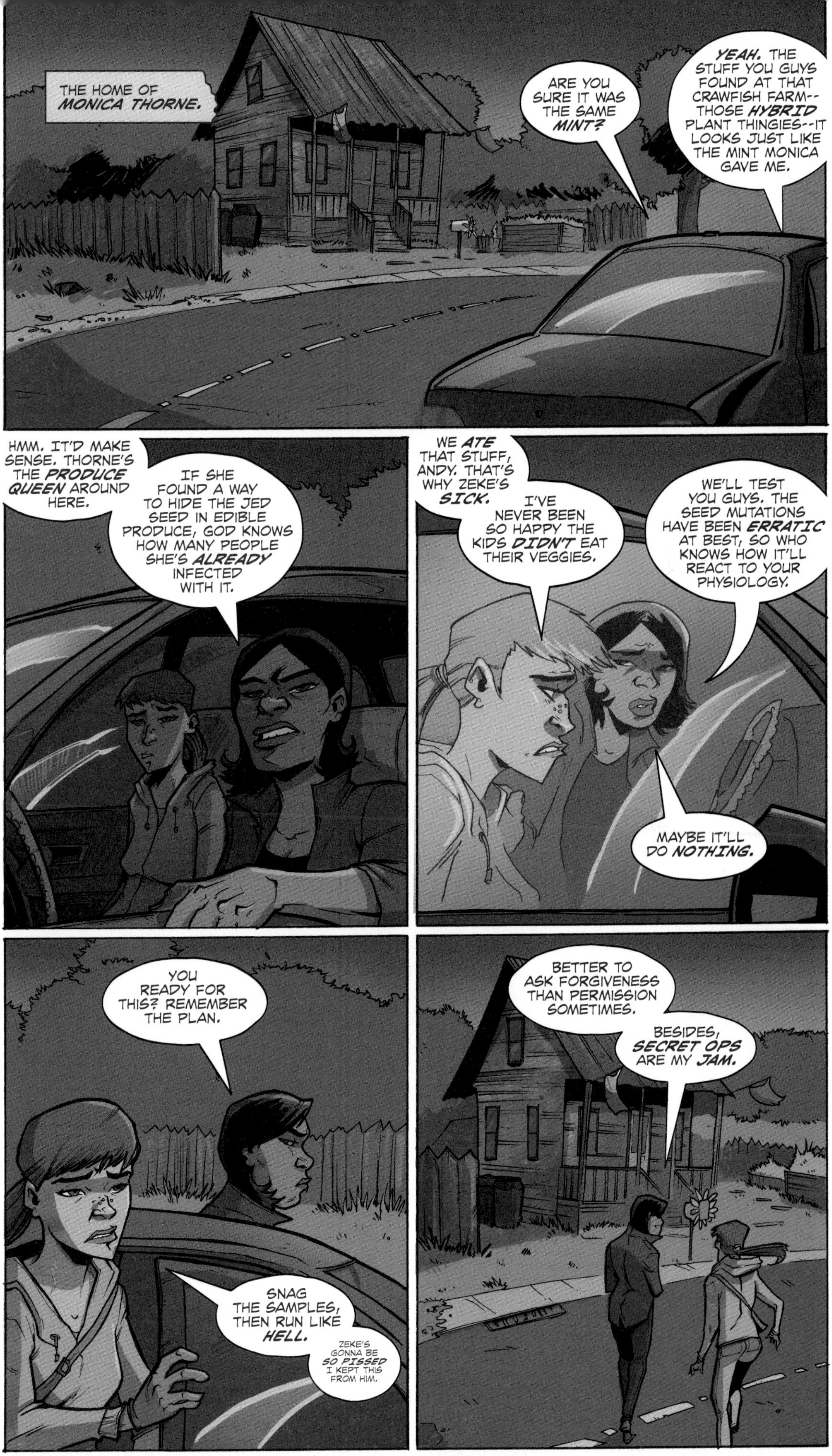
THE HOME OF MONICA THORNE.
ARE YOU SURE IT WAS THE SAME MINT?
YEAH. THE STUFF YOU GUYS FOUND AT THAT CRAWFISH FARM--THOSE HYBRID PLANT THINGIES--IT LOOKS JUST LIKE THE MINT MONICA GAVE ME.
HMM. IT'D MAKE SENSE. THORNE'S THE PRODUCE QUEEN AROUND HERE.
IF SHE FOUND A WAY TO HIDE THE JED SEED IN EDIBLE PRODUCE, GOD KNOWS HOW MANY PEOPLE SHE'S ALREADY INFECTED WITH IT.
WE ATE THAT STUFF, ANDY. THAT'S WHY ZEKE'S SICK.
I'VE NEVER BEEN SO HAPPY THE KIDS DIDN'T EAT THEIR VEGGIES.
WE'LL TEST YOU GUYS. THE SEED MUTATIONS HAVE BEEN ERRATIC AT BEST, SO WHO KNOWS HOW IT'LL REACT TO YOUR PHYSIOLOGY.
MAYBE IT'LL DO NOTHING.
YOU READY FOR THIS? REMEMBER THE PLAN.
SNAG THE SAMPLES, THEN RUN LIKE HELL.
ZEKE'S GONNA BE SO PISSED I KEPT THIS FROM HIM.
BETTER TO ASK FORGIVENESS THAN PERMISSION SOMETIMES.
BESIDES, SECRET OPS ARE MY JAM.

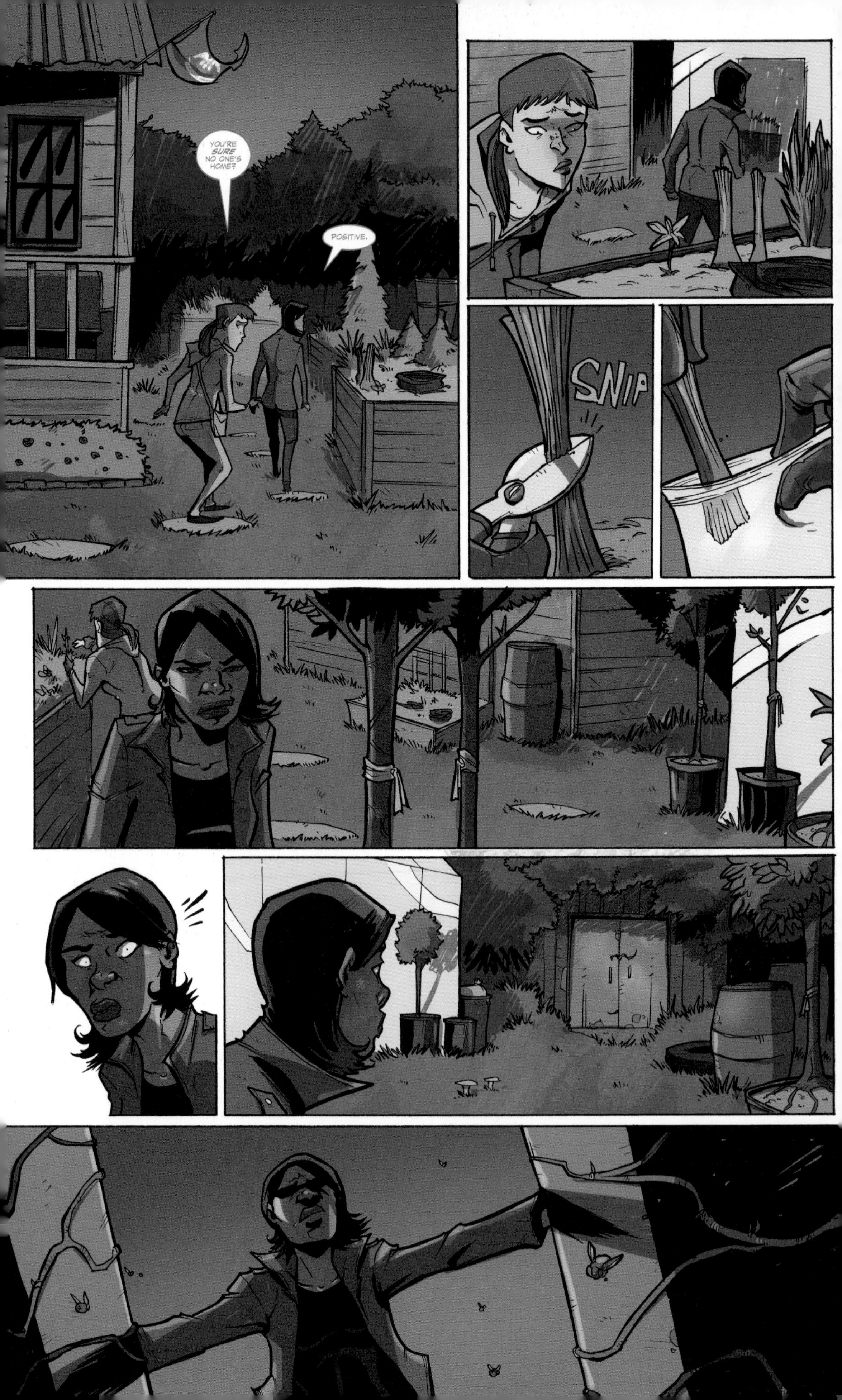
YOU'RE SURE NO ONE'S HOME?
POSITIVE.
SNIP

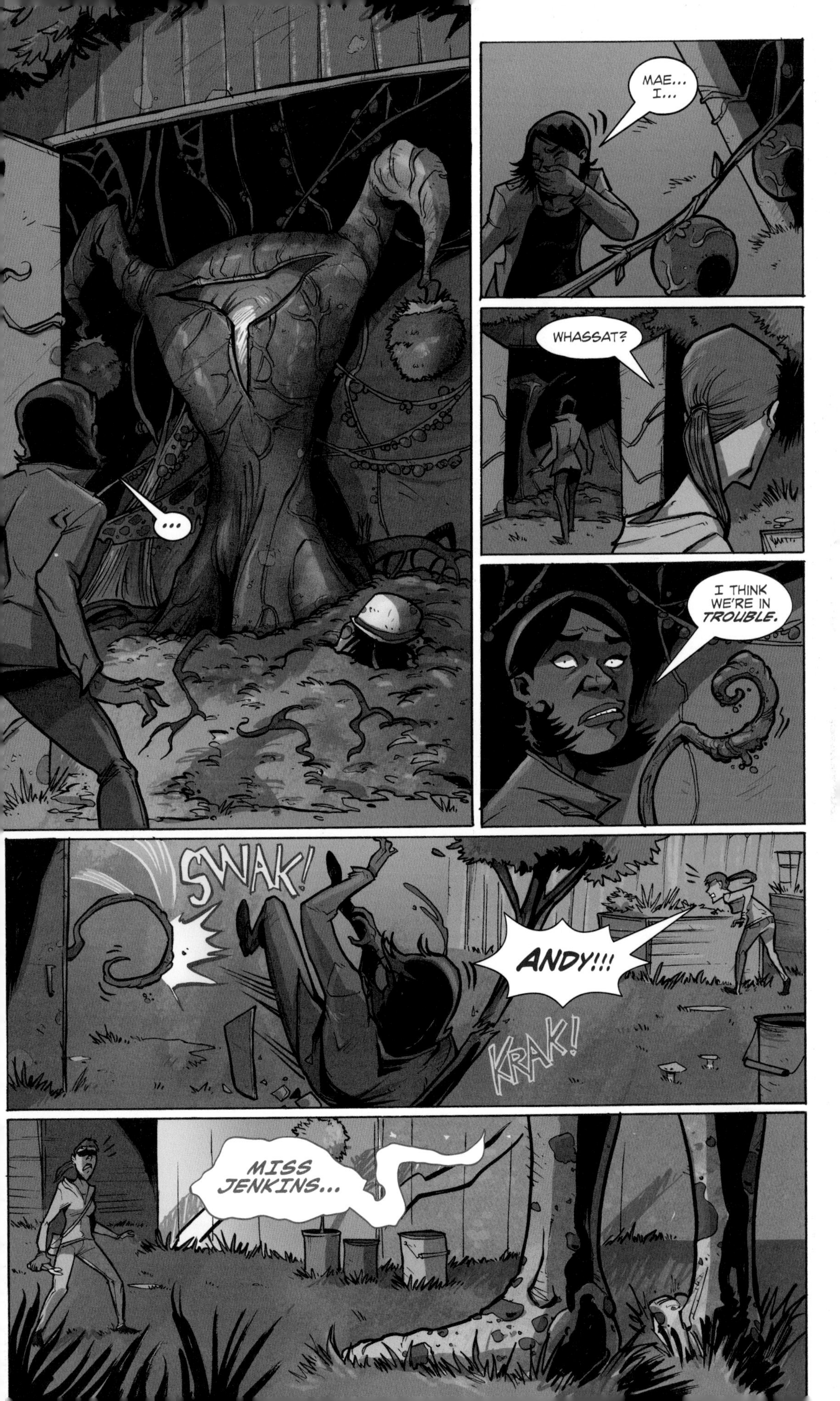
...
MAE... I...
WHASSAT?
I THINK WE'RE IN TROUBLE.
SWAK!
ANDY!!!
KRAK!
MISS JENKINS...

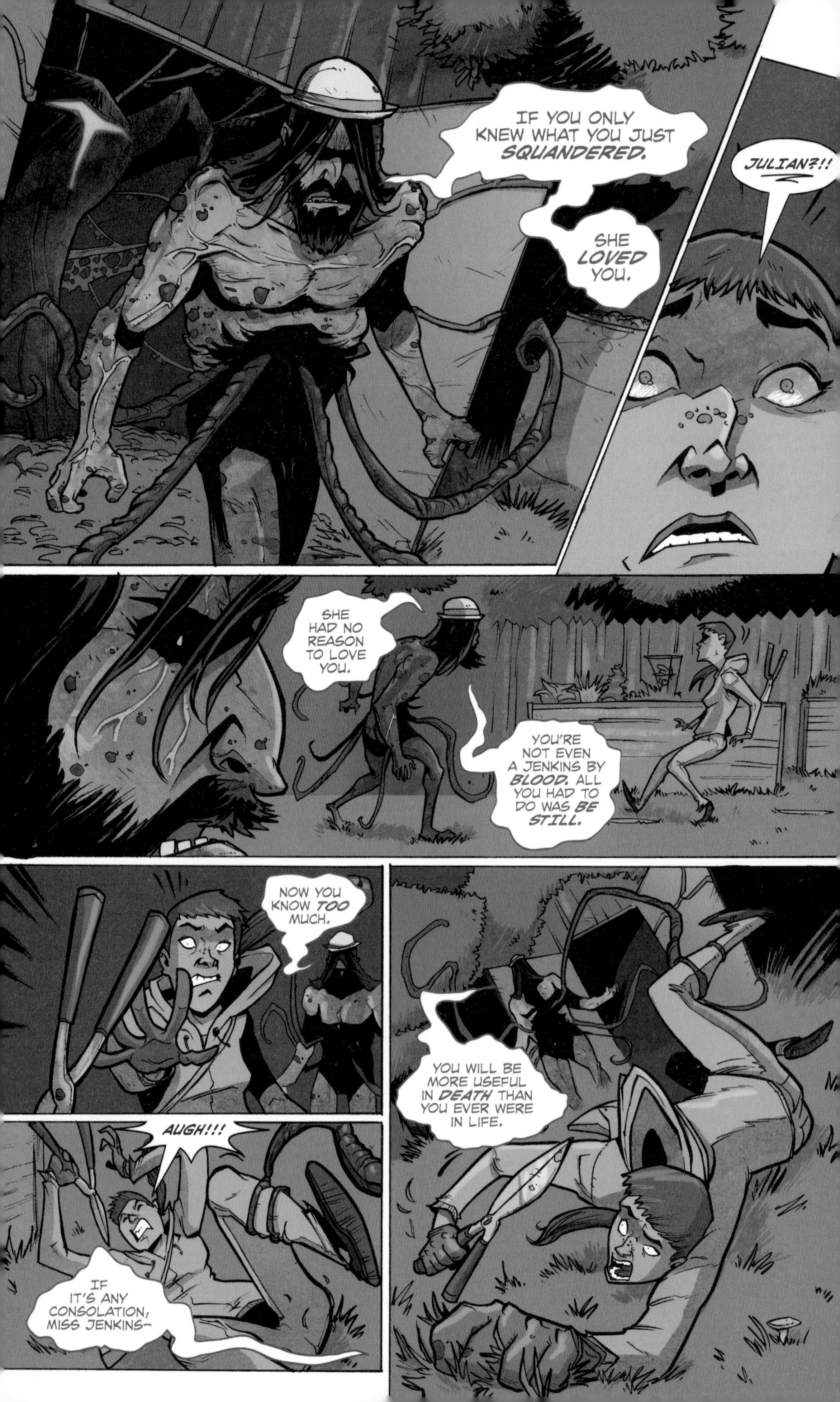
IF YOU ONLY KNEW WHAT YOU JUST SQUANDERED.
SHE LOVED YOU.
JULIAN?!!
SHE HAD NO REASON TO LOVE YOU.
YOU'RE NOT EVEN A JENKINS BY BLOOD. ALL YOU HAD TO DO WAS BE STILL.
NOW YOU KNOW TOO MUCH.
AUGH!!!
IF IT'S ANY CONSOLATION, MISS JENKINS–
YOU WILL BE MORE USEFUL IN DEATH THAN YOU EVER WERE IN LIFE.

BANG!!

?

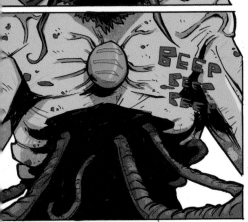

BEEP BEEP BEEP

GUUUUH... WHAT...?

DEHYDRATOR GUN, YOU OLD-TIMEY HAT-WEARING BITCH.

SOIL.

MAE! YOU GOOD?

SNIP!

DEFINITELY NOT.

WE FINALLY GOT HER.

HEAR THAT, PUNKASS? THORNE AIN'T EXPLAINING THIS AWAY. GAME'S OVER.

HARDLY.

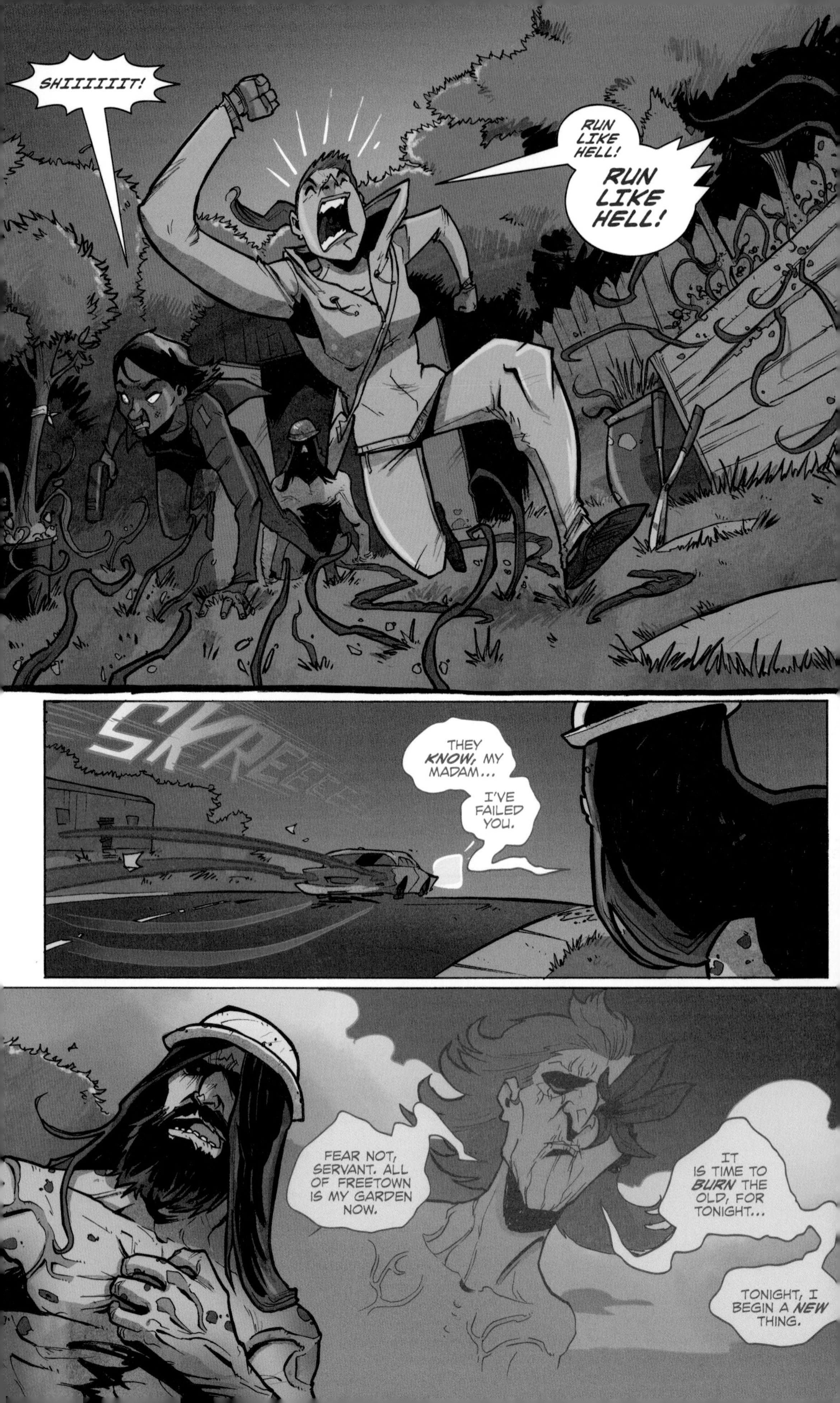
SHIIIIIIT!
RUN LIKE HELL!
RUN LIKE HELL!
SKREEEEE
THEY KNOW, MY MADAM...
I'VE FAILED YOU.
FEAR NOT, SERVANT. ALL OF FREETOWN IS MY GARDEN NOW.
IT IS TIME TO BURN THE OLD, FOR TONIGHT...
TONIGHT, I BEGIN A NEW THING.

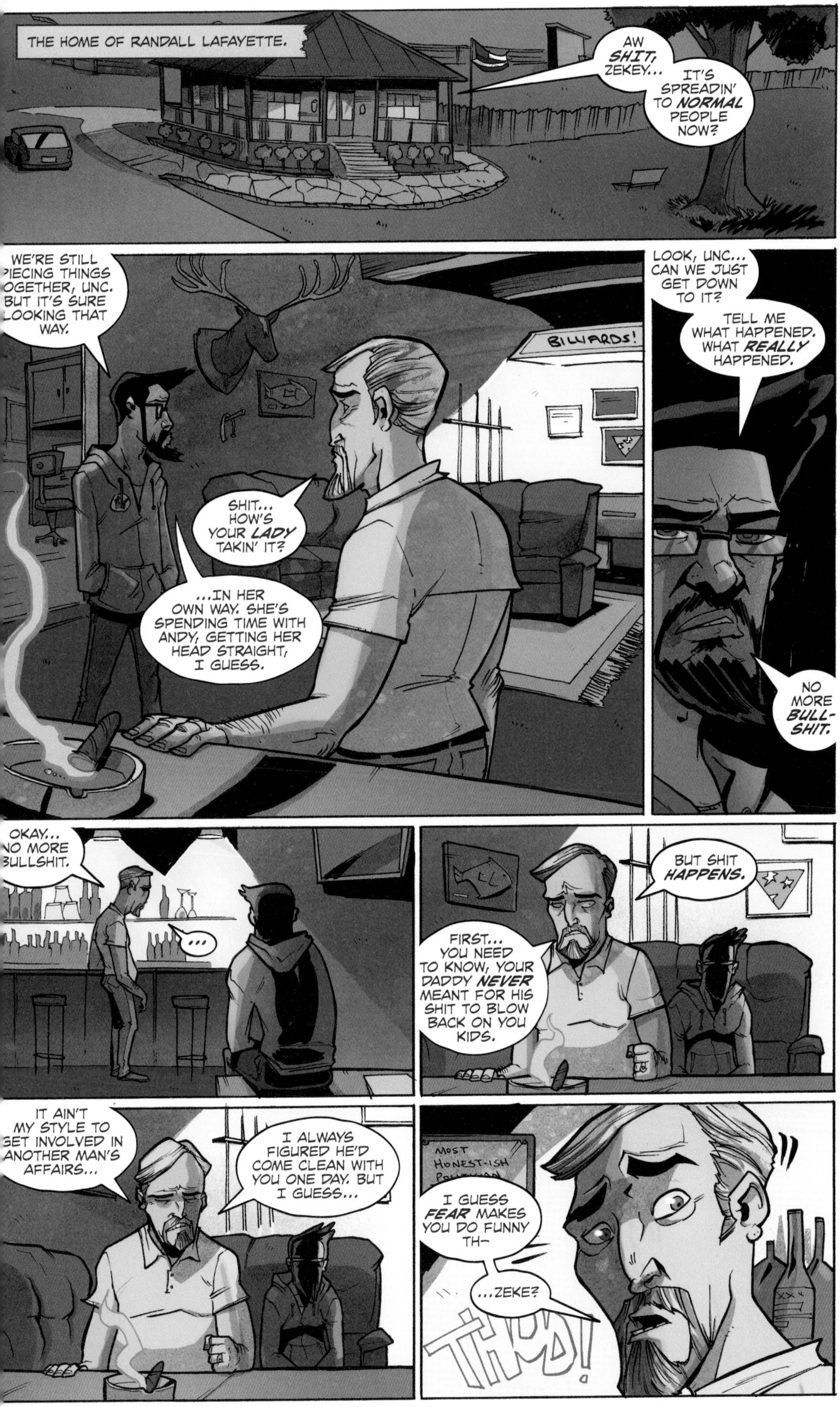
THE HOME OF RANDALL LAFAYETTE.
AW SHIT, ZEKEY...
IT'S SPREADIN' TO NORMAL PEOPLE NOW?
WE'RE STILL PIECING THINGS TOGETHER, UNC. BUT IT'S SURE LOOKING THAT WAY.
BILLIARDS!
SHIT... HOW'S YOUR LADY TAKIN' IT?
...IN HER OWN WAY. SHE'S SPENDING TIME WITH ANDY, GETTING HER HEAD STRAIGHT, I GUESS.
LOOK, UNC... CAN WE JUST GET DOWN TO IT?
TELL ME WHAT HAPPENED. WHAT REALLY HAPPENED.
NO MORE BULL-SHIT.
OKAY... NO MORE BULLSHIT.
...
BUT SHIT HAPPENS.
FIRST... YOU NEED TO KNOW, YOUR DADDY NEVER MEANT FOR HIS SHIT TO BLOW BACK ON YOU KIDS.
IT AIN'T MY STYLE TO GET INVOLVED IN ANOTHER MAN'S AFFAIRS...
I ALWAYS FIGURED HE'D COME CLEAN WITH YOU ONE DAY. BUT I GUESS...
MOST HONEST-ISH
I GUESS FEAR MAKES YOU DO FUNNY TH-
...ZEKE?
THUD!

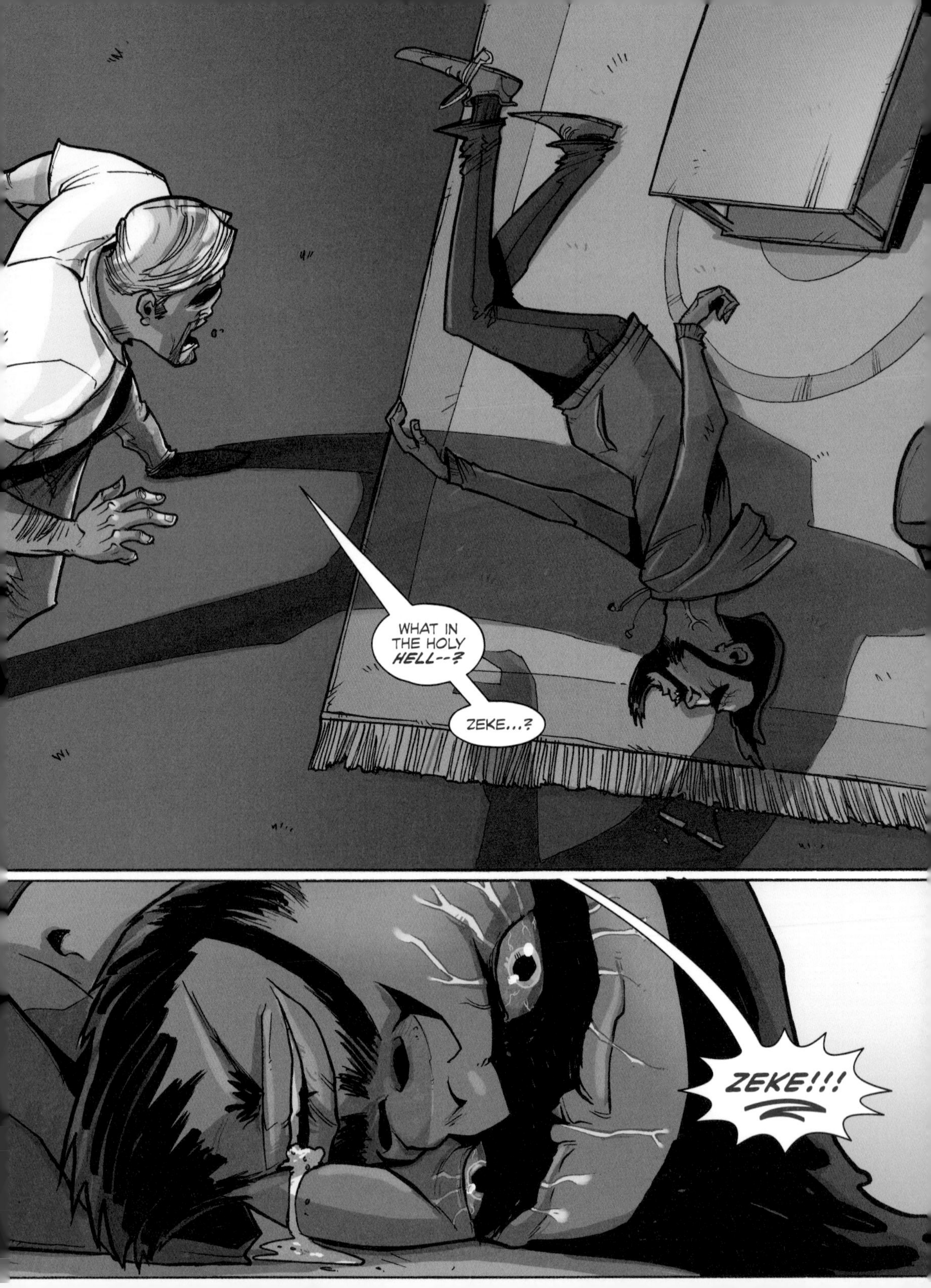
WHAT IN THE HOLY HELL--?
ZEKE...?
ZEKE!!!

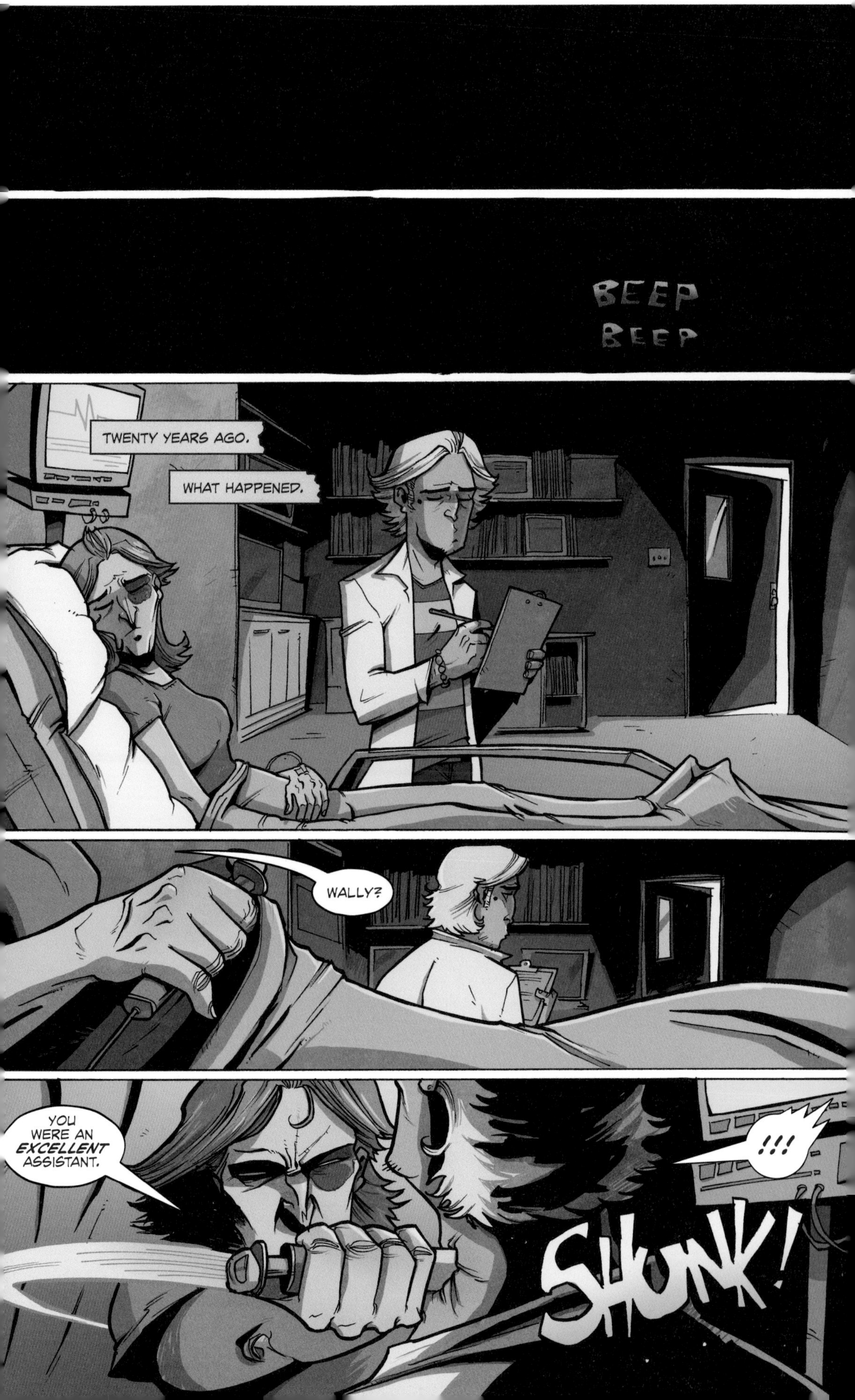
BEEP
BEEP
TWENTY YEARS AGO.
WHAT HAPPENED.
WALLY?
YOU WERE AN *EXCELLENT* ASSISTANT.
!!!
SHUNK!

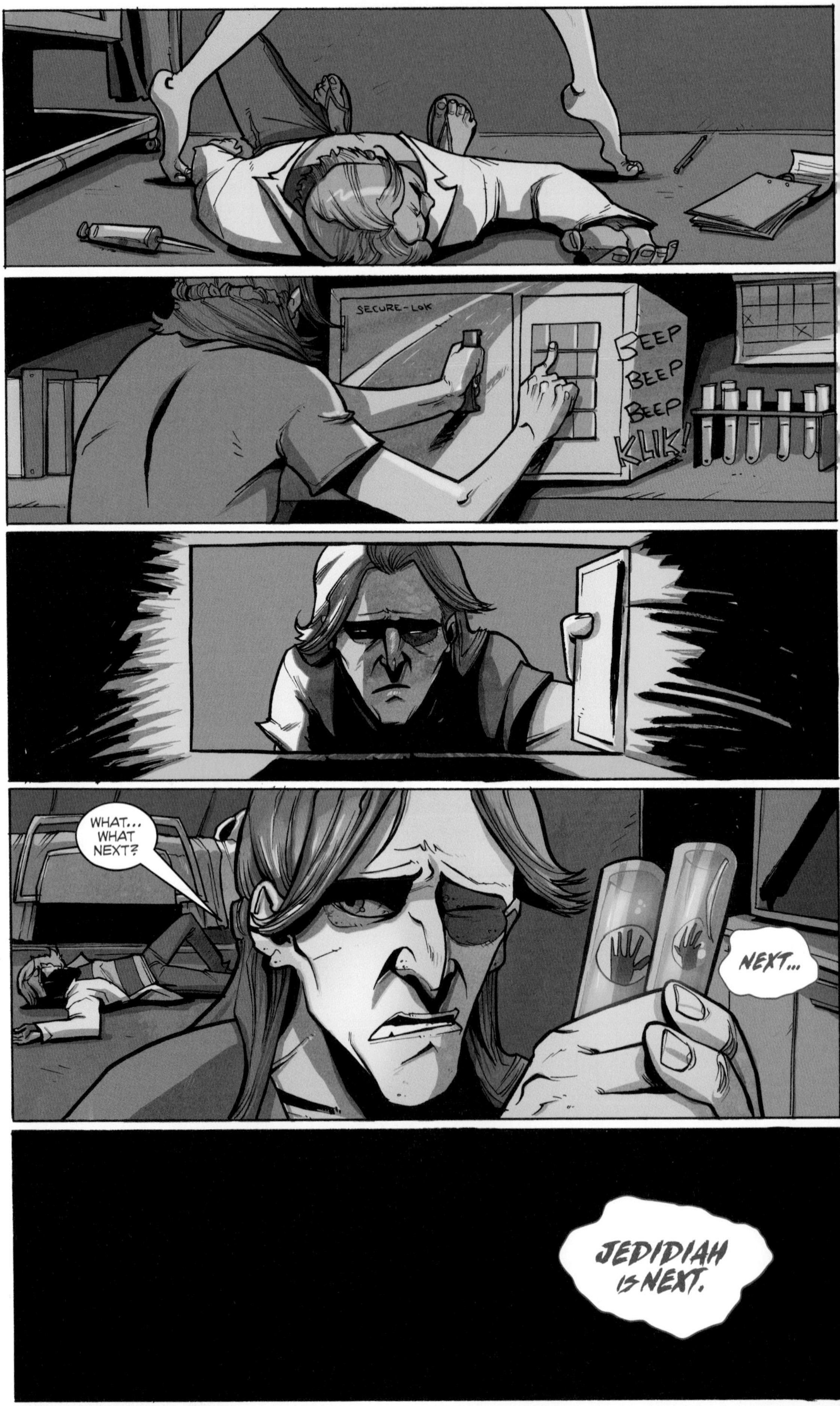
SECURE-LOK
BEEP
BEEP
BEEP
KLIK!
WHAT... WHAT NEXT?
NEXT...
JEDIDIAH IS NEXT.

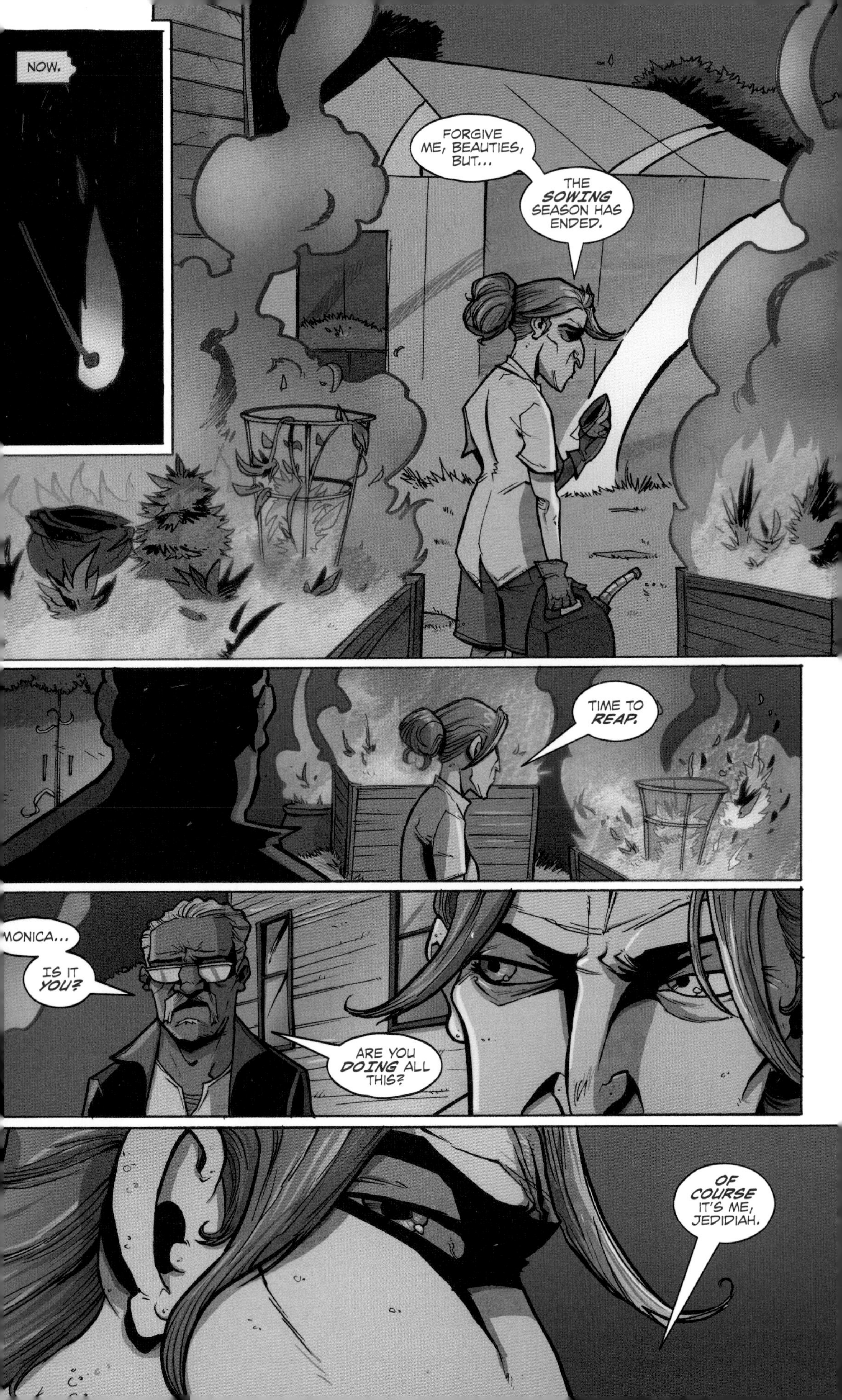
NOW.
FORGIVE ME, BEAUTIES, BUT...
THE *SOWING* SEASON HAS ENDED.
TIME TO *REAP.*
MONICA...
IS IT *YOU?*
ARE YOU *DOING* ALL THIS?
OF COURSE IT'S ME, JEDIDIAH.

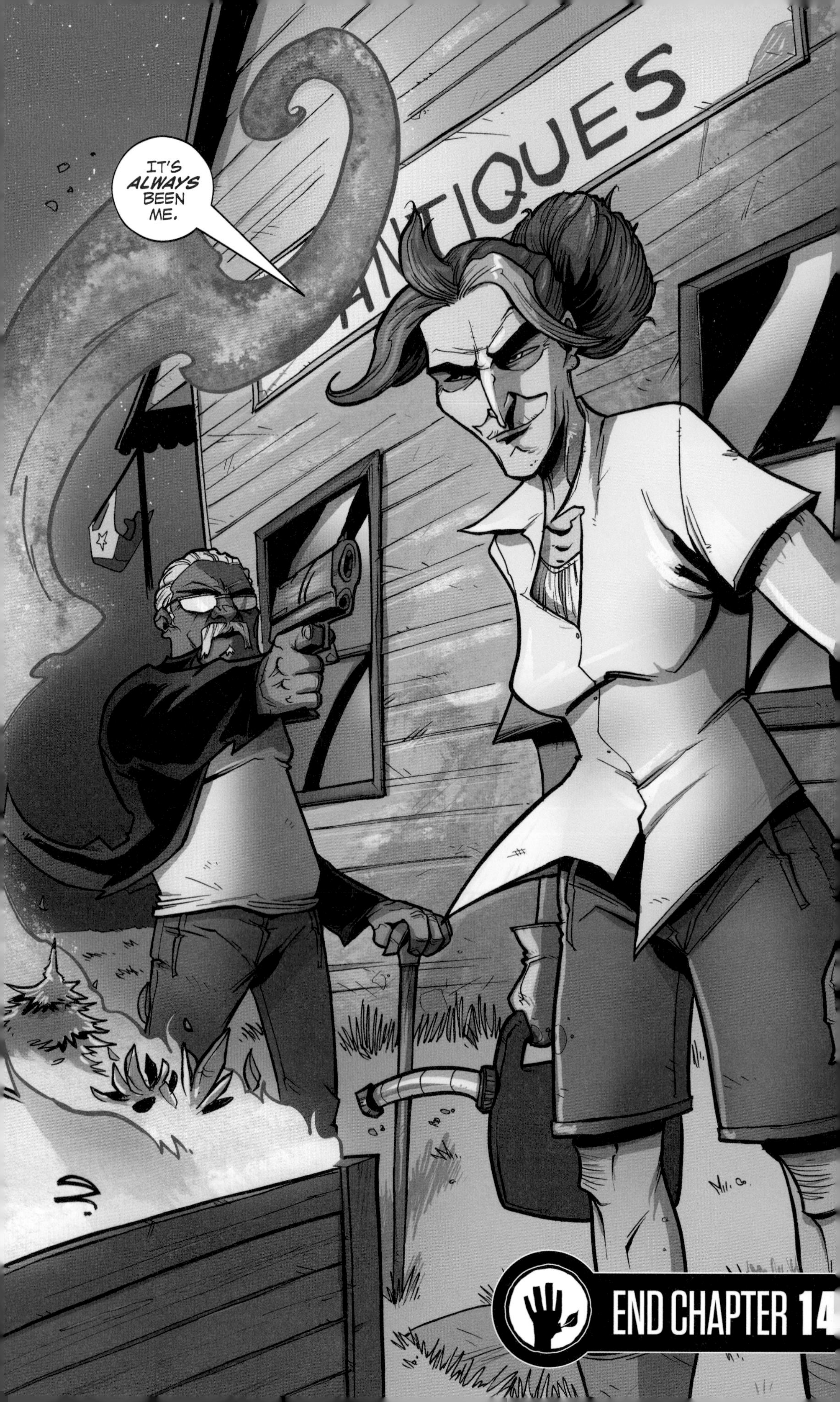
IT'S ALWAYS BEEN ME.
ANTIQUES
END CHAPTER 14

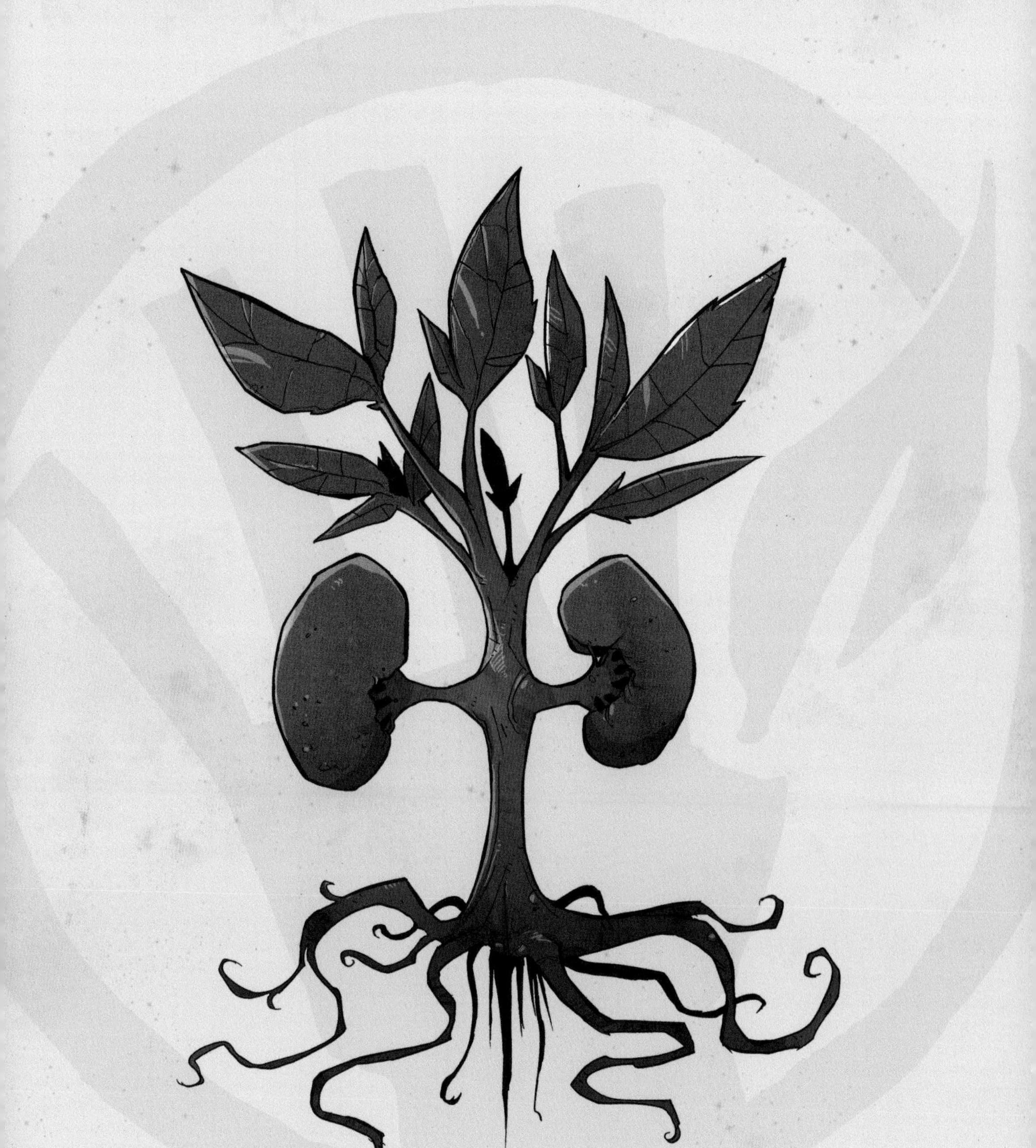

CHAPTER 15

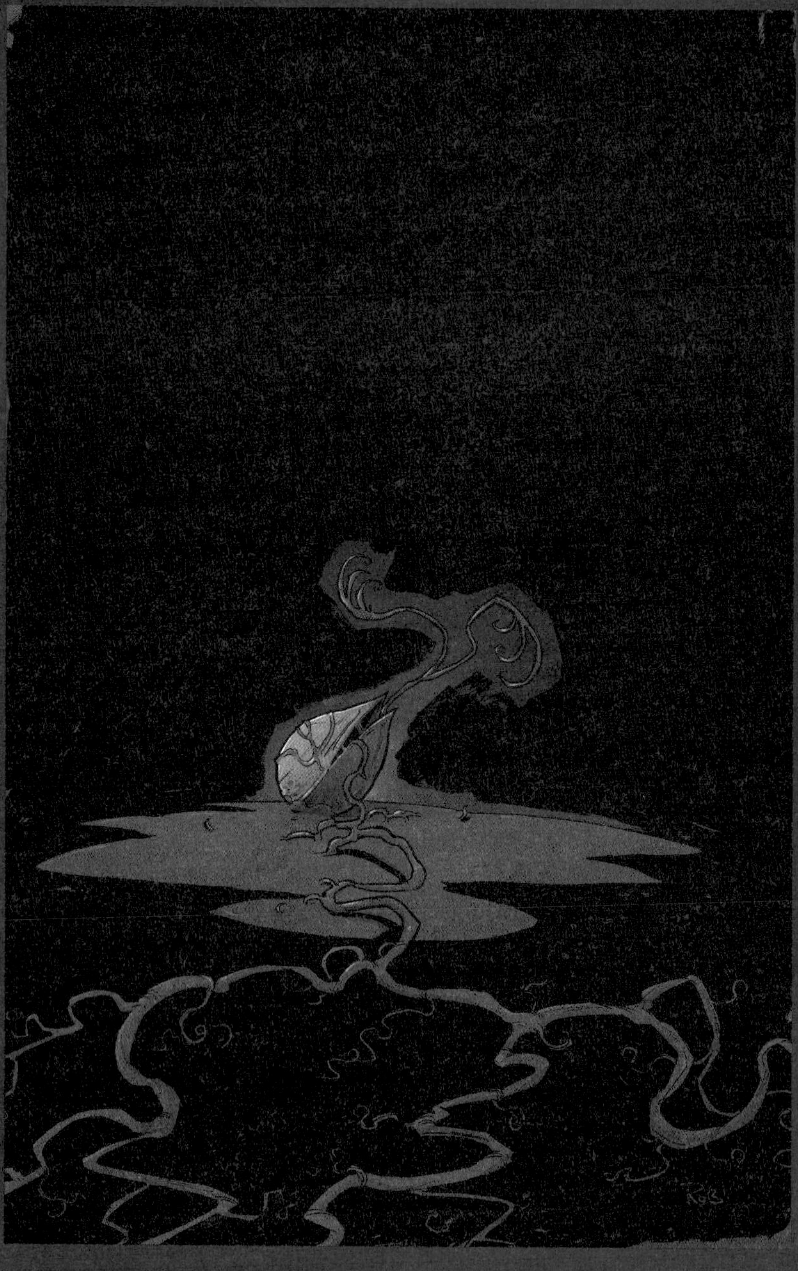

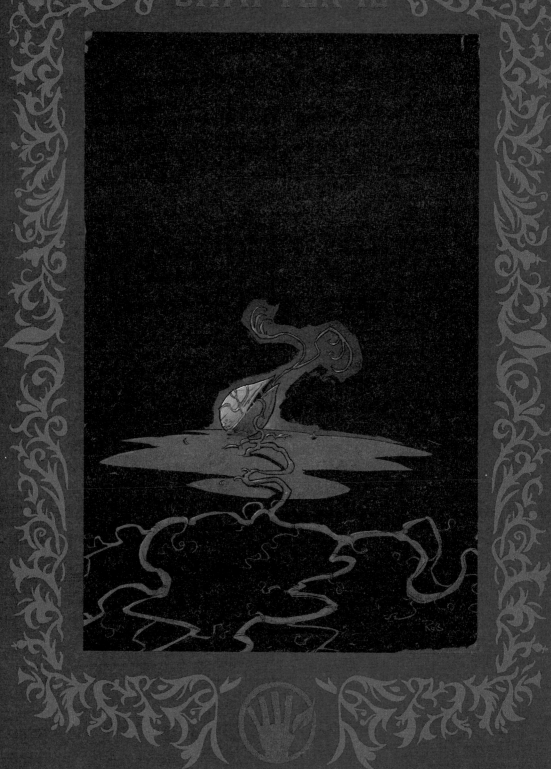

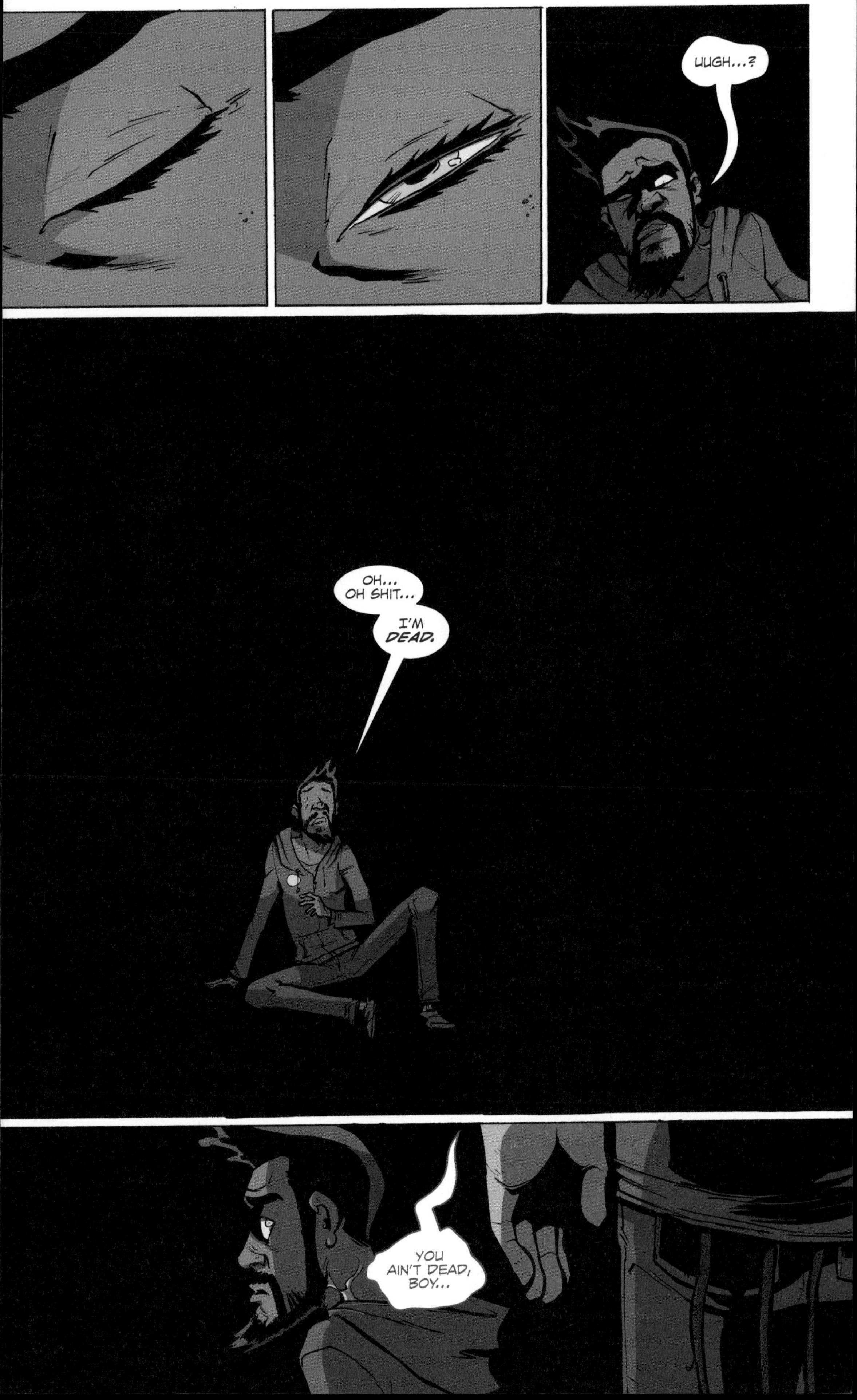

UUGH...?
OH... OH SHIT...
I'M DEAD.
YOU AIN'T DEAD, BOY...

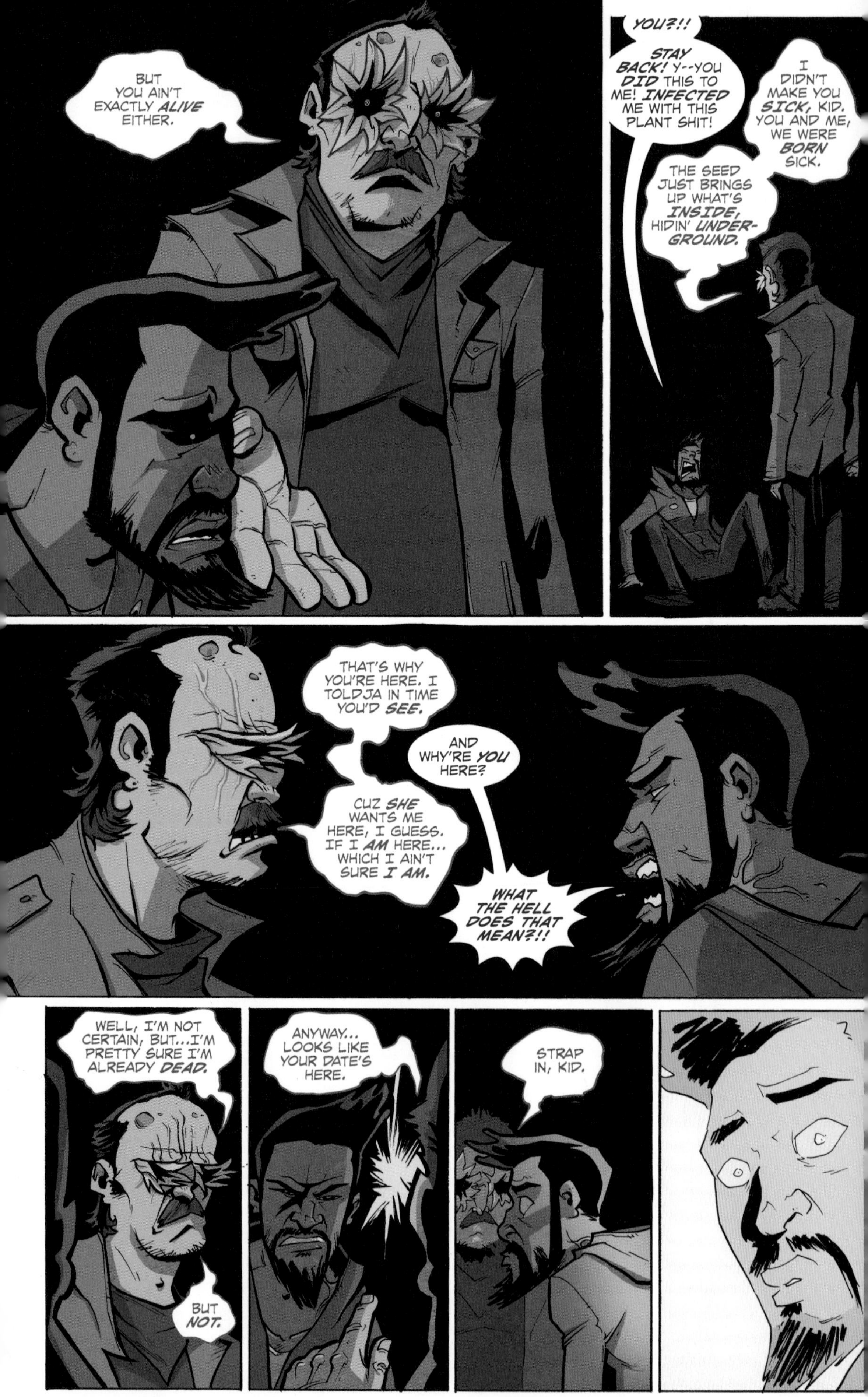
BUT YOU AIN'T EXACTLY ALIVE EITHER.
YOU?!!
STAY BACK! Y--YOU DID THIS TO ME! INFECTED ME WITH THIS PLANT SHIT!
I DIDN'T MAKE YOU SICK, KID. YOU AND ME, WE WERE BORN SICK.
THE SEED JUST BRINGS UP WHAT'S INSIDE, HIDIN' UNDER-GROUND.
THAT'S WHY YOU'RE HERE. I TOLDJA IN TIME YOU'D SEE.
AND WHY'RE YOU HERE?
CUZ SHE WANTS ME HERE, I GUESS. IF I AM HERE... WHICH I AIN'T SURE I AM.
WHAT THE HELL DOES THAT MEAN?!!
WELL, I'M NOT CERTAIN, BUT...I'M PRETTY SURE I'M ALREADY DEAD.
BUT NOT.
ANYWAY... LOOKS LIKE YOUR DATE'S HERE.
STRAP IN, KID.

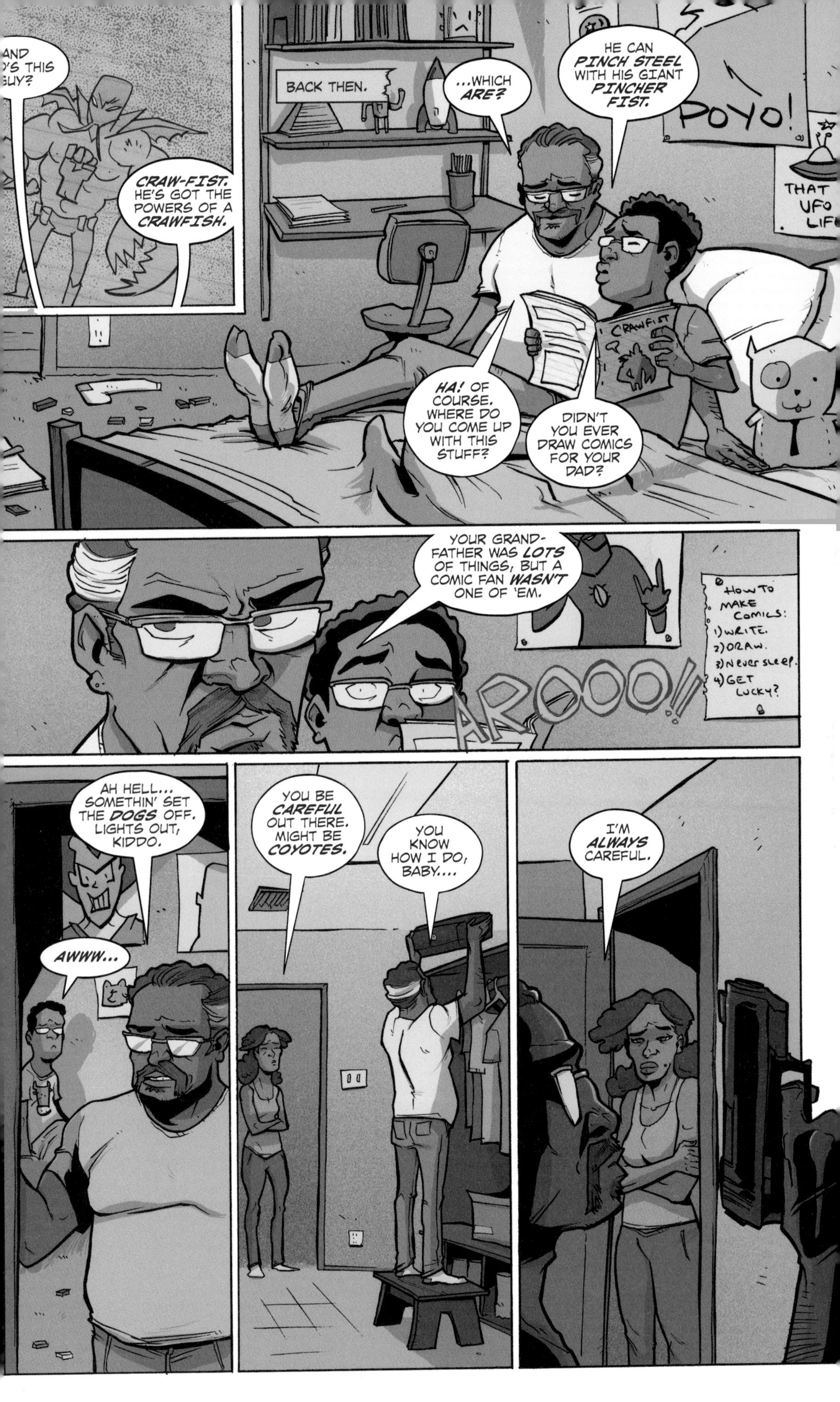
AND ...'S THIS GUY?
CRAW-FIST. HE'S GOT THE POWERS OF A CRAWFISH.
BACK THEN.
...WHICH ARE?
HE CAN PINCH STEEL WITH HIS GIANT PINCHER FIST.
POYO!
THAT UFO LIF
CRAWFIST
HA! OF COURSE. WHERE DO YOU COME UP WITH THIS STUFF?
DIDN'T YOU EVER DRAW COMICS FOR YOUR DAD?
YOUR GRAND-FATHER WAS LOTS OF THINGS, BUT A COMIC FAN WASN'T ONE OF 'EM.
HOW TO MAKE COMICS: 1) WRITE. 2) DRAW. 3) NEVER SLEEP. 4) GET LUCKY?
AROOOO!!
AH HELL... SOMETHIN' SET THE DOGS OFF. LIGHTS OUT, KIDDO.
AWWW...
YOU BE CAREFUL OUT THERE. MIGHT BE COYOTES.
YOU KNOW HOW I DO, BABY....
I'M ALWAYS CAREFUL.

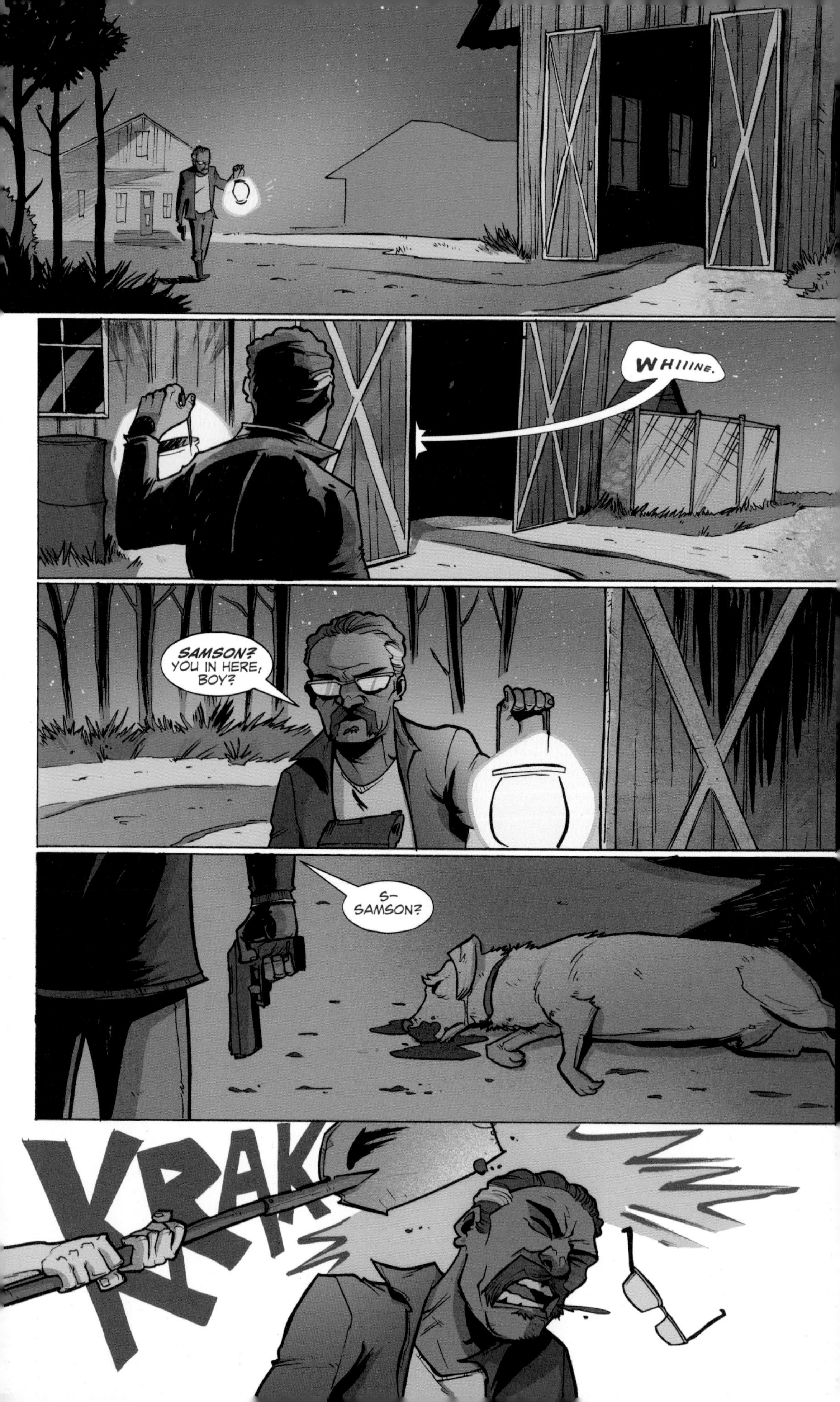
WHIIINE.
SAMSON? YOU IN HERE, BOY?
S— SAMSON?
KRAK

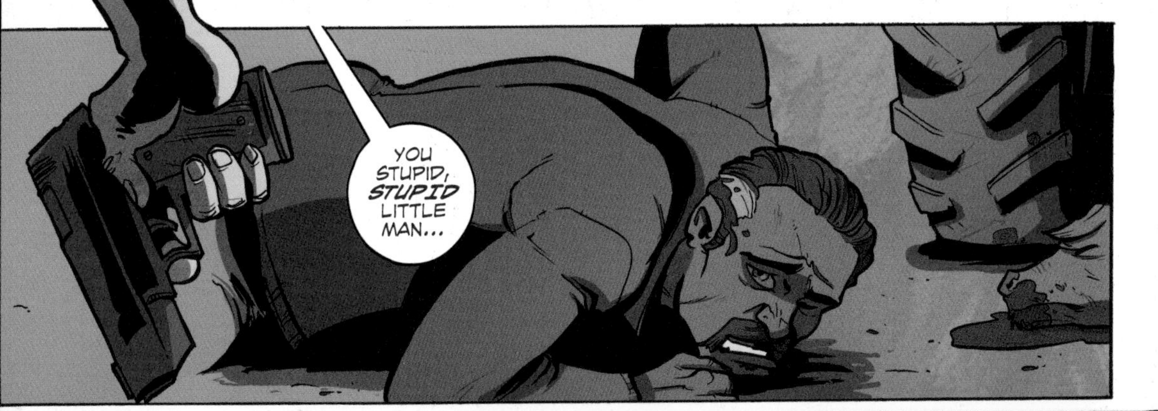
YOU STUPID, STUPID LITTLE MAN...

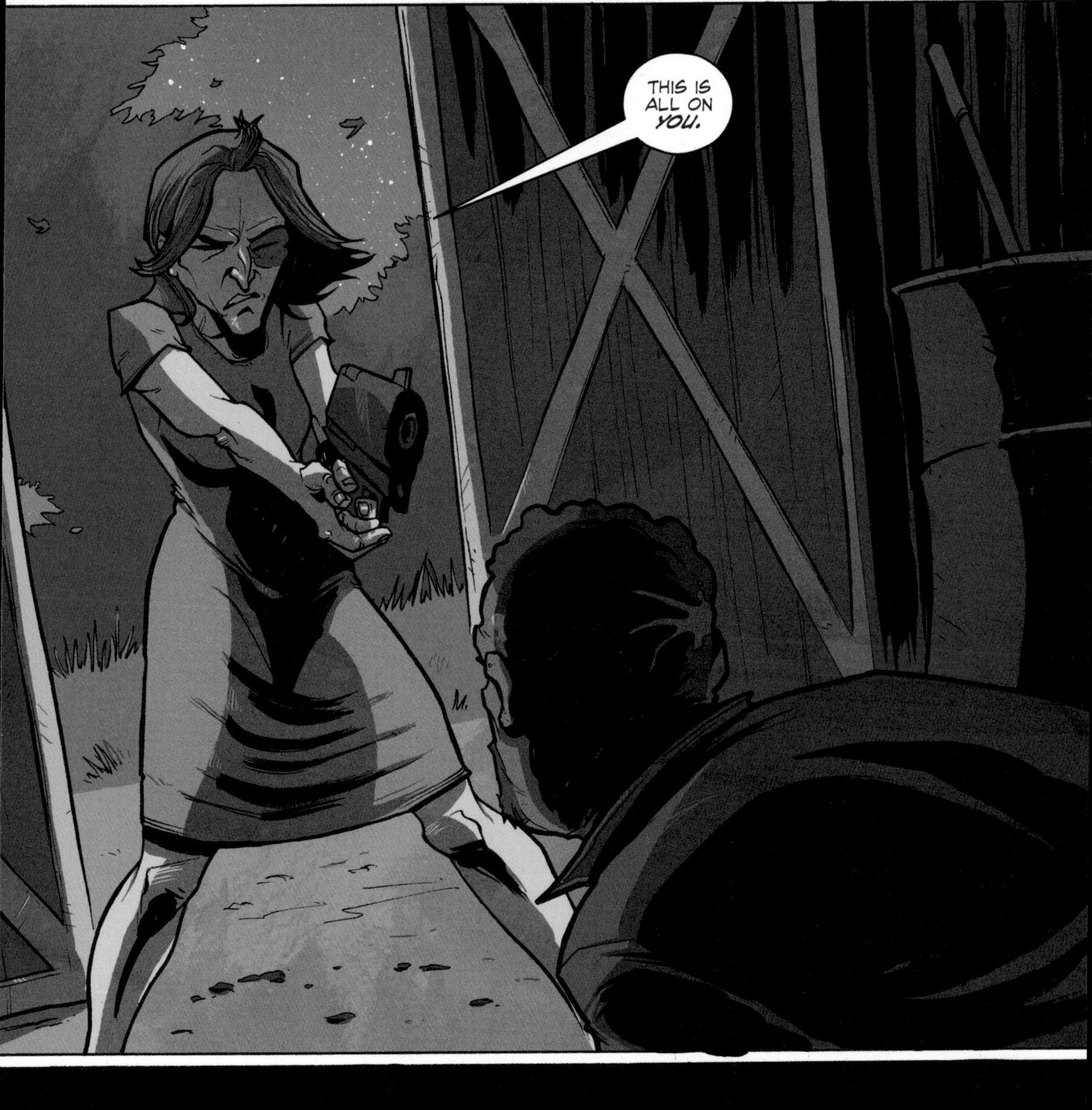
THIS IS ALL ON YOU.

CHAPTER 15: THE KNOWLEDGE OF GOOD AND EVIL.

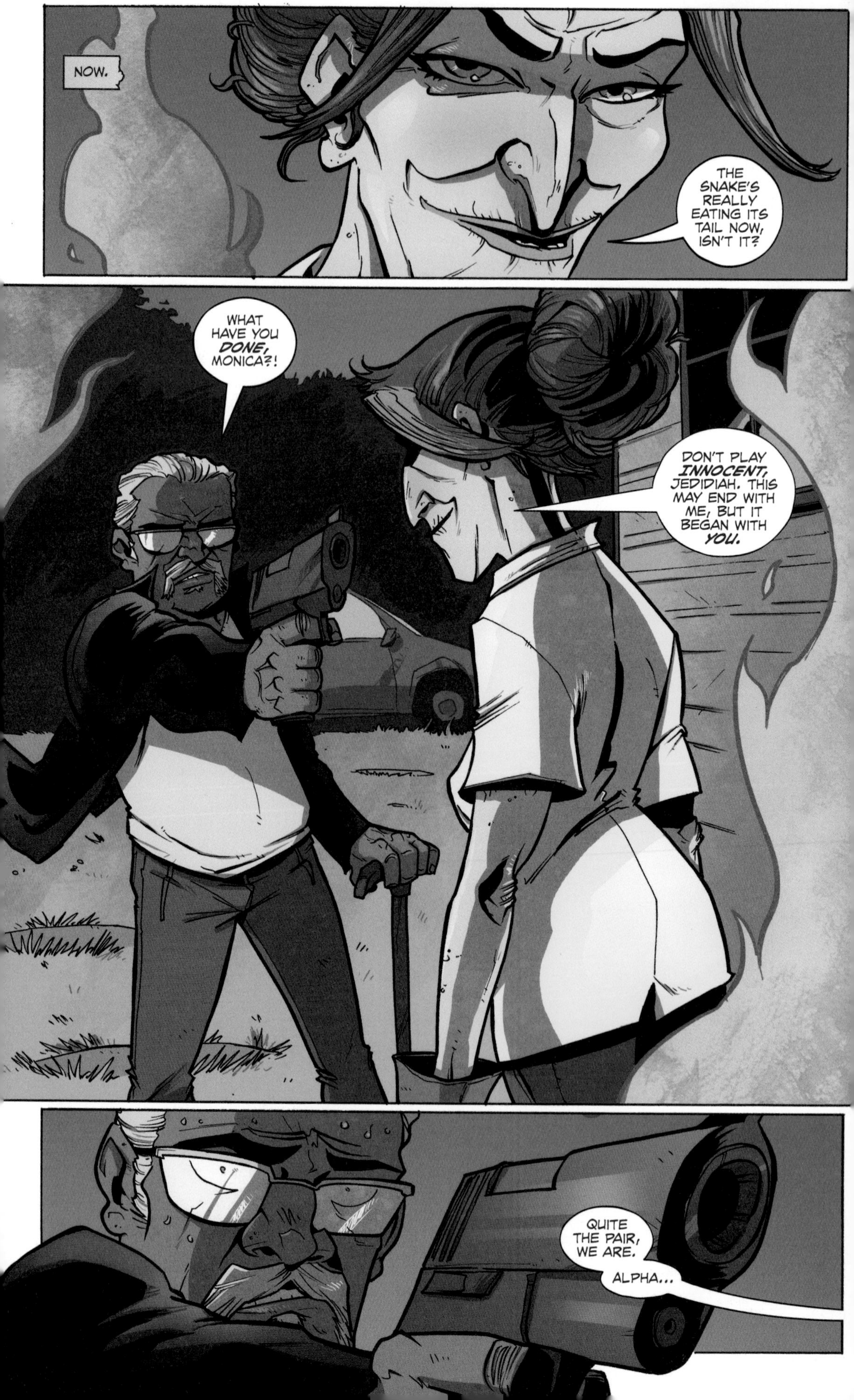
NOW.
THE SNAKE'S REALLY EATING ITS TAIL NOW, ISN'T IT?
WHAT HAVE YOU *DONE,* MONICA?!
DON'T PLAY *INNOCENT,* JEDIDIAH. THIS MAY END WITH ME, BUT IT BEGAN WITH *YOU.*
QUITE THE PAIR, WE ARE.
ALPHA...

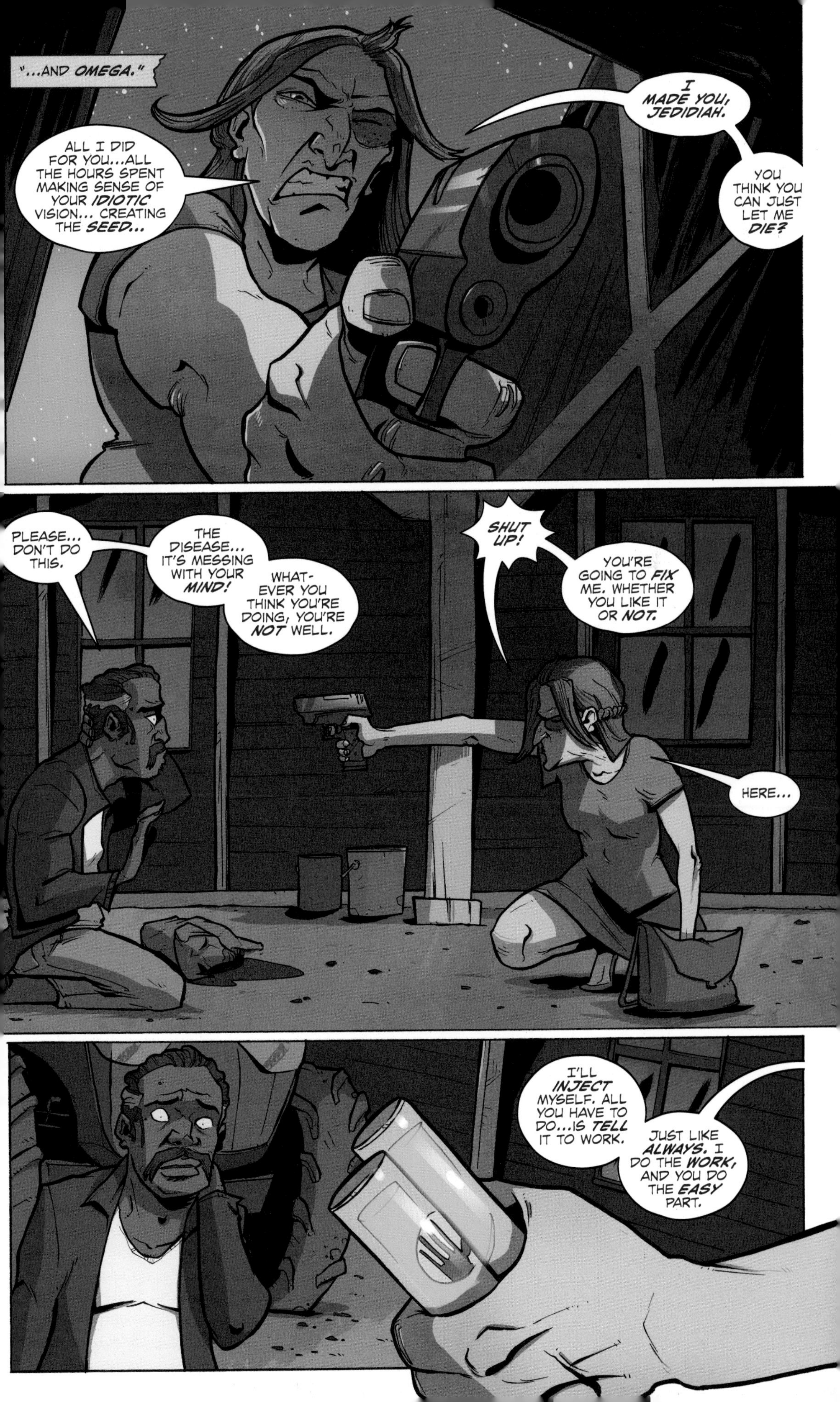
"...AND OMEGA."
ALL I DID FOR YOU...ALL THE HOURS SPENT MAKING SENSE OF YOUR IDIOTIC VISION... CREATING THE SEED...
I MADE YOU, JEDIDIAH.
YOU THINK YOU CAN JUST LET ME DIE?
PLEASE... DON'T DO THIS.
THE DISEASE... IT'S MESSING WITH YOUR MIND!
WHAT-EVER YOU THINK YOU'RE DOING, YOU'RE NOT WELL.
SHUT UP!
YOU'RE GOING TO FIX ME. WHETHER YOU LIKE IT OR NOT.
HERE...
I'LL INJECT MYSELF. ALL YOU HAVE TO DO...IS TELL IT TO WORK.
JUST LIKE ALWAYS. I DO THE WORK, AND YOU DO THE EASY PART.

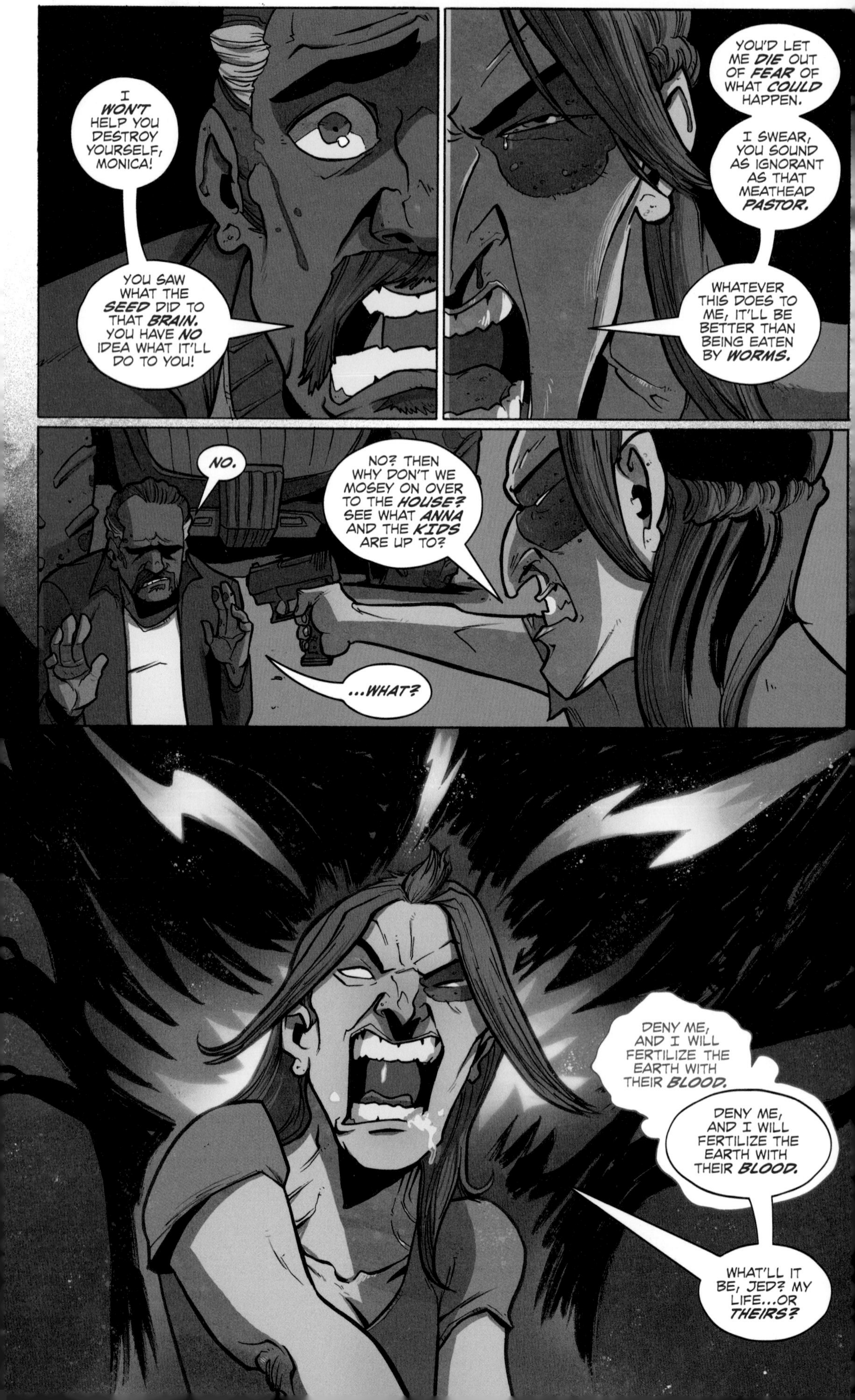
I WON'T HELP YOU DESTROY YOURSELF, MONICA!
YOU SAW WHAT THE SEED DID TO THAT BRAIN. YOU HAVE NO IDEA WHAT IT'LL DO TO YOU!
YOU'D LET ME DIE OUT OF FEAR OF WHAT COULD HAPPEN.
I SWEAR, YOU SOUND AS IGNORANT AS THAT MEATHEAD PASTOR.
WHATEVER THIS DOES TO ME, IT'LL BE BETTER THAN BEING EATEN BY WORMS.
NO.
NO? THEN WHY DON'T WE MOSEY ON OVER TO THE HOUSE? SEE WHAT ANNA AND THE KIDS ARE UP TO?
...WHAT?
DENY ME, AND I WILL FERTILIZE THE EARTH WITH THEIR BLOOD.
DENY ME, AND I WILL FERTILIZE THE EARTH WITH THEIR BLOOD.
WHAT'LL IT BE, JED? MY LIFE...OR THEIRS?

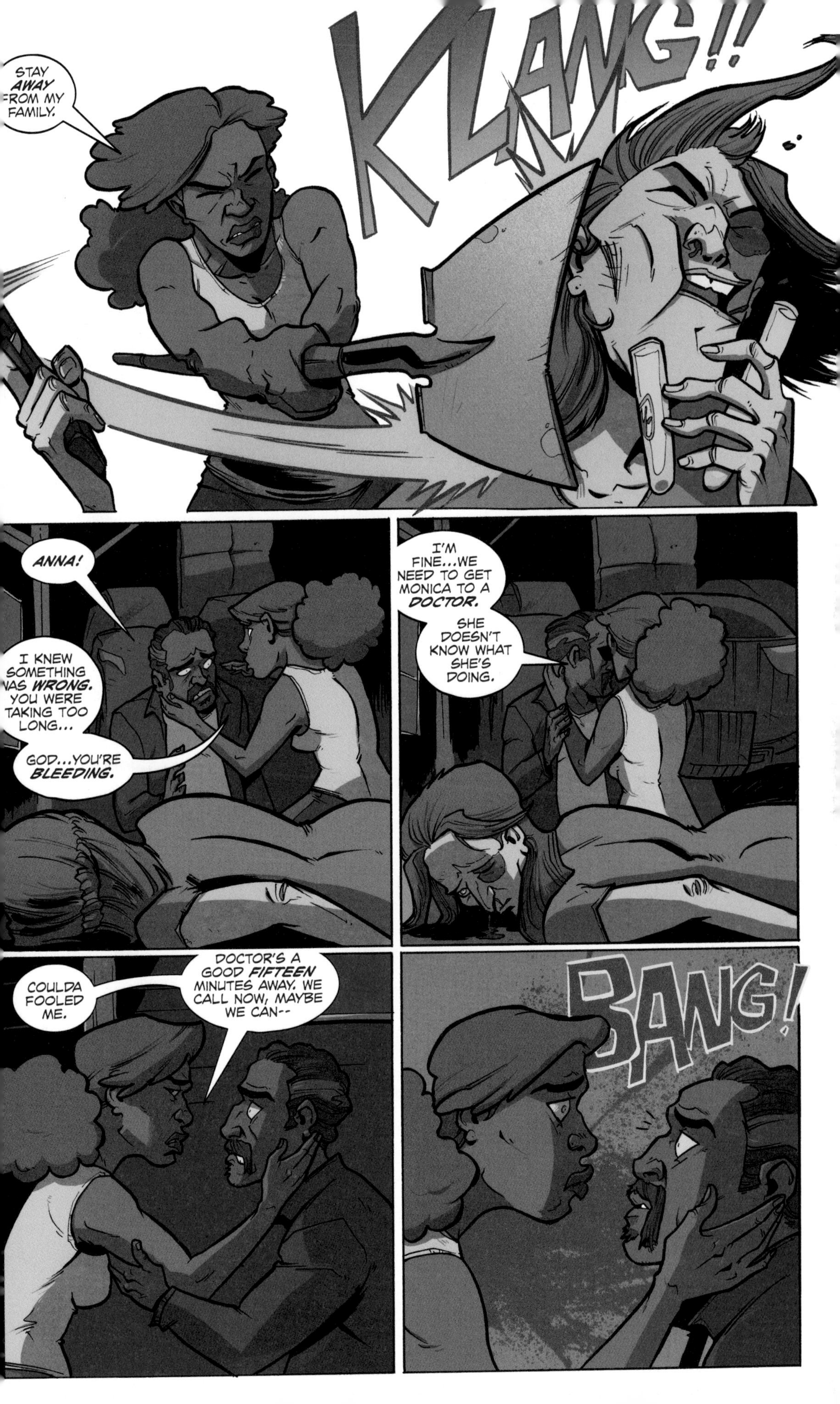
STAY AWAY FROM MY FAMILY.
KLANG!!
ANNA!
I KNEW SOMETHING WAS WRONG. YOU WERE TAKING TOO LONG...
GOD...YOU'RE BLEEDING.
I'M FINE...WE NEED TO GET MONICA TO A DOCTOR.
SHE DOESN'T KNOW WHAT SHE'S DOING.
COULDA FOOLED ME.
DOCTOR'S A GOOD FIFTEEN MINUTES AWAY. WE CALL NOW, MAYBE WE CAN--
BANG!

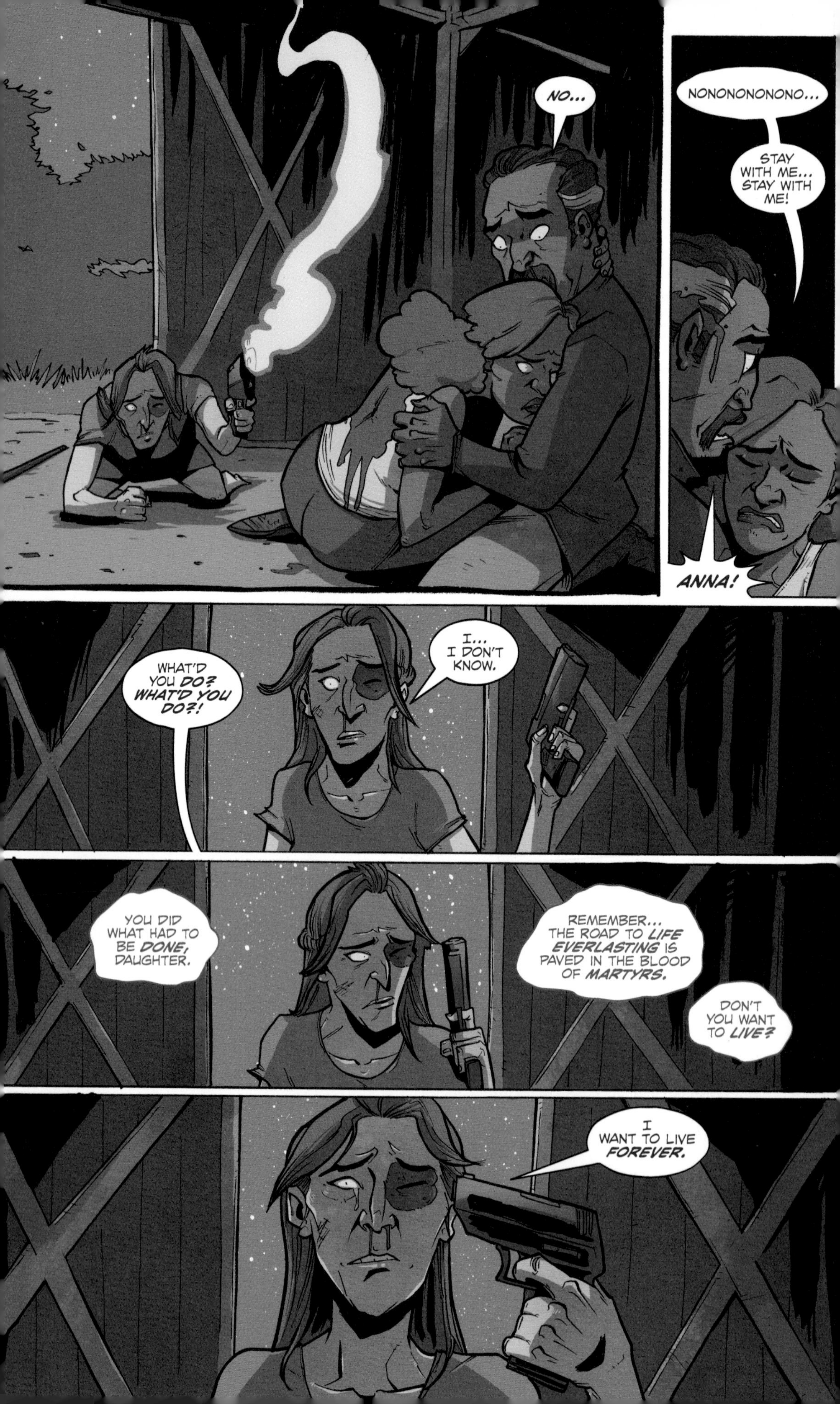
NO...
NONONONONONO...
STAY WITH ME... STAY WITH ME!
ANNA!
WHAT'D YOU DO? WHAT'D YOU DO?!
I... I DON'T KNOW.
YOU DID WHAT HAD TO BE DONE, DAUGHTER.
REMEMBER... THE ROAD TO LIFE EVERLASTING IS PAVED IN THE BLOOD OF MARTYRS.
DON'T YOU WANT TO LIVE?
I WANT TO LIVE FOREVER.

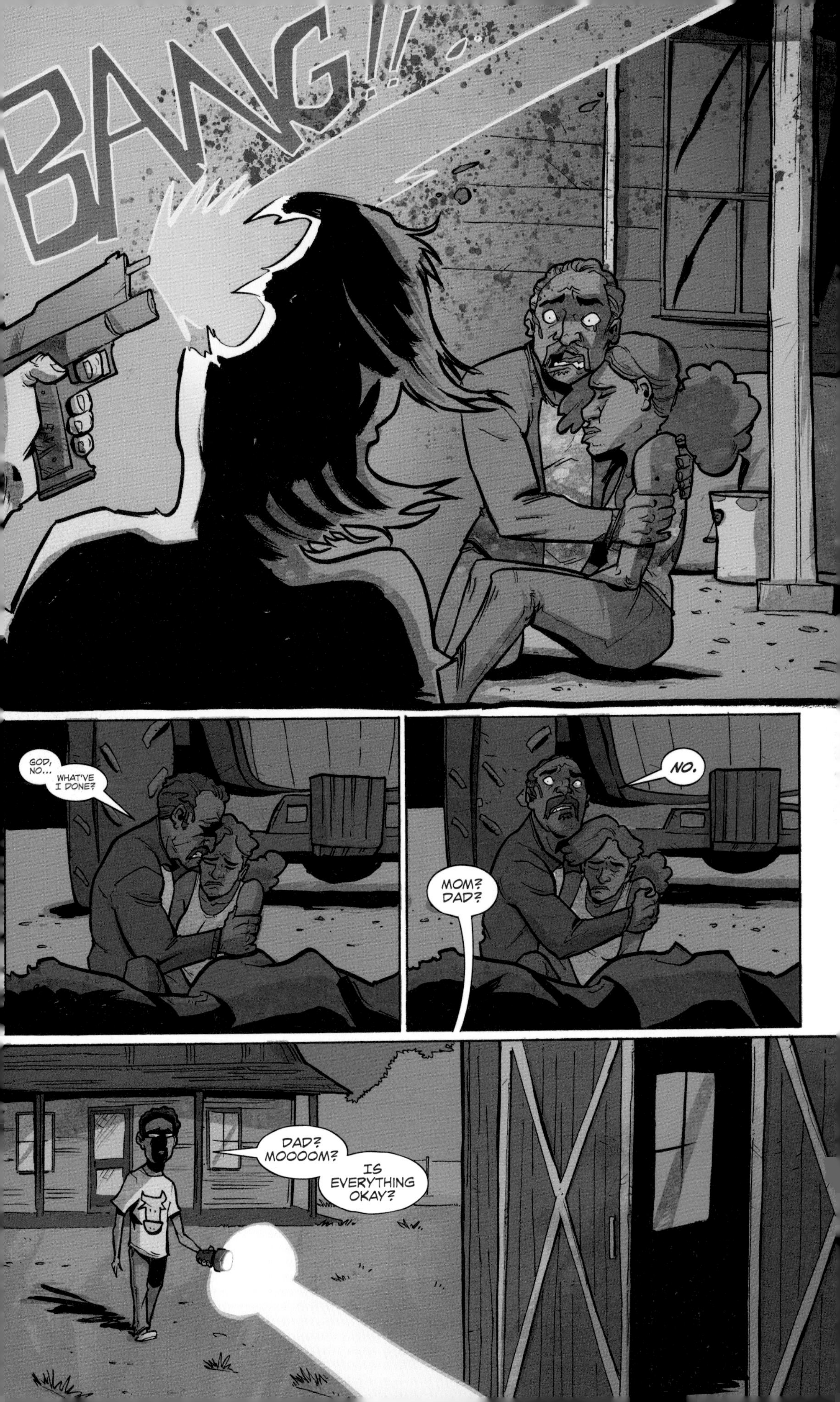
BANG!!
GOD, NO... WHAT'VE I DONE?
NO.
MOM? DAD?
DAD? MOOOOM?
IS EVERYTHING OKAY?

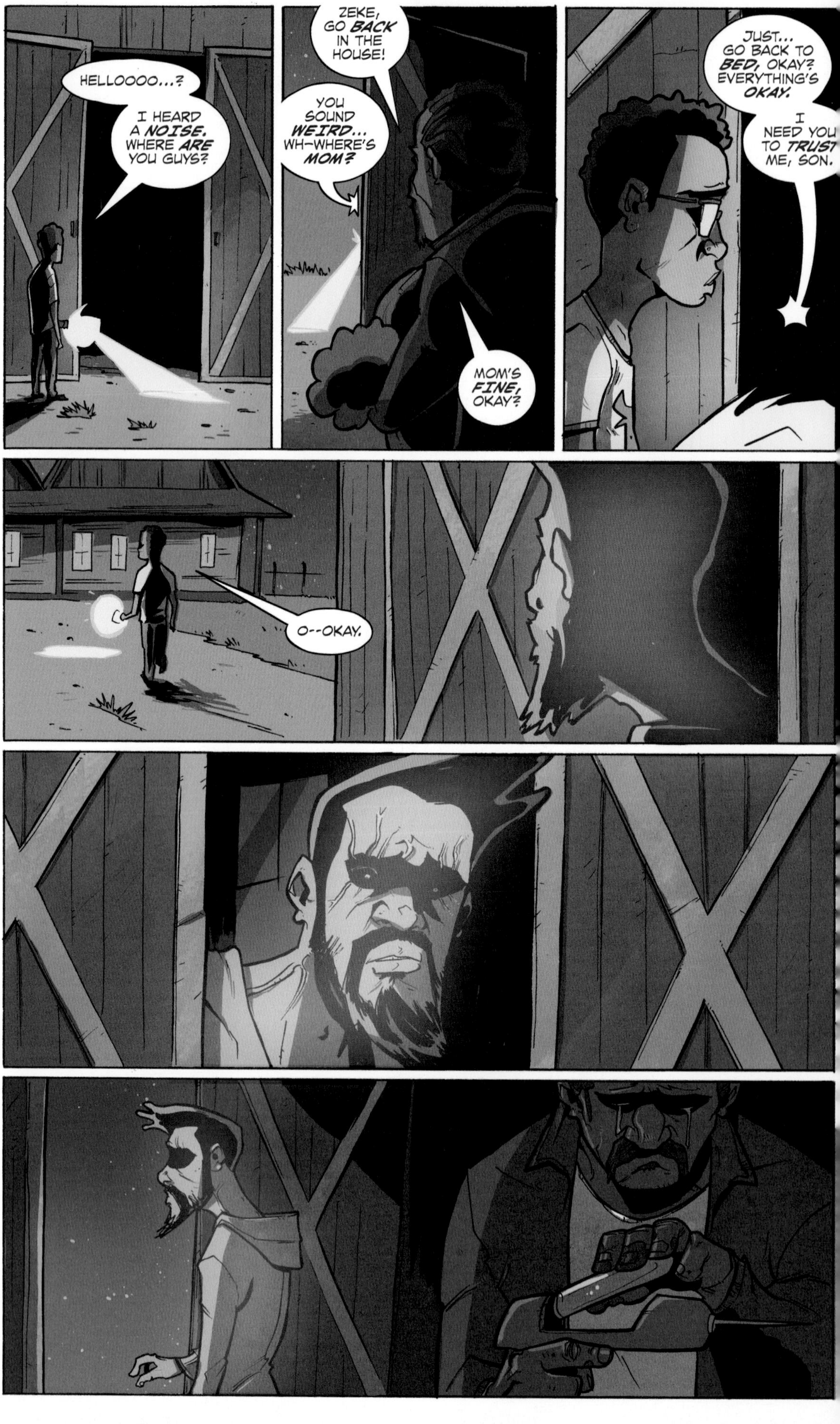

HELLOOOO...?
I HEARD A NOISE. WHERE ARE YOU GUYS?
ZEKE, GO BACK IN THE HOUSE!
YOU SOUND WEIRD... WH-WHERE'S MOM?
MOM'S FINE, OKAY?
JUST... GO BACK TO BED, OKAY? EVERYTHING'S OKAY.
I NEED YOU TO TRUST ME, SON.
O--OKAY.

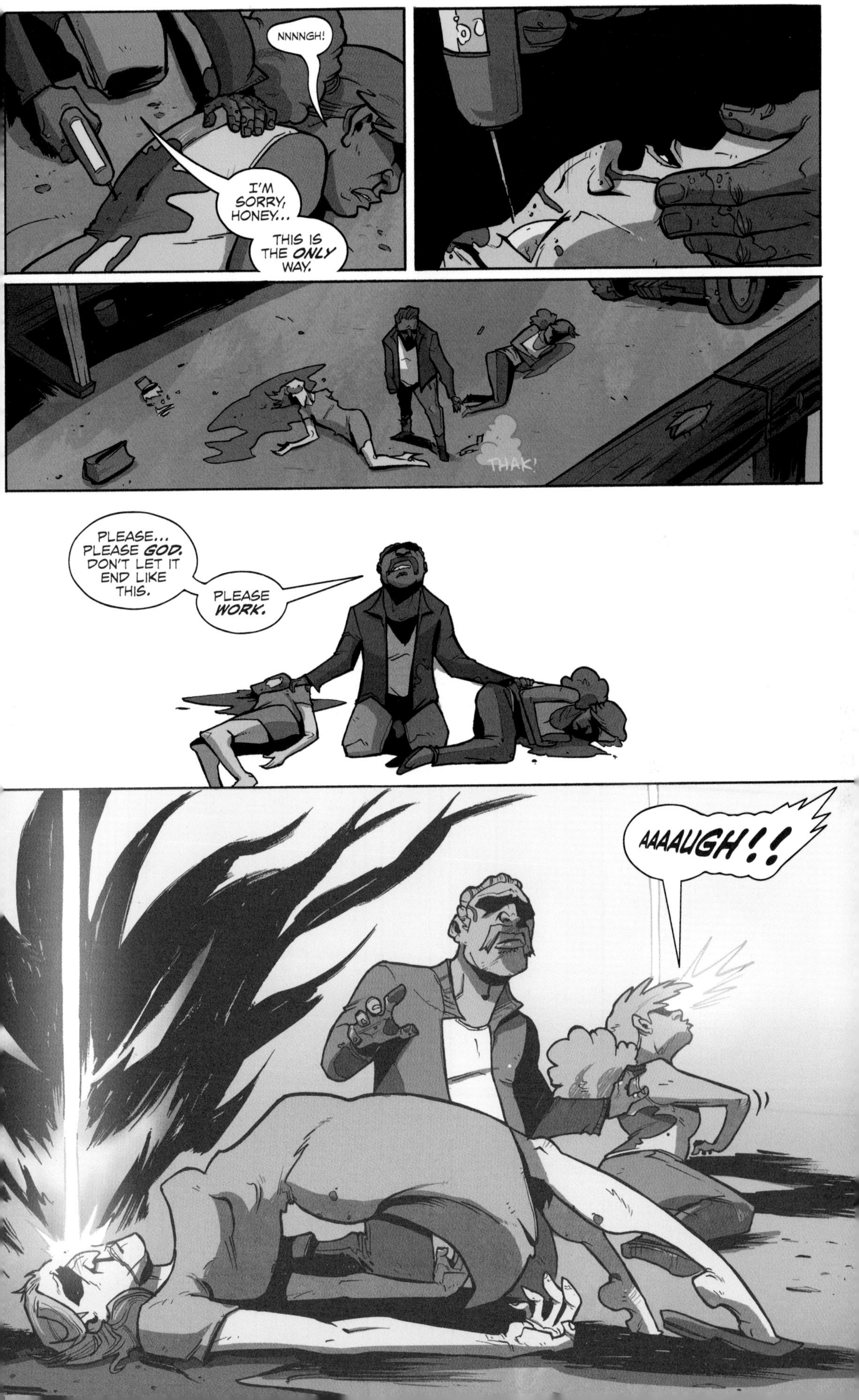
NNNNGH!
I'M SORRY, HONEY...
THIS IS THE ONLY WAY.
THAK!
PLEASE... PLEASE GOD. DON'T LET IT END LIKE THIS.
PLEASE WORK.
AAAAUGH!!

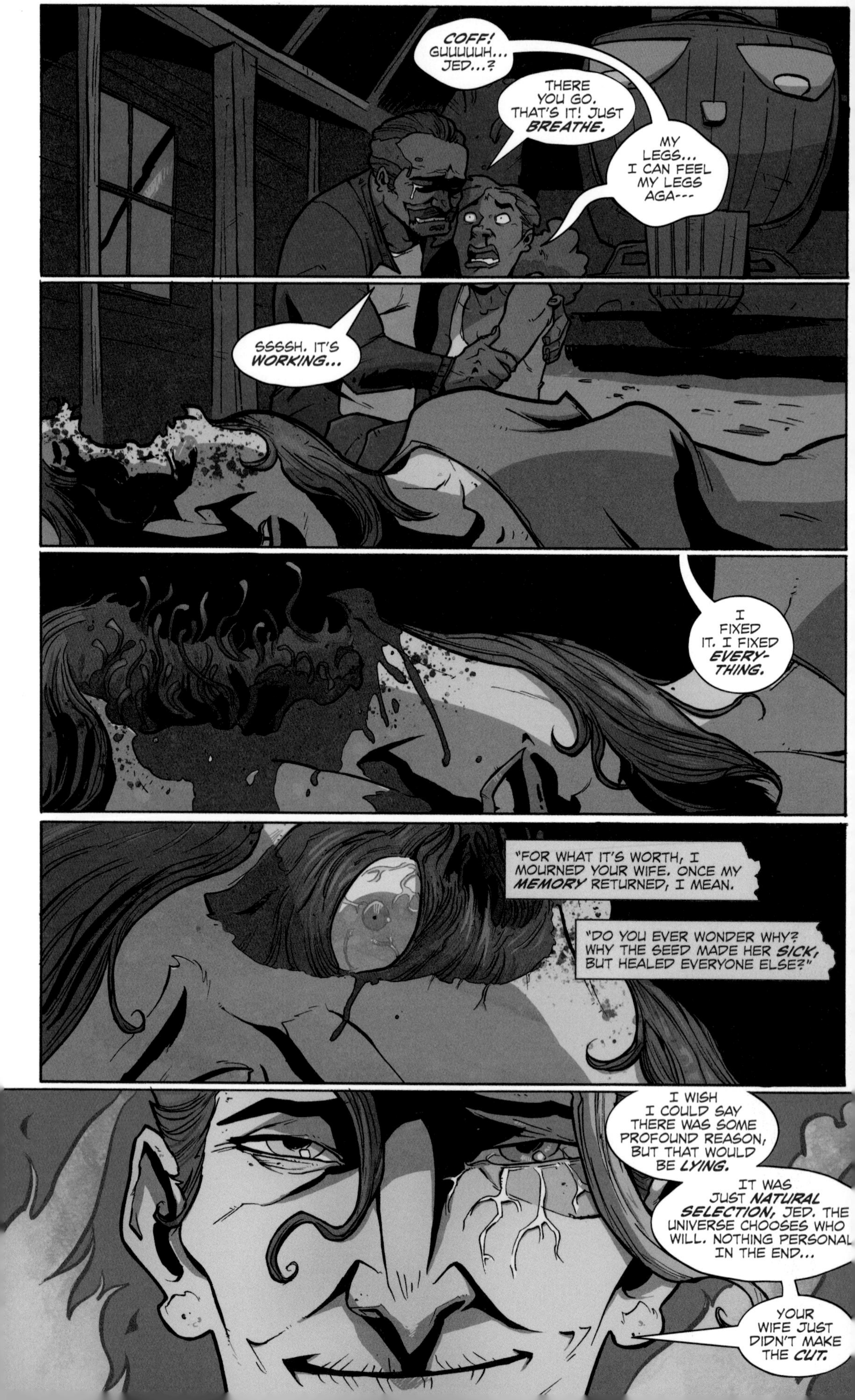
COFF! GUUUUUH... JED...?
THERE YOU GO. THAT'S IT! JUST BREATHE.
MY LEGS... I CAN FEEL MY LEGS AGA---
SSSSH. IT'S WORKING...
I FIXED IT. I FIXED EVERY-THING.
"FOR WHAT IT'S WORTH, I MOURNED YOUR WIFE. ONCE MY MEMORY RETURNED, I MEAN.
"DO YOU EVER WONDER WHY? WHY THE SEED MADE HER SICK, BUT HEALED EVERYONE ELSE?"
I WISH I COULD SAY THERE WAS SOME PROFOUND REASON, BUT THAT WOULD BE LYING.
IT WAS JUST NATURAL SELECTION, JED. THE UNIVERSE CHOOSES WHO WILL. NOTHING PERSONAL IN THE END...
YOUR WIFE JUST DIDN'T MAKE THE CUT.

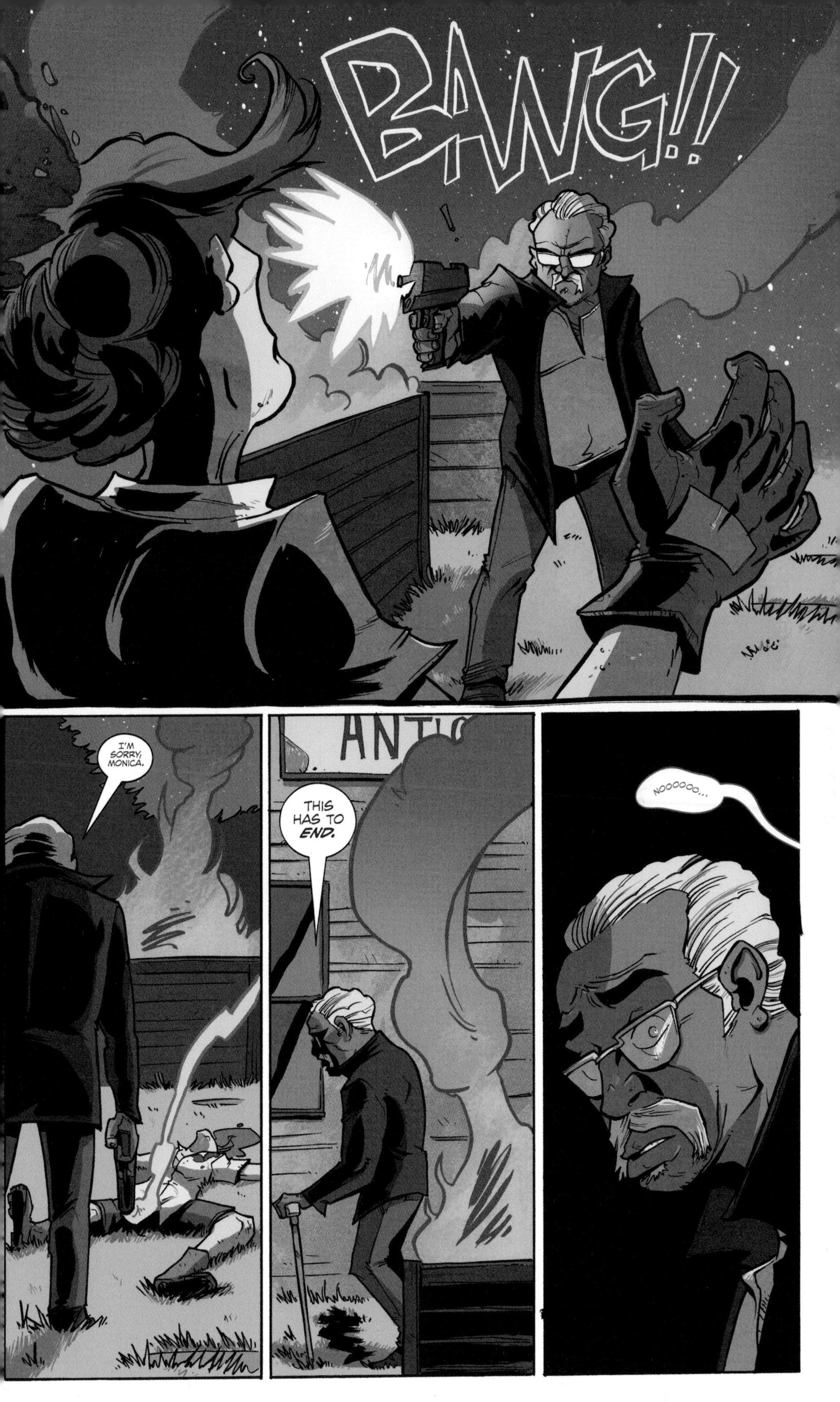
BANG!!
!
I'M SORRY, MONICA.
ANTI
THIS HAS TO END.
NOOOOOO...

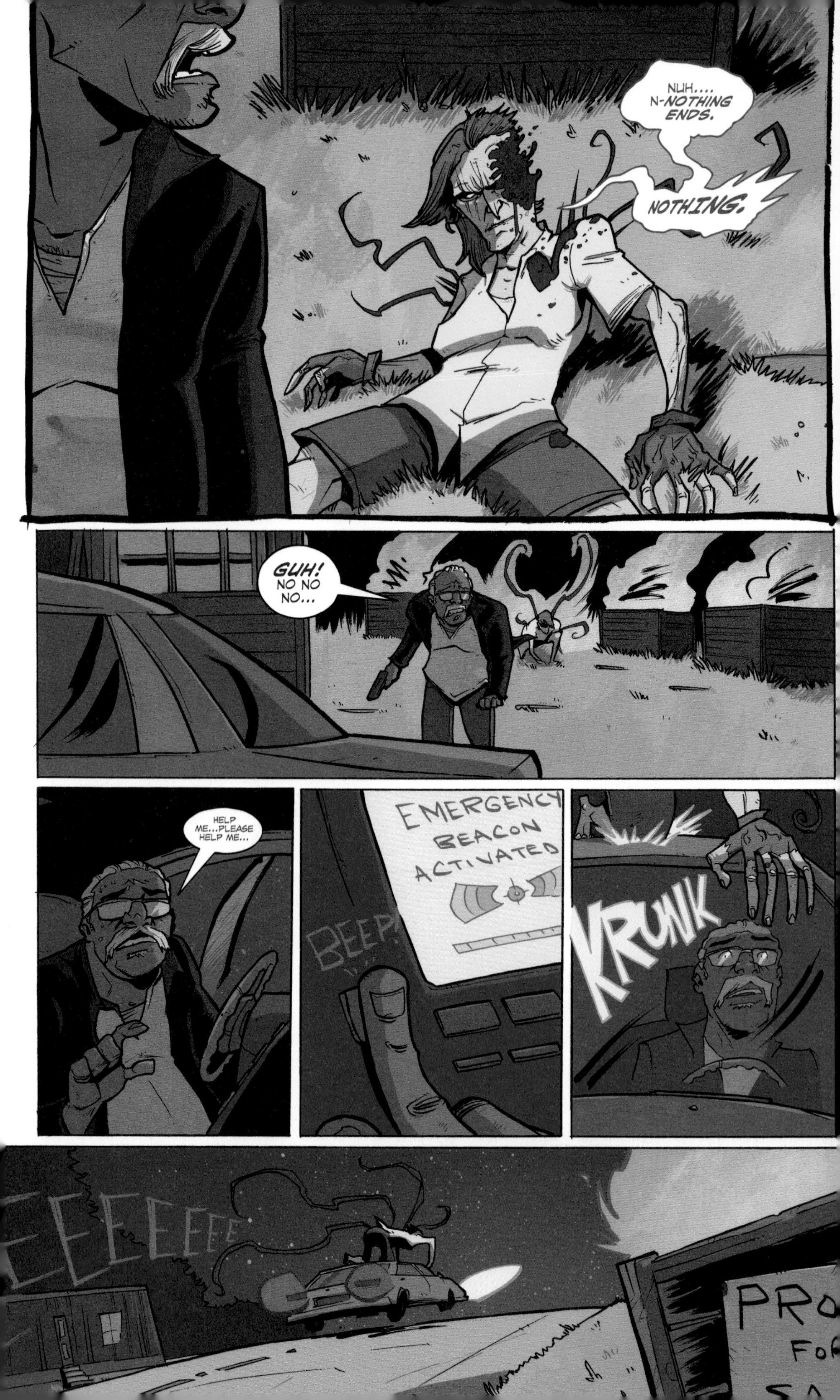
NUH....
N-NOTHING
ENDS.
NOTHING.
GUH!
NO NO
NO...
HELP
ME...PLEASE
HELP ME...
EMERGENCY
BEACON
ACTIVATED
BEEP!
KRUNK
EEEEEEE
PRO
FO

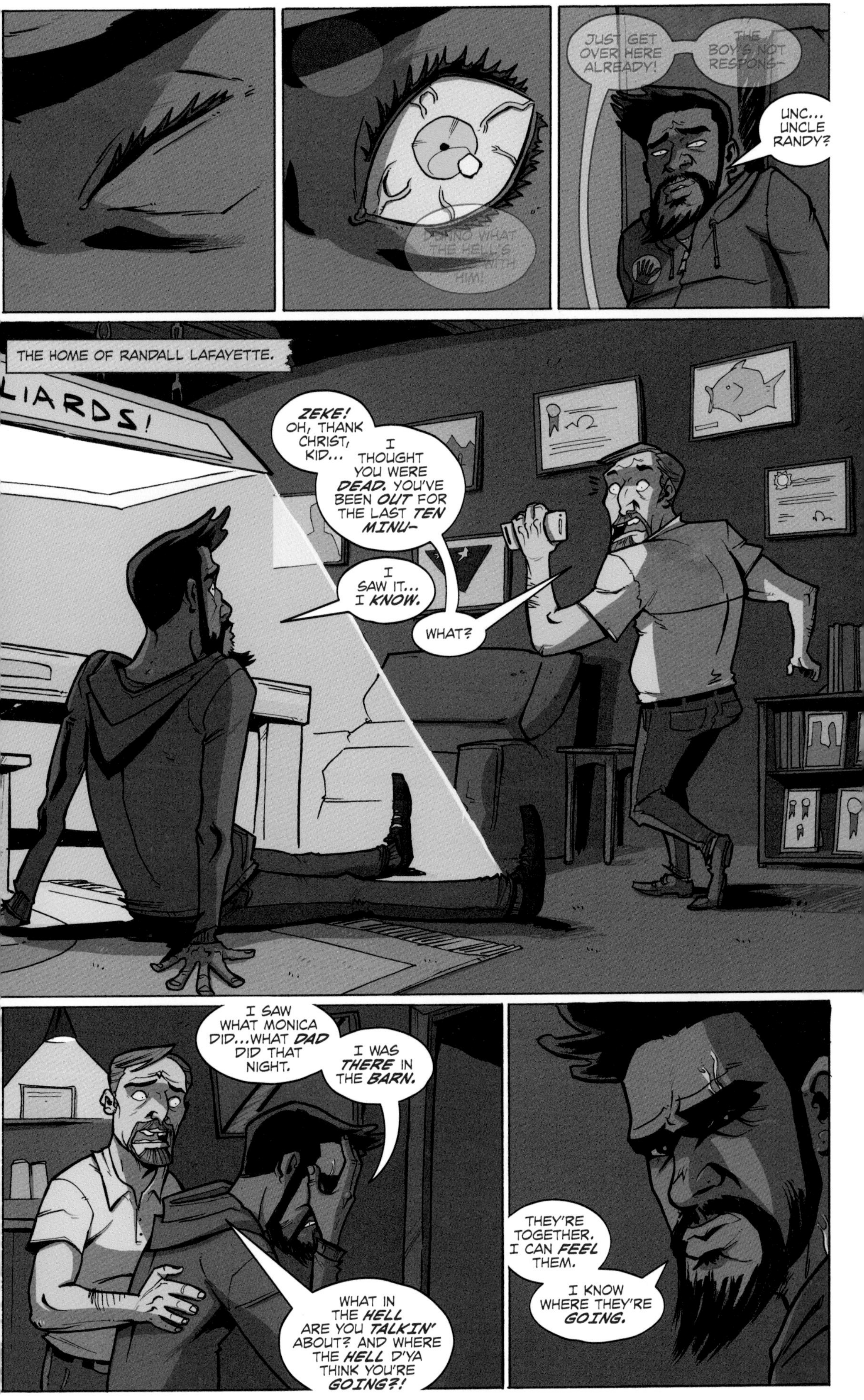
DUNNO WHAT THE HELL'S
WITH HIM!
JUST GET OVER HERE ALREADY!
THE BOY'S NOT RESPONS—
UNC... UNCLE RANDY?
THE HOME OF RANDALL LAFAYETTE.
LIARDS!
ZEKE! OH, THANK CHRIST, KID...
I THOUGHT YOU WERE DEAD. YOU'VE BEEN OUT FOR THE LAST TEN MINU-
I SAW IT... I KNOW.
WHAT?
I SAW WHAT MONICA DID...WHAT DAD DID THAT NIGHT.
I WAS THERE IN THE BARN.
WHAT IN THE HELL ARE YOU TALKIN' ABOUT? AND WHERE THE HELL D'YA THINK YOU'RE GOING?!
THEY'RE TOGETHER. I CAN FEEL THEM.
I KNOW WHERE THEY'RE GOING.

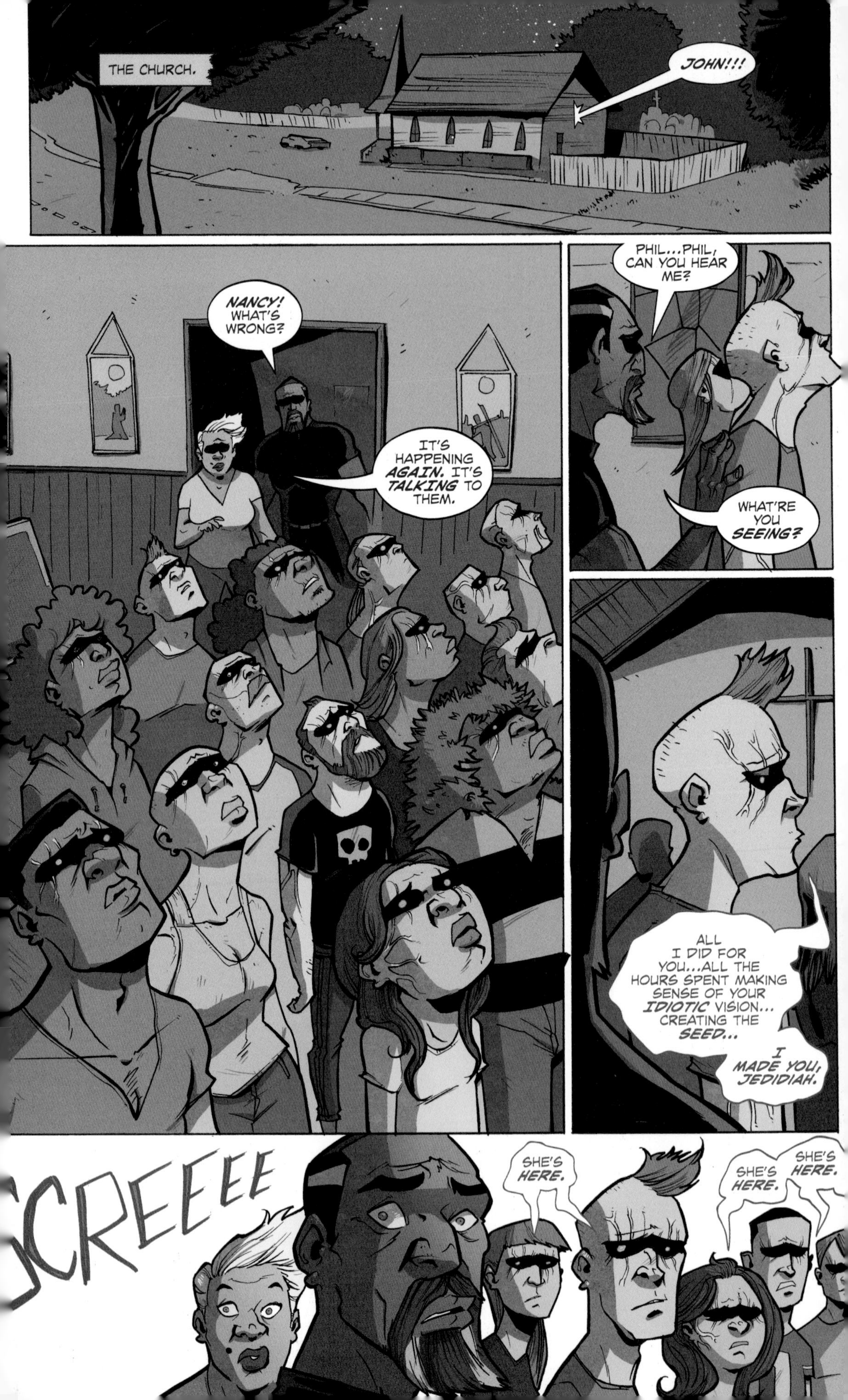
THE CHURCH.
JOHN!!!
NANCY! WHAT'S WRONG?
IT'S HAPPENING AGAIN. IT'S TALKING TO THEM.
PHIL...PHIL, CAN YOU HEAR ME?
WHAT'RE YOU SEEING?
ALL I DID FOR YOU...ALL THE HOURS SPENT MAKING SENSE OF YOUR IDIOTIC VISION... CREATING THE SEED...
I MADE YOU, JEDIDIAH.
SCREEEE
SHE'S HERE.
SHE'S HERE.
SHE'S HERE.

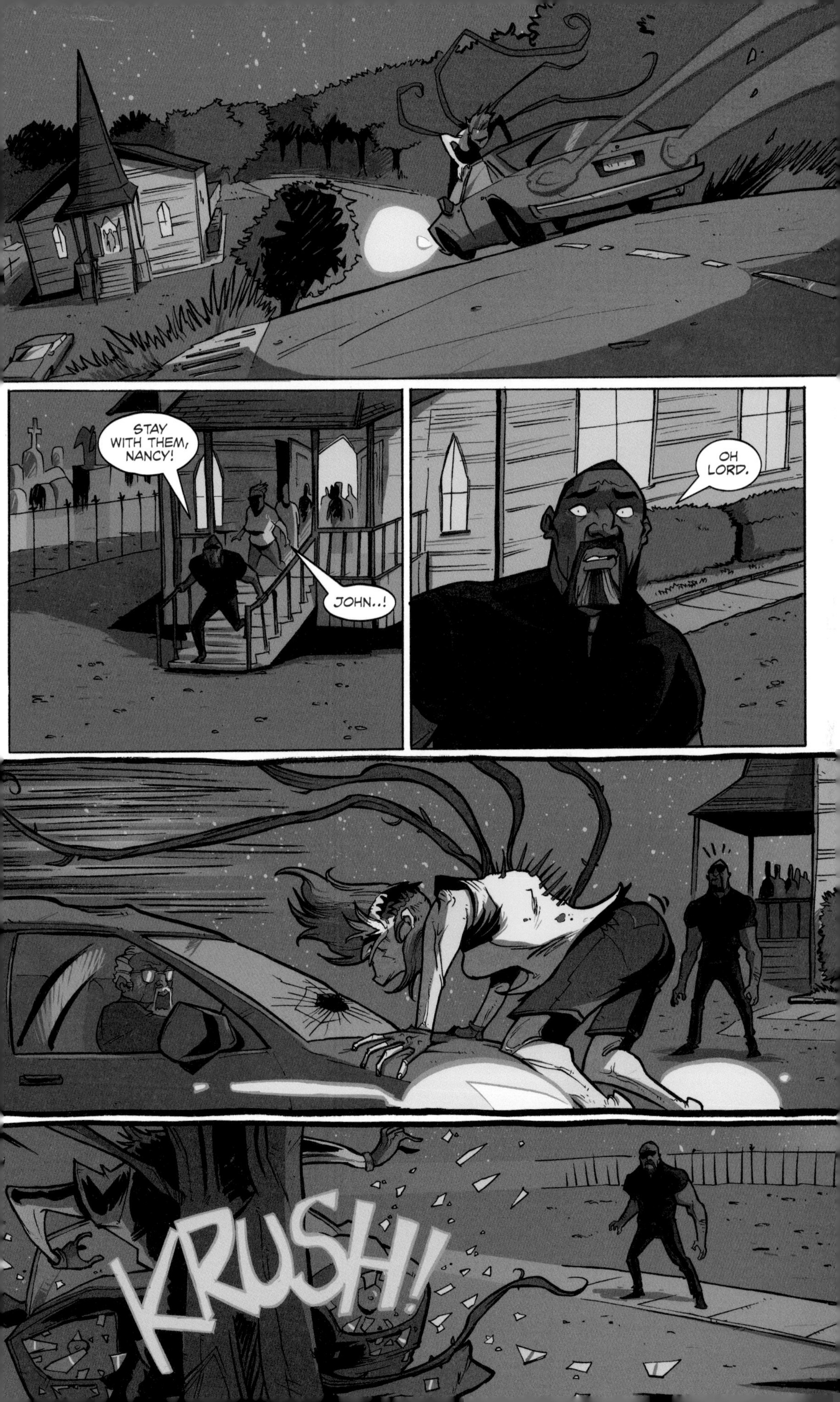
STAY WITH THEM, NANCY!
JOHN..!
OH LORD.
KRUSH!

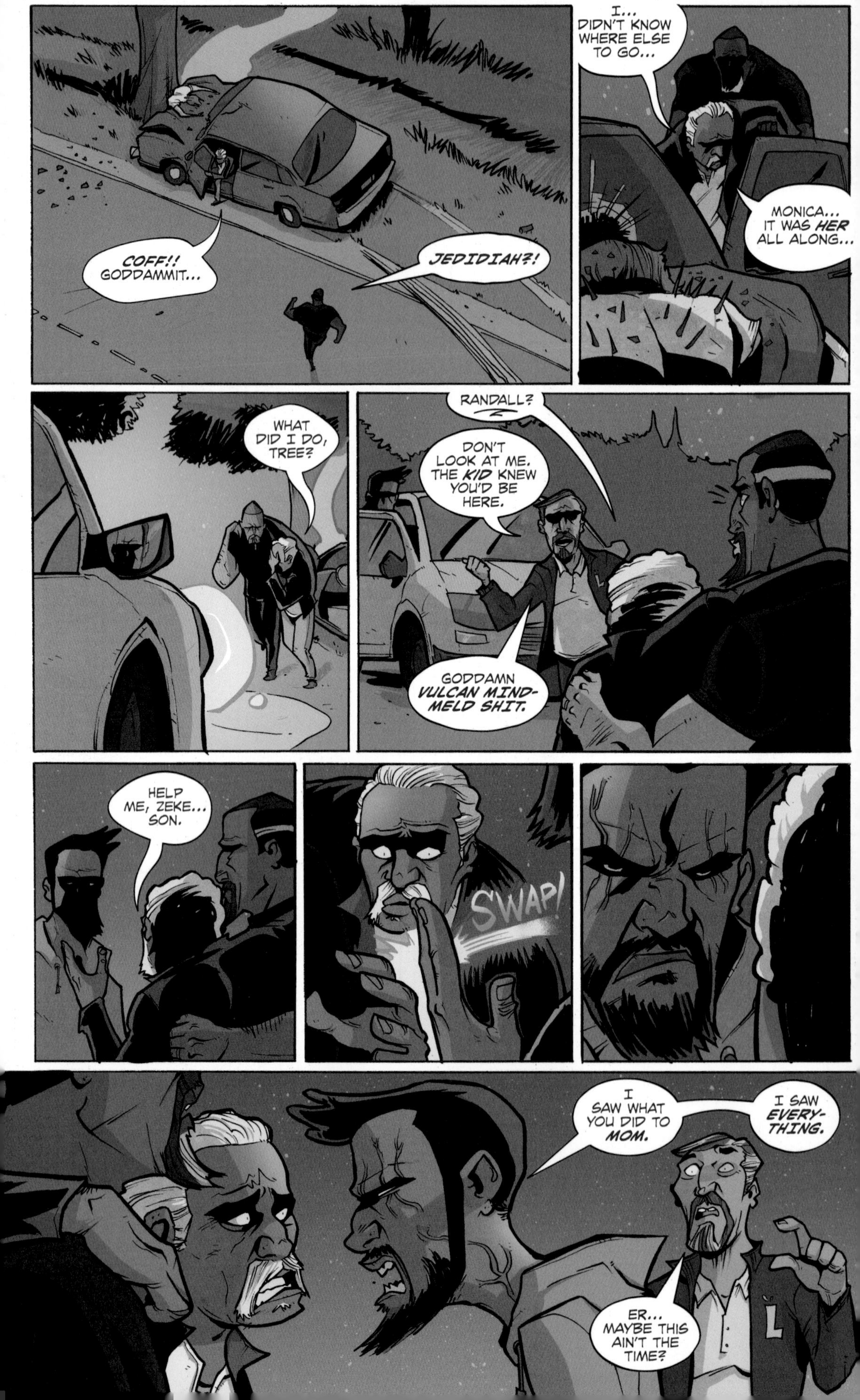
COFF!! GODDAMMIT...
JEDIDIAH?!
I... DIDN'T KNOW WHERE ELSE TO GO...
MONICA... IT WAS HER ALL ALONG...
WHAT DID I DO, TREE?
RANDALL?
DON'T LOOK AT ME. THE KID KNEW YOU'D BE HERE.
GODDAMN VULCAN MIND-MELD SHIT.
HELP ME, ZEKE... SON.
S'WAP!
I SAW WHAT YOU DID TO MOM.
I SAW EVERY-THING.
ER... MAYBE THIS AIN'T THE TIME?

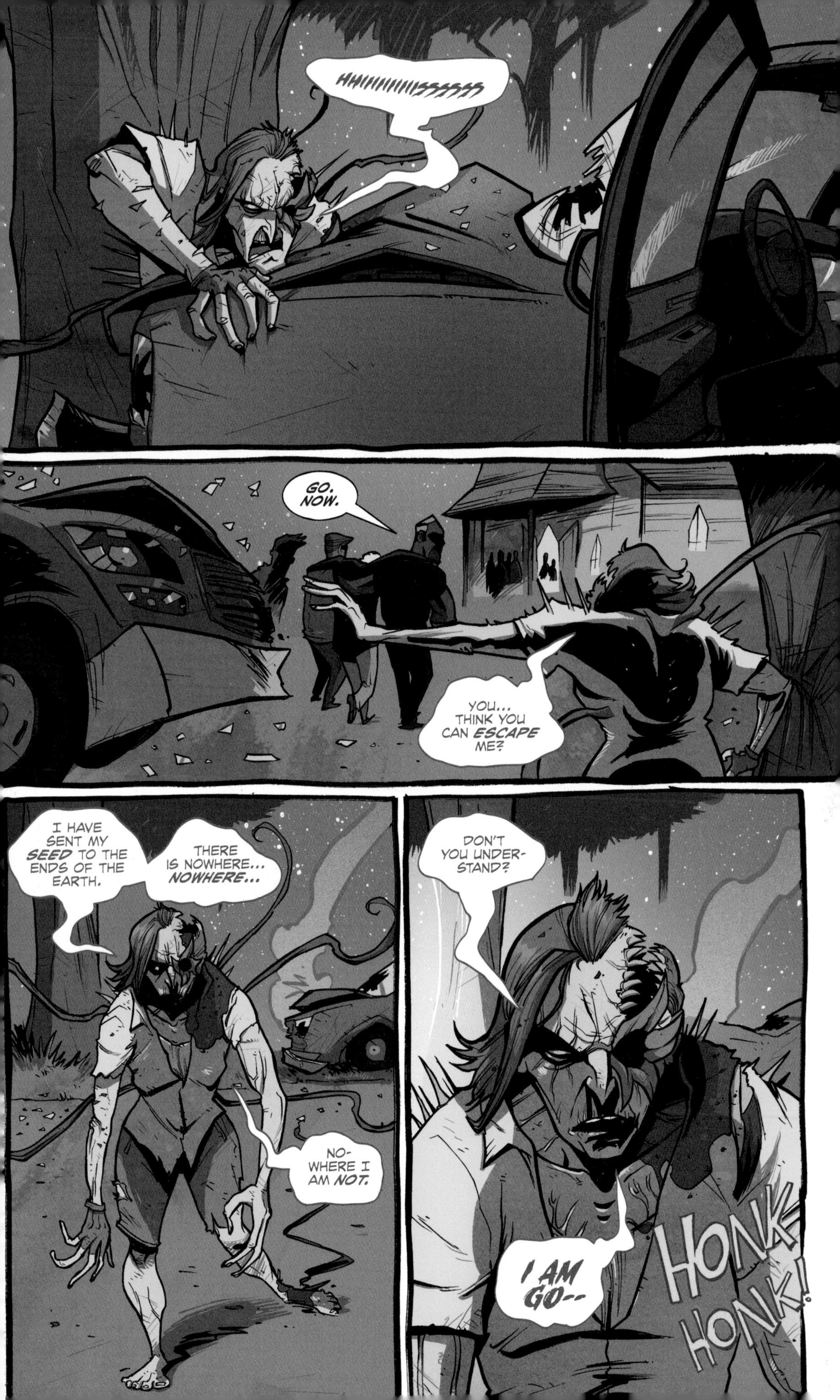
HHIIIIIIIIISSSSSSS
GO. NOW.
YOU... THINK YOU CAN ESCAPE ME?
I HAVE SENT MY SEED TO THE ENDS OF THE EARTH.
THERE IS NOWHERE... NOWHERE...
NO-WHERE I AM NOT.
DON'T YOU UNDER-STAND?
I AM GO--
HONK HONK!

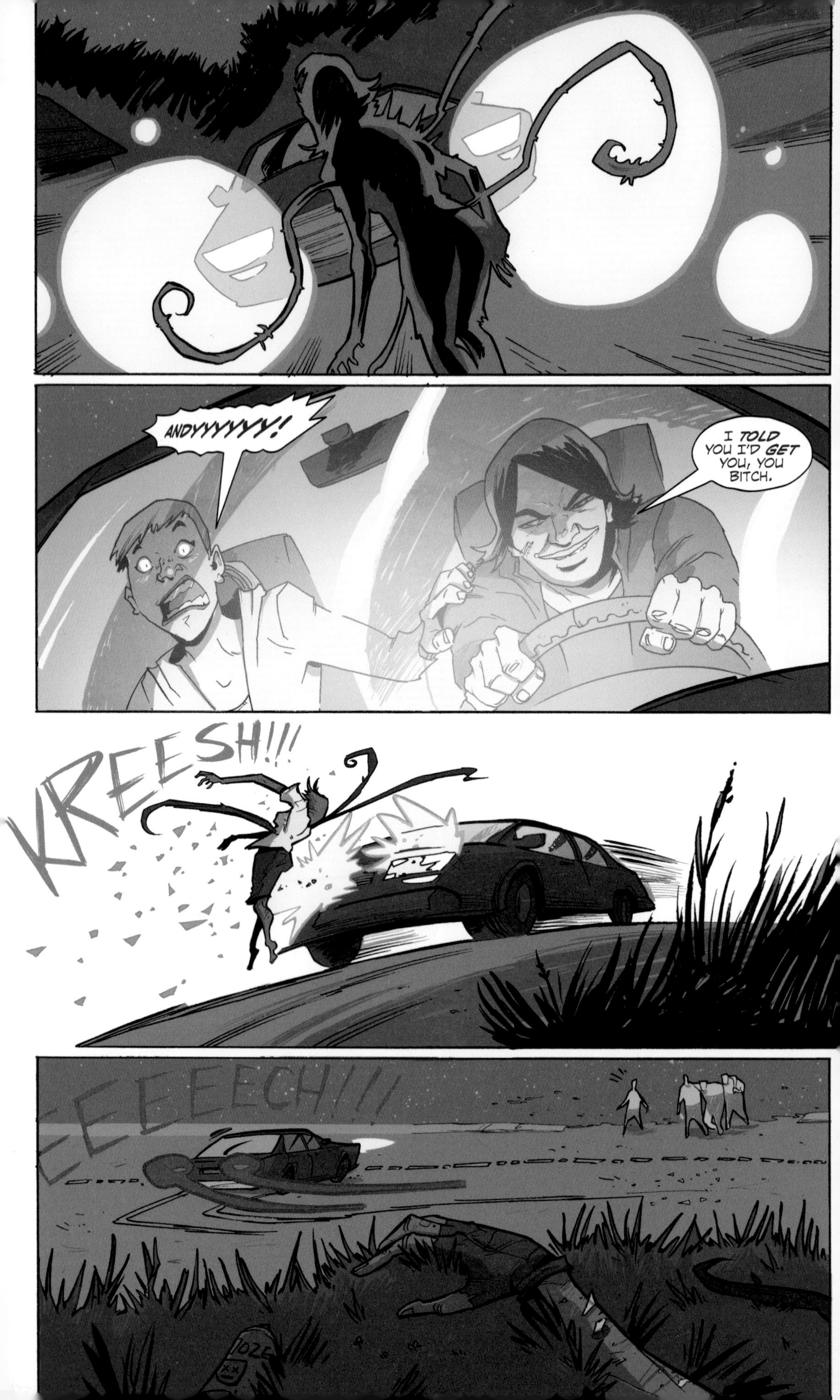

ANDYYYYYY!
I TOLD YOU I'D GET YOU, YOU BITCH.
KREESH!!!
EEEEECH!!!

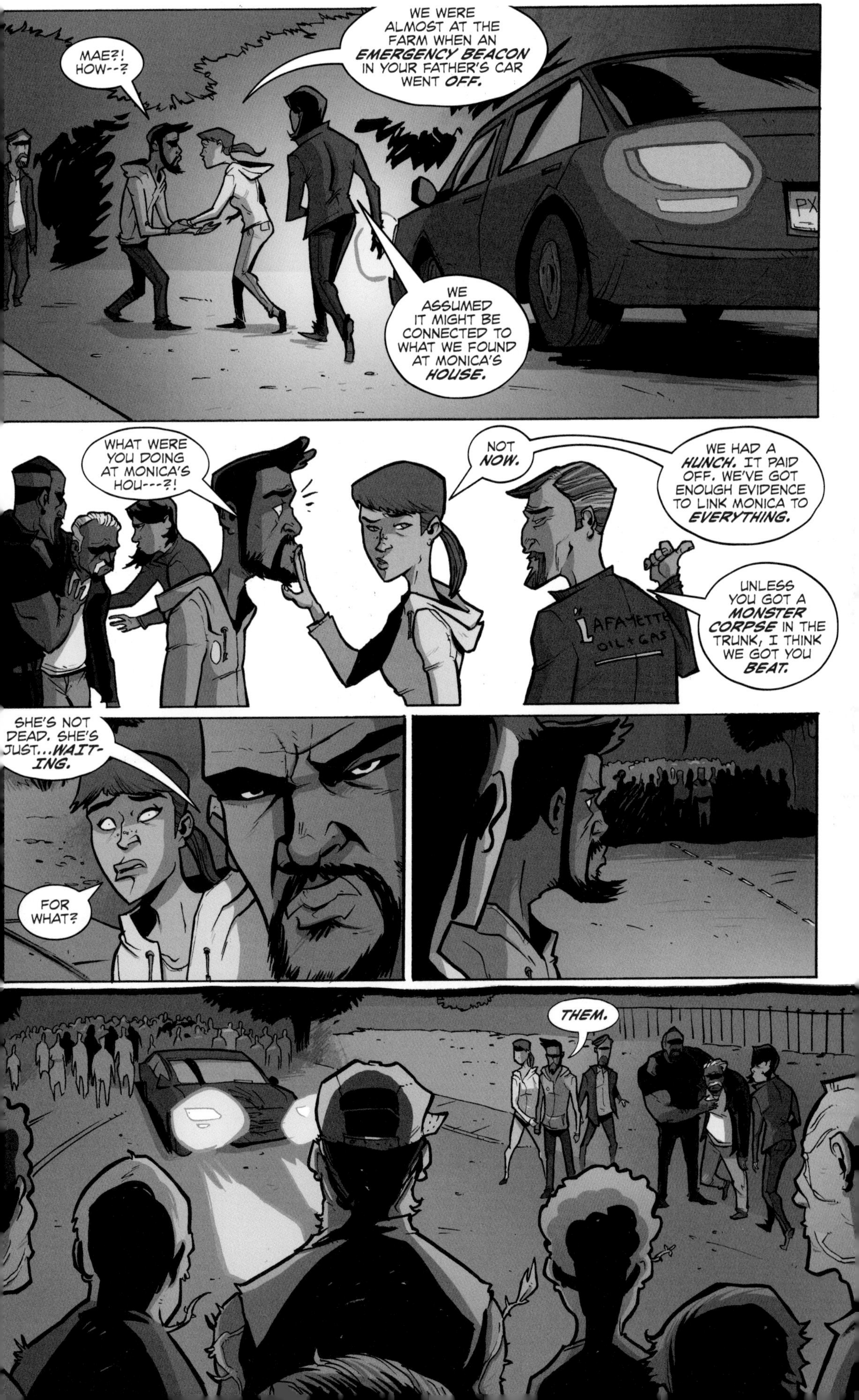
MAE?! HOW--?
WE WERE ALMOST AT THE FARM WHEN AN EMERGENCY BEACON IN YOUR FATHER'S CAR WENT OFF.
WE ASSUMED IT MIGHT BE CONNECTED TO WHAT WE FOUND AT MONICA'S HOUSE.
WHAT WERE YOU DOING AT MONICA'S HOU---?!
NOT NOW.
WE HAD A HUNCH. IT PAID OFF. WE'VE GOT ENOUGH EVIDENCE TO LINK MONICA TO EVERYTHING.
LAFAYETTE OIL + GAS
UNLESS YOU GOT A MONSTER CORPSE IN THE TRUNK, I THINK WE GOT YOU BEAT.
SHE'S NOT DEAD. SHE'S JUST...WAIT-ING.
FOR WHAT?
THEM.

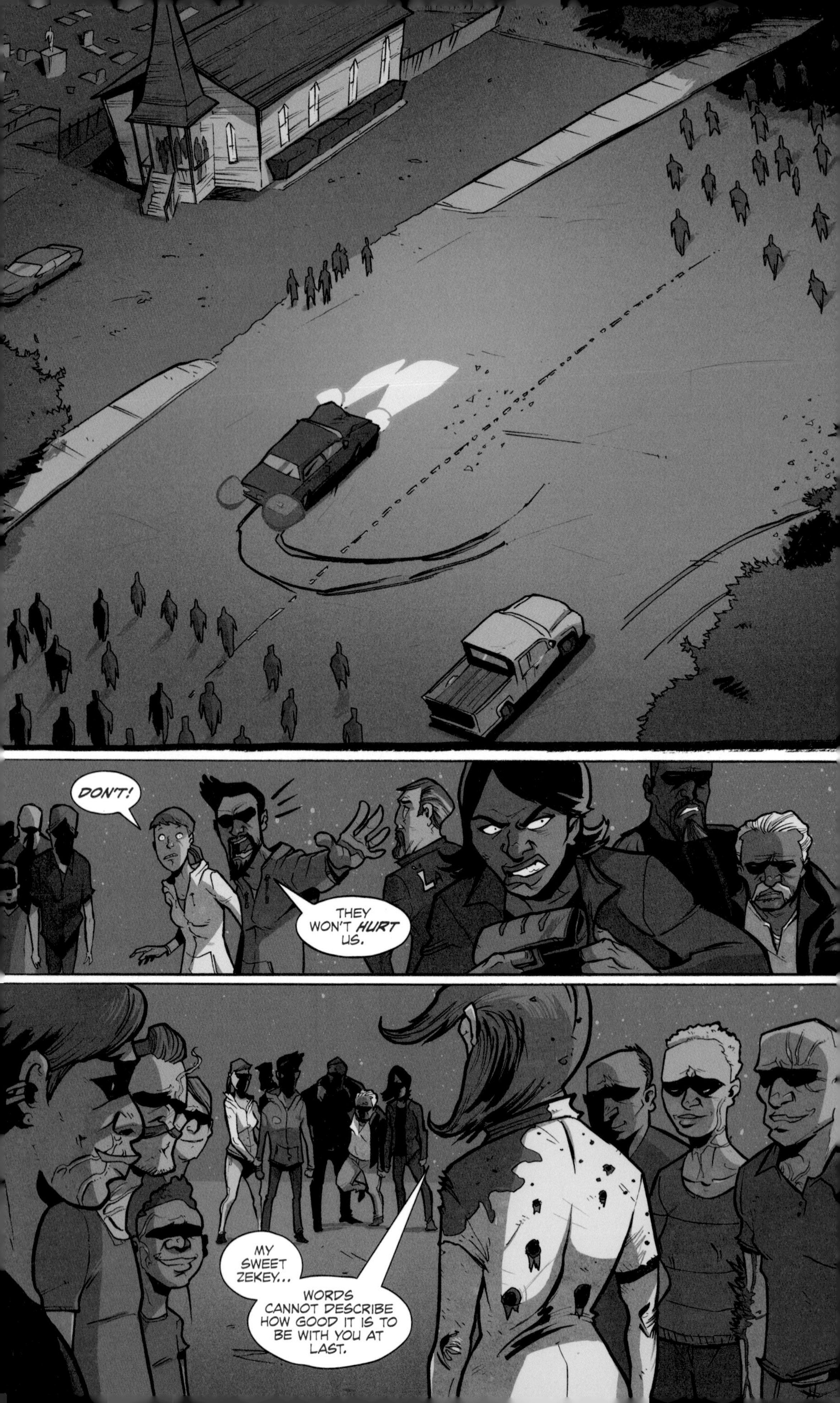
DON'T!
THEY WON'T HURT US.
MY SWEET ZEKEY... WORDS CANNOT DESCRIBE HOW GOOD IT IS TO BE WITH YOU AT LAST.

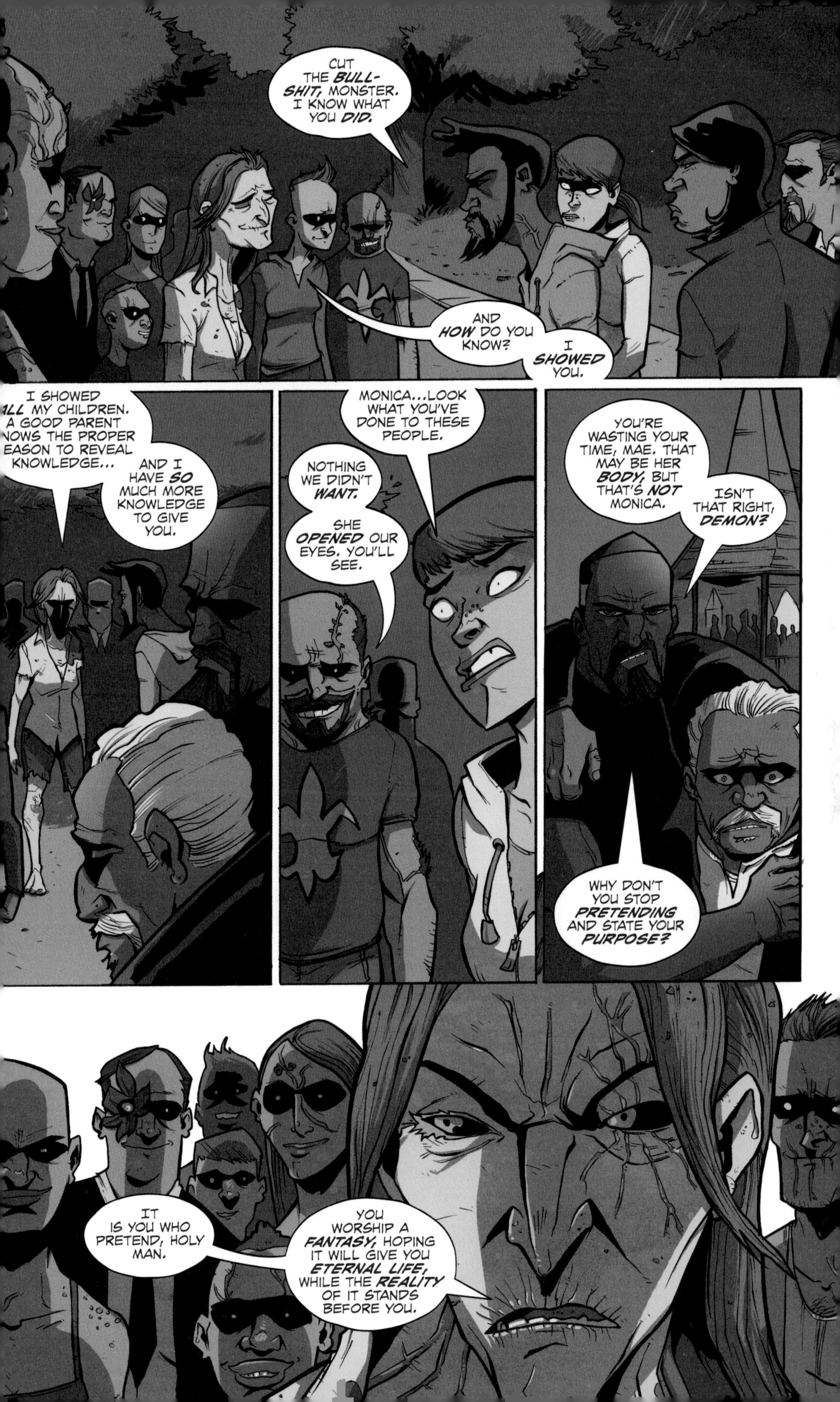
CUT THE BULL-SHIT, MONSTER. I KNOW WHAT YOU DID.
AND HOW DO YOU KNOW?
I SHOWED YOU.
I SHOWED ALL MY CHILDREN. A GOOD PARENT KNOWS THE PROPER SEASON TO REVEAL KNOWLEDGE...
AND I HAVE SO MUCH MORE KNOWLEDGE TO GIVE YOU.
MONICA...LOOK WHAT YOU'VE DONE TO THESE PEOPLE.
NOTHING WE DIDN'T WANT.
SHE OPENED OUR EYES. YOU'LL SEE.
YOU'RE WASTING YOUR TIME, MAE. THAT MAY BE HER BODY, BUT THAT'S NOT MONICA.
ISN'T THAT RIGHT, DEMON?
WHY DON'T YOU STOP PRETENDING AND STATE YOUR PURPOSE?
IT IS YOU WHO PRETEND, HOLY MAN.
YOU WORSHIP A FANTASY, HOPING IT WILL GIVE YOU ETERNAL LIFE, WHILE THE REALITY OF IT STANDS BEFORE YOU.

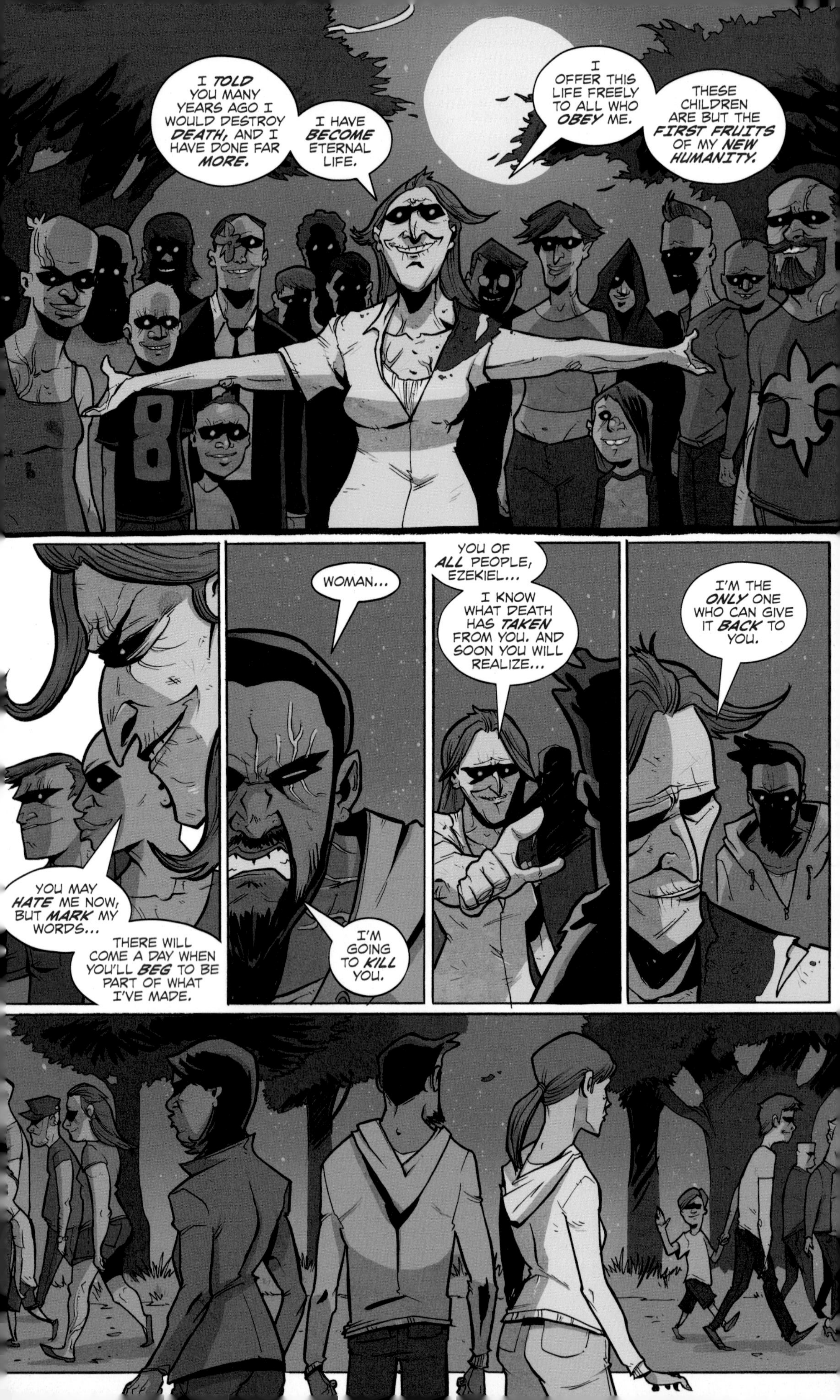

I TOLD YOU MANY YEARS AGO I WOULD DESTROY DEATH, AND I HAVE DONE FAR MORE.
I HAVE BECOME ETERNAL LIFE.
I OFFER THIS LIFE FREELY TO ALL WHO OBEY ME.
THESE CHILDREN ARE BUT THE FIRST FRUITS OF MY NEW HUMANITY.
YOU MAY HATE ME NOW, BUT MARK MY WORDS...
THERE WILL COME A DAY WHEN YOU'LL BEG TO BE PART OF WHAT I'VE MADE.
WOMAN...
I'M GOING TO KILL YOU.
YOU OF ALL PEOPLE, EZEKIEL...
I KNOW WHAT DEATH HAS TAKEN FROM YOU. AND SOON YOU WILL REALIZE...
I'M THE ONLY ONE WHO CAN GIVE IT BACK TO YOU.

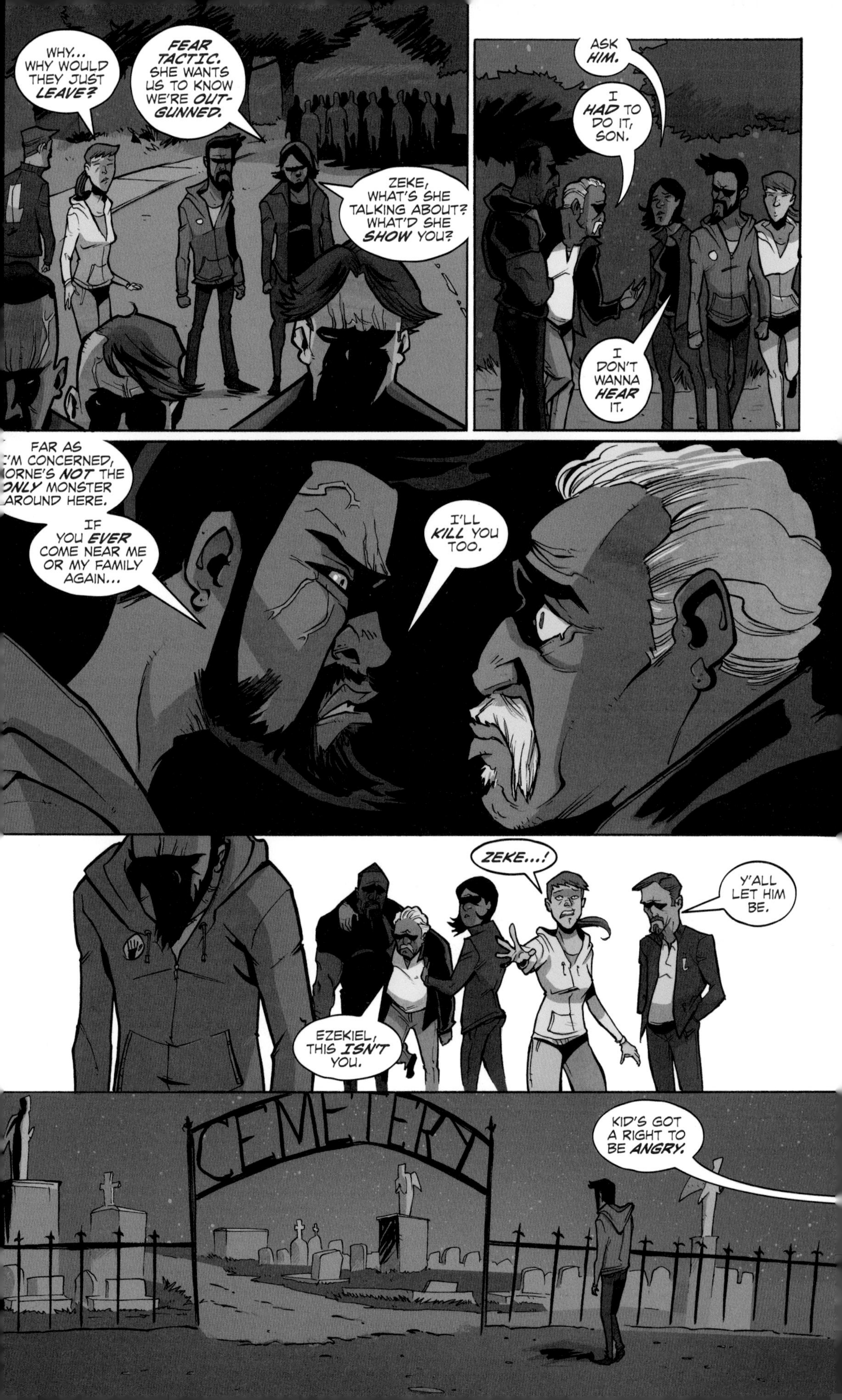
WHY... WHY WOULD THEY JUST LEAVE?
FEAR TACTIC. SHE WANTS US TO KNOW WE'RE OUT-GUNNED.
ZEKE, WHAT'S SHE TALKING ABOUT? WHAT'D SHE SHOW YOU?
ASK HIM.
I HAD TO DO IT, SON.
I DON'T WANNA HEAR IT.
FAR AS I'M CONCERNED, HORNE'S NOT THE ONLY MONSTER AROUND HERE.
IF YOU EVER COME NEAR ME OR MY FAMILY AGAIN...
I'LL KILL YOU TOO.
ZEKE...!
Y'ALL LET HIM BE.
EZEKIEL, THIS ISN'T YOU.
CEMETERY
KID'S GOT A RIGHT TO BE ANGRY.

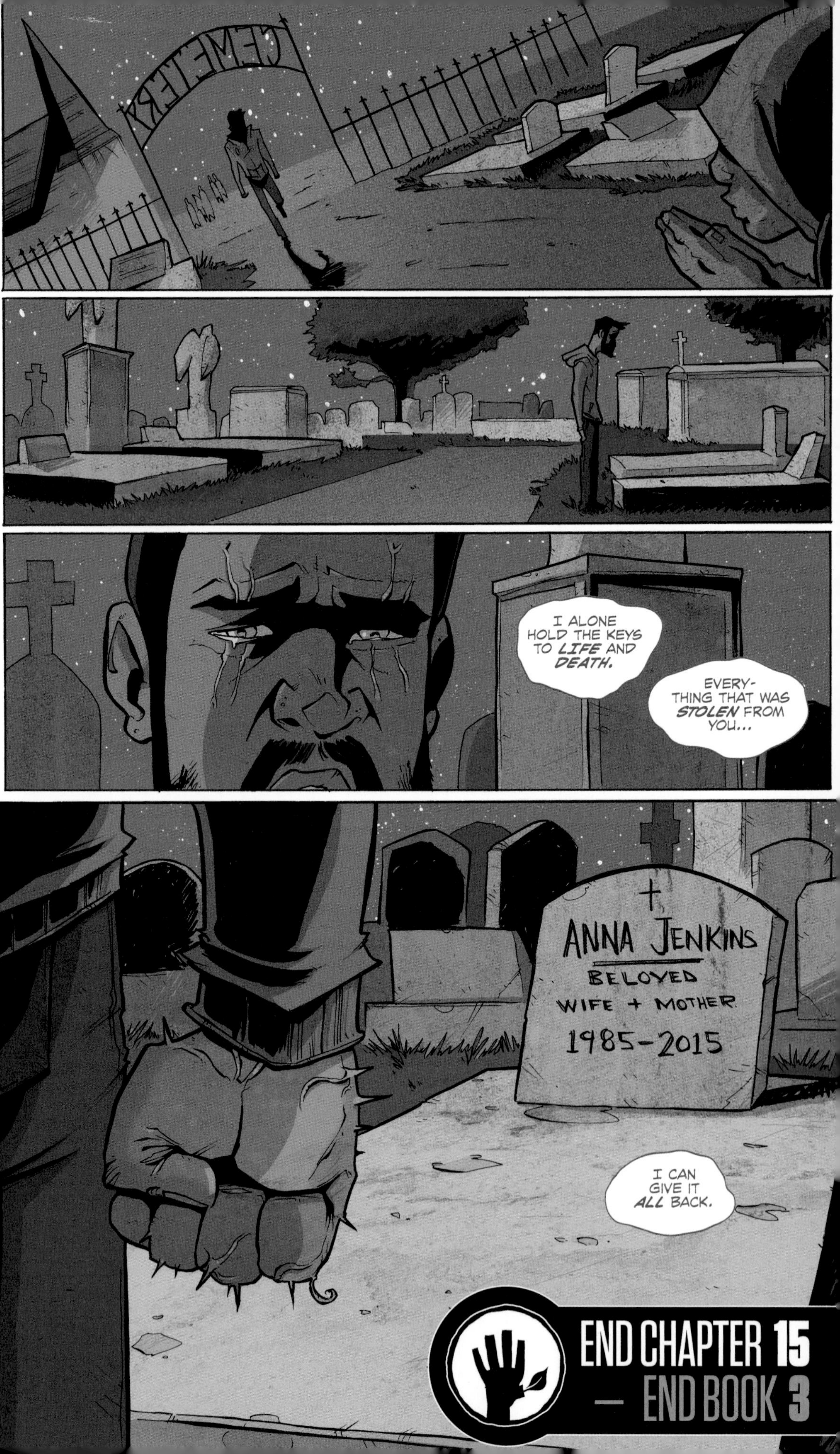
CEMETERY
I ALONE HOLD THE KEYS TO LIFE AND DEATH.
EVERY-THING THAT WAS STOLEN FROM YOU...
ANNA JENKINS
BELOVED
WIFE + MOTHER
1985–2015
I CAN GIVE IT ALL BACK.
END CHAPTER 15
— END BOOK 3

And to Adam he said,

"Because you have listened to the voice of your wife

and have eaten of the tree

of which I commanded you,

'You shall not eat of it,'

cursed is the ground because of you;

in pain you shall eat of it all the days of your life;

thorns and thistles it shall bring forth for you;

and you shall eat the plants of the field.

By the sweat of your face

you shall eat bread,

till you return to the ground,

for out of it you were taken;

for you are dust,

and to dust you shall return."

Genesis 3:17-19

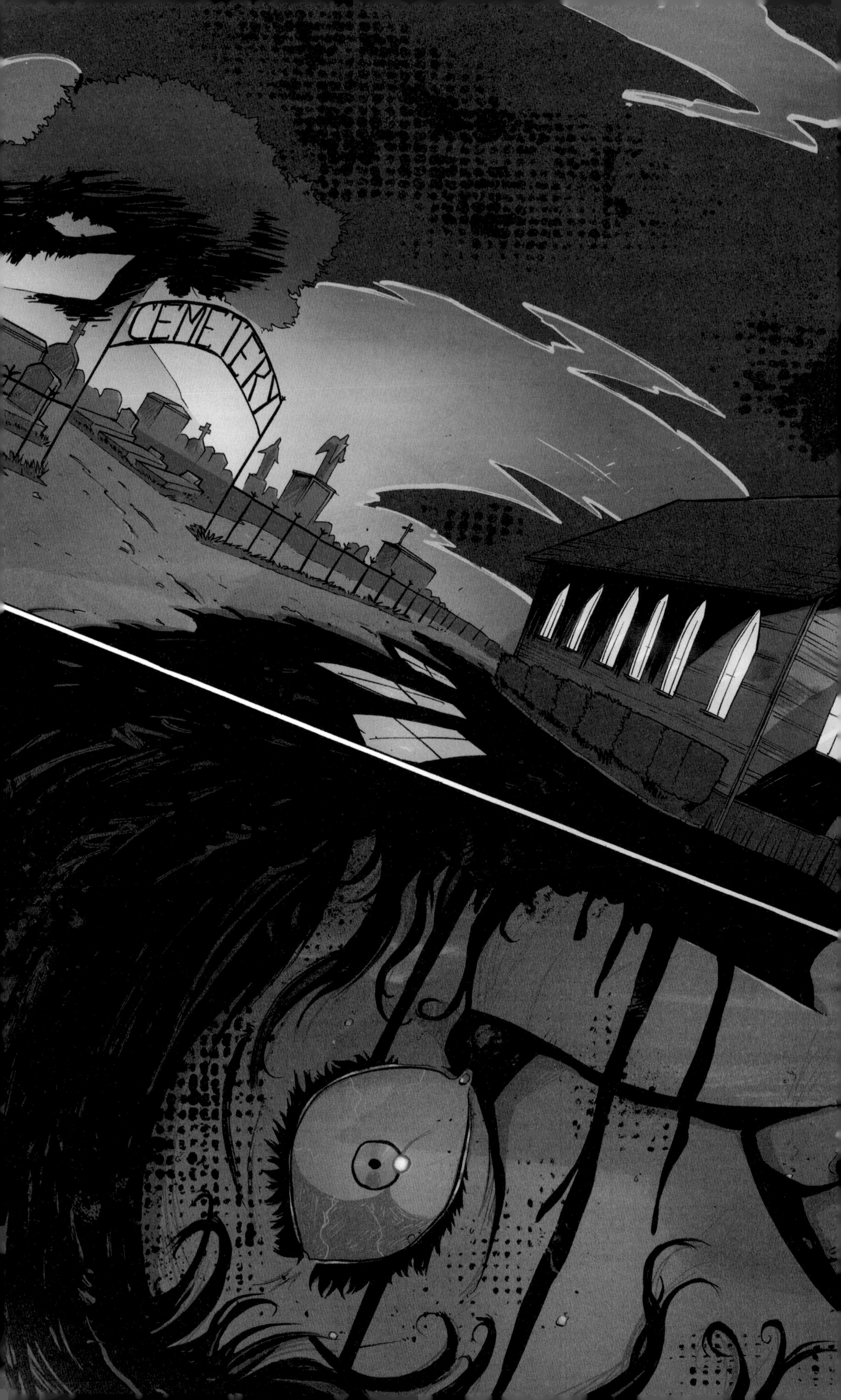
CEMETERY

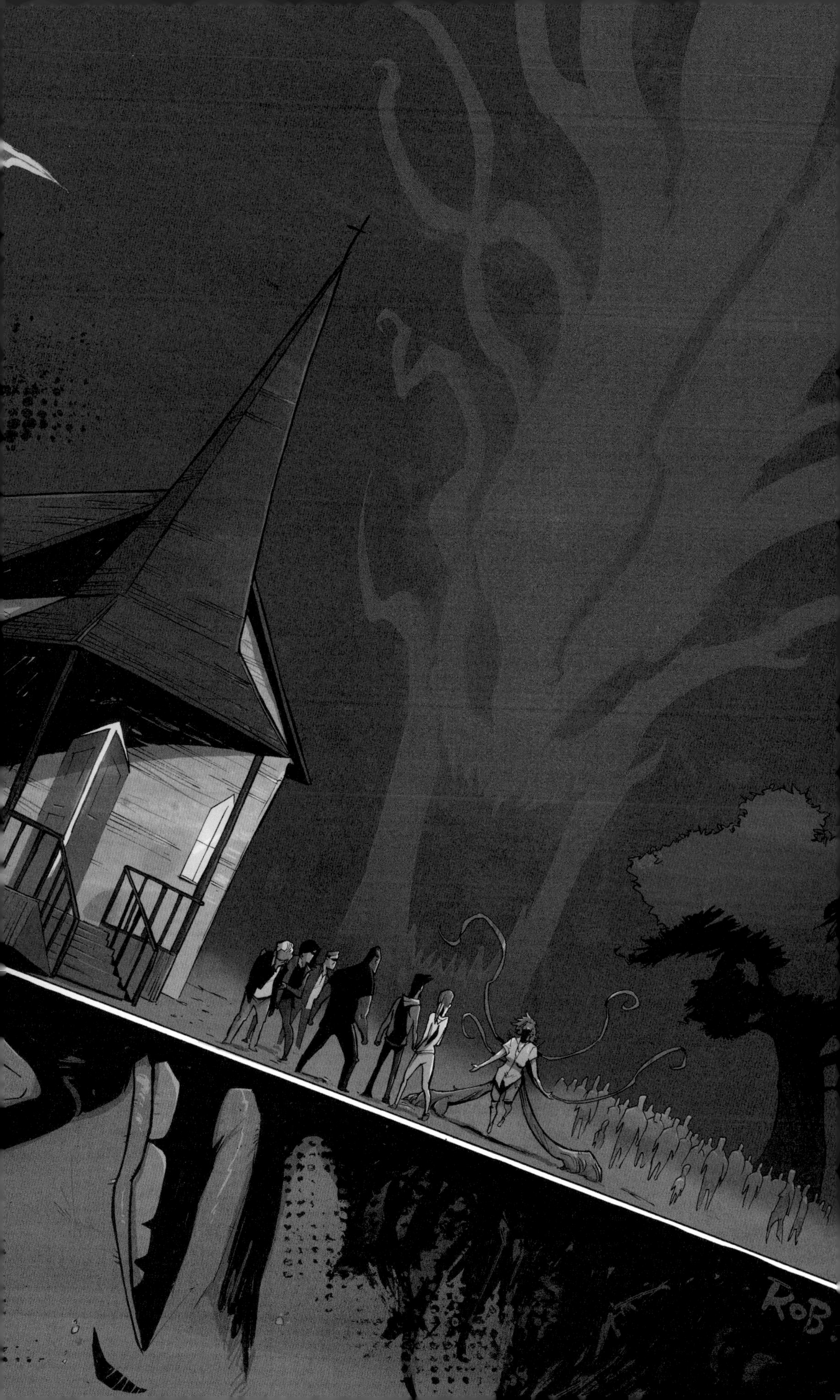
ROB.

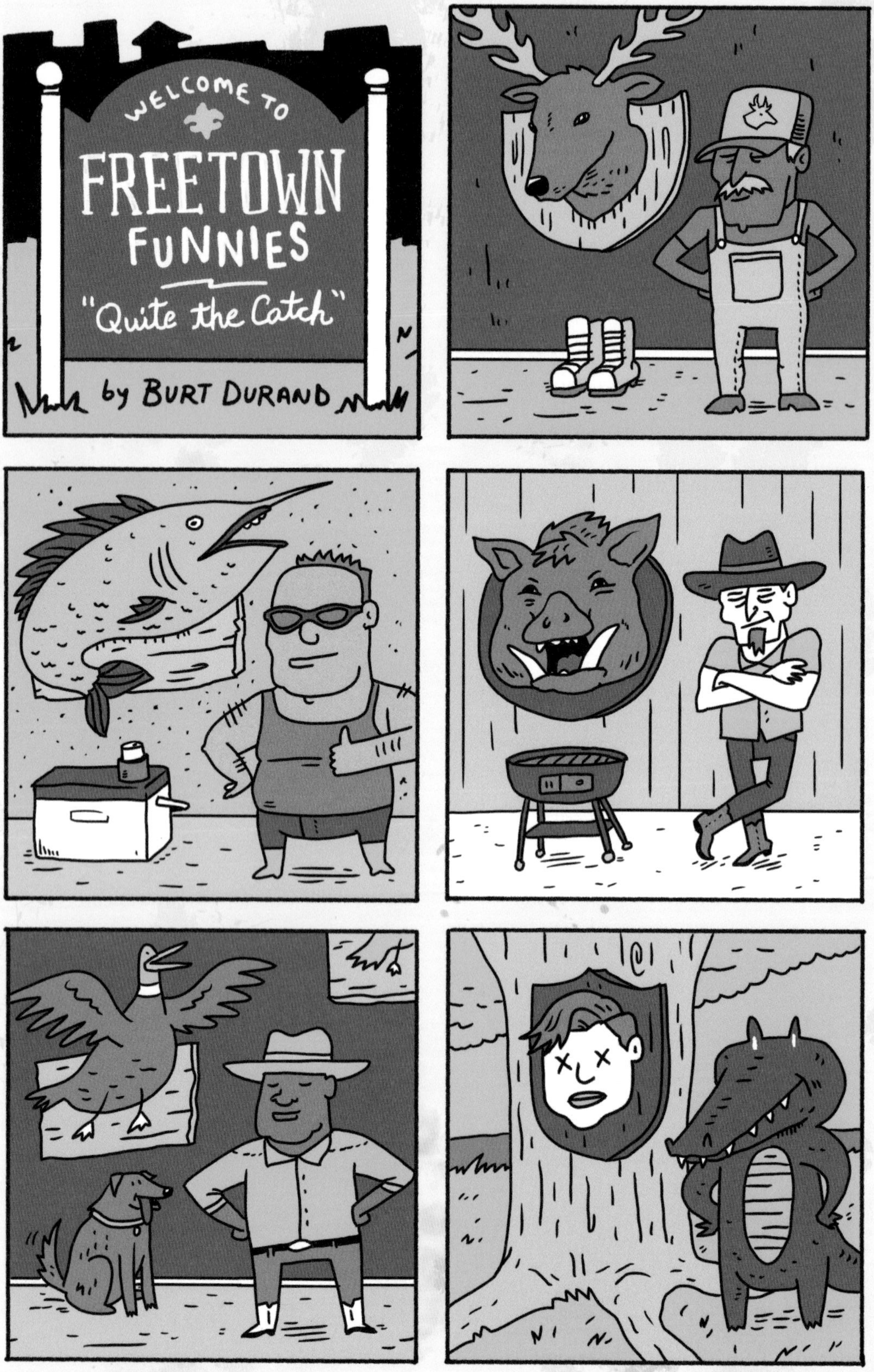
WELCOME TO
FREETOWN FUNNIES
"Quite the Catch"
by BURT DURAND

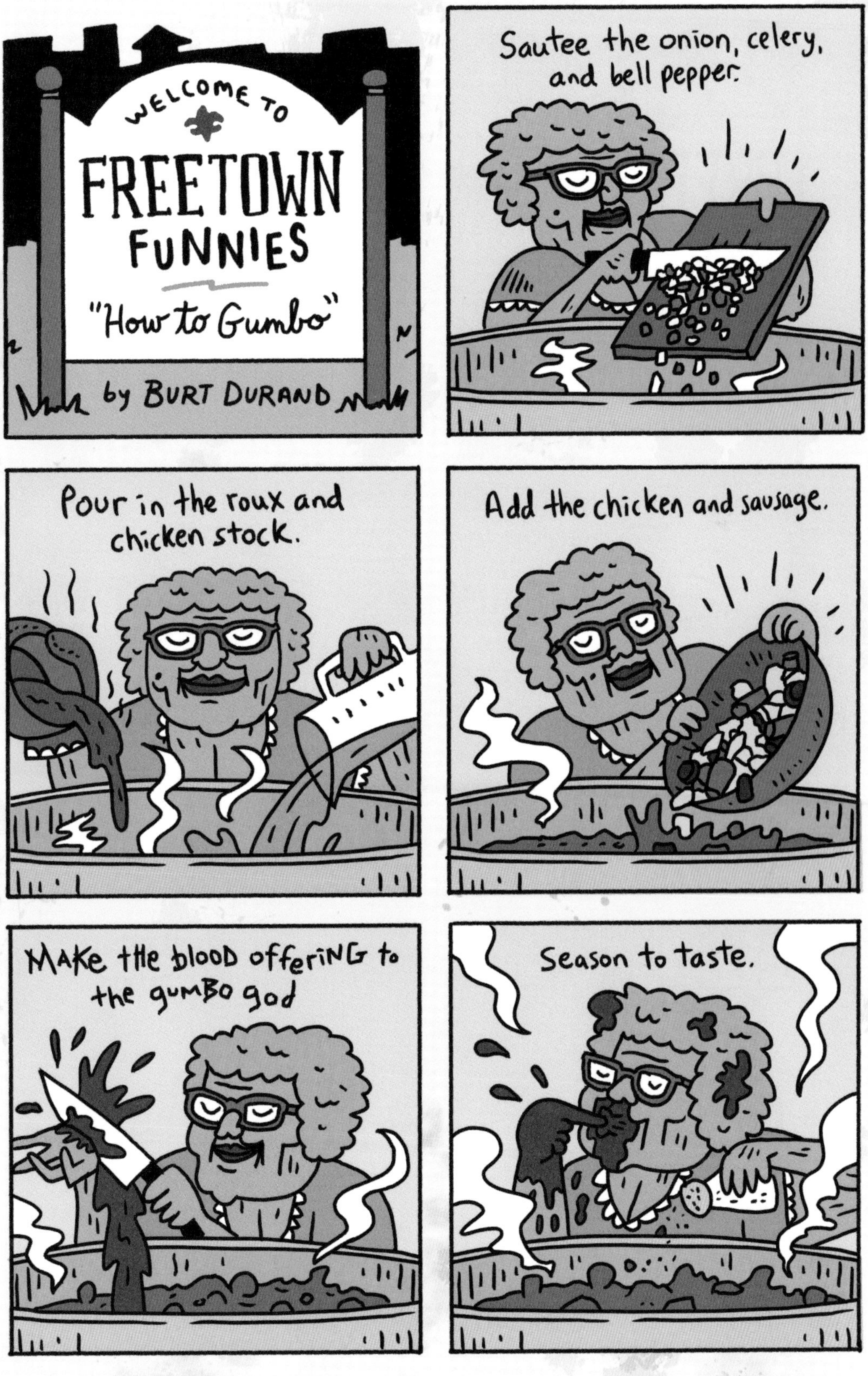
WELCOME TO
FREETOWN FUNNIES
"How to Gumbo"
by BURT DURAND
Sautee the onion, celery, and bell pepper.
Pour in the roux and chicken stock.
Add the chicken and sausage.
MAKE tHE BLOOD offeriNG to the gumBo god
Season to taste.

WELCOME TO
FREETOWN FUNNIES
"Ain't That Quaint"
by BURT DURAND
SIGH
nothin' ever happens in this dang town! sheesh
hey boy, what's up?
woo woo
SLURP
SLURP
dang ole nothin'

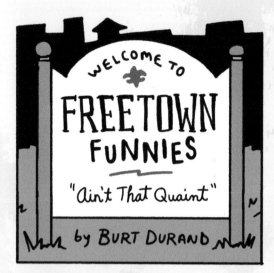

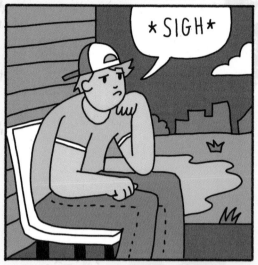

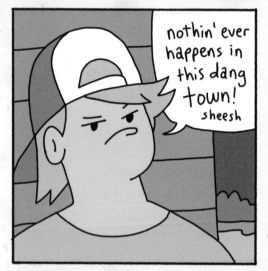

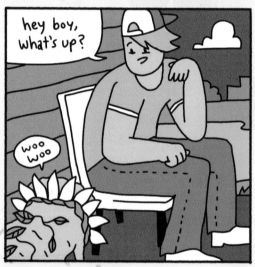

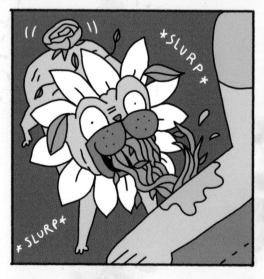

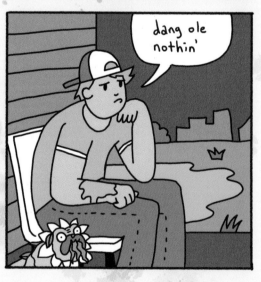

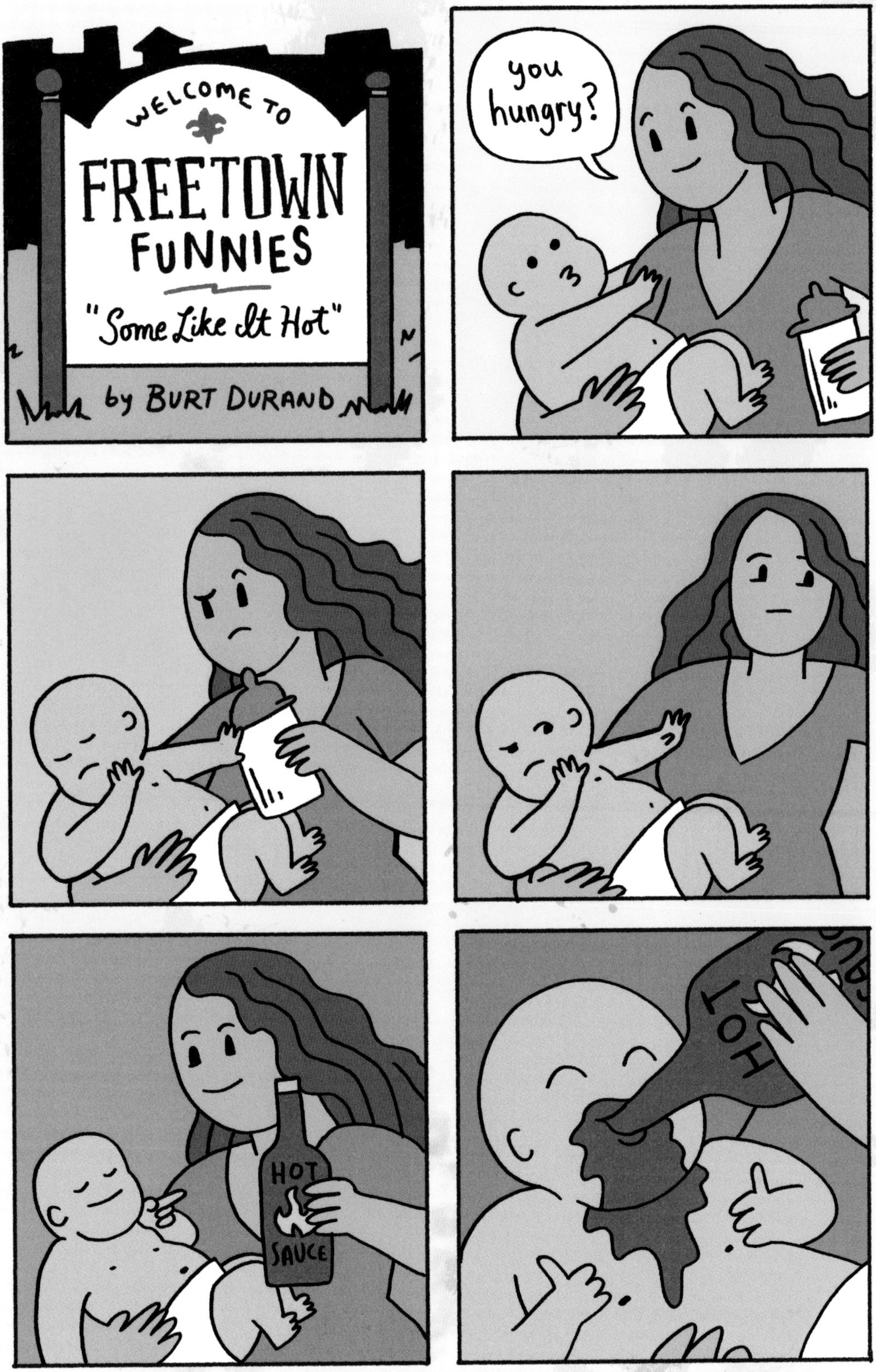
WELCOME TO
FREETOWN
FUNNIES
"Some Like It Hot"
by BURT DURAND
you hungry?
HOT
SAUCE
HOT

@BURTDURAND | BURTONDURAND.COM

RobGuillory.com

Original Art + Merch + Signed Books

⁓⁓ GRASSROOTS ⁓⁓

The Official FARMHAND Letters Column!

Accepting fan mail, gardening tips, haiku poems and random pictures of your dog.

You can email letters to:	Or go the snail mail route:
FARMHAND@robguillory.com	FARMHAND | P.O. Box 304 | Scott, LA 70583

 @ROB_GUILLORY    @ROB_GUILLORY   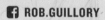 ROB.GUILLORY